The Complete Works of Álvaro de Campos

The Complete Works of Álvaro de Campos

Fernando Pessoa

Edited by Jerónimo Pizarro & Antonio Cardiello

Translated from the Portuguese
by Margaret Jull Costa & Patricio Ferrari

A NEW DIRECTIONS
PAPERBOOK ORIGINAL

 FLAD LUSO-AMERICAN DEVELOPMENT FOUNDATION *Book supported within the scope of the Open Call for Translation of Literary Works by the Luso-American Development Foundation.*

Manufactured in the United States of America
First published as New Directions Paperbook 1569 in 2023

Library of Congress Cataloging-in-Publication Data
Names: Campos, Alvaro de, 1888–1935, author. | Pizarro, Jerónimo, editor. |
Cardiello, António, editor. | Costa, Margaret Jull, translator. | Ferrari, Patricio, translator.
Title: The complete works of Álvaro de Campos / edited by Jerónimo Pizarro and
Antonio Cardellio ; translated by Margaret Jull Costa and Patricio Ferrari.
Other titles: Works. English
Description: New York, NY : New Directions Publishing Corporation, 2023. |
"A New Directions book." | Translated from the Portuguese.
Identifiers: LCCN 2023001769 | ISBN 9780811229883 (paperback) |
ISBN 9780811229890 (ebook)
Subjects: LCSH: Portuguese literature—20th century.
Classification: LCC PQ9261 .P417 2023 | DDC 869.1/41—dc23/eng/20230310
LC record available at https://lccn.loc.gov/2023001769

10 9 8 7 6 5 4 3 2 1

New Directions Books are published for James Laughlin
by New Directions Publishing Corporation
80 Eighth Avenue, New York 10011

Contents

"Álvaro de Campos," by Almada Negreiros (c. 1959)

A Brief Biographical Note

Fernando Pessoa devoted his life to literature, producing an extensive and extraordinarily varied body of work that went far beyond any dominant literary traditions or creeds—leaving to posterity two trunks filled to the brim with thousands upon thousands of unpublished writings. Born in Lisbon in 1888 and practically unknown outside of Portugal at the time of his death in 1935, he knew from an early age that his calling was the written word—exploring it across languages and genres while radically challenging the boundaries of authorship and subject. As a young boy he set out on his process of "self-othering" in English, a language he learned in the decade he spent in the British-governed town of Durban, where his stepfather João Miguel Rosa (1857–1919) had been appointed Portuguese Consul. What Pessoa gained as an individual and in literary prowess during his formal education within the British Empire at the end of the Victorian era inexorably shaped his fate in Lisbon, where he spent the rest of his life.

That short yet prolific life may be divided neatly into three periods. In a letter to the *British Journal of Astrology* dated February 8, 1918, Pessoa wrote that there were only two dates he remembered with absolute precision: July 13, 1893, the date of his father's death from tuberculosis (when Pessoa was only five); and December 30, 1895, the day his mother remarried, which meant that, shortly afterwards, the family moved to South Africa. In that same letter, the twenty-nine-year-old Pessoa mentions a third date, too: August 20,

1905, the day he left South Africa and returned to Lisbon for good.

That first brief period was marked by two losses: the deaths of his father and of a younger brother. And perhaps a third loss too, that of his beloved Lisbon. During the second period, despite knowing only Portuguese when he arrived in the racially and ethnically diverse coastal city in eastern South Africa's KwaZulu-Natal province, Pessoa rapidly became fluent in English and, to a lesser degree, in French. He was clearly no ordinary student. When asked years later, a fellow pupil described Pessoa in laudatory terms:

> [A]s a boy of 17 he wrote the article on Macaulay … which I always regarded of exceptional merit. His English composition was generally remarkably good and sometimes approached to genius. He was a great admirer of Carlyle … I was always very good friends with the boy and found him loyal and public-spirited. He was not athletic himself in ordinary English games; but I have been told by some of his contemporaries he was very easily excited after watching a game of football.*

In 1902, just six years after arriving in Durban, Pessoa won first prize for an essay on the British historian Thomas Babington Macaulay. Indeed, he appeared to spend all his spare time among books, and had already started creating the fictional alter egos—or as he later described them, *heteronyms*—for which he is now celebrated, writing poetry and prose under such names as Karl P. Effield, David Merrick, Charles Robert Anon, Horace James Faber, Alexander Search, and more. In a recent book, Jerónimo Pizarro and Patricio Ferrari introduced and anthologized nearly 140 fictitious authors, some with their own specific biographies, literary influences, political views, and philosophical idiosyncrasies. Only toward the end of the 1920s did Pessoa formally write of his self-othering:

> What Fernando Pessoa writes belongs to two categories of works, which we could call orthonymic works and hetero-

---

* Quoted in Hubert D. Jennings. *The Poet with Many Faces: a Biography and Anthology*, edited by Carlos Pittella (Providence: Gávea-Brown, 2018), 46.

nymic works. It is not possible to say that they are autonomous works and pseudonymous works because they are truly not. Whereas the pseudonymous work is done by the author in his own person (the only difference being the name chosen for the signature), the heteronymic work is done by the author outside his personality. This is to say that it is the work of an individuality completely crafted by him as would be the sayings of characters in any of his dramas.*

The third period of Pessoa's life began when, at the age of seventeen, he returned alone to Lisbon, never to set foot on African soil again. He returned ostensibly to attend college, initially living with Anica, his maternal aunt and godmother, not far from the Curso Superior de Letras (School of Arts and Letters). For different reasons—chief among them ill health and a student strike—he abandoned his studies in 1907 and became a regular visitor to the National Library (which he had already begun frequenting during his second semester in 1906, keeping a diary of his readings). There, he resumed his regime of voracious reading: philosophy, psychology, sociology, history, and, particularly, literature. During those first few years back in his native city, Pessoa reread his English masters (Shakespeare, Milton, Byron, Shelley, Keats), while also becoming acquainted with the works of Portuguese poets (Almeida Garrett, Antero de Quental, Cesário Verde, António Nobre, Guerra Junqueiro) and leading French symbolist poets (Baudelaire, Mallarmé, Verlaine), as well as the works of Walt Whitman, whose *Leaves of Grass* would have a great impact on his heteronymic work—primarily in Alberto Caeiro and Álvaro de Campos.†

* Featured in *Presença—Folha de Arte e Crítica* (Coimbra, n. 17, Dec. 1928), 10. The Portuguese magazine was published from 1927 until 1940.
† Alberto Caeiro is Pessoa's main poetic heteronym. Pessoa's other two major heteronyms, Ricardo Reis and Álvaro de Campos, and Pessoa himself considered Caeiro to be their literary Master. While the first two wrote exclusively in Portuguese, Campos used English and French sparingly in his poetry. The three heteronyms emerged in 1914.

Late in the summer of 1907, Dionísia Estrela de Seabra (1823–1907), Pessoa's paternal grandmother, left him a small legacy, and in the second half of 1909 he used that money to buy a printing press for his publishing house, Empreza Íbis, which he set up a few months later. Empreza Íbis closed in 1910, having published not a single book. Needing to fend for himself, he turned to one of the skills that set him apart from his Portuguese contemporaries: foreign languages. Throughout the rest of his life he would work as a freelance commercial translator (Portuguese, English, French) for various Lisbon-based import-export firms, never committing to the drudgery of a fixed schedule. Interestingly, it was around this time, in his early twenties, that the Portuguese (would-be English poet) finally embraced his mother tongue as his main literary language.

In 1912 he met the poet and fiction writer who would become his closest artistic ally and friend, Mário de Sá-Carneiro (1890–1916). That same year, Pessoa turned down an invitation by the American editor and publisher Warren F. Kellogg to travel and sojourn in London as a literary translator.* In April 1912, Pessoa published his first piece of criticism in Portugal, the lengthy and provocative article entitled "The New Portuguese Poetry Sociologically Considered," in the review *A Águia*, founded in Oporto two years earlier. From 1915 on, Pessoa would continue contributing essays, as well as his own writings and translations, to various journals, including the literary magazine *Orpheu*, which he cofounded with artists and poets such as Almada Negreiros (1893–1970) and Sá-Carneiro. Through this collaboration he became part of Lisbon's literary avant-garde and was involved in various ephemeral literary movements such as Intersectionism and Sensationism. Alongside his day job, he wrote prolifically, producing poetry, fiction and plays. Considering the sheer quantity of writings that never made it into print during

---

* Pessoa made his debut as a literary translator in the *Biblioteca Internacional de Obras Célebres* (1911–1912) with translations from English and Spanish.

Pessoa's lifetime, it is fair to say that very little of his own poetry or prose was made available to his contemporaries—especially in England, where he managed to publish only one poem ("Meantime," in the *Athenaeum*, London, January 30, 1920).

At the end of the First World War, Pessoa printed two of his English works that he had written during that decade: *Antinous*, a long poem that celebrates the homoerotic love between Antinous and the Emperor Hadrian, and *35 Sonnets*, inspired by Shakespeare's sonnet series. Both chapbooks were self-published in Lisbon in 1918. Three years later, in 1921, he self-published *English Poems I–II*—which included a revised version of "Antinous" and "Inscriptions," a series of epitaphs motivated by his reading of *The Greek Anthology*, translated into English by William Roger Paton—and *English Poems III* (*Epithalamium*, twenty-one poems infused with explicit scenes of heterosexual love set in Rome). These two slim volumes were released by Olisipo, a commercial agency and publishing house that Pessoa had founded that same year.

Literary fame came to Pessoa only posthumously. Besides these English chapbooks, which received some disparaging reviews, he managed to publish just one slender volume of forty-four poems in Portuguese, *Mensagem* (*Message*), in December 1934—which secured him the recently established Antero de Quental Award. When Pessoa died in 1935, at the age of forty-seven, he left behind the famous trunks (there are at least two) stuffed with writings—nearly thirty thousand pieces of paper—and only then, thanks to some of his devoted literary friends and to the numerous scholars who have since spent years excavating the archive, did he come to be recognized as the prolific genius he was.

Pessoa lived to write, writing, typing, or hastily scribbling on anything that came to hand: scraps of stationery, used envelopes, leaflets, advertising flyers, the backs of business letters, flyleaves and margins of books in his personal library, dust jackets, tiny notebook sheets he would tear off and drop into the midst of his literary forest.

The creator of the heteronyms wrote voluminously, under his own name or another: poetry, prose, drama, philosophy, criticism, political theory—even if it was incomplete or unpolished. It is not unusual to find texts by different heteronyms on either side of a verso, commingling across the years. "All passes and remains," we read in the middle of loose sheets, between unfinished lines of an English poem titled "Elegy," which he probably wrote prior to the heteronymic eruption of 1914; a passage that, years later, will resonate with the closing line of Caeiro's penultimate poem in *The Keeper of Sheep*: "Passo e fico, como o Universo" (I pass and I remain, like the universe). All literary archived materials are dormant possibilities to be awakened, as one rummages through a multilayered visual and acoustic space, one where any reader, as is the case with Pessoa's papers, may also stumble upon his deep interest in esoterica—from occultism, theosophy, and astrology, to Indian mysticism, Kabbalistic, and Rosicrucian traditions. Yes, Pessoa drew up horoscopes not only for himself and his friends, but also for many dead writers and historical figures, among them Shakespeare, Wilde, and Robespierre, as well as for his heteronyms, a term he eventually chose over "pseudonym" because it more accurately described their stylistic and intellectual independence from him, their creator, and from each other. They sometimes interacted, even prefacing or criticizing each other's works. Pessoa's most active early fictitious authors wrote mostly in English, leaving metered poetry in various forms (sonnet, rondeau, epigram, epitaph), as well as an astonishingly eclectic range of prose texts (philosophical notes, essays, short stories) mostly in the form of first drafts; but others, like semi-heteronym Bernardo Soares, created around 1920, who is associated with the posthumous *Book of Disquiet*, and his three main poetic heteronyms (Alberto Caeiro, Ricardo Reis, Álvaro de Campos), produced a very solid body of work.

In an unfinished poem dated August 1, 1918, when Pessoa's focus was also on his English "Inscriptions," we find what could be read as his own epitaph: "Genius, the greatest curse / That the Gods bless us with."* Pessoa wrote literature both out of necessity and conviction. May posterity judge his calling to the Gods.

PATRICIO FERRARI & MARGARET JULL COSTA

* Quoted in Patricio Ferrari, ed., *Inside the Mask: The English Poetry of Fernando Pessoa* (Providence: Gávea-Brown, 2018), 16.

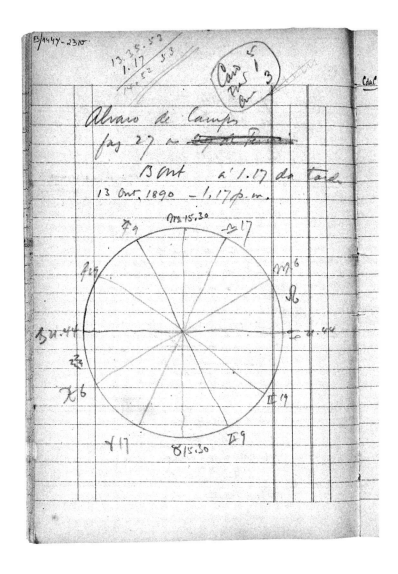

Horoscope for Álvaro de Campos's date, time, and place of birth

Introduction

Pessoa's heteronym Álvaro de Campos was not the first author to make an appearance in Pessoa's fictitious coterie, but he was the first to be brought to light, in 1915, in the short-lived literary magazine *Orpheu*, as well as the first heteronymic voice to affirm that, "properly speaking," Pessoa did not exist. Pessoa gave March 8, 1914, as the date of his heteronym Alberto Caeiro's poetic arrival in life, describing it as a "triumphal day" in a letter from 1935—the year of his death—to his friend, the Portuguese literary critic Adolfo Casais Monteiro. The two other heteronyms who followed shortly after were Álvaro de Campos and Ricardo Reis—both during the spring and summer of 1914.

This volume provides readers with the opportunity to read Campos's complete works in English—his "Book of Verses," which Pessoa at one point called "Intervals," and his "Book of Prose," which, in the end, he named "Episodes." Now, these "intervals" could refer to Campos's poems following the great odes; as for the "episodes," they consist of the prose texts that Campos sometimes considered accidents of fate. Álvaro de Campos was quite ironic about fate, and perhaps he would agree with Pessoa when he wrote, quoting Carlyle, "*disjecta membra* are what we have of any poet, or of any man." As an introduction to Campos's "books," Pessoa left the following note in Portuguese: "Alvaro de Campos is a character in a play; what's missing is the play."*

---

* Sometimes Pessoa wrote the name "Alvaro" without the accent, as in this note.

There are several incomplete pen portraits of Campos, as if both Pessoa and subsequent critics felt the need to give him a minimal fictional substance. Pessoa himself did so on various occasions, whether in the 1915 pamphlet about the Lisbon School attributed to Frederico Reis (here Tavira is not Campos's birthplace and Campos "is what the futurists wanted to be, plus something else"); or, as Pessoa wrote in the "Bibliographic Table" published in the magazine *Presença* in 1928: "Alvaro de Campos, born in 1890 ... closed off what you might call his emotional side [under the influence of Caeiro], which he called 'sensationist' ..." In this latter portrait, Pessoa links Campos to a range of literary influences, "in which Walt Whitman predominates, albeit less so than Caeiro," and he states that Campos had produced "various compositions, generally scandalous and provocative in nature, especially to Fernando Pessoa, who, nevertheless, has no option but to publish them, however much he disagrees with them."*

In the aforementioned letter dated January 13, 1935, we find the most complete description of Campos: "Alvaro de Campos was born in Tavira, on October 15, 1890 ... He is a naval engineer (educated in Glasgow) ... tall (5 feet, 7 inches—almost one inch taller than me), thin and slightly hunched ... [He is] neither very pale nor very dark, vaguely like a Portuguese Jew; [his] hair, however, is straight and he normally has a side parting, [he wears a] monocle ... He received an average high-school education; then he was sent to Scotland to study engineering, first mechanical engineering, then naval." Reading the incendiary prose/poetry work "Ultimatum," published in the first and only number of *Portugal Futurista* (1917), or another piece of provocative writing such as the one-page prose text "Message to the Devil," the reader will agree that it was not mere chance that Campos shared a birthday (October 15) with Friedrich Nietzsche—whose *Thus Spoke Zarathustra* Pessoa had read in Spanish translation around 1911–1912.

* Fernando Pessoa. "Tabua Bibliográfica." In *Presença, Coimbra*, n. 17 (1928): 10.

In the most positive portrait, so to speak, extant in Pessoa's archive, Campos is the naval engineer and Futurist poet harking back to the days of the magazines *Orpheu* and *Portugal Futurista*. Then, at the fictitious age of twenty, he became known for his "Maritime Ode," one of the longest poems in the Portuguese language with its 904 lines, and the incendiary "Ultimatum." Campos is also the author of two somewhat intemperate letters: one in French, unsent, to Marinetti—the Italian poet, editor, and founder of the Futurist movement; and the other, addressed to the director of *A Capital*, generated a public controversy, though the newspaper ended up only reproducing an inconsequential excerpt. But Campos is also the lyric self of "Tobacconist's Shop," protagonist of that long, disenchanted "Song of Myself," as well as the hero of an "[a]potheosis turned on its head …" (from which a much less triumphant portrait emerges), and myriad other poems drawing on a number of literary traditions from across Europe and America.

In the same letter from January 1935, Pessoa writes: "I am, in fact, a mystic nationalist, a rational Sebastianist. But I am, apart from that, and even in contradiction with that, many other things." By so doing, he confirms the patriotic position taken in his book *Mensagem* (*Message*). And yet, stressing how contradictory and diverse he may be, Campos, at the outset of "Tobacconist's Shop" declares: "I'm nothing. / I'll always be nothing. / I can't even hope to be nothing. / That said, I have inside me all the dreams of the world." While Pessoa assumes that he is "someone," but insists on being "many other things," Campos claims to be "nothing," but to have in him "all the dreams of the world." But what is it that Campos assures us he is not? The opening line is not an affirmative "I'm nothing," but rather "Não sou nada" (which could be read literally as "I am not nothing"). This type of structure gives rise to a possible inference: if he's nothing, then is he everything? Not necessarily, for one can be nothing without being everything; but this inference is reinforced because of the "[t]hat said"—in the Portuguese text, *aparte isso*, literally "besides that"—and it is always "besides that" that Campos claims to have in him "all the dreams of the world." He claims to be Whitman's "brother in the Universe" or a "globetrotter of the Divine." Campos can be defined by what he is, but also by what he is "besides that." He has "dreamed far more than Napoleon ever did"; he is "nothing," yet he is "a foreigner, a tourist, a passerby"; he has "clutched to [his] hypothetical bosom more humanities than Christ ever did"; he slips "through the interstices of everything" and has "secretly written philosophies that no Kant ever wrote." Campos's poetic cosmopolitanism converges with the same telluric landscape of a Dino Campana (a contemporary of Pessoa). When feeling low in spirits, he is closer to a Samuel Beckett, full of a painful and cynical nihilism that suggests making a blank slate of any previous paradigm. Campos fulfills in poetry what Ludwig Wittgenstein set out in prose when he said: "We are asleep. Our life is like a dream. In our better hours, though, we wake up just enough to realize that we are dreaming." Campos is a vagrant, an outlaw, an outsider. ("But I am, and perhaps always will be, a tenant in one of those garrets."). He refuses to be like the others ("You wanted me married, futile, ordinary, and taxable?"), and he denies any classification or confinement:

> A patient in a lunatic asylum is at least someone.
> I'm a patient in a lunatic asylum but without the lunatic asylum.
> I'm rationally mad,
> I'm both lucid and loony[.]

Campos is neither a genius nor a madman, but "rationally mad"; he is not simply this or that, and therefore attacks those who line up to be part of a literary current or a poetic school of thought:

> Why is there a limit if to be limited, existence is quite enough?
> To create is to free the self!
> To create is to substitute oneself!
> To create is to be a defector!

Campos is the most extroverted and irreverent Pessoan double, conceived to embody, more deeply than any other of his fictitious authors, the mission of living life to a supreme level of vertigo in a feverish outpouring of dysphoric emotions. He is a being who is not sufficient unto himself. Faced with the multiform world set out before him, as a horizon at the same time real and unattainable, Campos is possessed by the fury that strives to contain it, trying to embrace all the brouhaha of the modern world—both people and objects, culture and machinery. The whole he pursues encompasses not just the full range of imaginative possibilities, nor the landscapes he has seen or dreamed of. He's also a Calatrava bridge between the past and the present over human abysses, or between John Keats's negative capability and the anthropological psychoanalysis of Wilfred Bion.

All things considered, Campos is also the synthesis of a poetic and fictional evolution. As for his poetic evolution, there is: (1) the premodernist poet of "Opiary," whom Pessoa calls "an Alvaro in the making," and to whom he attributes an indefinite series of "Poems before waking," which means "before [Campos] had met Caeiro and fallen under his influence"; (2) the modernist poet of the book of verse entitled *Triumphal Arch*, the book of his great odes, containing at least "five apotheoses in verse"; and (3) the late-modernist poet— the poet of a second modernism already closer to postmodernity— of a set of unconnected poems that Pessoa had planned to gather under the title *Intervals*, or, alternatively, *Accessories*. The question that inevitably arises is whether this evolution—allowing for the imperfections of such a term—finds a parallel in his prose. After all, we do not know Campos's decadent prose, nor his sensationist prose, nor is there a late-modernist prose. Apart from certain futurist passages in *Ultimatum*, the prose is more or less always identical, very similar to what Fernando Pessoa himself wrote, albeit with some differences that seem to be to do with a "character," that the style—sometimes more provocative, more aphoristic, sometimes more emotional—tries to re-create and define. Is this because historiography tends to rely more on poetry than on prose? Is it because formalist theories have always been more concerned with poetry than with prose? Could it be because Campos was only seen as a

prose writer of some letters and a series of critical and intervention-
ist texts until Bernardo Soares reappeared around 1928, Barão de
Teive emerged, and Campos took on the task of writing the "Notes
in Memory of my Master Caeiro" between 1929–1930? What is cer-
tain is that the modernity of Campos's prose remains to be stud-
ied—from the mixed poetry/prose of "Ultimatum" to the "Notes."
It's a modernity of which Pessoa, around 1929, wrote a brief analysis
comparing his heteronyms:

> The assistant bookkeeper Bernando Soares and the Barão de
> Teive are both me and not-me, in that they write in substan-
> tially the same style, with the same grammar, the same use
> of language: they write in a style which is, for good or ill, my
> own. I compare these two because they are examples of the
> same phenomenon—an inability to adapt to the reality of life,
> and for the same motives and reasons. However, while the
> Portuguese of the Barão de Teive and Bernardo Soares is the
> same, their styles differ ... On the other hand, while there are
> notable similarities between Bernardo Soares and Álvaro de
> Campos, the Portuguese of Álvaro de Campos is looser, his
> imagery more extravagant, more personal and more sponta-
> neous than that of Soares.

In 1935, Pessoa said that he wrote poetry as Campos when he felt
"a sudden impulse to write without knowing exactly what," adding
in parentheses: "My semiheteronym Bernardo Soares, who in many
ways resembles Alvaro de Campos, appears whenever I am tired or
drowsy, so that the qualities of reasoning and inhibition are some-
what suspended ... What's difficult for me is writing Reis's prose—as
yet unpublished—or that produced by Campos. The simulation is
easier, also, because it is more spontaneous, in verse." Pessoa had
made this last assessment around 1931, in the draft of a preface he
wrote for the anthology of his heteronyms, *Fictions of the Interlude*,
left among the thousands of other unpublished manuscripts and
typescripts:

Among the authors of *Fictions of the Interlude*, it is not only their ideas and feelings that distinguish them from mine: the actual technique of composition, the style, is different too. There, each character is not just conceived differently, but created to be a wholly distinctive persona. That's why poetry predominates in *Fictions of the Interlude*. In prose, it's harder to *other* oneself.*

Affirmations of the sort can also be found in Campos's "Notes in Memory of my Master Caeiro," and lead us to wonder if Pessoa othered himself less, in terms of style, in the Engineer's prose, and in prose in general.

I [Álvaro de Campos] am exasperatingly sensitive and exasperatingly intelligent. In this respect (apart from a smidgeon more sensibility and a smidgeon less intelligence) I resemble Fernando Pessoa; however, while in Fernando, sensibility and intelligence interpenetrate, merge and intersect, in me, they exist in parallel or, rather, they overlap. They are not spouses, they are estranged twins.

*

Through Campos's radicalism we can understand how Fernando Pessoa was an intemperate writer who had no disciples or followers, but imitators. That his only true heir was no more or less than himself. And the limits of his genius perhaps coincide with those of modernism; although, curiously, it is within these same limits that his uncategorizable ascent to poet-thinker—both multiple and absent from himself—takes place.

Considering the temporal existence of Alvaro de Campos and all the fictitious authors Pessoa brought to poetic life for almost three

* *Fictions of the Interlude* is the general title Pessoa originally gave to the collected works of his heteronyms, which he planned to publish in several separate volumes. In the end, it served only as the title for five poems published under his own name in 1917.

decades is important, especially if we are to read his heteronymic works in the context of a whole—and ever-expansive—literary space. For instance, whether by coincidence or not, the writing of one of the greatest poems in the Portuguese language, "Tobacconist's Shop," coincides with the beginning of the second phase of *The Book of Disquiet*. This invites us to read the late Campos in parallel with this second *Book of Disquiet*. Just as the apotheotic *Triumphal Arch*, with its odes, gave way to rather simpler and more continuous accessory-poems, if we can call them that, the "grand" or "grandiose" excerpts from *The Book of Disquiet* gave way to anonymous, less decadent fragments. Additionally, it is essential to enter the works that make up Pessoa's oeuvre and consider them in a global context, relating it to the works of other contemporary authors—in Europe, the United States, and beyond.

*

This volume is based on the second edition of the first complete critical edition of Campos's writings published by Tinta-da-China in Portugal (2021). That Portuguese edition respects the original spellings and reproduces all the variants Pessoa left behind in his manuscripts and typescripts. It also corrects and improves on transcriptions by previous editors in Portugal. Given Campos's prolific output, just the English translations are contained in this print edition. Since this edition is not a critical one, variants other than the last are not reproduced. It does not include certain incomplete or unfinished poems and prose texts. Some of these, however, may still be found in translation on the New Directions website (ndbooks. com). This edition features poetry and prose never before translated into English, as well as facsimiles of some poems and prose texts from the Pessoa Archive housed at the National Library of Portugal in Lisbon.

JERÓNIMO PIZARRO & ANTONIO CARDIELLO

Acknowledgments

The editors wish to thank José Barreto, Marco Pasi, Patricio Ferrari, and Sofia Rodrigues for all the support they received while working on the first Portuguese edition of *The Complete Works of Álvaro de Campos* in Lisbon back in 2014. They are grateful to Pedro Serpa, Vera Tavares, Rita Almeida Simões, Madalena Alfaia, Inês Hugon, and Bárbara Bulhosa at Tinta-da-China, where the Pessoa Collection, directed by Jerónimo Pizarro, continues to grow.

The translators wish to acknowledge the publications where the following texts appeared:

"[My poor friend ...]" in *Asymptote*, Lee Yew Leong, editor in chief (Winter 2023)

"Note," "[Almost unwittingly ...]," "Lisbon (1926)"in *Bomb*, Benjamin Samuel, editor (Summer 2023)

"Carry Nation [My Joan of Arc ...]," "Carry Nation [Not an aesthetic saint ...]," "[With this misty day ...]," "[I'm weary of the intellect ...]," "Bicarbonate of Soda," in *The Brooklyn Rail*, Anselm Berrigan, poetry editor (June 2023)

"[Ah, how refreshing ...]" in *The New York Review of Books*, Jana Prykril, poetry editor (June 22, 2023)

"Three Sonnets" in *The Paris Review*, Vijay Seshadri, poetry editor (Spring 2022)

"[No, you're right, I'm wrong ...]" in *Poetry*, Charif Shanahan, guest editor (May 2023)

"[Lisbon with its houses ...]," "[I'm beginning to know myself ...]," "Álvaro de Campos, Naval Engineer and Futurist Poet. Interview" in *The Southwest Review,* Greg Brownderville, editor (Spring 2023)

The translators are also indebted to Rita Almada, Catarina Almada, and Silvia Costa for the reproduction of Almada Negreiro's artwork.

The editors and translators extend their gratitude to Barbara Epler and Declan Spring at New Directions for enthusiastically opening their literary home to the works of Fernando Pessoa—beginning with the publication of *The Book of Disquiet* in 2017, followed by *The Complete Works of Alberto Caeiro* in 2020. We are grateful, too, to the rest of the New Directions team—especially Brittany Dennison, codirector of publicity—for their professionalism, diligence, and continuous dedication to modern U.S. and world literature.

The translators would particularly like to acknowledge the help of our dear late friend, the poet Ana Luísa Amaral, who gladly took the time to read all the English translations of the poetry and made so many intelligent and helpful comments.

The Complete Works of Álvaro de Campos

The beginning of the Álvaro de Campos

The beginning of Álvaro de Campos: "Life is so very unheraldic!" (Text 1)

Poems

1   [c. 1914]

Life is so very unheraldic!
So lacking in thrones and everyday pinchbeck!
So essentially hollow, so self-evidently naked,
Drown me, O noise of action, in the roar of your oceans!

Blessèd be, [...]* the carts and the trains and the automobiles,
The regular breathing of factories, the thunder of shuddering
          engines
With your chronic [...]
Blessèd be you, for you conceal me from myself...

You conceal the whole and real silence of the Hour
You diffuse into methodical noise the mystery,
The mystery that almost screams, almost, almost weeps inside me,
Rocked to sleep by your mechanical lullabying,

Carry me far away from knowing I'm alive and can feel,
Stuff my ears—which are also yours—with the banal and material.
The life I live—O [...]—is the lie of a life I tell myself,
I only have what I [...], and only want what I cannot have.

* Missing text is indicated throughout by an ellipsis inside brackets.

2

[c. 1915]

Three Sonnets

I.

When I look at myself I see a stranger.
So obsessed am I with feeling
That I sometimes lose my way when I step free
From all the sensations I receive.

The air I breathe, the liquor I imbibe
Both belong to my way of existing,
And I never quite know how to conclude
The sensations I so unwillingly conceive.

Nor have I ever properly ascertained
If I do actually feel what I feel. Am I
Really the person I seem to be?

Am I really who I believe I am?
Even in my sensations I'm a semi-atheist,
Unsure that I am the one who in me feels.

II.

The Praça da Figueira in the morning,
When it's a sunny day (as it always is
In Lisbon), is never far from my mind,
However futile that memory might be.

There are so many more interesting things
Than that logical, plebeian place!

4

And yet for some reason I love it ... do I
Know why? Who cares anyway? ... Onwards!

Sensations are only worth our while
If we don't waste our time studying them.
Not one of those that exist in me is serene ...

Besides, nothing in me is ever certain or
In agreement with my self ... Beautiful hours
Belong to others, or simply don't exist.

III.
Listen, Daisy: be sure, when I die,
To tell my friends in London,
That you feel, even if it's a lie,
Real grief at my death. You will go

From London to York, where you were born (So you say ...
Not that I believe anything you say),
To tell that poor young lad
Who gave me so many happy hours,

Of which you know nothing, that I died ...
Even he, whom I thought I loved so much,
Won't give a damn ... Then go and share

The news with that strange creature Cecily
Who believed I would one day be great ...
Oh, to hell with life and everyone in it!

Opiary   *For Senhor Mário de Sá-Carneiro*

It's before the opium that my soul falls sick.
Feeling life both fortifies and etiolates
And I seek in that consoling opium
An East to the east of the East.

This life on board will be the death of me.
Each day my head pounds with fever
And, though I search until I drop,
I can find no impulse to adapt.

I live in paradox, astral ineptitude,
I live in the golden folds of my life,
Where self-respect is a slippery slope,
Even pleasures are the ganglia of what ails me.

Through a mechanism of disasters,
A series of cogs with fake flywheels,
I walk among visions of gallows
In a garden where flowers float in the air, stemless.

I stagger through the neat stitching
Of an inner life of lace and lacquer.
I believe that at home I have the knife
That slit the throat of John the Baptist.

I am atoning for a murder in a trunk
Casually committed by a grandfather of mine.
My nerves are in the noose, dozens of them,
And I fell into opium as if into a ditch.

At the drowsy touch of the morphine
I lose myself in throbbing transparencies
And in a night laden with diamonds
The moon rises glittering, like my Fate.

I was always a bad student, now
I simply watch the ship travel
Down the Suez Canal steering
My life, an amphora in the dawn light.

I have lost the days I once enjoyed.
I only worked so as to feel the same fatigue
That is now like an arm about my neck
Which both chokes and comforts me.

I was a child just like everyone else,
Born in a Portuguese province,
And I've known English people
Who say I speak English perfectly.

I'd like to have poems and stories published
By Editions Plon and the *Mercure de France*,
But this life cannot possibly continue
On a voyage untroubled by storms!

Life on board is a sad thing
Although we do occasionally have fun.
I speak with Germans, Swedes, and Brits
But the pain of living still persists.

After all, what use was it to me to have
Gone to the East and seen India and China?
The Earth is all the same and very tiny,
And there's only one way to live.

That's why I take opium. As a remedy.
I am a convalescent of the Moment.
I live on the ground floor of my thoughts
And watching Life pass by just fills me with ennui.

I smoke. I grow weary. If only there were an earth
Where the east didn't always become the west!
Why did I visit the India that exists
If the only India is the soul within me?

For inheritance all I have is misfortune.
The gypsies made off with my Fate.
Perhaps, even at death's door, I'll find
No shelter from my own cold self.

I pretended to study engineering.
I lived in Scotland. I visited Ireland.
My heart is a poor grandmother
Begging at the doors of Joy.

O iron ship, don't ever reach Port Said!
Turn right instead, heading who knows where.
I spend the days in the smoking room with the count—
A French *escroc*, who is only a count at funeral teas.

I return to Europe feeling discontented, and
minded to become a somnambulic poet.
I am a monarchist but not a Catholic
And would like to be something stronger.

I would like to have beliefs and money,
To be various insipid people I've seen.
However, here, today, I am nothing
But a passenger on some ship or other.

I have no personality at all.
The cabin boy is far more striking than me,
He has the wonderfully haughty manner
Of a Scottish laird who's been fasting for days.

I cannot be anywhere. My country
Is wherever I am not. I am ill and weak.
The purser is an old rogue. He saw me
With the Swedish woman ... and can guess the rest.

One day I will cause a scandal here on board,
Just to get the other passengers talking about me.
I simply cannot cope with life, and cannot help
The rages into which I sometimes fall.

I've spent the day smoking and drinking,
American drugs that dizzy the mind,
And I was already drunk on nothing!
My rose-like nerves deserve a better brain.

I write these lines. It seems impossible
That even though I do have talent, I barely feel it!
The fact is, this life is a farmstead
Where any sensitive soul would grow bored.

The English are made for existence.
No other people are so clearly intended
For the Quiet Life. Put a coin in the slot
And out comes a beaming Englishman.

I belong to the long line of Portuguese
Who, once India had been discovered,
Were left with nothing to do. Death is certain.
How that thought has assailed me.

Oh to hell with life and having to live it!
I don't even read the book by my bedside.
I'm sick of the Orient. It's like a rug which,
Once rolled up, ceases to be beautiful.

I have no choice but to take opium. You can't
Expect me to lead one of those clean-living lives,
To become one of those honest souls
With fixed hours for sleeping and eating,

The devil take them! Deep down, though, I envy them.
Because these nerves will be the death of me.
If only some ship could carry me off
To a place where I only want what I can see.

No, I would still be just as bored.
I need a far stronger opium to plunge me
Into dreams that would finish me off
And throw me into some muddy ditch.

Fever! If what I have isn't fever,
Then I don't know what fever must feel like.
What it comes down to is this: I am ill.
This hare has run out of road, my friends.

Night fell. The first bell rang
Calling us to get dressed for supper.
Social life calls! So off we go socializing
Until we slip our collar and lead!

Because it will end badly, and there's sure to be
(Hooray!) blood and a revolver at the end
Of this terrible inner disquiet
For which there's no solution.

Yet anyone looking at me would think me banal,
Me and my life ... Just another young man ...
Even my monocle labels me
As belonging to some universal type.

Ah, how many souls must there be, like me,
Who always toe the Line, but, like me, are mystics!
How many beneath the inevitable dinner jacket
Also feel, like me, a horror of life?

If only I were as interesting
Internally as I am externally!
I ride the Maelstrom, ever closer to the center.
Doing nothing will be my ruination.

A good-for-nothing. Yes, and why not?
If only we could look down on others
And, even with our jacket out at the elbows,
Be a hero, a madman, doomed and handsome!

I feel like pressing my hands to my mouth
And biting down very hard on them.
It would be an unusual thing to do
And would amuse the others, the supposedly sane.

The absurd, like the flower from that India
I did not find in India, is the child
Of my brain grown tired of being bored.
May God either change my life or end it ...

Leave me sitting here, in this chair,
Until they come and put me in my coffin.
I was born to be some classy mandarin,
But I lack the peace of mind, the mat, the tea.

And how good it would be just to drop
Into the grave through some trick trapdoor!
Life tastes to me of blonde tobacco.
All I've ever done is smoke my life away.

Ultimately, what I want is faith, peace.
Not all these confusing sensations.
I wish God would just end it! Open the floodgates—
And be done with these comedies played out in my soul!

On board ship in the Suez Canal.

4 CARNIVAL
4a   [c. 1915]
Life is one long drinking spree.
I can never see it as anything else.
When I walk down the street, it feels
Like a carnival full of color and dust …

Whatever the hour, I have the painful
Yet nonetheless pleasant sensation
Of barging my way through the glee
Of a dense, clownishly plebeian mob …

Every moment is a vast carnival,
In which I find myself unwittingly caught up.
Whenever I think this, life seems tedious
And I, who love intensity, find this all too

Intense … A hubbub that enters the mind
Of anyone who cares to stop for a moment
And see what it's doing to his thoughts
Before being and lucidity slough it off …

Automobiles, vehicles, […]
The crowded streets, […]
A film strip constantly running
And never with any clear meaning.

I feel as if I were drunk, confused,
I stagger inside my own sensations,
Feel a sudden need for banisters
In the full glare of the city […]

This whole existence is one long party …
Utter bafflement creeps into me
And dislocates the credulous center
Of my ever-circling psyche …

And yet perhaps more than anyone
I'm in amorous accord with all of this …
I find in myself, when I analyze myself,
No difference between me and

This whole silly carnival hooha,
This blend of European and Zulu,
This garish, vulgar drumming
So elegantly unconsoling …

What creatures! At once friendly and unpleasant!
And though I am one of them, I loathe them too!
We share the same European complexion
And the same air conjoins us […]

Sometimes I find the ennui of being me
Combines with this way and manner of existence …
And I spend long, futile hours
Trying to discover who I am; and my search

Always comes to nought ... If I evolve
A plan in the life I'm carving out for myself,
Before I've even brought that plan to a conclusion
Things will be just as they were before. It's a delusion

To trust in anyone who has being ...
[...]

4b   [c. 1915]

Ah, all this is just to say that
I am not at ease in life, I want to go
To a quieter place, to hear
Rushing rivers and have no more sorrows.

Yes, I'm fed up with the body and the soul
This body contains, or is, or pretends to be ...
Each coming moment is a nascent body ...
But what matters is that I know no peace.

I don't intend to write another poem,
I intend only to say that I'm bored
With measuring out my life hour by hour
And find it a most regrettable strategy

On God's part to use the scrap of material
He decided to choose for my body ...
Everything inside me is pure filth
And the most monotonous of miseries.

The only decent thing is to be someone else,
But that is because we view things from outside ...
There is something in me that seems now
[...]

4c   [after 1915]

It's Carnival, and the streets are full
Of people who still experience sensations,
While I have only intentions, thoughts, ideas,
But can have neither mask nor bread.

They are all the same, but I am diverse—
I wouldn't be accepted even among poets.
Sometimes I don't dare put this into verse—
And I say things in a way they never would.

How measly are the many people here!
I am tired, brain-tired and weary.
I see this and I stand, totally here,
But alone with time and with space.

Behind the masks our being watches,
Behind the mouths a mystery emerges
That my anodyne verses reject.
[…]

Am I major or minor? I have hands and feet
And a mouth that speaks and I move around in the world.
Today, when all are masked, you are
A being all masks-cum-gestures, and so deep …

4d   [after 1915]

That sad, false resemblance between
The person I think I am and the person I am.
I am the mask that becomes a child again,
But which I recognize as an adult wherever I am.

This is neither Carnival nor me.
I feel like sleeping, and yet I walk.
What ripples about around me
Passes […]

Sleeping, taking off this outrageous world
As if taking off a stolen Carnival costume,
Removing a fake soul as if it were a suit
[…]

My fate fills me with a kind of carnal nausea.
I grow almost tired of being tired. And so I go,
Anonymous, […] a child,
Setting off into my being in search of who I am.

5   [1914]

Triumphal Ode
By the painful glare of the factory's electric lights
I sit in a fever, writing.
I write grinding my teeth, greedy for the beauty of it all,
For a beauty of which the ancients knew nothing.

O wheels, O gears, O eternal *r-r-r-r-r-r*!
O powerful spasm contained in those furious mechanisms!
Furious inside me and furious outside,
In every one of my dissected nerves,
In every one of the papillae through which I feel!
My lips have gone dry, O great modern noises,
Just to hear you so horribly close,
And my head burns with desire to sing you with an excess
Of expression welling up from all my sensations,
With an excess contemporaneous with you, O machines!

Feverish and gazing at the engines as if at some tropical Nature—
Great human tropics of iron and fire and energy—
I sing, and I sing the present, as well as the past and the future,
Because the present is all of the past and all of the future
And Plato and Virgil are there in the machines and the electric lights
Only because there was once another age and Virgil and Plato were
       human,
Along with bits of some Alexander the Great from perhaps the
       fiftieth century,
Atoms that will burn with fever in some Aeschylus's brain from the
       hundredth century.
There they all are in those transmission belts and pistons and steer-
       ing wheels,
Roaring, creaking, whispering, booming, clanking,
Showering my body with an excess of caresses in one single caress
       of the soul.

Oh to be able to express my whole self the way an engine expresses
       itself!
To be as complete as a machine!
To be able to go through life as triumphantly as the very latest
       model of car!
To be able at least to let all this penetrate me physically,
To tear my flesh, to open up completely, to become permeable
To all the perfumes of oil and heat and coal
Given off by that stupendous flora, black, artificial, insatiable!

Fraternity with all that is dynamic!
A promiscuous fury to be part-participant
In the cosmopolitan iron rumble
Of those diligent trains,
In the freight-bearing toil of ships,
In the slow, slippery turning of cranes,

In the disciplined tumult of factories,
And in the whispering, monotonous, near-silence of transmission
    belts!

Productive European hours spent immersed
In mechanisms and useful tasks!
Big cities taking a break in cafés,
In cafés—oases of noisy futility
Where the murmurings and gestures of the Useful
Jostle and crystallize
Along with the wheels and cogs and bearings of Progress!
A new soulless Minerva of wharves and train stations!
New enthusiasms worthy of the Moment!
Iron-plated keels smiling as they lean against the dock
Or else raised up on the inclined planes of ports!
International activity, transatlantic, *Canadian-Pacific*!
Lights and feverish hours wasted in bars, in hotels,
At Longchamps and Derbies and Ascots,
And in Piccadillies and Avenues de l'Opéra that enter
My very soul!

Hey there streets, hey there squares, he-e-e-y *la foule*!
Everything that passes, everything that pauses at shop windows!
Traders; tramps; overdressed con men;
Blatant members of aristocratic clubs;
Sleazy, dubious individuals; heads of households vaguely happy
And paternal even down to the gold watch chain that crosses their
    vest
From pocket to pocket!
Everything that passes, everything that passes and never passes!
The rather obvious presence of ladies of easy virtue;
Bourgeois women, usually mother and daughter,
Banal but interesting (and who knows what else inside),
Who walk down the street heading somewhere or other;
The false, feminine grace of pederasts sauntering slowly by;

And all the other simply elegant people out for a stroll and out to be
     seen
And who do, after all, have a soul!
(Ah, how I would love to be the *souteneur* for the whole lot of them!)

The marvelous beauty of political corruption,
Delicious financial and diplomatic scandals,
Political riots in the streets.
And now and then the blazing comet of a regicide
That lights up with Furor and Fanfare the
Usually limpid skies of day-to-day Civilization!

News *passez* à-la-caisse in the newspapers,
Insincerely sincere political articles,
Headline news, heinous crimes—
Two whole columns continued on the next page!
The fresh smell of printer's ink!
The posters newly pasted, still damp!
Yellow books with a white wrapper—*vients-de-paraître*!
How I love you all, all, all,
How I love you in every possible way,
With eyes and ears and smell
And touch (ah, what merely touching you means to me!)
And with my intelligence like an antenna you set vibrating!
Ah, how jealous all my senses are of you!

Fertilizers, steam-driven threshing machines, agricultural progress!
Agrarian chemistry, and commerce made almost a science!
The sample cases of traveling salesmen,
Yes, traveling salesmen, the knights errant of Industry,
The human extensions of factories and quiet offices!

O fabrics in shop windows! O mannequins! O the latest fashions!
O all those useless items that everyone wants to buy!
Hi there, big department stores with your many departments!

Hi there, neon signs that come on and are there and then gone!
Hi there, all the stuff they use in construction now, so different from
      yesterday!
You know, reinforced concrete, cement, new processes!
Advances in gloriously deadly weapons!
Bulletproof vests, cannons, machine guns, submarines, airplanes!

I love you all, everything, ferociously.
I love you carnivorously,
Pervertedly and fixing my gaze
Upon you, O great, banal, useful, useless things,
O all things modern,
O my contemporaries, the present and soon-to-be
Brand-new system of the Universe!
New metallic, dynamic Revelation of God!

O factories, laboratories, *music-halls, Luna-Parks,*
O battleships, O bridges, O floating docks—
In my troubled, incandescent mind
I possess you as one would a beautiful woman,
I possess you completely as one would a beautiful woman one
      doesn't love,
Whom one meets by chance and finds really fascinating.

Hey there façades of big shops!
Hey there, elevators in big buildings!
Hey there, cabinet reshuffles!
Parliaments, policies, budget reports,
Falsified budgets!
(A budget is as natural as a tree
And a parliament as beautiful as a butterfly.)

Howdy-do, zest for everything in life,
Because everything is life, from the diamonds in the shop windows

To the night, that mysterious bridge between the stars
And the ancient, solemn sea that washes the coasts
And is mercifully just the same
As it was when Plato was Plato,
In his actual presence and in his flesh with his soul inside it,
And when he used to talk to Aristoteles, who would not become his disciple.

With a woman's delicious sense of sexual surrender
I could be chopped into little pieces by an engine.
Fling me into the furnaces!
Throw me under the trains!
Thrash me on the decks of ships!
Masochism through mechanisms!
A modern kind of sadism along with me and the noise!

Huzzah, *jockey* who won the *Derby*,
Oh to sink my teeth into your bi-colored cap!

(Being too tall to get through any door!
Ah, looking, for me, is a sexual perversion!)

Hello, hello, hcllo, cathedrals!
Let me crack my head open on your corners,
And be picked up from the street covered in blood
With no one knowing who I am!

O tramways, funiculars, and metros,
Bring me to orgasm just by rubbing up against me!
Hallo, halloo, hallay!
Go on, laugh in my face,
O automobiles crammed with partygoers and prostitutes,
O quotidian crowds in the streets, neither happy nor sad,
An anonymous, multicolored river in which I cannot bathe as I would
        wish!

Ah, what complex lives, what behind-closed-doors existences!
Ah, if only I could know each of those lives, the problems with money,
The domestic disputes, the unsuspected debauchery,
The thoughts each person thinks alone in their room
And the gestures they make when no one else is there!
Not knowing all this is to know nothing, O fury,
A fury which, like a fever and a jealousy and a hunger,
Hollows my cheeks and sometimes makes me wildly clench
And unclench my fists even as I'm walking through the crowds
On the streets rife with collisions!

Ah, the grubby, ordinary people, who always seem the same,
Who use expletives as if that were normal,
Whose sons steal from the stalls outside grocery stores
And whose eight-year-old daughters—and this I just love!—
Jerk off seemingly respectable gentlemen in stairwells.
The rabble who climb scaffolds for a living and head home
Down almost unbelievably pinched and putrid alleyways.
Marvelous human beings who live like dogs,
Who belong to no moral system,
For whom no religion was made,
No work of art created,
No political ideology designed!
But how I love you all, precisely because of that,
For not being immoral however low you sink, neither good nor bad,
Impervious to all progress,
Marvelous fauna from the seabed of life!

(The mule walks round and round and round
The waterwheel in my garden,
And that's about the size of the mystery of the world.
Wipe the sweat from your brow with your arm, disgruntled laborer.
The light of the sun muffles the silence of the spheres
And we all have to die,

O dark pinewoods in the gloaming,
Pinewoods where my childhood was something very different
From what I am today ...)

But there's that constant mechanical rage again!
Again the obsessive bustle of the buses.
Again the furious desire to be traveling simultaneously in every train
All over the world,
To be waving goodbye on board all the ships,
Which, at this very moment, are weighing anchor or sailing away
        from the docks.
O iron, O steel, O aluminium, O sheets of corrugated iron!
O wharves, O ports, O trains, O cranes, O tugboats!

All hail, major rail crashes!
All hail, mining disasters!
All hail, delicious shipwrecks of great transatlantic liners!
All hail, revolutions here, there, and everywhere,
As well as constitutional changes, wars, treaties, invasions,
Noise, injustice, violence, and perhaps, very shortly, the end.
The great invasion of Europe by the yellow-skinned barbarians,
And another Sun on the new Horizon!

What does all this matter, what does it actually matter
To the blazing red clamor of contemporary life,
To the deliciously cruel clamor of today's civilization?
All of this erases everything else, except for the Moment,
The Moment, hot and bare-chested as a furnace-man,
The Moment, stridently noisy and mechanical,
The Moment, the dynamic passing of all the Bacchantes
Of iron and bronze and other intoxicating metals.

Hurrah for the trains, hurrah for the bridges, for the hotels at
        suppertime,

Hurrah for every kind of machine, metallic, brutal, minimal,
Precision instruments made to crush and dig,
Mills and drills and all things rotary!
Hurrah! Hurrah! Hurrah!
Hurrah for electricity, the ailing nerves of Matter!
Hurrah for the radiophone, the metallic sympathy of the
        Unconscious!
Hurrah for tunnels, canals, Panama, Kiel, and Suez!
Hurrah for all the past contained in the present!
Hurrah for all the future already contained in us! Hurrah!
Hurrah! Hurrah! Hurrah!
Useful iron fruits from the cosmopolitan tree-factory!
Hurrah! Hurrah! Hurrah! Hurrah ho-o-o!
I don't even know that I exist inside. I turn, I spin, I engineer myself.
I'm coupled up to all the trains.
I'm hoisted up onto all the wharves.
I spin inside the propellers of all the ships.
Hurrah! Hooray! Hurrah!
Hurrah! I'm mechanical heat and electricity!
Hurrah! As well as the *rails* and the powerhouses and Europe!
Hurrah and hooray for every-me and everything, with all engines
        firing. Hurrah!

Leaping with everything over everything! Hup-up-up!

Hup la, hup la, hup-la-ho, hup-la!
Hey-ha! Hey-ho! Ho-o-o-o-o!
Z-z-z-z-z-z-z-z-z-z-z!

Ah to be everyone and everywhere!

6

[30 June 1914]

Two Excerpts from Odes
(The end of two Odes, of course)

I.

Come, ancient and ever-identical Night,
Night Queen born and instantly dethroned,
Night as silent inside as silence itself. Night
With the stars like glittering sequins
On your dress fringed with Infinity.

Come faintly,
Come lightly,
Come solitary and solemn, with your hands hanging
At your sides, come
And bring the far-flung hills close to the nearest trees,
Make all the fields I see into one field, your field,
Make the mountain one with your body,
Erase all the differences I see there by day,
All the roads that rise up,
All the various trees that turn it dark green,
All the white houses and the smoke drifting up among the trees,
And leave only one light, then another, and another,
In the vague and vaguely troubling distance,
In the distance suddenly impossible to traverse.

Our Lady
Of the impossible things we seek in vain,
Of the dreams that come to us by the window, at dusk,
Of the plans that caress us
On the spacious terraces of cosmopolitan hotels overlooking the sea,
To the European sound of music and voices distant and near,
And that wound us with the knowledge that they will never be
        realized.

Come cradle us,
Come caress us,
Kiss us silently on our brow,
So lightly that we only know we've been kissed
Because of a slight shift in our soul
And a faint sob emerging oh so tenderly
From what is most ancient in us
Where all those marvelous trees take root
Whose fruits are the dreams we coddle and adore
Because we know they bear no relation to real life.

Come most solemnly,
Solemnly and full
Of a hidden desire to weep,
Perhaps because the soul is large and life is small,
And none of our gestures ever leave our body,
And we can only reach as far as our arm can reach
And only see as far as our eyes can see.

Come sorrowfully,
Mater Dolorosa of the Anguish of the Timid,
Turris Eburnea of the Griefs of the Despised,
Cool hand on the fevered brow of the Humble,
Spring water on the dry lips of the Weary.
Come from afar,
From the gray horizon,
Come pluck me
From the soil of the anguish in which I thrive,
From the soil of disquiet and too-much-life and false-sensations
From which I naturally sprang.
Uproot me from that soil, a forgotten daisy,
Overshadowed by tall weeds,
Read in me, petal by petal, some sign or other,
And remove my petals one by one purely for your pleasure,

For your cool, silent pleasure.
Throw one petal to the North,
Home to the cities of Today, whose hustle and bustle I loved as
        though it were a body.
Throw another petal to the South
Home to seas and dreamed adventures.
Throw yet another petal to the West,
Where everything that might be the future blazes red,
Home to large raucous machines and vast rocky deserts
Where souls grow wild and morality does not penetrate.
And another petal, the other petals, all the other petals—
O secret call-to-arms inside my soul—
Throw them to the East,
To the East from which everything comes, the day and religion,
To the East, sumptuous, fanatical, warm,
To the excessive East that I will never see,
To the Buddhist, Brahmanist, Shintoist East,
To the East that is everything we do not have,
That is everything we are not,
To the East where—who knows?—Christ is perhaps living to this day,
Where perhaps God exists in bodily form, organizing everything ...

Come over the seas,
Over the endless seas,
Over the sea with no precise horizons,
Come run your hand over its animal back,
And instill in it a mysterious calm,
O hypnotic tamer of unruly things!

Come thoughtfully,
Come maternally,
On tiptoe, O ancient nurse, you who sat
At the bedside of the gods of lost faiths,
And who saw the birth of Jehovah and Jupiter

And smiled, because for you all is false, apart from darkness and
    silence,
And the great Mysterious Space beyond them ...

Come, silent, ecstatic Night,
Come wrap your light blanket
About my heart ...
As serenely as a slow evening breeze,
As tranquilly as a motherly caress,
With the stars shining (O Masquerade from the Beyond!)
Gold dust on your black hair,
And the waning moon on your cheek.

All sounds sound different
When you come.
When you enter all voices are lowered.
No one sees you enter.
No one knows when you arrive,
Or only suddenly, when they see that everything is closing,
Losing shape and color,
And that, high in the sky, still clearly blue and white on the horizon,
Already a crisp crescent or a yellowish circle or a mere sparse white
    face,
The moon is beginning its day.

II.
Ah, dusk, nightfall, the coming on of lights in the big cities,
And the mysterious hand muffling the hubbub,
And the weariness of everything in us that turns us away
From a precise, active sense of Life!
Every street is a canal in a Venice of tediums
And how mysterious the unanimous depths of the streets,

Of the streets as night falls, O Cesário Verde, my Master,
O "The Feeling of a Westerner!"

What profound disquiet, what desire for other things,
Which are neither countries or moments or lives,
What longing perhaps for other ways of feeling or being
Make the slow, distant instant moist with desire!

A somnambular horror among the lit lamps,
A tender, liquid terror leaning on street corners
Like a beggar for impossible sensations
With no idea who could possibly provide them …

When I die,
When—stiff and different like everyone else,
Ignoble outside and who knows what other-self inside—
When I set off down that road the very idea of which we cannot bear,
Through that door, through which, had we the choice, we would
        not look,
To that port unknown to the Captain of the Ship—
May it be at this hour worthy of the tediums I've endured,

At this same mystical, spiritual, and most ancient of hours,
At this hour when, perhaps, far longer ago than seems possible,
A dreaming Plato saw the idea of God
Carve out a clearly plausible body and existence
Inside his mind as wide open as a field.

May it be at this hour that you take me to be buried,
At this hour that I do not know how to live,
In which I do not know what sensations to have or pretend to have,
At this hour so tormentingly, excessively merciful,
Whose shadows come from some thing that is not a thing,

Whose vestments, as it passes, do not even brush the floor of the
    Feeling Life
Nor leave a trace of perfume on the paths of the Gaze.

Fold your hands on your lap, O dear companion I neither have nor
    want to have,
Fold your hands on your lap and look at me in silence,
At this hour when I cannot see you looking at me,
Look at me in silence and in secret and ask yourself
—You who know me—who I am ...

7 DEPARTURE

7a   [c. 1914]

Now that I can feel Death's fingers around my throat
Beginning to apply the final pressure,
And, realizing this, with eyes agape,
Looking behind me to gaze back at the past,
I see who I was and, above all, who I was not,
I lucidly review my motley past
And conclude that there must have been some mistake
Either in my having lived at all or in my having lived that way.

Is it always like this when Death enters the room
And locks the door behind her,
And the thing is final and fixed,
With no *Cour de Cassation* for your sealed fate,
Is it always like this when midnight strikes in life,
This same exasperating calm, this unwanted lucidity
That awakes in my departure something that predates childhood?
A final impulse, the last flicker of a flame that then burns out,
The cold splendor of the firework before it turns to ashes,
The massive crack of thunder above our heads, by which
We know that the storm has reached its peak and is on the wane.

I turn to the past.
My flesh feels young again.
With the kind of joy that comes with that utter lucidity
I observe the instinct for failure that was there in my life.
They're about to put out the last lamp
In the dawning street of my Soul!
It's the sign of a very old friendship
That last lamp being extinguished,
But even before I see the truth of this, I sense it
Even before I know it, I love it.
I look back at the past, at that past unlived;
I look and the past is a kind of future for me.

My Master, Alberto Caeiro, who I met at the start
And who I later discarded like some paltry jotting,
Today I recognize how wrong I was, and I weep inside,
I weep with joy to see how lucidly I weep
And I put out flags to celebrate my death and my unending failure,
I put out flags to celebrate this discovery, this knowledge of Death.
And at last I sit up among these almost comfortable pillows
And return to my healthy state of remorse.

7b   [c. 1914]

Ave atque vale, O amazing universe!
Ave atque vale, how very differently
I will look at you, and always will,
Should there still be more life, more ways of knowing you,
More angles from which to view you—and, who knows, I may never
        see you from the One-and-only—
Whatever happens, though, ave atque vale, O World!

I will set off for whatever side of you that Death may reveal to me
With my heart aching, my soul yearning, my gaze vague,

With the thrill of the adventure making waves in my blood …
I will set off for Death expecting to find nothing
But ready to see prodigious things from the other side of the World.

Ave atque vale, O spontaneous Universe!
The green leaves of grass in the happy meadows,
The darker green in the tops of the wind-rocked trees,
The dark white of the water,
The invisible down of the moorlands,
The impalpable shadowy claws of the storms,
The vast expanse of the seas,
The clear-cut course of the rivers,

Ave atque vale! Even God! Even Me! Even You!

When I step out from my individual self as if getting out of a chair,
When I step away from the universe as if leaving a room,
When I abandon all forms, senses, thoughts, all ways of feeling,
As if taking off a bothersome cape,
When my soul finally reaches the surface of my skin
And scatters my being throughout the external universe,
Then may I joyfully realize that Death
Has come like a distant Sun at the dawn of my new being.

On an oblique journey from my deathbed,
A journey diagonal to the dimensions of things,
The bed will rise up from the floor to the highest point on the ceiling,
Rise up like an absurd balloon and race
Off along the rails like a train …

[…]

I'm not afraid, O Death, of what the forbidden hatch
In your door to the world may be concealing from view.

I hold out my arms to you the way a child does,
Sitting on his nursemaid's knee, when he sees his Mama appear ...
For you I will happily leave my grown-up toys,
For you I will leave all family ties, for nothing binds me
To this prodigious, constant, ailing universe ...
The Definitive lies in You or it lies nowhere.

7c [c. 1914]

And I the complex, I the numerous,
I the saturnalias of all possibilities,
I the bursting dike of all personae,
I the excessive, I the successive, I the [...]
I the prolix even in moderation and stasis,
I who have felt in my blood and my nerves
All the sensibilities corresponding to all the metaphysics,
I who have disembarked in every port of the soul,
And flown in a plane over all the lands of the mind,
I the explorer of all the wastelands of reason,
The [...]
The creator of *Weltanschauungen*,
The prodigal sower of my own indifference
Of all modern trends, every one of them different,
And all at the very moment they are deemed to be true,
All of them different, all of them me—
Will I die like this? No: the universe is large
And any number of things could happen.
No: everything is better and bigger than we think
And death will reveal some truly extraordinary things ...
God will be happier.
Greetings, O new things that will happen when I die,
A newly mobile universe appearing over my horizon
When, once and for all,
Like a steamship leaving harbor on a long voyage,

With the ship's band playing the national anthem of the Soul,
I set off for X, troubled by my departure
But full of the vague, ignorant hope of all emigrants,
Full of faith in the New, of pure Belief in Abroad,
Yes—off I go, imprisoned by those seas,
In search of my future either in the lands, lakes, and rivers
That connect the round earth—the whole Universe—
Or else hidden from view. Yes, off I go …
Ave atque vale, O clamorous Universe …

[…]

First, there will be
A great acceleration of sensations, a […]
With major *dérapages* on the roads of my consciousness

(And even the final *atterrissage* of my airplane […])
A great englobement of noncontiguous sensations,
A swift, voracious whistle from the space between soul and God
From my […]
My successive states of soul will become simultaneous,
My whole individual self will be crumpled up into one small dot,
And when, just as I'm ready to depart,
Everything I experience, and will experience beyond the world,
Will be fused into one homogeneous, incandescent whole
And with such a crescendo of noise from the engines
That it will become a noise no longer metallic, but merely abstract,
I will set off through the Unknown in a whispering dream of velocity,
Leaving behind me on either side meadows, landscapes, villages
And moving ever closer to the edge, to the most far-flung parts of
        the knowable,
Driving a furrow of motion through the shipyard of things,
A new kind of dynamic eternity whistling through static eternity—
s-s-s-ss-sss
z-z-z-z-z-z divine automobile

7d   [c. 1914]

And when my bed is almost touching the ceiling
And I'm looking back through this porthole at the room with all its
    wardrobes,
And feeling in my soul the whirring of the ship's propellor,
Everything will seem far off and different and cold …
My sensations are in a distant city on a hill
And beyond, behind them, lies the entire universe, a broken bridge
    …

7e   [c. 1914]

Death—that inevitable worst-of-all-things,
That plunge to the bottom of a bottomless well;
That universal night descending inside us;
That final judgement of the consciousness with the fall of all the stars—
Will one day be mine,
And that day which moves ever nearer, ever nearer,
Paints all my sensations black,
And both thoughts and life
Are like incorporeal sand running through my fingers.

The train station in the desert, deserted;
The dumb interpreter;
The human doll with neither eyes nor mouth,
A will-o'-the-wisp hanging
Over a sea that is nothing but pure space
Beneath a sky shaken by black lightning …
May it sinisterly sail, the sentient keel audibly gnawed at by worms,
May the masts be like long, long amber fingers,
Pointing out the void in all things (the abyss in everything) …
May the sails, like a red curtain, lovely and dark,
Open to the wind blowing through an enormous, bottomless chasm,
And outside of time, may they all set off on a voyage to the end of
    everything.

A tightening sense of horror in the groaning of the ropes ...
The sound of the creaking wood is pure soul ...
The swift advance is all that's missing ...
And if life is horizontal, then this is happening vertically ...

7f   [1914–1915]
When it's time for the Great Departure,
When we finally set sail from our beings and our feelings
In the good steamship Death (what label will be on our suitcases ...
What terrifying foreign name and place, what destination?)
When, emigrants once and for all, we set off on that irreparable
        journey,
And abandon this hollow, terrifying world so [...] for the nerves,
These sensations of things so connected and mysterious,
These human feelings so natural and inexplicable,
These torments, these desires to be out of here (and out of now),
        this sudden aimless nostalgia,
This rising up of our feminine side into our gaze which watches
        maternally over the smallest things,
Over the lead soldiers, and the clockwork trains and the buckles on
        the shoes of our childhood,
When, finally and for ever, irretrievably [...]

8   [13 December 1914]
The dead! Who, so prodigiously
And with what awful reminiscency,
Live on in our memories of them!

My old aunt in her old house in the country,
Where I was the child that I was and happy and at ease ...
I think of this and am filled by a furious nostalgia
And yet, I think, she died years ago ...

36

This, after all, is as mysterious as the dusky dusk ...
I think and am filled by the whole enigma of the universe.
I see it all again in my imagination and it's so real
That, afterwards, when I realize it's all over
And that she's dead,
The mystery grows paler before me,
Seems more obscure, crueler, farther off,
And so aware am I of the terror of life that I do not even weep.

———————

How I would love to be part of the night,
A formless part of the night, some place in space
Not even really a place, because it would have neither shape nor
        location
But a night within the night, a part of it, belonging to it wholly and
        completely,
A close and distant companion of my absence of existence ...

———————

Everything about that time was so real, so vivid, so present! ...
And when I once again see it in myself, it lives again in me ...
I'm astonished that something so real could end ...
And not exist today and today be so different ...
The waters of the river run down to the sea, far from my sight,
They reach the sea and are lost in the sea,
But does the water lose its self?
Does something that clearly exists cease to be
Or do they lack life, our eyes and ears,
And our external awareness of the Universe?
Where is my past today?
In what trunk did God pack it away so that I can never find it?
When I once again see it in myself, where is what I am seeing?
All of this must have some meaning—perhaps a very simple one—
But however hard I think, I cannot grasp it.

[c. 1915]

My imagination is a Triumphal Arch
Under which passes all of Life.
The commercial life of now, automobiles, trucks,
Traditional life in the uniforms of certain regiments,
All the social classes, and every form of life,
And in the moment when they pass under its shadow,
They are, momentarily, the triumph I make of them.
Something triumphal falls on them,
And they are, for a moment, small and great.

The Triumphal Arch of my Imagination
Is based, on the one hand, on God and on the other
On the quotidian, on the petty (depending on one's viewpoint),
On everyday drudgery and everyday sensations,
And the short-lived intentions that die before they even become
        gestures.

I myself, apart from and except for my imagination,
And yet also part of it,
I am the triumphal figure gazing down from atop the arch,
Who both emerges from and belongs to the arch,
And lofty and still, monstrous and beautiful,
I observe whoever passes.

However, at the high points of my sensation,
When instead of rectilinear, it is circular
And spins vertiginously upon itself,
The Arch disappears, merges with the people passing,
And I feel that I am the Arch, and the space it occupies,
And all the people who pass,
And all the past of the people who pass,
And all the future of the people who pass,
And all the people who will pass,

And all the people who have already passed.
I feel this, and as I feel it, I become more and more
The sculpted figure emerging from the top of the arch
Staring down
At the universe passing.
But I myself am the Universe,
I myself am subject and object,
I myself am Arch and Street,
I myself surround and allow to pass, encompass and liberate,
I gaze down from above and gaze up from below at myself gazing
     down,
I pass underneath the arch and remain above, outside,
I am all things and transcend all things,
I embody God in a piece of triumphal architecture,
A Triumphal Arch placed upon the universe,
A Triumphal Arch built
On all the sensations of all those who feel
And on all the sensations of all the sensations ...

Poetry of impulse and gyration,
Of vertigo and explosion,
Dynamic, sensationist poetry whistling
Out through my imagination in torrents of fire,
Great rivers of flame, great volcanoes of light.

10   [1915]
Maritime Ode

                                        For Santa Rita Pintor
Alone, on the deserted quayside, on this summer morning,
I look towards the bar, I look towards the Indefinite,
I look and take pleasure in seeing
The small shape, black and clear, of a steamship hoving into view.
It's still a long way off, clean and classic in its own way.

It leaves in the distant air behind it the futile fringe of its smoke.
It enters, and the morning enters with it, and on the river,
Here and there, maritime life is waking up,
Sails are raised, tugs advance,
Small boats emerge from behind the ships already in port.
There is a vague breeze.
But my soul is caught up in what I can see least clearly,
The steamship about to arrive,
Because the ship belongs to Distance and the Morning,
To the maritime feel of this Hour,
To the painful sweetness that rises in me like a nausea,
Like a beginning of seasickness, although only in the mind.

With great independence of soul, I look at the steamship from afar,
And inside me a wheel slowly starts to turn.

The steamships that reach the bar in the morning
Bring to my eyes
The sad, joyful mystery of all who arrive and depart.
They bring memories of distant quaysides and other moments
Of a different sort of the same humanity in other ports.
All that coming in to dock, all that setting sail,
Is—I feel it inside me like my blood—
Unconsciously symbolic, terribly,
Threateningly full of metaphysical meanings
That startle in me the person I once was ...

Ah, the whole quayside is nostalgia set in stone!
And when the ship leaves the quay
And I notice suddenly that there's a space
Between quay and ship,
I'm filled, for some reason, with a renewed sense of anguish,
A mist of sad feelings
That shine in the sun of my mossy anguishes

Like the first window struck by the dawn light,
And it wraps about me like a memory belonging to someone else
But which is somehow mysteriously mine.

Ah, who knows, who knows,
Perhaps I once set off, before I was me,
From some other quayside; perhaps I, a ship
In the slanting dawn rays,
Left another kind of port?
Who knows, perhaps there was a time,
Before the external world as I see it now
First dawned for me,
When I left some broad quayside full of just a few people,
The quayside of a big city only half-awake,
A vast commercial city, overgrown, apoplectical,
If that can possibly exist outside of Space and Time?

Yes, from a quayside, from some physical quayside,
Real and visibly a quayside, a real quayside,
The Absolute Quayside that we men unconsciously imitated,
Unwittingly evoked,
When we built our quays in our ports,
Our real stone quaysides on actual water,
Which, once built, announce themselves suddenly
As Real-Things, Mind-Things, Stone-souled Entities,
At certain moments of deep-rooted feeling
When, in the outside world, it's as if a door is opened
And, without anything actually changing,
Everything reveals itself to be different.

Ah, the Great Quayside from which we depart in
          Ships-cum-Nations!
The Original Great Quayside, eternal and divine!
From which port? On which waters? And why do I think this?

The Great Quayside like all other quaysides, but Unique.
Full, like them, of murmurous silences in the early hours,
And blossoming with the morning into the sound of cranes
And the arrival of freight trains,
And beneath the occasional wispy cloud of dark
Smoke from the chimneys of nearby factories
That casts a shadow over the ground black with fine, sparkling coal,
As if it were the shadow of a cloud passing over somber waters.

Ah, what essence of mystery and arrested senses
Gripped by some divine revelatory ecstasy
At hours the color of silence and anguish
Forms a bridge between any quayside and *The* Quayside!

A quayside blackly reflected in the still waters,
Hustle and bustle on board the ships,
O wandering, restless soul of those people already embarked,
Of the symbolic people who pass and for whom nothing lasts,
For when the ship returns to port,
There is always some change on board!

O continual flights, departures, the intoxication of the Diverse!
Eternal soul of navigators and navigations!
Hulls reflected adrift on the waters
When the ship leaves port!
To float as a living soul, to depart like a voice,
To live the moment tremulously on eternal waters.
To wake to days more straightforward than European days,
To see mysterious ports on the solitude of the sea,
To round remote capes and chance upon vast landscapes
And innumerable astonished slopes ...

Ah, distant beaches, quaysides spotted from afar,
And then the beaches suddenly close, the quaysides closer.

The mystery of every departure and every arrival,
The painful instability and incomprehensibility
Of this impossible universe
That with each passing maritime hour is felt more deeply on one's
    skin!
The absurd sob that spills forth from our souls
Over the great expanses of different seas dotted with far-off islands,
Over the remote outlines of coasts passed by,
Over the ports slowly growing more visible, with their houses and
    their people,
As the ship approaches.

Ah, the coolness of the mornings when you arrive,
And the paleness of the mornings when you depart,
When your stomach contracts
And a vague feeling resembling fear
The ancestral fear of going away, of leaving,
The mysterious ancestral dread of Arrival and the New—
Makes our skin prick and our stomach churn,
And our whole anguished body feels,
As if it were our soul,
An inexplicable desire to be able to feel this differently:
A longing for something,
A shiver of affection, but for what vague fatherland?
What coast? What ship? What port?
Then the thought sickens and dies,
Leaving only a great vacuum inside us,
A hollow satiety of maritime minutes,
And a vague anxiety that might be tedium or grief
If it knew how to be such things ...

Still, the summer morning is almost cool.
A faint night torpor lingers in the buffeting air.
Inside me, the wheel turns slightly faster.

And the steamship continues its approach, as it must,
And not just because I'm watching it moving in the far, far distance.

In my imagination, it is already close and visible
From first porthole to last,
And everything in me, flesh and skin, trembles,
Because of that person who never arrives on any ship
And for whom, as if obeying some oblique order, I'm waiting today.

The ships that cross the bar,
The ships that leave the ports,
The ships that pass in the distance
(I imagine watching them from a deserted beach)—
All these ships, almost abstract in their departure,
All these ships move me as if they were something else
And not just ships, ships coming and going.

And the ships seen from up close, even if you're not about to embark,
Seen from below, from the boats, like high metal walls,
Seen from inside, through the cabins, the lounges, the storerooms,
Looking closely at the masts tapering up into the sky,
Brushing past the cables, going down the narrow stairs,
Smelling the greasy, metallic, maritime smell of it all—
The ships seen from up close are both different and the same,
They provoke the same nostalgia and the same longing only in a
        different way.

All of maritime life! Everything about maritime life!
Slips insinuatingly, seductively into my blood
And I brood vaguely on voyages.
Ah, the outline of distant coasts, squat on the horizon!
Ah, the capes, the islands, the sandy beaches!
The maritime solitudes, like certain moments in the Pacific
When, thanks to some idea learned at school,

You feel, weighing on your nerves, the fact that this is the largest of the
  oceans
And, inside us, the world and the taste of things are transformed into a
  desert!
The more human, saltier size of the Atlantic!
The Indian Ocean, the most mysterious of all!
The Mediterranean, classic, sweet, and utterly unmysterious, a sea
  made to break
On esplanades gazed upon from nearby parks by white statues!
All the seas, all the straits, all the bays, all the gulfs,
I felt like clutching them to me so as to feel them properly and then die!

And you, all things nautical, the toys I played with in my childhood
  dreams!
Create outside of me my inner world!
Keels, masts and sails, helms, rigging,
Smokestacks, propellers, topsails, pennants,
Tiller ropes, portholes, boilers, pipes, valves,
Fall inside me in a great heap, a pile,
Like the jumbled contents of a drawer emptied onto the floor!
Be the treasure of my febrile miserly greed,
Be the fruits of the tree of my imagination,
The subject of my songs, the blood in the veins of my intelligence.
Be the aesthetic tie that binds me to the outside world,
Furnish me with metaphors, images, literature,
Because really, truly, literally,
My sensations are a ship with its keel in the air,
My imagination a half-submerged anchor,
My longing a broken oar,
And the fabric of my nerves a net left to dry on the beach!

From the river comes a whistle, just one.
The whole ground of my psyche is trembling now,
The wheel inside me turning ever faster.

Ah, the steamships, the voyages, the not-knowing-the-whereabouts
Of So-and-so, a mariner of our acquaintance!
Ah, the glory of knowing that a fellow traveler
Was drowned near an island in the Pacific!
We, his companions, will tell everyone about this
With legitimate pride, with an invisible confidence
That all this has a vaster, more beautiful meaning
Than just the sinking of the ship on which he was traveling
And him having sunk to the bottom because water entered his lungs!

Ah, the steamships, the collier ships, the sailing ships!
They're becoming scarce now—alas!—those sailing ships!
And I who love modern civilization, I who lovingly embrace
          machines,
I, the engineer, I, the civilized man, I the person educated abroad,
Would like to see again, up close, only sailing ships and wooden ships,
And to know only the maritime life on the seas of old!
Because the seas of old are Absolute Distance,
Pure Far-off-ness, free from the weight of the Present ...
And ah, how everything here reminds me of that better life,
Those seas, larger because we traveled more slowly,
Those seas, more mysterious because we knew less about them.

Every far-away steamship is a sailing ship close to shore.
Every ship seen in the distance now is a ship from the past seen
          close up.
All the invisible sailors on board the ships on the horizon
Are visible sailors from the days of the old ships,
From the slow, sailing-ship age of dangerous voyages,
From the age of wood and canvas on voyages that lasted months.

I am gradually gripped by the delirium of all things maritime,
The quayside and its atmosphere enter me physically,
The lapping of the Tejo overwhelms my senses,

And I begin to dream, begin to wrap myself in the dream of the waters,
The transmission belts begin to wind tightly about my soul
And the accelerating wheel sets me shaking.

The waters are calling to me,
The seas are calling to me,
The far-off is calling to me in a corporeal voice,
The maritime age of the past is calling to me.

It was you, an English sailor, you, my friend Jim Barns,
Who taught me that ancient English cry,
Which so venomously sums up
For complex souls like mine
The bewildering call of the waters,
The rare, implicit voice of all things maritime,
Of shipwrecks, distant voyages, perilous crossings,
That English cry, made universal in my blood,
Not that it sounded like a cry, lacking human form or voice,
That tremendous cry that seems to come
From inside a cave whose vault is the sky
And seems to tell of all the disasters
That can happen Far Off, on the Sea, at Night …
(You always pretended you were calling to a schooner,
And you said it like this, cupping your mouth with both hands,
Making a loudspeaker out of those dark, weatherbeaten hands:

Aho-o-o-o-o-o-o-o-o-o-o - - - -yyyy …
Schooner aho-o-o-o-o-o-o-o-o-o-o-o-o-o - - - -yyyy …)

I can hear you from here, now, and I awaken to something.
The wind trembles. The morning stirs. The heat opens.
I feel my cheeks grow red.
My conscious eyes grow wide.
Ecstasy rises up in me, grows, advances,

And with the blind roar of a street riot
The wheel inside me begins to spin still faster.

O clamorous call
In whose heat, in whose fury, all my longings
Burn inside me in one explosive unit,
My own tediums made dynamic, all of them!...
The appeal launched into my blood
By a past love, from where I don't know, and which returns
And still has the power to lure me and draw me,
And still has the power to make me hate this life
Which I spend caught up in the impenetrability, physical and
        psychological,
Of the real people among whom I live!

Ah, simply to leave, for whatever reason and to wherever it might be!
To set off through the waves, the danger, the sea,
To go Far Away, to go Elsewhere, into the Abstract Distance,
Indefinitely, through deep, dark, mysterious nights,
Carried along, like dust, by the winds, by the storms!
To go, to go, simply to go!
Every drop of my blood is furious for wings!
Every inch of my body is lunging forwards!
I bound and gallop through my imagination!
I stumble, I roar, I hurl myself!...
My longings crumble into foam
And my flesh is a wave crashing against the rocks!

When I think this—and what rage I feel to think this—what fury!
When I think this from my narrow little life so full of longings,
Suddenly, tremulously, extraorbitally,
With a vicious, vast, violent tremor
From the living wheel of my imagination,

There breaks in me, whistling, hissing, spinning,
The somber, sadistic oestrus of the strident maritime life.

Hey, mariners and topmen! Hey, sailors and pilots!
Navigators, seafarers, sea dogs, adventurers!
Hey, ships captains! Men at the helm and up the masts!
Men sleeping in rough berths!
Men sleeping with Danger peering in through the portholes!
Men sleeping with Death as their pillow!
Men with decks and bridges from which to gaze upon
The immense immensity of the immense sea!
Hey, crane operators!
Hey, trimmers of sails, stokers, stewards!
Men who load the cargo into the hold!
Men who coil the ropes on deck!
Men who polish the brass on the portholes!
Men of the helm! Men of the machines! Men of the masts!
He-e-e-e-e-e-y!
Men in straw hats! Men in string vests!
Men with anchors and crossed flags embroidered on their chests!
Men with tattoos! Men with pipes! Men at the ship's rail!
Men with skin burned by so much sun, seared by so much rain,
Clear-eyed from the immense immensity before them,
Bold-faced from so much battering by the winds.
Hey-e-e-e-e-e-y!
You men who saw Patagonia!
You men who sailed past Australia!
Who gazed your fill on coasts I will never see!
Who landed on lands where I will never set foot!
Who bought crudely made artefacts in colonies-cum-wildernesses!
And you did all this as if it were nothing,
As if it were natural,
As if that were how life was,

As if you weren't even fulfilling a destiny!
Hey-e-e-e-e-e-y!
Men of the present-day sea! Men of seas past!
Stewards! Galley slaves! Men who fought at Lepanto!
Pirates from Roman times! Explorers from Greece!
Phoenicians! Carthaginians! Portuguese men setting off from Sagres
For an adventure into the unknown, for the Absolute Sea, to do the
      Impossible!
Hey-e-e-e-e-e-e-y!
You men who built monuments to your discoveries, who named
      Capes!
You men who negotiated for the first time with Blacks!
You who first sold slaves from those new lands!
Who gave the first European orgasm to astonished Black women!
Who brought back gold, beads, perfumed wood, arrows
From hillsides exploding with lush green vegetation!
You men who plundered tranquil African villages,
Who put the people to flight with the boom of your cannon,
Who killed, robbed, tortured, who won
The prize for Novelty awarded to those who, head down,
Launch themselves upon the mystery of new seas! He-e-e-e-e-y!
You, who are all men in one, you who are one man in all,
You, who are all mixed and mingled,
You bloody, violent, loathed, feared, sacred men,
I salute you, I salute you, I salute you!
He-e-e-e-y! H-e-e-e-y! He-e-e-e-e-e-y!
Hey-laho-laho-laHO-laha-a-a-a!

I want to go with you, I want to go with you,
At the same time and with all of you
To wherever it was you went!
I want to meet your dangers head on,
To feel on my face the winds that weathered yours,
To spit out the salt from the same seas that kissed your lips,

To labor alongside you, to share your storms,
And finally arrive with you at extraordinary ports!
To flee with you from civilization!
To lose with you all notion of morality!
To feel my humanity move off into the distance!
To drink with you in southern seas,
New savageries, new upheavals of the soul,
New fires ablaze in my volcanic spirit!
To go with you, to remove—off with you, now!—
My civilized suit, my mild manners,
My innate fear of chains and shackles,
My peaceful life,
My sedentary, static, rule-bound, scrutinized life!

To the sea, to the sea, to the sea, to the sea,
Yes, send my life off to the sea, to the wind,
To the waves!
Temper with salty, wind-blown foam
My taste for great voyages.
Flail with whipping water the flesh of my adventure,
Soak in oceanic cold the bones of my existence,
Flagellate, slash, wither with winds, with foam, with suns,
My cyclonic, atlantic self,
My nerves taut as shrouds,
A lyre in the hands of the winds!

Yes, yes, yes … Crucify me as we sail the seas
And my shoulders will relish their cross!
Bind me to those voyages as if to a stake
And the feeling of that stake will enter my spine
And I will experience it instead like one vast, passive orgasm!
Do what you will with me as long as I can be on the seas,
On decks, to the sound of the waves,
Knife me, kill me, wound me!

What I want is to carry into Death
A soul overflowing with Sea,
Roaring drunk on things maritime,
On sailors and anchors and capes,
On distant coasts and the sound of the winds,
On the Far-Away as well as the safe Harbor, on shipwrecks
As well as on a little tranquil trading,
On masts as well as waves,
To carry into Death painfully, voluptuously,
A body covered in leeches, sucking, sucking,
Strange green absurd maritime leeches!

Make shrouds of my veins!
Hawsers of my muscles!
Flay my skin and nail it to the keel.
And may I feel the pain of the nails and never cease to feel it!
Make of my heart an admiral's pennant
When the old ships go into battle!
Put out my eyes and trample them underfoot!
Batter my bones against the ship's rail!
Tie me to the masts and flog me, flog me!
To all the winds on every latitude and longitude
Spill my blood on the waters hurled
Over the ship, over the quarterdeck, everywhere,
During the wild turmoil of storms!

To be as bold as the sails are in the wind!
To be, like the topsails, the whistle of the winds!
The old guitar playing the Fado about the perilous seas,
A song for sailors to hear and not repeat!

The mutinous mariners
Hanged the captain from a spar.
They abandoned another on a desert island.
Marooned!

The sun of the tropics has set the fever of the old pirates
Burning in my tense veins.
The Patagonian winds have tattooed my imagination
With images tragic and obscene.
Fire, fire, I'm on fire inside!
Blood! Blood! Blood! Blood!
My whole brain is exploding!
My world torn asunder is entirely red!
My veins are snapping with the sound of the hawsers!
And inside me bursts out, fierce and voracious,
The song of the Great Pirate,
The Great Pirate's death howl which he sings
Until his men feel fear run down their spines.
Lying astern and dying, howling, singing:

> *Fifteen men on the Dead Man's Chest.*
> *Yo-ho-ho and a bottle of rum!*

And then shouting in a now unreal voice that bursts upon the air:

Darby M'Graw-aw-aw-aw aw!
Darby M'Graw-aw-aw-aw-aw-aw-aw-aw!
Fetch a-a-aft the ru-u-u-u-u-u-u-u-um, Darby!

Ah, what a life this is! What a life that was!
Hey-e-e-e-e-e-e-e-y!
Hey-laho-laho-laHO-laha-a-a-a-a!
Hey-e-e-e-e-e-e-e-y!

Shattered keels, ships on the sea bottom, blood on the seas!
Decks running with blood, fragments of bodies!
Lopped off fingers on the ship's rail!
Here and there the heads of children!
Eyeless people, shouting, screaming!
Hey-e-e-e-e-e-e-e-e-e-y!

Hey-e-e-e-e-e-e-e-e-e-y!
I wrap myself in all this as if in a cloak against the cold!
I rub up against all this like a cat in heat rubbing against a wall!
I roar at all this like a starving lion!
I charge at all this like a mad bull!
I dig in my nails, break my claws, bite until my gums bleed!
He-e-e-e-e-e-e-e-e-e-y!

Suddenly there breaks about my ears,
Like a bugle right beside me,
The old cry, angry now, metallic,
Announcing the prize on the horizon,
The schooner about to be taken:

Aho-o-o-o-o-o-o-o-o-o - - - -yyyy…
Schooner aho-o-o-o-o-o-o-o o-o-o-o-o - - - -yyyy…

The world does not exist for me! I burn red!
I roar in the fury of boarding the ship!
Pirate Chief! Pirate Caesar!
I pillage, I kill, I slash, I hack!
I feel only the sea, the prize, the plunder!
Pounding inside me I feel only the pounding
Of the veins in my temples!
My eyes feel as if they were running with warm blood!
Hey-e-e-e-e-e-e-e-e-e-y!

Ah, pirates, pirates, pirates!
Pirates, love me and loathe me!
Make me one with you, O pirates!

How your fury, your cruelty, how they speak to the blood
In the body of a woman who once was mine and whose lust survives!

I want to be a creature representative of all your gestures,
A creature that would sink its teeth into ship's rails and keels,
That would devour masts and drink the blood and tar from the decks,
Bite sails, oars, rigging, and blocks,
A monstrous female sea serpent feasting on crimes!

And now comes a symphony of incompatible, analogous sensations,
An orchestration in my blood of a pandemonium of crimes,
An orgasmic clamor of orgies of blood on the seas,
As furious as a heatwave in the mind,
A cloud of hot dust clouding all clarity of thought,
And making me see and dream all this with only my skin and my veins!

The pirates, piracy, the ships, the hour,
That maritime hour when the ships are boarded,
And the terror of the captives verges on madness—that hour,
With all the murders, terror, ships, people, sea, sky, clouds,
Breeze, latitude, longitude, yelling,
I wish All of this were my own body suffering All of this,
That it was my body and my blood, my very being written in red,
Blossoming like an itchy wound on the unreal flesh of my soul!

Ah, to be all things in all crimes! To be every component part
Of every raid, massacre, and rape!
To be everything that happened in those attacks!
To be everything that lived or died in those bloody tragedies!
To be the very essence of pirate when piracy was at its peak,
The very synthesis of the flesh-and-blood victims of all the pirates of
     the world!

To be, in my passive body, the woman-and-all-women
Who were raped, killed, wounded, butchered by pirates!
To be in my subjugated self the female that has to be theirs!
And to feel all this—simultaneously—in my very spine!

Oh my rough, hairy heroes of adventure and crime!
My seaborne brutes, husbands of my imagination!
Casual lovers of my oblique sensations!
I would like to be She who waits for you in port,
You, loathèd lovers dreamed of by her pirate blood!
Because she, in spirit at least, would have rampaged alongside you
Over the naked bodies of your victims at sea!
Because she would have followed your every crime, and in the
        oceanic orgy
Her witch-like spirit would dance invisibly above every move
Made by your body, your cutlass, your strangling hands!
And she, on land, would be waiting for you when you returned, if
        you returned,
And in your amorous bellowings she would drink in all the vast,
Misty, sinister perfume of your victories,
And in your orgasms would hear the hiss of a whole witches' sab-
        bath in reds and yellows!

Torn flesh, bodies ripped open, eviscerated, blood gushing!
Now, at the very peak of my dream of what you did,
I lose myself entirely, I no longer belong to you, I am you,
My female self, your companion, becomes your souls!
I am there inside your savagery, your every savage act!
I absorb your consciousness of your sensations
When you stain the high seas with blood,
When you occasionally throw to the sharks
The still living bodies of the wounded, the pink flesh of children,
And force their mothers over to the ship's rail to witness their fate!

I am there with you in the carnage and the pillage!
I am part of the orchestra of the symphony of your lootings!
Ah, I can't say how or how much I want to be yours!
Not just to be your woman, your women, your victims,
Yes, your victims—men, women, children, ships—

Not just to be the hour and the ships and the waves,
Not just to be your souls, your bodies, your fury, your plunder,
Not just to be, in reality, your abstract act of orgy,
No, that isn't all I want—it is more than that, to be the very God of it!
I need to be God, the God of a reverse cult,
A monstrous, satanic God, a God of a pantheism of blood,
To be able to fill up my whole imaginative fury,
To be able never to exhaust my desire to identify
With each, with all, and the more-than-all, of your victories!

Ah, torture me in order to heal me!
My flesh—make of it the air through which you slice with your
        cutlasses
Before letting them fall on heads and shoulders!
May my veins be the clothes your knives pierce!
My imagination the bodies of the women you rape!
My intelligence the deck on which you stand to kill!
May my whole life, my whole being, nervous, hysterical, absurd,
Be the great organism of which each act of piracy
Is a conscious cell—and may all of me churn about
Like a great swirling putrescence, yes, may I be all those things!

With rampant, terrifying speed,
The febrile machine of my unfettered visions
Is spinning now that my volatile consciousness
Is merely a misty circle whistling in the air.

Fifteen men on the Dead Man's Chest.
Yo-ho-ho and a bottle of rum!

Hey-laho-laho-laHO----lah-a-aaa----aaa ...

Ah! the savagery of that savagery! To hell
With all lives like ours, so utterly different!

Here I am, an engineer, obliged to be practical, sensitive to
    everything,
Here I stand, and compared to you, I'm static even when I walk;
Inert even when I act; feeble even when I impose my will;
Static, broken, a dissident coward compared to your Glory,
Your great, hot, strident, bloody dynamism!

Why the hell can't I act in accordance with my own mad self!
Why the hell must I always cling to the skirts of civilization!
Why must I walk around with the *douceur des moeurs* on my back
    like a bundle of lace!
We are all of us the mere errand boys of modern humanitarianism!
Tubercular, neurasthenic, lymphatic sluggards
Lacking the courage to be violently, boldly men,
Our souls like a chicken tied by one leg!

Ah, pirates, pirates!
The yearning for the illegal and the savage,
The yearning for the totally cruel and abominable
That gnaws like an abstract lust at our sickly bodies,
At our feminine, delicate nerves,
And fills our empty eyes with mad fevers!

Make me kneel before you!
Humiliate and beat me!
Make me your slave and your creature!
And may you never cease to despise me!
O my lords! O my lords!

Have me always gloriously take the submissive role
In any bloody events or acts of boundless sensuality!
Fall on me, like great heavy walls,
O barbarians of the ancient sea!
Cut me and wound me!

From east to west of my body
Smear my flesh with blood!
Embrace with cutlasses and whips and rage
My blithe carnal terror of being possessed by you,
My masochistic longing to submit to your fury,
To be the inert, sentient object of your omnivorous cruelty,
Dominators, gentlemen, emperors, warhorses!
Ah, torture me,
Slash me and cut me open!
Slice me into still-conscious pieces
And tip me out onto the decks,
Scatter me to the seas, leave me
On the greedy beaches of islands!

Slake in me all my mystical feelings about you!
Engrave my soul with blood!
Cut, slash!
O tattooers of my corporeal imagination!
Beloved flayers of my carnal submission!
Subdue me like someone kicking a dog to death!
Make me the recipient of all your lordly disdain!

Make of me every one of your victims!
Just as Christ suffered for all men, I want to suffer
For all those who have died at your hands,
Your calloused, bloody hands, minus a few fingers
Sliced off when boarding ships!

Make of me a mere thing as if I had been
Dragged—O pleasure, O blessed pain!—
Dragged behind horses urged on by you …
But at sea, at sea, at S-E-E-EA!
Hey-e-e-e-e-e-y! Hey-e-e-e-e-e-e-y! HEY-E-E-E-E-E-E-E-E-Y!
    AT S-E-E-EA!

59

Ya-a-a-a-a-y! Ya-a-a-a-a-y! Ya-a-a-a-a-y!
Everything is bellowing! Bellowing! Winds, waves, ships,
Seas, topsails, pirates, my soul, my blood, and the air, and the air!
Hey-e-e-e-y! Ya-a-a-a-y! Ya-a-a-a-a-y! Everything is bellowing
    out a song!

FIFTEEN MEN ON THE DEAD MAN'S CHEST.
YO-HO-HO AND A BOTTLE OF RUM!

Hey-e-e-e-e-e-y! Hey-e-e-e-e-e-e-y! Hey-e-e-e-e-e-y!
Hey-laho-laho-laHO-O-O-oo-lah-a-a---aaa!

AHO-O-O-O-O-O-O-O-O-O-O - - - - yyyy! . . .
SCHOONER AHO-O-O-O-O-O-O-O-O-O-O-O-O-O-O - - -
    - yyyy! . . .

Darby M'Graw-aw-aw-aw-aw-aw!
DARBY M'GRAW-AW-AW-AW-AW-AW-AW!
FETCH A-A-AFT THE RU-U-U-U-U-UM, DARBY!

Hey-e-e-e-e-e-e-e-e-e-e-y!
HEY-E-E-E-E-E-E-E-E-E-EY!
HEY-E-E-E-E-E-E-E-E-E-EY!
HEY-E-E-E-E-E-E-E-E-E-EY!
HEY-E-E-E-E-E-E-E-E-E-EY!

Something inside me breaks. The red has grown dark as night.
I felt too much to be able to go on feeling.
My soul is exhausted, leaving only an echo inside me.
The wheel slows perceptibly.
My dreams make me uncover my eyes a little.
Inside there's only a void, a desert, a nocturnal sea.
And as soon as I feel that nocturnal sea,
There rises up from the sea's far distances, born out of their silence,
Again and again, a vast, ancient cry.

Suddenly, like a lightning flash of sound that provokes no noise,
      only tenderness,
Suddenly, embracing the whole horizon,
A damp, sombre lapping, human and nocturnal,
The voice of a distant siren, weeping, calling,
Comes from the depths of the Far-away, from the depths of the Sea,
      from the soul of the Abyss,
And on the surface, like seaweed, bob my shattered dreams …

Aho-o-o o o o-o-o o o o- - - -yy …
Schooner aho-o-o o-o o o o o o-o-o-o - - - -yy … … …

Ah, I can feel the dew on my excitement!
The cool night air on my inner ocean!
And all of me is suddenly looking out at a night sea
Full of the enormous and utterly human mystery of the nocturnal
      waves.
The moon rises on the horizon
And inside me my happy childhood wells up like a tear.
My past resurfaces, as if that sailor's cry
Were an aroma, a voice, the echo of a song
Summoning up from my past
The happiness I will never have again.

It was in the hushed, peaceful old house by the river …
(My bedroom windows, and the dining room windows too,
Looked out over the roofs of a few low houses to the nearby river,
To the Tejo, the same Tejo, but not here, further downstream.
But if I were to go over to those same windows now, I couldn't.
That time has passed like the smoke from a steamship on the high
      seas …)

An inexplicable tenderness,
A profound, tearful remorse,
For all those victims—especially the children—

Who I dreamt when I dreamed myself to be an ancient pirate,
Genuine emotion, because they were my victims;
But a tender, gentle emotion because they weren't;
A confused tenderness, like a piece of blurred blue glass,
Sings old songs in my poor grieving soul.

Ah, how could I have thought, have dreamt such things?
How far I am from the person I was only moments ago!
The hysteria of sensations—now these, now those!
In the blond day now dawning, my ear chooses only
Those things that accord with that new emotion—the lapping of
      the water,
The light lapping of the river against the quay ...
The sailboat passing near the other bank,
The distant hills, Japanese blue,
The houses of Almada,
And how much sweetness, how much childhood there is in this
      morning hour!...

A seagull passing,
And that feeling of tenderness grows.

But during all that time I wasn't actually aware of anything.
It was just an impression that brushed my skin, like a caress.
During all that time I didn't once take my eyes off my distant dream,
My house near the river,
My childhood near the river,
My bedroom windows looking out over the river at night,
And the peace of the moonlight scattered over the waters!...
My old aunt, who loved me because she had lost her own child ... ,
My old aunt used to sing me to sleep
(Even though I was already much too old for that) ...
I remember, and the tears fall on my heart and wash it clean of life,
And a light sea breeze rises inside me.
Sometimes she would sing "The Good Ship Catrineta":

There goes the Good Ship Catrineta
Over the watery main ...

And sometimes a very nostalgic, medieval tune,
"The Fair Princess" ... I think back, and her poor old voice rises up
      inside me
And reminds me how rarely I thought of her afterwards, she who
      loved me so much!
How ungrateful I was—and what did I make of my life in the end?
Yes, "The Fair Princess" ... I would close my eyes, and she would sing:

While the Fair Princess
Was sitting in her garden ...

I would open my eyes slightly and see the window full of moonlight,
Then I would close them again, and I felt so happy.

While the Fair Princess
Was sitting in her garden,
Combing her hair
With her golden comb ...

My childhood past, a doll someone broke!

Ah, to be able to travel back to the past, to that house and that fond
      affection,
And to stay there forever, forever a child and forever content!

But all that was the Past, a lamp on the corner of an old street.
This thought chills me, fills me with a hunger for something I
      cannot have.
Leaves me with a kind of absurd feeling of remorse.
O slow swirl of jarring sensations!
A slight confused whirl of feelings within the soul!
Shared tantrums, affections like the cotton reels children play with,

Great crumblings of the imagination over the eyes of the senses,
Tears, idle tears.
Light contradictory breezes brushing the soul's cheek …

I make a deliberate effort to evoke all this as a way out of this emotion,
I make a desperate effort, dull, ineffectual, to evoke all this,
The song of the Great Pirate, when he was about to die:

Fifteen men on the Dead Man's Chest.
Yo-ho-ho and a bottle of rum!

But the song is a rather wobbly straight line drawn inside myself …

I make an effort and again manage to summon up to the eyes of my
    soul,
Again, but using an almost literary imagination,
The savagery of the pirates, of the slaughter, of the almost palpable
    greed, of the raid.
The futile slaughter of women and children,
The pointless torture of the poor passengers, purely for our own
    amusement,
And the sensual pleasure of destroying and breaking things dear to
    other people,
But I dream all this with a fear of something else breathing down
    my neck.

It occurs to me that it would be interesting
To hang the children while their mothers watch
(But I can't help feeling sorry for the mothers),
Or burying the four-year-olds alive on desert islands
And rowing the parents close to shore to see this happen
(But I shudder, thinking of a child I don't have and who is sleeping
    peacefully at home).

I try to prod into life a cold yearning for maritime crimes,
For an inquisition with not even the excuse of Faith,
Crimes that cannot even be justified by evil and anger,
Cold-blooded crimes, lacking even the intention to wound or harm,
Or to amuse ourselves, but simply as a way of passing the time,
Like someone playing patience at a provincial dining table after
       supper, with the cloth pushed to one side,
Just for the sweet pleasure of committing abominable crimes as if it
       didn't matter,
Of seeing someone suffer to the point of madness and death-by-
       pain, but always stopping just short of that ...
But my imagination refuses to go with me.
A shiver runs through me.
And suddenly, more suddenly than before, more distantly, more
       profoundly,
Suddenly—ah, the terror that runs through my veins!—
A sudden blast of cold air from the door to the Mystery opening
       inside me!
I remember God, the Transcendental side of life, and suddenly
The old voice of the English sailor Jim Barns, who I used to talk to,
Becomes the voice of the mysterious tendernesses inside me, of the
       small things recalling a mother's lap, the ribbon in a sister's hair,
But, extraordinarily, that voice comes from beyond the mere ap-
       pearance of things,
That faint, remote Voice becomes the Absolute Voice, the Mouth-
       less Voice,
Emerging from above and below the nocturnal solitude of the seas,
And it calls to me, calls to me, calls to me ...

A very faint, almost muffled voice, as if I were hearing it
In the far distance, as if it were speaking somewhere else and could
       not be heard here,
Like a suppressed sob, a doused light, a silent out-breath,

Coming from nowhere in space, from nowhere in time,
The eternal, nocturnal cry, the deep, obscure sigh:

Aho-o-o-o-o-o-o-o-o-o-o-o—yyy ......
Aho-o-o-o-o-o-o-o-o-o-o-o-o-o-o-o——yyy ......
Schooner aho-o-o-o-o-o-o-o-o-o-o-o-o-o-o-o-o——yy ....

A shiver runs through body and soul
And suddenly I open my eyes, which I hadn't closed.
Ah, what a joy to escape from dreams once and for all!
Here again is the real world, so good for the nerves!
Here is this morning hour, when the early steamships arrive in port.

I don't care now about the steamship arriving. It's still some ways off.
Only the one that's nearest washes my soul clean.
My sensible, strong, practical imagination
Is only interested now in useful modern things,
In cargo ships, steamships, and passengers,
In sturdy, immediate things, modern, commercial, real.
The wheel inside me turns more slowly.

What a marvelous thing it is, the modern maritime life,
All cleanliness, machines and health!
All so neatly arranged, so spontaneously ordered,
All the parts of the machines, all the ships on the seas,
All the elements of the business of import and export
So perfectly dovetailed
That everything works as if according to natural laws,
With nothing ever clashing with anything else!

Nothing has lost its poetry. And now there are machines
That have their own poetry, as well as the whole new way of life,
Commercial, worldly, intellectual, sentimental,

That the age of the machine has brought to our souls.
Journeys are just as beautiful as they were before
And a ship will always be beautiful, simply because it's a ship.
Traveling is still traveling, and the far-away is still where it always was—
Nowhere at all, thank God!

The ports full of all kinds of steamships,
Small, large, of various colors and various arrangements of portholes,
And such a deliciously large number of shipping companies!
Steamships in the ports, each so individual in their moorings!
And with the attractive quiet elegance of all things commercial that
        ply the sea,
The ancient and still Homeric sea, O Ulysses!
The kindly gaze of the lighthouses in the distance of night,
Or the sudden appearance of a lighthouse nearby in the dark, dark
        night
("How close to land we were!" And the sound of the water sings in
        our ears)!…

Everything today is as it always was, apart from commerce:
And the commercial fate of the big steamships
Makes me feel proud of the age I live in!
The mixture of people on board passenger ships
Fills me with a modern pride to be living in an age where it's so easy
To mingle races, to cross great distances, to see everything so easily,
And to enjoy life, thus realizing all kinds of dreams.

Clean and regular, as modern as an office with yellow mesh grilles on
        the counter windows,
My feelings are as natural and measured as gentlemen,
And are purely practical and not in the least hallucinatory, filling
        their lungs with sea air,
Like people who know just how healthy it is to breathe in sea air.

The day is all set now for working life.
Everything is beginning to move, to get organized.

With enormous pleasure, natural and straightforward, I review with
  my soul
All the commercial operations necessary for the embarkation of
  goods.
The age I live in is the stamp that appears on all the invoices,
And I feel that all the letters from all the offices
Should be addressed to me.

A bill of lading has so much personality,
And the signature of a ship's captain is so fine and modern!
Commercial rigor at the beginning and end of letters:
Dear Sirs—Messieurs—Amigos e Snrs,
Yours faithfully—... nos salutations empressées ...
All this is not only human and clean, it is beautiful too,
And ultimately enjoys a maritime fate, a steamship laden
With the goods of which the letters and invoices speak.

The complexities of life! The invoices are drawn up by people
Who feel love and hate, who have political passions, may even be
  criminals—
And yet they are well written, so neat, so independent of all this!
Some people may look at an invoice and feel nothing of this.
But I'm sure that you, Cesário Verde, would feel it.
I feel it so very humanly that it almost reduces me to tears.
Don't tell me there's no poetry in commerce, in office life!
No, it enters every pore ... I can breathe it in this sea air,
Because it all has to do with steamships, with modern shipping,
Because the invoices and the commercial letters are the beginning
  of the story
And the ships that carry the goods over the sea are the end.

Ah, and the voyages, the cruises, and so on,
The voyages by sea, where we are all, in a special way,
Each other's companion, as if a maritime mystery
Brought our souls closer together and transformed us for a moment
Into transitory compatriots of the same uncertain country,
Eternally moving over the immensity of the waters!
You, my transatlantic liners, are the Grand Hotels of the infinite!
So totally, perfectly cosmopolitan, never stopping anywhere
And containing all kinds of clothes, faces, and races!

Voyages, voyagers—and of every kind too!
So many nationalities in the world! So many professions! So many
        people!
So many diverse directions one can take in life,
Although life is basically always the same!
So many curious faces! But then all faces are curious
And nothing provokes more religious feeling than looking one's fill at
        people.
Fraternity is not, in the end, a revolutionary idea.
It's something we learn throughout life, where we have to tolerate
        everything,
And even learn to be amused by what we have to tolerate,
And almost shed fond tears over what we did tolerate!

Yes, all this is beautiful, all this is human and connected
To human feelings, so convivial and bourgeois,
So complicatedly simple, so metaphysically sad!
Fluctuating, diverse life ends up educating us in what it is to be
        human.
Poor things! Poor things, every one of us!

I bid farewell to this hour in the body of this other ship
Which is about to leave. It's an English *tramp steamer*,
As grubby as if it were a French ship,

With the pleasing air of a proletarian of the seas,
And doubtless mentioned yesterday on the back page of the papers.

This poor ship, so humble, so unassuming, touches my heart.
It seems to me like a ship with scruples, about what I don't know, an
	honest fellow,
Always ready to do its duty, whatever that might be.
There it goes, leaving the quay where I'm standing.
There it goes, very calmly, following the same routes taken by other
	ships
In the old days, the old days ...
Heading for Cardiff? For Liverpool? For London? It doesn't matter.
It's doing its duty. As we do ours. What a life!
Bon voyage! Bon voyage!
Bon voyage, my poor chance friend, who did me the favor
Of carrying off with you the febrile sadness of my dreams,
And restoring me to life in order to look at you and see you passing.
Bon voyage! Bon voyage! This is what life is ...
With what natural, early-morning aplomb
You leave the port of Lisbon, today!
I feel for you a strange, grateful affection because ...
Because of what? I've no idea ... Off you go ... Sail away ...
With a slight shudder,
(T-t--t---t----t-----t ...)
The wheel inside me stops turning.

Set sail, slow steamship, set sail, don't stay ...
Set sail from me and from my gaze,
Leave your place in my heart,
Lose yourself in the Far-away, in the Far-away, God's mist,
Lose yourself, follow your fate and leave me here ...
Who am I that I should weep and ask questions?
Who am I that I should speak to you and love you?
Who am I that I should feel troubled by the sight of you?

The ship moves off, the sun rises and grows golden,
The roofs of the buildings on the quayside glitter,
This whole side of the city glows ...
Set sail, leave me, become
First the ship in the middle of the river, clear and distinct,
Then the ship on its way to the bar, small and dark,
Then a vague dot on the horizon (such anguish!),
An ever vaguer dot on the horizon ...
Then nothing, only me and my sadness,
And the great city now full of sun
And the hour, real and deserted like a port with no ships,
And the slow turning of the crane like a turning compass
Traces a semicircle of some emotion or other
In the tremulous silence of my soul ...

11 SALUTE TO WALT WHITMAN
11a   [11 June 1915]
Portugal-Infinity, eleventh of June, nineteen hundred and fifteen ...
Hey-la-a-a-a-a-a!

From here, from Portugal, from every epoch in my brain,
I salute you, Walt, I salute you, my brother in the Universe,
You eternally modern and eternal singer of concrete absolutes,
Fiery concubine of the scattered universe,
Great pederast rubbing up against the sheer diversity of things,
Aroused by stones, trees, people, professions,
Lusting after passersby, chance encounters, mere observations,
My enthusiast for the contents of everything,
My great hero bounding into Death,
And bellowing, shrieking, screaming a greeting to God!

Singer of a fierce, tender brotherhood with everything,
Great democrat in skin and body and soul,

Carnival of all actions, bacchanalia of all intentions,
Twin soul of all impulses,
Jean-Jacques Rousseau of the world that would produce machines,
Homer of the *insaisissable* of the fluctuating flesh,
Shakespeare of sensation about to become steam-driven,
Milton-Shelley of the horizon of future Electricity!
Incubus of all gestures,
Inward spasm of all outward objects,
Souteneur of the entire Universe,
Whore of all the solar systems, God's faggot!

I, in my monocle and my absurdly waisted jacket,
I'm not unworthy of you, as you know, Walt,
I'm not unworthy of you, for all I need is to salute you ...
I, always so prey to inertia, so easily filled with tedium,
I am one of yours, as you know, and I understand you and love you,
And even though I never met you, having been born around the year
        you died,
I know that you loved me too, that you knew me, and I am content.
I know that you knew me, that you studied me and explained me,
I know that this is what I am, whether on Brooklyn Ferry ten years
        before I was born,
Whether walking up Rua do Ouro thinking about everything that is
        not Rua do Ouro,
And just as you felt everything, so I feel everything too, and here we
        are hand in hand,
Hand in hand, Walt, hand in hand, dancing the universe in our souls.

How often I kiss your portrait.
And wherever you are now (I don't know where, but wherever it is,
        is God)
You feel this, I know you do, and my kisses are much warmer in person
Which is how you want them, my old friend, and you thank me in
        the place where you are—

I know this for sure, something tells me that it is so, a shiver of plea-
sure in my mind,
An abstract, oblique erection in the depths of my soul.
You were never *engageant*, but cyclopean and muscular,
But as regards the universe, your attitude was that of a woman,
And every leaf of grass, every stone, every man was, for you, the
Universe.
Ave, old Walt, my great Comrade, evoe!
I belong to your bacchic orgy of sensations-set-free,
I am one of yours, from the sensation in my feet to the nausea of my
dreams,
I am one of yours, look at me, from your place in God you see me
back to front:
Inside out ... You sense my body, but see my soul—
You see that clearly and through my soul's eyes you see my body—
Look at me: you know that I, Álvaro de Campos, engineer,
Sensationist poet,
Am not your disciple, am not your lover, am not your singer,
You know that I am You and that pleases you!

I can never read your poems in one go ... There's too much feeling
there ...
I walk through your poems as if through a jostling crowd,
And it smells of sweat, of oil, of human and mechanical activity.
At a certain point in your poems, I don't know if I'm reading or living,
I don't know if my real place is in the world or in your poems,
I don't know if I'm here, standing on natural earth,
Or hanging upside down in some establishment or other,
From the natural ceiling of your teeming inspiration,
From the middle of the ceiling of your inaccessible intensity.

Fling wide all the doors!
I must be allowed through!
My password? Walt Whitman!

But I give no password ...
I simply walk in with no explanations ...
If necessary I break down the doors ...
Yes—feeble, civilized me, I break down doors,
Because at that moment, I am neither feeble nor civilized,
I am ME, a thinking universe of flesh and bone, demanding to be let
    in,
And I will be let in, because when I want to walk through that door,
    I am God!

Clear away this garbage from my path!
Stow those emotions in a drawer!
From here on in, politicians, the literati,
Smug merchants, policemen, whores and *souteneurs*,
All these are the letter that kills, not the spirit that brings life.
The spirit that gives life at this moment is ME!

Let no bastard get in my way!
My way takes me to infinity and to the end of infinity!
Whether I reach the end or not is none of your business, just let me
    through—
It's up to me and God and the meaning I give to the word Infinity ...
Onwards!
I put on my spurs!
I feel the spurs dig in, I am the horse I am riding,
Because I, in my desire to be consubstantiate with God,
Can be everything or nothing, or anything,
Depending on my mood ... This is no one else's business ...
Raving lunacy! A desire to yelp and leap,
To bellow, bray, skip, turn somersaults, let forth a visceral howl,
To cling to the wheels of vehicles and go under them,
To place myself before the whip just as it's about to fall,
To [...]
To be the bitch in heat of every dog and still not be satisfied,
To be the wheel on every machine, to be limitless speed,

74

To be all that is crushed, abandoned, discarded, killed,
And all this in order to sing you and to salute you in [...]
Dance with me, Walt, in that world beyond all this fury,
Jig up and down with me to the wild drumming that clashes with
      the stars,
Come with me and fall limply to the ground.
Hurl yourself unconscious against walls,
Shatter and splinter yourself into pieces
And [...]
In everything, through everything, around everything, without
      everything,
In an abstract bodily rage creating *maelstroms* in the soul ...

Hup! Onwards!
If God himself tries to stop us, we must still march onwards ... It
      makes no difference ...
Onwards!
Onwards even if we're going nowhere ...
Infinity! The Universe! With or without a goal! What does it matter?
Pum! Pum! Pum! Pum! Pum!
Yes, now, let's go, onwards, pum!
Pum
Pum
Yeah ... yeah ... yeah ... yeah ... yeah ...

I unleash myself like a thunderbolt
And my soul goes bounding towards you,
With military bands marching ahead to prolong my greeting ...
With a great cortège and a furore of bellows and leaps
I boom forth your name
And every cheer I give is for you, for me and you and God,
And the Universe circles around us like a carousel with music inside
      our heads,
And I decorate my outer epidermis with essential lights,
Me, mad with the drunken, sibilant music of machines,

You famous, you bold, you the [...] and the [...],
You both sensuality and port
You a sensuality curiously, nascently dead
You and intelligence [...]

11b   [c. 1915]

Door to everything!
Bridge to everything!
Road to everything!
Your omnivorous soul and [...]
Your bird soul, fish soul, beast, man, woman,
Your souls two when there are two,
Your soul the one which is two when two are one,
Your arrow-soul, lightning bolt, space,
Amplexus, nexus, sexus, Texas, Carolina, New York,
Brooklyn Ferry in the evening,
Brooklyn Ferry of outward journeys and returns,
Liberty! *Democracy!* The twentieth century somewhere in the
        distance!
Pum! Pum! Pum! Pum! Pum!
PUM!

You, what you were, what you saw, what you heard,
Subject and object, active and passive,
Here and there, everywhere you,
A circle enclosing all possible feelings,
Milestone of all possible things,
The god Terminus of all imaginable objects, that is you!
You the Hour,
You the Minute,
You the Second!
You intercalated, liberated, unfurled, dispatched,
Intercalation, liberation, dispatch, unfurling,

Intercalator, liberator, unfurler, dispatcher,
A stamp on every letter,
A name in every address,
Merchandise delivered, returned, forwarded ...
A train of sensations at soul-kilometers per hour,
Per hour, per minute, per second. PUM!

And all these natural noises, human, mechanical
All of them go together, the whole tumultuous lot,
Proud to be coming to meet you, to salute you,
Proud to be coming to meet you,
Futile human cries, futile earthly tears
Futile mountain peaks
Futile murmuring waters
Futile noise of war
Futile blasts of [...], the [...] of [...]
Futile roaring of wild beasts in the distance,
Futile feeble sighs in the darkness
And futile too, closer to me, surrounding me,
A far greater prize than being able to salute you
The noises, the whispering whistle of trains
The noisy noises of factories,
Of mills,
Wheels,
Rivets,
Propellors
Pum ...

11c   [c. 1915]
Listen, I'm going to summon up
For the noisy, deafening privilege of saluting you
All of the teeming human Universe,
Every form of every emotion,

Every mode of every thought,
Every wheel, every gear, every piston of the soul.
Hey there, I shout
And in a cortège of Me to you there will be such a clamor
Of real and metaphysical gibberish,
An inner hullaballoo of unconnected things.

Ave, salve, viva, O great bastard of Apollo,
Impotent, passionate lover of the nine muses and of the graces,
The funicular from Olympus to us and from us to Olympus,
Fury of the modern made real in me,
Translucent spasm of being,
Flower that blooms from others' actions,
Feast because Life exists,
Madness because there isn't life enough to be everyone
Because to be is to be limited and only God could help us.
And you who sang everything left everything unsung.
Who can include more than his body in his body
Or have more sensations than there are sensations to be had?
Who is enough when nothing is enough?
Who can be complete when one single blade of grass
Has its roots outside his heart?

11d   c. 1915
That is why it is to you that I am addressing
My poem-leaps, my poem-skips, my poem-pure-ecstasies,
My attack-of-hysteria-poems,
My poems that draw the carriage [...] of my nerves.

I stumble forward into inspiration,
Barely able to breathe, thrilled just being-able-to-stand,
And my poems are me unable to explode with life.

78

Fling open all the windows!
Tear the doors off their hinges!
Bring the house down on top of me!
I want to live freely in the air,
I want to make gestures that exist independently of my body,
I want to run like the rain down the walls,
I want to be trodden underfoot like the cobbles in the broad streets,
I want to sink, like all heavy things, to the bottom of the sea,
With a voluptuosity long since beyond me!

I don't want locks on the doors!
I don't want padlocks on the safes!
I want to interleave myself, insinuate myself, be carried off,
I want to be made someone else's painful possession,
To be emptied out of crates,
To be tossed into the sea,
To be tracked down at home for obscene ends,
Better that than to be always sitting here quietly,
Better that than to be merely writing these lines!

I don't want there to be intervals in the world!
I want objects to actually touch and penetrate!
I want physical bodies to be one with each other like souls,
Not just dynamically, but statically too!

I want to fly and to fall from a great height!
To be thrown like a grenade!
To end up in ... To be carried to ...
The abstract culmination of the end of me and of everything!

A climax of iron and engines!
A stairway without stairs speeding ever higher!
A hydraulic pump sucking out my festering innards!

Put chains on me just so that I can break them!
So that I can break them with my teeth and make my teeth bleed,
One of life's masochistic, blood-letting pleasures!

The sailors took me prisoner.
Their hands gripped me in the darkness.
I died momentarily when I felt this.
My soul then licked the floor of that private prison,
And the strident hum of impossibilities outlined my outrage.

Skip, leap, take the bit between your teeth,
You red-hot-iron-Pegasus of my restless longings,
Uncertain destination of my engine-driven fate!
Leap, skip, deck yourself with flags,
Leave a trail of blood in the vastness of night,
Hot blood, even from afar,
Fresh blood, even from afar,
Cold, living blood in the dynamic air of me!
Skip, leap, spring,
On your feet and start leaping, [...]

11e   [c. 1915]

To sing you,
To salute you,
I would have to write that supreme poem,
Where, more than in any other supreme poem,
There would live, in a complete synthesis consisting of a painstak-
        ing Analysis,
The whole Universe of things, lives, and souls,
The whole Universe of men, women, children,
The whole Universe of gestures, actions, emotions, thoughts,
The whole Universe of the things that humanity does,
Of the things that happen to humanity—

Professions, laws, regimes, medicines, Destiny,
Written crisscross, with constant intertwinings,
On the dynamic paper of Things that Happen,
On the rapid papyrus of social relations,
On the palimpsest of constantly renewed emotions.

11f   [c. 1915]

In order to salute you—
In order to salute you as you should be saluted–
I need to transform my verses into a swift steed,
I need to transform my verses into a train,
I need to transform my verses into an arrow,
I need to transform my verses into speed,
I need to transform my verses into the things of the world.

You sang everything, and everything sang in you—
Ah, the splendid, whorish tolerance
Of your sensations, legs spread wide
To the details and shapes of the system of the universe.

11g   [c. 1915]

Go for it? Go for what and why?
What do I get out of "go for it?" Or indeed out of anything,
What is the point of even thinking about going for it?

Decadent, my friend, that's what we are, decadent ...
Deep inside each of us is a Byzantium in flames,
And I feel neither the flames nor Byzantium,
But the Empire is dying in our watery veins
And our Poetry sprang from our inability to act ...
You, singer of energetic professions, you Poet of the Extreme, of the Strong,
You, muscular inspiration, dominated by masculine muses,

You are, after all, an innocent in full hysterical flow,
In short, a mere "caresser of life,"
An idle fop, a flamer at least in intent,
—Well … that's your business—but where is Life in all that?

I, an engineer by profession, fed up with everything and everyone,
I, absurdly superfluous, at war with things,
I, useless, spent, futile, pretentious, and amoral,
The buoy of my sensations cut adrift by the storm,
The anchor of my ship now lying wrecked on the seabed,
I, a singer of Life and Power—can you believe it?
I, like you, energetic and salutary in my poems—
And, at bottom, sincere like you, burning up with having all of
        Europe in my brain,
In my explosive brain, uncontained by dikes,
In my highly trained, dynamic intelligence,
In my rubber-stamped, signed-off, trademark, checkbook sensuality,
Why on earth are we living, why are we writing poetry?
Damn the idleness that makes us poets,
The degenerateness that fools us into being artists,
The fundamental tedium that makes us think we're energetic and
        modern,
When what we want is to amuse ourselves, to feel alive,
Because we do nothing and are nothing, life flows very slowly
        through our veins.
Let's be honest, Walt, and see things for what they are …
Let's drink this down like a bitter medicine
And agree to send the world and life to hell
Not out of scorn or loathing, but out of languor.

Is this any way to salute you?
Whatever it is, it's my way of saluting you,
Whatever it's worth, it's my way of loving you,

Whatever it might be, it's my way of agreeing with you ...
Whatever it is, that is what it is. And you understand, you're pleased,
You, my old friend, weeping on my shoulder, agree with me—
(When does the last train leave?—
A long holiday in God ...)
Let us go, let us confidently go ...
This must all have some other meaning
More than just living and having everything ...
There must be a point in our consciousness
When there's a shift in the landscape
And it begins to interest us, to welcome us, to move us ...
When there begins to be a welcome coolness in our soul
And sun and countryside in our newly awakened senses.
Wherever the Station is, we'll meet there ...
Wait for me at the door, Walt; I'll be there ...
I'll be there without the universe, without life, without myself, with-
        out anything ...
And with our respective griefs we will ponder, alone and in silence,
The great absurdity of the world, the coarse ineptitude of things,
And we will feel, we will feel the mystery so far, far, far away,
So absolutely, abstractly far away
Definitively far away.

11h [c. 1915]

Go for it? Go for what? Why? Where?
How far?
Go where, swift steed of my imagination?
Go where, entirely imaginary train?
Go where, arrow, haste, speed?
They are all just me grieving for them,
They are all just me regretting not having them here running
        through every nerve.

Go where, if there is no where or how?
Go where, if I'm always where I am and never ahead,
Never ahead, or even behind,
But always all-too-inevitably where my body is,
All-too-humanly at the thinking-point of my soul,
Always the same unsplittable atom of the divine persona?

Go where, O sad knowledge that I will never get what I want?
Go where, why, for what, if there is no what?
Go for it, go for it, go for it, but, O my uncertainty, where?

11i [c. 1915]

Futility, unreality, the static [...] of all art,
The curse of the artist condemned to not living!

Oh, Walt, if only we had
That third thing, the middle way between art and life,
The thing that you felt, and which is neither static nor dynamic,
Neither real nor unreal
Neither us nor the others—
But how can we even imagine it?
Or even learn it
Even if there's no hope of us ever having it?

Pure dynamics, pure speed,
Which is there so absolutely in things,
Which actually collides with the senses,
Let us build trains, Walt, and not sing them,
Let us dig, my old friend, and sing neither the digger nor the field
[...]
Let us endure and not write,
Let us love and not sing,
Let us put two bullets in the first hat-wearing head we see

And let us make no pointless, empty onomatopoeias in our poetry
In our poetry written cold, and then typed and then printed.

A poem that would sculpt a sculpture out of Motion and Eternity,
A poem that [...] the orchestra and that of the stage,
That [...] adds rhythm to the song, the dance and [...]
A poem that would be all poems,
That would dispense with all other poems,
A poem that would dispense with Life itself.
Damn it, whatever I do, however I twist and turn in the center of
        my being,
However hard I strain nerves trained and honed for everything,
However I conjure up rage and lucidity in my brain,
The thing I'm thinking about always escapes me,
The thing I miss always [...] and I go to see if it's missing,
I'm always lacking six sides on every cube,
Four sides on every square I attempted to express,
Three dimensions on the solidity I tried to project ...
A clockwork train set in motion by pulling a string, a thread,
Will always have more movement than my static, read-on-the-page
        poems,
The most worm-like of worms, the most chemical of living cells
Will always have more life, more God, than all the life of my poems,
All the vermilions I describe will never match those of a stone,
The rhythms I suggest will never be as rhythmical as a piece of music!
Never like [...]
And I will never do more than copy the echo of things,
The reflection of real things in the dim mirror that is me.

The death of everything in my sensibility (so vibrant too!)
The very real and eternal drying up of the lucid river of my
        imagination!
I want to sing you, Walt, and I cannot!
I want to give you the song you deserve,

But I have no song for you, for anything—not even for myself, alas—
I'm a deaf-mute bellowing forth his gestures,
A blind man looking around at an invisible whole.

This is how I sing you, Walt, by saying that I cannot sing you!
My old commentator on the multiplicity of things,
My comrade in feeling in my nerves the dynamic march
Of the profound physical-chemistry of the [...]
Of the fundamental energy of the appearance of things to God,
Of the abstract form of subject and object beyond Life.

We are playing hide-and-seek with our intentions ...
We are making art and yet what we want, after all, is to make life.
What we want to make has already been made and it is not in us to
        make it,
Indeed any member of the bourgeoisie would do it better than us,
        more closely,
More diversely and instinctively,
Yes, if what is in the poems is what vibrates and speaks,
Life's chastest gesture is more sensual than the most sensual of poems,
Because it is made by someone who is alive, because it is [...], be-
        cause it is Life.

11j   [c. 1915]

In my poems, I sing of trains and cars and steamships,
But whatever lofty heights I raise them to, they are only rhythms and
        ideas and in my poems
There is no iron, no steel, no wheels, no wood, no ropes,
They lack even the reality of the merest stone in the street
That anyone might step on without even noticing,
But which can be looked at, picked up, trodden on,
Whereas my poems are sounds and ideas merely to be understood.

What I want is not just to sing of iron: it's iron itself.
What I think gives only an idea of Steel—not the actual steel—
What infuriates me about all the emotions of the intelligence
Is that I cannot exchange my rhythm imitating the singing water
For the real coolness of the water on my hands,
For the visible sound of the river into which I can plunge and get wet,
That can leave my suit dripping,
Where I can drown if I want,
And which, in its unliterary nature, possesses natural divinity.
Shit, a thousand times shit, for everything that I cannot do.
Everything, Walt—do you hear?—but what is everything, every-
       thing, everything?

It's such a drag this need we have to be God
So as to have poems written to the Universe and to Realities by our
       own Flesh,
And to have idea-things and Infinite thoughts!
To have real stars inside my thought-self,
Name-numbers in even the most outer reaches of my
       Earth-emotions.

11k   [c. 1915]
Declare our vitality bankrupt!
We write poems, we sing things-bankrupt, we don't live them.
How can we live all lives and all epochs
And all the forms of all forms
And all the gestures of all gestures?
What is writing poetry but a confession that life is not enough,
What is art but a forgetting that it is just art?
Farewell, Walt, farewell!
Farewell until the indefinite that awaits beyond the End.
Wait for me, if you can wait there where you are,

When does the last train leave?
When does it leave? (When, Walt?)

11| [c. 1915]

Wherever I am not the first, I would prefer to be nothing, just not to
    be there at all,
Wherever I cannot be the first to take action, I prefer to watch oth-
    ers act.
Wherever I cannot be in command, I would prefer not even to obey.
I am so excessive in my desire for everything, so excessive that I
    never falter,
And I never do falter, because I never even try.
"All or Nothing" has a special meaning for me.
But I cannot be universal because I am individual.
I cannot be everyone because I am One, only one, only me.
I cannot be the first in anything, because there is no first.
I therefore prefer the nothing of being only that being nothing.

When does the last train leave, Walt?
I want to leave this city, the Earth,
I want to leave the country of Me once and for all,
To leave the world like a self-confessed failure,
Like a traveling salesman selling ships to people who live far from
    the sea.

To the scrapyard with all the broken-down engines!
What did my existence ever amount to? A great, futile longing—
The sterile realization of an impossible fate—
A mad inventor's attempt to build a perpetual motion machine,
An obsessive's theorem for squaring the circle,
Or for swimming the Atlantic without leaving the shore
Or even getting into the water, just by looking and calculating,
Throwing stones at the moon,
An absurd longing for the parallel lines of God and life to meet.

Megalomania of the nerves,
My stiff body's longing to grow limber,
My physical self's fury because it isn't the be-all-and-end-all
Sensuality's vehicle of abstract enthusiasm
The dynamic vacuum of the world.

Let's get away from Existing!
Let's leave, once and for all and for ever, the village of Life,
The suburb of God's World
And plunge into the city, impulsively,
Recklessly, crazily Going …
Let's leave once and for all.

When does the last train leave for your place, Walt?
What kind of God was I that my nostalgia should turn into such
         longings?
Perhaps by leaving, I'll return. Perhaps by ending, I'll arrive.
Who knows? Any moment could be the right moment. Let's go,
Come on! To stay is to delay. To leave is to have left already.

Let's leave for wherever you might be.
Oh, to stay in a place where there-is-no-staying!
A terminus where there are No-Stops!

12   [c. 1915]

I
Bags packed and everything on board
And with nothing more to hope for from the land we're leaving,
Already dressed in our light traveling clothes and leaning on the
         ship's rail,
Let us bid farewell, with a sense of rising joy, to what remains,
Farewell to affections, to domestic thoughts, to home fires, and to
         siblings,

And as the space between the slow ship and the dock widens
We enjoy a shiver of grand, indefinable hope,
A tremulous sense of future.

There lies the way ahead, and once we reach the middle of the river,
Our view of the land from the water,
The balconies and the cranes or the piles of merchandise unloaded
       on the dockside become still clearer,
And, fortunately, the family gathered at the end of the quay,
Taking sensible, visible care not to fall into the water while in full
       emotional flow,
Are not saying goodbye to us.

We look at our fellow passengers. How different they all are!
Some are merely in transit. No one is waving goodbye to them …
Others, with the wanly cheerful air of someone trying not to cry,
Are using their handkerchiefs to wave rather feebly and inelegantly
At handkerchiefs being waved by others left behind on the quay,
On the quay—have you noticed?—suddenly so much farther off than
       we thought.
The bright bitterness of leaving,
The special savor of the beginning of a sea voyage, mingling our senses
With luggage smells, ship smells, food smells,
And our soul is a confused compote of smells and tastes,
The vague journey we will make seen through palate and nose,
The whole sensual uncertainty of life felt down our spine …

And we are not leaving anyone behind …
If we were, ah, all those broken ties!, the ship as it moves away
Would be moving away from far more than just the land;
It would be moving away from our entire past, from ourselves, left
       standing on the quay and still en route
from the domestic feeling with which we kissed our mother,

from the playful glee with which we would sometimes tease our
    sisters …
To leave! To leave is to live excessively. What is everything but
    leaving …
We leave the quay of our own life every day, ships […]
And we head off into the future as if into the Mystery,
But what do we know about where we are going, O sorrow, and
    what we are,
And what fluid, protean God watches over those departures?
He gazes from afar at the cranes still stirring,
He gazes at the figures on the quayside, black but for the white
    stains of waving handkerchiefs.
He gazes at the corrugated zinc roofs of warehouses on the quays
    and docks, at the doors,
The casual, detached calm of the workers and the stevedores …
There is such anguish, such inexplicable anguish in my soul
That I don't know how, given my strident cries, they have the
    courage to stand
So calmly, on the dock, the stevedores and the customs officers!

Life turned tipsy … a slight twitchiness in our sensations …
An alcoholic dizziness afflicting our innermost senses …
Our soul creeps out from its usual place
And the wheels of our daily life begin to wobble as if about to come
    loose from the axle …

On deck, the people who are accustomed to being here on board
Are quite oblivious to all this and yet still interested.
(Ah, whenever I'm interested in others, my gaze is never calm,
The trembling nerves of all those sentient beings vibrate inside me,
My eyes overflow with the tears of all those who weep to be parted.
I hold in my hands the circular gestures of all those sadly waving
    handkerchiefs,

I am all the sorrows of all those people having to leave ...
I am the hopes they carry with them, hopes that intensify the pain
       of departure,
I am thinking with the same foolish pride that all of them feel about
       the clothes bought for the voyage,
About the small objects purchased late in the day ("Oh, I nearly
       forgot," they say about some entirely unnecessary thing),
Just before closing time, in some marvelous shop full of leather
       suitcases ...
Ah, how my nerves vibrate with the nerves of all those people ...
And with the shuddering ship's engines, and with the flag fluttering
       in the wind
And with the tumescent tremor of the shrouds and the flapping of
       the awnings
And our whole soul is a painful physical vibration set to my inner
       rhythms).

Cosmopolitan life thrown to the four winds ...
The life of so many real people on board so many ships ...
The intoxication of mixing with other people and knowing that
       they exist, have past lives, experienced, enjoyed, endured,
And how curious, interesting, and moral each person's clothes are,
Even the way they talk, so full of enigmas and metaphysics, the way
       they laugh, do their hair, rub along together ...
The metaphysical sensation of other people and their realities, their
       décor ...
Ah, the humanitarian malady of my vibrating nerves so full of other
       people,
The sensual pleasure of savoring and suffering through those hypo-
       thetical others ...
And yet still being me, only me eternally, and having no other lives
       but my own!
As if someone were suddenly to play a *fado* at midnight in some
       small American town.

A metaphysical patriotism with the nerves of all those people con-
    stantly vibrating inside me
When I look at others in that cosmopolitical way, and hear diverse
    languages
And see in gestures and clothes—which seem identical, but which
    are so very different—diverse countries, diverse costumes,
And glimpse different households, complex commercial lives, un-
    known loves, streets of cities I've never visited,
Like an animatograph in a theater the size of the Universe,
Where we know that, once the session is over and we leave,
There's no house to go home to, no car to take us anywhere,
But only Absolute Night, and God perhaps like a Vast Moon
    signifying

The End

IV[*]
The profound, religious solitude of the unbounded Universe,
Enormous vastness, neither broad nor high nor long, but merely
    space, the constellated space
Of this blue-black, starry mystery where the earth is a thing
And human lives appear like barges on the surface of the water ...
Rays of sun coming in through the half-open window of the bed-
    room in a country house,
Noontides on abandoned threshing floors,
Late-night assignations on other river banks,
Make of our inevitable end a consolation, a mantle
And lay it softly upon my soul ...
You easeful, untamed fields,
You rivers calmly flowing along a bed of disquiet,
You public parks visited in the afternoons,

* The author only numbered the beginning (I) and the end (IV).

You garden pools, you hearths in ancestral mansions,
And make of the silence of the night the disparate whispering of
    black silks.

13 THE PASSING OF THE HOURS
13a   [c. 1916]

To feel everything in every way,
To embrace every point of view,
To be sincere while constantly contradicting myself,
To disapprove of my own liberal thoughts,
And to love things as God loves them.

I, who have more fraternal feelings for a tree than for a workman,
I, who feel more intensely the imagined pain of the sea breaking on
    the shore
Than the real pain of children who are beaten
(Ah, this can't be right, poor beaten children—
And why do my sensations change so quickly?)
In short, I who am a continuous dialogue,
An incomprehensible talking-out-loud, a dark night in the tower,
When the bells sway slightly, untouched by any hand
And when one is saddened by the thought that there's still life to be
    lived tomorrow.
In short, I, both literally me,
And metaphorically me too,
I, the sensationist poet, sent by Chance
To live by Life's blameless laws,
I, the smoker of cigarettes as befits my profession,
The fellow who smokes opium, who drinks absinthe, but who
    actually
Prefers thinking about smoking opium to smoking it,
And looking at a glass of absinthe to drinking it ...
I, this superior degenerate with nothing filed away in my soul,

With no personality of any obvious value,
I, the solemn investigator of futile things,
Who would be capable of going to live in Siberia out of sheer
      cussedness,
And who is, I believe, quite right to think the land of his birth
      unimportant,
Because, unlike a tree, I have no roots …
I, who so often feel as real as a metaphor,
As the words written by a dying man in the book of the girl he met
      on the terrace,
Or a game of chess on the deck of an ocean liner,
I, the nursemaid who pushes perambulators round all the public parks,
I, the policeman who stands watching her from behind,
I, the child in the pram waving a rattle at that man's lucid
      unconsciousness,
I, the backdrop to all this, the urban peace
Sifted through the branches of the trees in the park,
I, what awaits them in the street,
I, what they don't know about themselves,
I, the thing you're thinking about and that makes you smile,
I, the contradictory, the fictitious, the tirade, the foam,
The newly pasted poster, the backside of that French woman, the
      gaze of the priest,
The square where two streets meet and where the chauffeurs doze off
      leaning against their cars,
The scar on the face of the evil-looking sergeant,
The greasy stain on the collar of the ailing teacher returning home,
The cup from which the little boy who died always drank,
And which has a crack on the handle (all of which fills a mother's
      heart to overflowing) …
I, the French dictation of the small girl who keeps fiddling with her
      garters,
I, the feet touching each other under the bridge table lit by a
      chandelier,

I, the hidden letter, the warmth of the sheet, the bay window with
the window ajar,
The tradesmen's entrance where the maid is discussing what her
cousin has been up to,
That rascal Jose, who promised to come, then didn't,
And we were going to play a trick on him too ...
I am all of this, as well as the rest of the world ...
So many things, the doors opening and the reason why they open,
And the things that the hands opening the doors did before ...
I, the innate-unhappiness of all expressions,
The impossibility of expressing all feelings,
And with no gravestone in the cemetery for the brother of all these
things,
And how what seems to mean nothing always means something ...
Yes, I, the naval engineer, as superstitious as a country-bumpkin
bridesmaid,
Sporting a monocle so as not to appear to be the same as the real
idea I have of myself,
The I who sometimes takes three hours to get dressed, not that I
find this normal,
But, rather, metaphysical, and if someone knocks at my door, I get
angry
Not so much because they've interrupted me tying my tie, as for
reminding me that there's life out there ...
Yes, I the addressee of sealed letters,
The trunk with the faded initials,
The cadence of voices we'll never hear again—
God keeps all this stowed away in the Mystery, and whenever we
feel it,
Life suddenly weighs heavy and it feels very cold and much closer
than our own body.
Brigida, my aunt's cousin,
The general they used to talk about—a general from when they
were small,

And life was civil war on every corner ...
Vive le mélodrame où Margot a pleuré!
Dead leaves drop to the ground at irregular intervals,
But the truth is, it's always fall in the fall,
And winter inevitably follows behind,
And there is only one road to life, which is life ...

That insignificant old man, who, it turns out, knew the Romantics,
That political pamphlet from the days of the constitutional
        revolutions,
And the pain all this leaves behind, without anyone knowing why,
Not that there's any reason to weep over it, yet reason enough to feel
        it.

All the lovers embraced in my soul,
All the tramps have, at some point, slept on me for a moment,
All the scorned and rejected have for a moment rested on my
        shoulder,
All the old and sick have crossed the road leaning on my arm,
And all the murderers told me the same secret.

(The woman whose smile suggests the peace I don't have,
And in whose lowered eyes lives a whole Dutch landscape,
Complete with feminine heads *coiffées de lin*
And all the hard daily grind of a peaceful, clean-living people ...
Or the woman who is the ring left on top of the chest of drawers,
And the ribbon caught in the drawer,
A pink ribbon, although it's not the color I like, but the trapped
        ribbon,
Just as while I may not like life, I still like to feel it ...

To sleep like a dog run over in the road in the sun,
Definitively dead to the rest of the Universe,
And to have the cars drive straight over me.)

I've been to bed with every sentiment,
I've been a *souteneur* for every emotion,
Every chance sensation has bought me a drink,
I've exchanged glances with all kinds of reasons to take action,
I've been hand-in-hand with every impulse to leave,
The intense fever of the passing hours!
The anguish of that forge of the emotions!
Rage, foam, the immensity too large for my handkerchief,
The bitch howling in the night,
The pool in the garden strolling around my insomnia,
The wood as it was when we used to walk there in the evening, the
     rose,
The indifferent lock of hair, the moss, the pine trees,
The rage at being unable to contain all of this, to hold on to all of this,
Oh, the abstract hunger of things, the impotent lust of the moment,
The intellectual orgy of feeling life!

To obtain everything through divine sufficiency—
Evenings, consents, warnings,
The beautiful things of life—
Talent, virtue, impunity,
The tendency to accompany others home,
How it feels to be a passenger,
The advisability of embarking early in order to reserve a place,
And there's always something missing, a glass, a breeze, a phrase,
And life hurts the more you enjoy it and the more you invent it.

To be able to roar with laughter and to laugh and laugh,
To laugh like an overturned glass,
Absolutely crazy with feeling,
Absolutely battered from bumping into things,
My mouth torn from biting things,
My nails bleeding from grasping things,
Then just choose me a cell where I can sit and remember life.

To feel everything in every way,
To live everything from every angle,
To be the same thing in every possible way at the same time,
To realize in yourself all the humanity of every moment
In one single diffuse, profuse moment, complete and remote.

I always want to be the thing I sympathize with,
Sooner or later, I always become
That thing, be it a stone or a desire,
Be it a flower or an abstract idea,
Be it a whole multitude or a way of understanding God,
And I sympathize with everything, I live from everything in
        everything.
I sympathize with superior men because they are superior,
And I sympathize with inferior men because they are superior too,
Because to be inferior is different to being superior,
And that's why, when viewed in a certain way, it is a form of
        superiority.
I sympathize with others for their lack of those same qualities,
And with others I sympathize simply so as to sympathize with them,
And there are certain absolutely organic moments when this applies
        to all men.
Yes, I am absolute monarch in my sympathy,
The fact that it exists is reason enough for me to live.
I clutch to my heaving bosom in a tremulous embrace
(In the same tremulous embrace)
The man who gives his shirt to a poor stranger,
The soldier who dies for his country without knowing what his
        country is,
As well as the matricide, the fratricide, the incestuous father, the
        pedophile,
The highwayman, the pirate,
The pickpocket, the shadow lurking in alleyways—

They are all my favorite lover, at least for one moment in life.
I kiss all the prostitutes on the mouth,
I kiss the eyes of all the pimps,
My passivity lies down at the feet of all the murderers,
And my Spanish cape conceals the retreat of all the thieves.
All these things are my life's raison d'être.

I have committed every crime,
I have lived inside every crime
(I myself was neither criminal nor crime,
But, rather, the vice personified inside each of them,
And those are the most triumphal-archest moments of my life).

I multiplied myself in order to be able to feel myself,
To feel myself I needed to feel everything,
I overflowed, I spilled over,
I stripped off, I surrendered,
And in every corner of my soul there is an altar to a different god.

The arms of every athlete embraced my suddenly female self,
And the very thought made me swoon in that imagined muscular
        embrace.

My mouth received the kisses of every meeting,
Every handkerchief waved in farewell waved inside my heart,
Every obscene gesture, word, and look
Strike my whole body as if thirsting for my erogenous zones.
I've been every ascetic, every no-hoper, everyone seemingly
        forgotten,
As well as every pederast—every single one (not one was missing).
A *rouge-et-noir* rendezvous in the infernal depths of my soul!

(Freddie, I used to call you Baby, because you were blonde and
        white and I loved you,

How many empresses yet to reign and how many dethroned prin-
cesses were you for me!
Mary, with whom I used to read Burns on days that were as sad as
feeling that one is still alive,
Mary, you have no idea how many respectable couples, how many
happy families,
Inhabited you through my eyes and my encircling arm and my hesi-
tant consciousness,
Their banal lives, their suburban houses and gardens, their unex-
pected half holidays ...
Mary, I'm unhappy ...
Freddie, I'm unhappy ...
All of you, every one of you, casual, belated,
How many times would you have thought of thinking about me, but
never did,
Ah, how insignificant I was in what you are, how insignificant, how
very insignificant—
Yes, and what have I been, O my subjective universe,
O my sun, my moonlight, my stars, my moment,
O external-me lost in God's labyrinths!)

Everything passes, everything parades past inside me,
And all the cities of the world murmur inside me ...
My tribunal-heart, my market-heart, my stock-exchange-heart, my
bank-counter-heart,
My rendezvous-heart with all of humanity,
My bench-heart in park, guesthouse, inn, cell number something-
or-other
(*"Aquí estuvo Manolo en vísperas de ir al patíbulo,"*)
My club-heart, room-stalls-doormat-box-office-gangway-heart
My bridge-gate-excursion-walk-voyage-auction-fair-fête-heart,
My hatchway-heart,
My order-heart,
My letter-luggage-satisfaction-delivery-heart,

My marginalized-limit-summary-index-heart,
Eh-la, eh-la, eh-la, my heart the bazaar.

Every morning is morning and life.
Every dawn shines on the same place:
Infinity ...
Every bird-like outpouring of joy comes from the same throat,
Every trembling of leaves comes from the same tree,
And everyone who gets up early to go to work
Leaves the same house for the same factory and takes the same
      route ...

Roll on, big ball, teeming world of consciousnesses, the earth,
Roll on, dawn-struck, evening-struck, plumb beneath the suns,
      nocturnal,
Roll on in abstract space, in the dimly-lit night
Roll on and [...]

I can feel in my head the speed of the earth's turning,
And all countries and all people turn inside me,
A centrifugal yearning, a furious desire to be able to travel through
      space to the stars
Beats against the inside of my skull,
Sticks pins all over my consciousness of my body,
Makes me get up a thousand times over and head for the Abstract,
For the Unfindable, the unbounded Beyond,
The invisible Goal being all the places where I am not, and all at the
      same time.

Ah, not to be standing even when I walk,
Not to be lying down even when I stand,
Or awake even when asleep,
Neither here nor anywhere else,
To solve the equation of this prolix restlessness,

To know where to be in order to be everywhere,
To know where to lie down so that I can walk along every street,
To know where […]

Ho–ho–ho–ho–ho–ho–ho
Ho–ho–ho–ho–ho–ho–ho
Ho–ho–ho–ho–ho–ho–ho
Ho–ho–ho–ho–ho–ho–ho

My winged cavalcade flying over everything,
My explosive cavalcade flying under everything,
My winged and explosive cavalcade because of everything…

Hup-la over the trees, hup-la under the pools,
Hup-la into the walls, hup-la scrambling up tree trunks,
Hup-la into the air, hup-la into the wind, hup-la, hup-la onto the beaches,
At an ever-increasing speed, insistent, violent,
Hup-la hup-la hup-la hup-la…

A pantheistic cavalcade inside everything,
An energetic cavalcade inside all the energies,
A cavalcade inside the red-hot embers, the burning lamp,
Inside every possible way of using energy
A cavalcade in amperes, in kilogram-meters
An explosive, exploded cavalcade, like a bomb that bursts,
A cavalcade bursting everywhere at the same time,
A cavalcade above space, a leap over time,
Ride on, electron-ion horse, solar system summarized
Inside the action of pistons, outside the turning wheels.
Inside the pistons, making speed abstract and mad,
I function entirely on iron and speed, coming-and-going, madness,
        repressed rage,
Tied to the trace left by every wheel, I spin astonishing hours,
And the whole universe creaks, cracks, and crumbles inside me.

Ho-ho-ho-ho-ho …
Ever faster, ever more mind over matter,
Ahead of the speeding idea of body-as-projectile,
With the mind both behind and ahead of the body, shadow, spark,
He-la-ho-ho … Helahoho …

All energy is the same and all nature is the same …
The sap of the sap of trees is the same energy that moves
The wheels of a locomotive, the wheels of the tram, the wheels of
    diesel cars,
And a cart drawn by mules or by gasoline all propelled by the same
    thing.

Pantheistic rage at the terrifying feeling inside me—
With all my senses at boiling point, with all my pores steaming—
That everything is one speed, one energy, one divine line
From itself to itself, stopped still, whispering of violent, crazy
    speeds …

Ho–ho–ho–ho–ho–ho–ho
Ho–ho–ho–ho–ho–ho–ho
Ho–ho–ho–ho–ho–ho–ho
Ho–ho–ho–ho–ho–ho–ho

Ave, salve, long live the speeding unity of everything!
Ave, salve, long live the sameness of everything-that-is-arrow!
Ave, salve, long live the great machine-universe!
Ave, you who are the same, trees, machines, laws,
Ave, you who are the same, worms, pistons, abstract ideas,
The same sap fills you, the same sap turns you,
You are the same thing, and everything else is external and false,
Everything, the static everything-else that lingers in eyes that don't
    look,
But not in my nerves-cum-piston-engine fueled by oil, heavy or light,

Not in my machine, gear-driven nerves,
In my locomotive-tram-automobile-steam-driven-thresher-nerves,
In my maritime-diesel-semi-diesel-Campbell-machine-nerves,
In my steam-gas-oil-electricity-fueled nerves,
Universal machine driven by the chains of each and every moment!
Train, smash into the buffers in the siding!
Steamship, crash, paf, into the dock!
Automobile driven by the craziness of the entire universe, hurl yourself
Down every precipice
And smash, bang, shatter into pieces in the bottom of my heart!

À moi, all projectile objects!
À moi, all directional objects!
À moi, all objects too swift to be seen!
Beat me, pierce me, surpass me!
The rage of all impulses closes in *moi*-the-circle!

Hela-hoho my train-automobile-airplane-yearnings,
Speed zooms through every idea,
Collides with every dream and reduces it to splinters,
Scorches every useful, humanitarian idea,
Runs down every normal, decent, concordant feeling,
Snatches up in the turn of your heavy, vertiginous wheel
The bodies of every philosophy, the rags of every poem,
And tears them to shreds, leaving only you, abstract, airy wheel,
Supreme master of the European hour, metal on heat.

Quick now, this cavalcade has no ending, not even in God!
Quick now, because even I am getting left behind,
Dragged along, clinging to a horse's tail, twisted, torn, lost
As I fall, my body and my soul trailing after my abstract desire,
My vertiginous longing to overtake the universe,
To leave God behind like some nonexistent milestone,
To leave the universe [...]

My imagination aches, I don't know quite how, but it does.
Inside me the noonday sun is setting.
There's already a hint of evening in the blue sky and in my nerves.
Let's go, cavalcade, who else do you want to run down?
Me, all velocity, voracity, greedy for abstract energy,
The one who wanted to eat, drink, scrape, and scratch at the world,
The one who wanted only to trample the universe underfoot,
Trample, trample, trample to the point of numbness …
Me who now feels locked out from my all-consuming imaginings,
Because although I wanted everything, I ended up with nothing,
[…]
[…]

Cavalcade disbanded at the peak of peaks,
Cavalcade dispersed beneath all the wells,
Cavalcade-flight, cavalcade-arrow, cavalcade-lightning-thought,
Cavalcade-me, cavalcade-me, cavalcade-universe-me.
Heloahoho-o-o-o-o-o-o-o …

My elastic being, spring, needle, vibration …

13c   [c. 1916]

I carry inside my heart,
As if in a coffer too full to close,
All the places I've ever been to,
All the ports I've ever arrived in,
All the landscapes seen through windows or portholes,
Or while dreaming on a ship's deck,
And all this, which seems so much, is too little for my wants.

Entering Singapore, with the green dawn breaking,
The coral of the Maldives in the heat of the day,
Macau at one in the morning … I wake suddenly …

Yacht-aho-o-o-o-o-o-o-oy ... Ghi- ...
And all of those things rise up from the depths of some other reality
    ...
The almost North African stature of Zanzibar in the sun ...
Dar es Salaam (a difficult port to leave) ...
Manjunga, Nosy Be, the lush greens of Madagascar ...
Storms breaking over Guardafui ...
And the Cape of Good Hope clear in the dawn light ...
And Capetown with Table Mountain in the background ...

I've traveled through more lands than those I set foot in ...
I've seen more landscapes than those I laid eyes on ...
I've experienced more sensations than all the sensations I've felt,
Because however much I felt, I always wanted to feel more,
And life always frustrated me, was always too little, and I unhappy.

At certain times of the day, I remember all this and feel afraid,
I wonder what will remain to me of this life lived in fragments, of
        this apogee,
Of this curving road, this automobile by the roadside, this warning,
This calm confusion of conflicting sensations,
This disquiet in the dregs of every glass,
This anxiety in the dregs of all pleasures,
This anticipated satiety in the handle of every cup,
This tedious game of cards between the Cape of Good Hope and
        the Canaries.

I don't know if life is too little or too much for me.
I don't know if I feel too much or too little, I don't know
If I lack spiritual scruples, some intellectual foothold,
Consanguinity with the mystery of things, the electric shock
Of contact, the blood beneath the blows, the shudder at the
        slightest noise,
Or if there is some other happier, more consoling meaning to all this.

Whatever the answer, it would have been far better not to have been
    born,
Because since life is so interesting at every moment,
It ends up hurting, nauseating, cutting, chafing, creaking,
Making me feel like shouting, leaping, keeping my feet firmly on
    the ground, abandoning
All houses, all logics and all balconies,
And heading off into death like a savage into the trees and into
    oblivion,
Through tumbles and dangers and an absence of tomorrows,
And all this ought to be something more closely akin to what I think,
To what I think or feel, O life, I don't know which.

I fold my arms on the table top and rest my head on my arms,
And I need to be able to cry, but don't know where to find the tears
    …
However hard I try to feel deeply sorry for myself, I cannot weep,
My soul lies torn asunder beneath the bent index finger touching it …
What is to become of me? What is to become of me?

They chased the fool out of the palace, whipped him, for no reason,
They made the beggar get up from the step where he'd fallen.
They beat the abandoned child and snatched the food from his hands.
Oh the immense pain of the world, what's needed is action …
So decadent, so decadent, so decadent …
I only feel all right when I listen to music, and even then …
Gardens from the eighteenth century before '89,
Wherever you are, I want to weep anyway.

Today's evening and that of every day falls gradually, monotonously,
Like a balm that brings comfort only because we think it is a balm.

The lights come on, night falls, life takes second place.
Yet somehow or other, we must continue to live.
My soul burns physically as if it were a hand.

I'm in everyone's way, I even bump into myself.
Ah, my house in the provinces,
All that stands between us is a train, a carriage, and the decision to
  depart.
But I stay, I stay ... I'm the one who always wants to leave,
And who always stays, always stays, always stays,
Even if I die, even if I leave, I stay, I stay, I stay ...

Make me human, O night, make me fraternal and solicitous.
One can only live in a humanitarian way.
Only by loving mankind, action, the banality of work,
That—alas—is the only way one can live.
That, O night, is the only way, and I cannot be like that!

I have seen everything and marveled at everything,
But everything was either too much or too little—I don't know
  which—and so I suffered.
I experienced every emotion, every thought, every gesture,
And I felt as sad as if I'd wanted to experience them and couldn't.
I loved and hated just like other people,
But for other people that was normal and instinctive,
And for me it was always an exception, a shock, a valve, a spasm.

Come, O night, extinguish me, come, drown me in your darkness.
O friend from the Beyond, lady of endless mourning,
Earth's outer covering of sorrow, the World's silent grief.
Gentle, ancient mother of unexpressed emotions,
Older sister, virginal and sad, of vacuous ideas,
Bride always waiting for us to make some decision,
The constantly abandoned direction of our fate,
Our joyless pagan uncertainty,
Our faithless Christian frailty,
Our inert Buddhism, with no love of things and no ecstasies,
Our fever, our pallor, our weakling impatience,
Our life, O mother, our wasted life ...

I don't know how to feel, I don't know how to be human, how to
    coexist
From within my sad soul with other men, my brothers on the earth.
I don't know how to be useful even by feeling, to be practical, every-
    day, clear-cut,
To have a place in life, to have a destiny among men,
To have work, strength, will, a garden,
A reason to rest, a need for distraction,
Something that comes directly from nature to me.

For all those reasons, be, then, like a mother to me, O tranquil night…
You, who take the world from the world, you who are peace,
You who do not exist, you who are only the absence of light,
You who are nothing, not a place, not an essence, not a life,
Penelope of the web of your darkness, undone each morning,
Unreal Circe of the febrile, the baselessly fearful,
Come to me, O night, reach out your hands to me,
And bring coolness and relief, O night, to my fevered brow…

You, whose coming is so gentle that it resembles a departure,
Whose ebb and flow of darkness, when the moon exhales,
Contains waves of dead affection, cold as a sea of dreams,
Breezes from landscapes fashioned to calm our excess of anxiety…
You, palely, you, feebly, you, liquidly,
The smell of death among flowers, the whiff of fever on river banks,
You, the queen, you, the chatelaine, you, the pale lady, come…

13d   [c. 1916]
Every day I turn every corner of every street,
And whenever I'm thinking about one thing, I'm thinking about
    another,
I subordinate myself only out of atavism,
And there are always reasons to emigrate for anyone not confined to
    bed.

From the *terrasses* of all the cafés of all the cities
Accessible to the imagination
I observe life as it passes, I follow it without moving from the spot,
I belong to it without taking a single gesture out of my pocket,
Nor do I make a note of what I saw so as to pretend that I saw it later on.

Someone's definitive wife rides by in a yellow car,
I'm sitting beside her, although she doesn't know it.
On the *trottoir* outside they meet perhaps by prearranged chance,
But before they even met, I was already there alongside them.
There's no way they can avoid meeting me, there's no way I can fail to
        be everywhere.
My privilege is everything
(*Brevetée, Sans Garantie de Dieu*, that is my Soul).

I am present at everything, absolutely everything.
There's no women's jewelry that wasn't bought by me and for me,
There's no intention to sit waiting that isn't in some way mine,
There's no conclusion to a debate that isn't also mine,
There's no peal of bells in Lisbon thirty years ago, no night at the
        theater fifty years ago
That wasn't intended for me as a belated compliment.

I was brought up by the Imagination,
I've traveled hand in hand with her,
I've always loved, loathed, failed, and thought according to her,
And so each and every day has that window before it,
And thus each and every hour seems to be mine.

13e   [c. 1916]
A clear morning bugle call sounds somewhere
On the cold semicircle of the horizon,
A faint, far-off bugle call like not quite discernible flags
Unfurled at a point beyond which colors are no longer visible ...

A tremulous bugle call, dust in the air suspended, where the night
    ends,
Golden dust suspended at the very limits of visibility ...

A carriage creaking loudly past, a steamship sounding its siren,
The noise in my ear of a crane beginning to turn,
The dry cough of someone just leaving his house,
A faint morning shiver of joy to be alive,
A sudden guffaw muffled somehow by the mist outside,
A seamstress fated for something worse than she feels on this dread
    morning,
The consumptive workman ill-prepared for joy at this
Inevitably vital hour,
When the outline of all things is soft, clear, simpatico,
When the walls are cool to the touch, and where, here and there,
The houses are opening their white-curtained eyes ...

The whole dawn is a quivering curtain,
Reviving illusions and memories in my pedestrian soul,
In my heart stripped of all epidermal feelings,
In my weary and veiled [...]
[...]
[...] and everything is strolling
Towards the light-filled hour when the shops lower their lids
And noise traffic carriage train I-feel sun roars

The vertigo of midday framed in vertigos—
Sun in every vertex and in the [...] of my striated vision,
The stopped carousel of my dried-up memory,
The fixed, foggy gleam of my consciousness of being alive.

And noise traffic carriage train car I-feel sun street
Hoops crates *trolley* car shop street windows skirt eyes
Quick now gutters carriages crates street cross street

Walk storekeepers "'scuse me" street
Street walking along me walking along the street along me
The stores over here inside the stores over there are all mirrors
The speed of the cars back to front in the oblique mirrors of the
      windows,
The ground in the air the sun under our feet street water flowers in
      the basket street
My past life street trembles truck street I don't remember street
Me head down in the center of my consciousness of myself
Street unable to find a single sensation every time street
Street behind and street ahead beneath my feet
Street in X in Y in Z inside my embrace
Street seen through my monocle in small cinematographic circles,
Kaleidoscope in bright rainbow curves street.

The intoxication of the street and feeling seeing hearing everything
      at the same time.
My temples pound to be walking over here at the same time as I'm
      going over there,
[...]*

13f   [1915–1916]
I fall headlong into the whole of life
And howl inside in my ferocious desire to live ...
There are no valid gestures of pleasure in the world
The astonished joy of someone who has no other way to express it
Than to roll around on the ground among the grass and the daisies
And luxuriate in the earth until suit and hair are filthy ...
No poetry can do that ...
Pull up a blade of grass and bite into it and then you'll understand,
You'll understand completely what I so incompletely express.

* Poem left incomplete.

I feel a furious desire to be a root
And chase after my own innermost sensations like sap ...
I'd like to have all the senses, including intelligence,
Imagination, and inhibition
Just beneath my skin so that I could roll around on the rough earth
Inside, and feel the roughnesses and irregularities more keenly.
I would only be happy if my body was my soul ...
Thus all the winds, all the suns, and all the rains
Would be felt by me in the only way I want ...
Since this is impossible, I despair, I rage,
I feel like tearing off my suit with my teeth
And then to have a lion's heavy claws so that I could rip myself to
        pieces
Until the blood ran, ran, ran, ran ...
I suffer because all this is absurd
As if someone were afraid of me,
With my aggressive feelings towards fate and God,
Who is born of our own confrontation with the Ineffable
And having suddenly to take the measure of our own weakness and
        smallness.

13g   [c. 1918]

I walk on, not noticing anything; I'm a stranger.
The women who hurried to their doors
Saw only that I passed.
I am always just around the corner from those who want to see me,
Invulnerable to metals and incrustations.

Ah, evening, what memories!
Only yesterday, I was a child gazing into a well,
And with what joy I would see my face beyond the distant water.

Now, a grown man, I see my face in the deep water of the world,
But if I laugh, it's only because I once was
That child joyfully seeing his own face at the bottom of the well.

———————

I feel that everyone is the substance of my own skin.
I touch my arm and there they are.

The dead—they never leave me!
Not dead people, past places, or the days.
And sometimes, amid the noise of the factory machinery,
A nostalgia taps me lightly on the shoulder
And I turn ... and there in the garden of my former home
Is the child I was, in the sun, unaware of who I would become.

Ah, be maternal!
Ah, be silent and mellifluous
O night in which I forget myself
Remembering [...]

14 MARTIAL ODE
14a   [c. 1914]
Bugles in the night,
Bugles in the night,
Bugles suddenly sounding clearly in the night ...

(Is that distant noise from the cavalcade, the cavalcade, the cavalcade?)

What is it that sends such a different tremor through the grass and
        through souls?
What is it that is about to change and already is changing far off—
In the distance, in the future, in our anguish—who knows where—?

Bugles in the night,
Bugles ... in the night,
Bu-u-u-u-ugles ...

It's the cavalcade,
It's the cavalcade, the cavalcade,
It's the cavalcade, the cavalcade, the cavalcade
The sound, sound, sound, now so clear.

I see them in my heart and in the horror that grips me:
Valkyries, witches, amazons of amazement ...
They are a great shadow—a close cluster of shadows moving in the
        night.
A whole cavalcade of them, and the earth trembles twice,
And my heart, like the earth, also trembles twice.

They are coming from the far side of the world,
They are coming from the abyss of all things,
They are coming from the place whence come the laws governing
        everything;
They are coming from where injustice spills over onto all beings,
They are coming from where it's clear that all love and affection are
        pointless,
And only war and evil are the inside and outside of the world.

Hela-ho-hooo ... helaho-hooooo ....

14b   [Nov. 1915]
Hail war, the sound of light and fire
Hail, hail, hail, your arsenals and your squadrons,
Hail, hail, hail, your ships and your factories,
Hail your whole metallic civilization hard at work,
Hail all your steel!

Hail all your aluminum!
Hail all your machines, hail!
Hail, hail, hail, to you, the driving force!

Lighthouse of Diligence!
Floodgate [...]
Great bridge perfectly constructed over [...]

14c   [c. 1914]

Numberless waterless river—only people and things,
Terrifyingly waterless!

In my ear the sound of distant drums,
And I don't know if I can see the river or hear the drums,
As if I couldn't hear and see at the same time!

Helahoho! Helahoho!

The sewing machine of the poor widow who was bayonetted to
        death ...
She used to spend the evenings endlessly, aimlessly sewing ...
The table where the old men used to play cards,

All mixed up, all mixed up with bodies, with blood,
All just one river, just one wave, one long drawn-out horror.

Helahoho! Helahoho!

I retrieved the toy train lying flattened in the middle of the road,
And I wept like all the mothers of the world over the horror of life.
My pantheistic feet stumbled on the sewing machine of the widow
        bayonetted to death
And that poor instrument of peace put a lance through my heart.

Yes, I was guilty of everything, I was all the soldiers
Who killed, raped, burned, and destroyed,
It was me, and my shame and my remorse like a misshapen shadow
Wander the world like Ahasuerus,
Behind my footsteps, though, echo other footsteps the size of infinity
And a physical horror of being accountable to God makes me sud-
    denly close my eyes.

Absurd Christ of the expiation of all crimes and all acts of violence,
I carry my cross inside me, stiff and red-hot and at breaking point,
And in my soul as large as a Universe everything hurts.

I snatched the pathetic toy from the child's hands and beat him,
His frightened eyes, like those of the son I might have and whom
    they will also kill,
Were begging me somehow or other to have pity on everyone.

In the old woman's room I grabbed the photo of her son and tore it up,
She, full of fear, wept and did nothing …
I felt suddenly that she was my own mother and the breath of God
    ran like a shiver down my spine.

I smashed the poor widow's sewing machine.
She was sitting in a corner weeping, without a thought for her sew-
    ing machine.
Will there be another world where I will have a daughter who will
    be widowed and suffer the same fate?

Captain, I ordered the terrified peasants to be shot,
I allowed the daughters of all the fathers tied to trees to be raped,
I see now that all this happened inside my heart,
And everything scalds and smothers and I can do nothing to stop
    this happening again.
May God have pity on me who never pitied anyone!

14d

♂ □ ♄

The noise for some reason both far and near
Of the European war ... The noise of the universe-as-catastrophe ...
What is about to die beyond where we can hear and see?
On which frontiers did death agree to a rendezvous
For the fate of nations?

Imperial Eagle, will you fall?
Will you hurl yourself, amorphous, black and bloodied,
Onto the earth where, beneath your fall,
You have already left the trace of your talons before setting off
For your flight over this muddled Europe?

Will you fall, too, O early-rising French cockerel,
Always saluting the dawn? Which masters do you salute now,
Which blood-red sun in the pale blue of the morning horizon?
Which shadowy shortcuts, which path do you seek,
Which path and where to?
O civilizations reaching the nocturnal crossroads
Where the signpost has been removed,
And from which various snaking paths lead who knows where,
With no moon to shed light on their indecisions ...

May God be with us ...
At night, Our Lady of Mercy weeps,
Wringing her hands so hard they can be heard
In the deep silence.

May God be with us in heaven and on earth,
O Tutelary God of the Future, O Bridge
Over the abyss of we know not what ...
May God be with us, and let us never forget
That the sea is eternal and ultimately calm

And the earth is large and maternal and kind
Because we can always rest our weary head on her
And sleep leaning against something or other.

Bugles in the night, bugles in the night … O Mystery
Which, like the sun, is setting on Europe, on the Empire …
Motley troupe of enemy races clashing
More profoundly than their armies and their squadrons,
More physically than man against man and nation against nation …

Bugles of cold, tremulous horror in the depths of night …
And what else? Drums beating somewhere beyond the mystery of
      the world?
Drums that … you sleep lying down, tiny folds sleeping on what?
One gloomy step rings out in the night, that of a vast indivisible
      army …
Bugles suddenly sounding closer in the Night …
O Man with hands bound, being led who knows where
By the guards, why do you fall, and at whose feet?
At whose feet, and what are those bugles warning us about?

(Tityrus, your flute and the fields of Italy under Caesar Augustus
Ah, why do your eyes fill with absurd tears
And what grief is this, for the past and the present and the future.
Which aches in the soul like a feeling of exile?
Tityrus your flutes—distant Eclogues …
Virgil worshipping the Caesar who won.)

Per populum dat juri … A poor man at war,
O my unquiet heart … O silences that would have been known
By bridges leading to fortresses in ancient times,
You know and see how the earth trembles beneath the marching
      armies,
The divine, eternal ebb and flow of the waves beneath the battle
      cruisers and the torpedo boats …

Ah, the still worse horror of the bugles falling silent,
What indecisive sounds are borne to us on what was once the wind
In the deathly pallor of a man about to kill?
Who goes there? What will happen?
Who is starting to sob in the calm, untranquil night,
My brother? Whose sister? O childhood years
When I would watch the soldiers from the window and see only their
        uniforms,
And when the bloody, carnal reality of things did not yet exist for
        me!...

A clash of cavalries, where?
Artillery, where, where, where?
    O pain of indecision like inexplicable stirrings in stagnant water ...
O incomprehensible murmurings of death like the wind in the leaves ...
O the undoubted terror of a reality drawn by indecisive mirrors ...

(Your hands wet with tears
Your eyes calm ...
And you, love, are you also a reality ...
Ah, not to be everything, but a painting, any painting ...
And who knows, perhaps everything is a painting, and grief and joy
And uncertainty and terror
Are things, mere things, nothing but things with nowhere to go, but
        that we can see ...
Your hands wet with tears, on the terrace looking out over the blue
        mountain lake
And the dusk slowly falling on the high peaks of our two souls
And a desire to weep clutching both of us to its bosom ...)

War, war, yes, really war.
All-too-present horror, real war ...
With its reality of people really dying,
With its strategy really applied to real armies made up of real people
And its consequences, not things told in books,

But cold truths, real human destruction, the deaths of people who
    really died,
And the also-real sun shining on the also-real earth
Really real and in the midst of all this—the same shit!

Genuine danger, the genuine deaths of the sick and the victims,
And the sounds that blossom mysteriously forth from their
    groaning …
The canary's cage at your window, Maria,
And the gentle murmur of water burbling in the pool …

The body … And the other bodies, not so very different from that
    one,
Death … And the opposite of all this is life …
My soul aches and I don't understand …
I find it hard to believe in what exists …
Pale and troubled, I don't move, I suffer.

14e [c. 1914]

II
War!
The warrior civilizations parade past me …
The warrior civilizations of every time and every place …
A confused yet lucid panorama,
In squadrons mixed and unmixed, separate and compact, but always
    squadrons
Parading past, both one after the other and simultaneously too,
They pass …
They pass, and I, I'm lying on the grass
And only the cars pass and pass—then cease to pass for us
I see them and my amazement feels not a flicker of calm or interest,
I neither see nor stop seeing them,

And they pass me by like a shadow on some internal wall.
Ah, ancient pomp and modern pomp, the uniforms of the engines of war,
The eternal, irremediable fury of battles
The deaths, always the same mysterious deaths—the body on the
       ground (and what is the world, after all, and where?)
The wounded groaning in the same way in the same bodies
And above all this, the sky, the eternal, unfeeling sky!

14f [c. 1915]

Hela hoho, helahoho!

The warrior civilizations parade past me ...
On a triumphant morning,
In a long line as if they were painted on my very soul,
One after the other, indeterminately,
Breastplates, lances, helmets gleaming,
Shields turned to face me,
Visors down, chainmail coats,
The battles, the jousts, the fighting, the ambushes,
Archers of Crécy and Agincourt!
Arms of Arras.

And everything is an uncertain dust, a cloud of anonymous people
Lifted up in various ways by the winds of strategy,
And blown in waves over their attentive eyes
And over the Sun of eternal truth, a sinister covering.
A triumphal march, where time both exists and does not exist,
In which, simultaneously, seamlessly overlapping,
There arise, appear, and gather in my consciousness
The warriors of all times, the soldiers of all races,
The breastplates of all nations,
The weapons forged in all forges,
The hosts composed of the martial practices of all armies.

14g

Woe to you, to you and to us!
Behind these fierce, inflexible laws of life
Is there some divine love that makes up for all this?

You still keep his cradle in one corner at home ...
You still keep his baby clothes ...
You still keep a few broken toys in a drawer somewhere ...
Go and look at them now, yes, go and weep over them ...
You don't even know where your son's grave is ...
He was Number so-and-so in such-and-such a regiment,
He died somewhere beyond the Marne ... He died ...
The son you held so close, whom you breastfed and raised ...
Who once stirred in your womb,
The big, sturdy boy who used to make you laugh at the funny things
     he said ...
Now he's food for the worms ... All it took on the German lines
Was a piece of lead the size of a nail, and your life was plunged into
     sadness ...

You received a medal from the State. They'll say your son was a hero
(No one knows, though, whether he was or not)
It's yet one more enigma for history ...
"Twenty, or a hundred men died in such-and-such a battle ... " He
     was one of them ...
And your mother's heart bled profusely for that hero of which his-
     tory will say nothing ...
But for you, that was the most important event in the war ...

14h

For those, mother, for those who died, who fell in battle ...
Ding-dong-ding-dong ...
For those, my mother, who lost arms and legs in the fighting

Ding-dong-ding-dong ...
For those whose fiancée will wait for ever in vain ...
Ding-dong-ding-dong ...
Seven times seven times the flowers will wither in the garden
Ding-dong-ding-dong ...
And their corpses will be nameless, universal dust
Ding-dong-ding-dong ...
And, who knows, my mother, perhaps they still love us, still live in
      hope ...
No, that's madness, mother, utter madness, because bodies die and
      grief does not ...
Ding-dong-ding-dong-ding-dong ...
What has become of the child you held at your breast?
Dong ...
Who knows which of the anonymous dead is your son
Dong ...
You still keep his baby clothes in a chest of drawers ...
In a drawer in the pantry you still keep his old toys ...
Now he lies in a state of orphaned decay somewhere in France.
He who was so important to you, who was everything everything
      everything ...
But really he's nothing in the great holocaust of history
Dong-dong ...
Dong-dong-dong-dong ...
Dong-dong-dong-dong ...
Dong-dong-dong-dong-dong-dong ...

15   [c. 27 June 1916]
It was on one of my voyages ...
At sea and in the moonlight ...
On board, the noises of night had stopped.
One by one, group by group, the passengers withdrew,
The band was just a music stand left for some reason in one corner ...

And in the smoking room a chess game being played out in silence...
Life continued to emerge through the open door to the engine room...
That was all ... And I was a soul naked before the Universe...
(O my native village in far-off Portugal!
Why did I not die when I was still a child and knew only you?)

Ah, when we finally set out to sea,
When we leave land, when we gradually lose sight of it,
When everything slowly fills with purely sea air,
When the coast becomes a shadow line,
A line that grows even fainter at nightfall (hovering lights)—
Ah, what a joyous sense of freedom for those who can feel.
Any reason to exist as a social being ceases.
There are no longer reasons to love, to hate, to feel duty-bound,
There are no longer any laws, no human sorrows...
There's only the Abstract Departure, the movement of the water,
The moving off, the sound
Of waves lapping against prow,
And a great unquiet peace creeping nervously into the mind.

Ah to have my whole life
Unstably fixed in such a moment,
To have the whole sense of my life on land
Become a moving away from that coast where I left behind everything—
Loves, irritations, sadnesses, collaborations, duties,
The restless anxiety of remorseful feelings,
The weariness with the futility of everything,
The satiety even of imagined things,
The nausea, the lights,
The eyelids closing heavily on my wasted life...

I will go far away, far away! Far away, O motiveless ship,
To the prehistoric irresponsibility of the eternal waters,
Far away, for ever far away, O death.
When I know where far away is and why, O life...

16 [c. 1916]

After all, the best way to travel is to feel.
To feel everything in every way.
To feel everything excessively,
Because truth be told, every thing is excessive
And the whole of reality is an excess, a violence,
An extraordinarily vivid hallucination
That we all share along with the fury of our souls,
The center that draws in the strange centrifugal force
That is the human psyche when all its senses are in accord.

The more I feel, the more I feel like various people,
The more personalities I have,
The more intensely, stridently, I have them,
The more simultaneously I feel with them all,
The more unifiedly diverse, disparately attentive,
I am, feel, live, will be,
The more I will possess the total existence of the universe,
The more complete I will be in the whole of space,
The more analogous I will be to God, whatever he may be,
Because whatever he is, he is definitely Everything,
And beyond Him there is only Him, and for Him Everything is too
 little.

Every soul is a step up to God,
Every soul is a corridor-Universe to God,
Every soul is a darkly whispering river flowing
Past the External towards God and in God.

Sursum corda! Lift up your souls! All Matter is Spirit,
Because Matter and Spirit are merely vague names
Given to the great shadow that drenches the External in dreams
And plunges the Excessive Universe into Night and Mystery!
Sursum corda! I wake in the night to a vast silence,
Things, arms folded, nobly, sadly,

Notice that I have my eyes open,
Eyes that see them like vague nocturnal shapes in the black night.
Sursum corda! I wake in the night and feel I am various people.
Everything in the World in its usual visible form
Lies at the bottom of a well and makes a muffled noise,
I listen, and in my heart a great sense of astonishment sobs.

Sursum corda! O Earth, hanging garden, cradle
That rocks the scattered Soul of sequential humanity!
Green, flowering mother of every new year,
Of every vernal, aestival, autumnal, hibernal year,
Every year spent wildly celebrating the feasts of Adonis
In a ritual that predates all meanings,
In a great tumultuous festival in mountains and in valleys!
Great heart beating in the bare chest of volcanoes,
Great voice singing in waterfalls and seas,
Great drunken Bacchante of Movement and Change,
Lusting for vegetation and blossoms bursting forth from
Your own body of earth and rocks, your body submissive
To your own unsettling, eternal will!
Fond, unanimous mother of the winds, the seas, the fields,
Vertiginous mother of storms and cyclones,
Capricious mother who causes things both to flourish and to wither,
Who upsets the very seasons and jumbles up
In one ethereal kiss the suns and the rains and the winds!

Sursum corda! I see you and the whole of me is a hymn!
Everything in me, like a satellite of your inner dynamic,
Spins and snakes, forming a kind of haze, a ring
Of mist, of vague, recollected sensations,
Around your tumescent, fervid inner shape.

Use all your strength and all your red-hot power to occupy
My heart, which stands here open to you!

Like a sword piercing my erect, ecstatic being,
Penetrate my blood, my skin, my nerves,
With your continuous movement, in constant contact with your
	own self.

I am a tangled heap of forces filled with infinity
Stretching in all directions to every point in space,
Life, that vast thing, is what captures and binds everything
And ensures that all the forces raging inside me
Do not go beyond me, do not shatter my being, split open my body,
Do not hurl me like a spiritual bomb that explodes
Among the stars in a distillation of blood and flesh and soul,
Beyond the suns of other systems and distant planets.

Everything inside me tends to return to being everything.
Everything inside me tends to scatter me on the ground,
On the vast, supreme ground that is neither above nor below
But beneath the stars and the suns, beneath souls and bodies
Through a kind of oblique possession of our intellectual senses.

I am a flame ascending, but I ascend downwards and upwards,
I ascend simultaneously in every direction, I am a globe
Of explosive flames seeking God and burning
The crust of my own senses, the wall of my logic,
My frozen, confining intelligence.

I am a great machine propelled by huge chains
Of which I can see only the part that beats on my drums,
The rest zooms off beyond the stars, beyond the suns,
And never seems to reach the drum, its starting point ...

My body is the center of a stupendous, infinite wheel
Always dizzyingly turning upon itself,
Intersecting in every direction with other wheels,

Which penetrate and mingle, because this isn't space
But the spatial somewhere of another-sort-of-God.

All the movements that make up the universe
Are imprisoned inside me and tethered to the ground,
The meticulous and [...] fury of the atoms
The fury of all the flames, the rage of all the winds,
The furious foam of all the rushing rivers,
And the rain like stones hurled from the catapults
Of enormous armies of dwarves hidden in the sky.

I am a formidable dynamism obliged by equilibrium
To be inside my body and not overflow my soul.
Roar, burst, conquer, break, seethe, shake,
Tremble, shudder, foam, storm, rape, explode,
Lose yourself, transcend yourself, encircle yourself, live yourself,
        shatter and flee,
Be with my whole body the whole of the universe and life,
Ignite with my whole being every light and lamp,
Illumine with my whole soul every lightning bolt, every fire,
Live on in my life in all possible directions!

17   [c. 1917]
And if everyone treats death as if it were of little importance, and if,
        even while
Suffering, they lack the necessary concentration to suffer,
That is because life does not believe in death, because death is
        nothing.

Multicolored flags and bunting flapping in the wind
Beneath the earth's vast, blue, luminous sky ...
Dances and songs,
Merry music,
Sounds of laughter and chatter, and banal conversations,

Welcome approaching death, because death does not approach,
And life feels this in all its veins,
The body believes in every part of its soul
That life is everything, and death is nothing, and that the abyss
Is merely the inability to see,
That all this cannot possibly exist if it then ceases to exist,
Because to exist is to be, and to be cannot be reduced to nothing.
Ah, if this whole bright world, these flowers and this light,
If this whole world with earth and sea and houses and people,
If this whole natural, social, intellectual world,
These naked bodies underneath their natural clothes,
If all this is mere illusion, why is it all here?
O my master Caeiro, you alone were right!
If all this does not exist, why then does it exist?
If all this cannot be, why then can it be?

Welcome her, when she arrives,
Death, I mean, that optical illusion,
With the smells of the fields, and the cut flowers carried home in
        one's arms,
With the festivals and evenings spent out in the streets,
With festive crowds, and happy homes,
With joy and sorrow, with pleasure and pain,
With all the vast, vital sea of life.
Welcome her without fear,
Just as someone waiting at a provincial station, a country stop,
Welcomes the traveler about to arrive on the train from Beyond.
Welcome her gladly,
Children singing and laughing, youthful bodies on fire,
The rough, natural good cheer of taverns,
And the embraces and kisses and smiles of young girls.

Flags and bunting blood-red and green,
Flags and bunting the colors of light and fire,
For death is life in disguise,

And that's what the beyond will be, like our present day
But made new and different.
Shout it to the heavens,
Shout it to the valleys,
That death is of no importance at all,
That death is a mistake,
That death is a […]
And if life is just a dream, then death is a dream too.

18 [c. 1917]

There are no abysses!
No sinister side!
There is no mystery, no truth!
There is no God, or life or a soul remote from life!
You, my master Caeiro, you were right!
But you didn't see everything; there is still more!
You gaily sang the joy of everything,
But without thinking, you sensed
That this is because the joy of everything is essentially immortal.
How gaily would you sing your future death
If you could think of it as death,
If you could truly feel the night and the end?
No, no: you knew this
Not with your thoughts, but with your whole body,
With all your senses so alert to the world,
That nothing dies, that nothing ceases to be,
That no moment ever passes,
That the plucked flower remains for ever on its stem,
That a kiss given is given eternally,
That in the essence and universe of things
Everything is joy and sun
And that only in error and in our gaze is there sorrow and doubt
      and darkness.
Put out the flags in songs and roses!

And at the provincial station, the country stop,
—There comes the train now!
With handkerchiefs waving, with eyes eternally bright
Let us greet approaching death with gold and flowers!

No, you can't fool us!
Fond grandmother of the already pregnant earth!
Disguised godmother of spoken feelings!

And the train comes round the bend, slows down, and is about to
          stop ...
And with a great explosion of all my hopes
My heart-universe
Enfolds all the suns in gold,
Embroiders all the stars in silver,
Grows tumescent with flowers and greenery,
And death when she arrives concludes that they've already met
And on her grave face appears
The human smile of God!

19 [c. 1917]

From the house in the hills, eternal, perfect symbol,
I see the fields, all the fields,
And I salute them at last in my true voice,
I greet them with cheers, weeping, with precisely the right tears and
cheers—
I clutch them to my breast, like a son finding his lost father.

Here's to you,
Hills, plains, grass!
Here's to you, rivers, springs!
Here's to you, flowers, trees, and stones!
Here's to you, living beings and tiny creatures,
Creatures that run, insects, and birds,

All the animals, so real without me,
Men, women, children,
Families and non-families equally!
Everything that feels without knowing why!
Everything that lives without knowing that it lives!
Everything that ends and ceases without a trace of anguish,
Knowing, better than I, that there's nothing to fear,
That there is no ending, no abyss, no mystery,
And that everything is God, everything is Being, everything is Life.

Yes, I am free!
Yes, I have cast off
The chains of thought.
I, the self-imposed cloister and cave of myself,
I, the abyss I myself dreamed,
I, who saw roads and shadowy paths in everything,
And yet the shadows and the roads and the paths were all in me!
Yes, I am free ...
Master Caeiro, I returned to your house in the hills
And I saw what you saw, but with my eyes,
Really and truly with my eyes,
Really and truly and for real ...
And I saw that there is no death!
I saw that [...]

20 [c. 1917]

My lost love, I weep for you no more, because I never lost you!
I might lose you in the street, but I cannot lose your actual being,
Because being is the same in you and in me.

There is much absence but nothing is lost!
All the dead—people, days, desires,
Loves, hates, sorrows, joys—

Are all merely on another continent …
The time will come for me to leave and go to meet them.
To be reunited with family and lovers and friends
Abstractly, really, perfectly,
Definitively and divinely.

I will be reunited in life and death
With the dreams never realized
I will give the kisses never given,
I will receive the smiles once refused to me,
I will receive the griefs I suffered in the form of joy …

Ah, captain, how long before
Our ocean liner leaves?
Have the ship's orchestra strike up—
A happy tune, banal and human like life itself—
Have the ship leave, because I want to leave now …

The clank of the anchor, ah, when
Will I finally hear my own death rattle?
The ship's sides shaken by the pulsating engines—
My heart giving its final, convulsive beat—
The lookouts sound their whistles, the port sighs
[…]
Handkerchiefs waving to me from the quay …
See you later, until the next time, farewell!
See you in the eternity of the joyful Now …
See you in […]

21   [c. 1921]
What emperor has the right
To smash the doll belonging to the worker's daughter?
What Caesar with his legions is justified

In breaking the old lady's sewing machine?
If I went out into the street
And snatched the grubby ribbon from the little girl's hand
And made her cry, where would we ever find a Christ figure?

If I were to knock the cheap slice of cake
From the mouth of some poor child
Where would I find justice in the world,
Where would I hide myself from the eyes of the Invisible
Figure watching from among the stars
When the heart sees with its own eyes the mystery eyeing the
    universe?
My genuine emotion, a child's toy,
The small legitimate joys of obscure, ordinary people,
The poor, meager wealth of the nobodies of this world …

The furniture bought with so many sacrifices,
The carefully darned tablecloths,
The small household items all in their proper places
But if the wheel of one of the conquering king's thousand cars
Breaks everything, then everyone loses everything.

22   [before February 1923]

Lisbon Revisited (1923)
No: I don't want anything.
I already said I don't want anything.

Don't come to me with conclusions!
The only conclusion is death.

Don't come to me with aesthetics!
Don't talk to me about morality!
And I want no truck with metaphysics!

Don't preach to me about complete systems, don't boast about the
        conquests
Of science (of science, my God, of science!)—
Of science, the arts, modern civilization!

What harm did I ever do to the gods?

If they do have the truth, they can keep it!

I'm a technician, but my technique is confined to things technical.
Apart from that, I'm crazy, and have every right to be.
Every right, you hear.

Don't pester me, for God's sake!

You wanted me married, futile, ordinary and taxable?
You wanted me to be the opposite of that, the opposite of
        something?
Were I a different person, I would do as you ask.
Being who I am, though, you have no chance!
You can go to the devil without me,
Or let me go to the devil alone!
Why should we go together?

Don't take my arm!
I don't like people taking my arm. I want to be alone,
Like I said, I only exist alone!
It's such a bore being expected to be companionable!

O blue sky—the same blue sky of my childhood—
Eternally empty and perfect truth!
O gentle Tejo ancestral and silent,
A small truth in which the sky is reflected!
O grief revisited, Lisbon of a time other than today!

You give me nothing, take nothing from me, are nothing that I can
   feel.

Leave me in peace! I won't be late, I never am …
And while I'm waiting for the Abyss and for Silence, I want to be alone!

23   [10 April 1923]
Nothing holds me, nothing binds me, I belong to nothing.
Every sensation grips me, but none linger.
I'm more varied than a random multitude,
I'm more diverse than the spontaneous universe,
All ages belong to me, for a moment,
All souls, for a moment, have their place in me.
A flow of intuitions, a river of suppositions—but,
Always in successive waves,
Always the sea—now, not recognizing itself,
Always, indefinitely, diverging from the river.

O quay from which I set off, once and for all, to the Truth,
O ship, complete with captain and sailors, in symbolic form,
O placid waters, like those of a river that exists in the twilight
In which I dream myself possible—
In which place, if any, are you, at which hour?
I want to leave and find myself,
I want to go back to find out where I came from,
Like someone returning to their home, like someone welcomed back,
Like someone still loved in his old village,
Like someone brushing past his dead childhood in every stone in the
   wall,
And seeing before him the wide eternal fields of long ago,
And a nostalgia, like a lullaby sung by his mother, drifts
Over the tragedy of the past having passed,

O sunny lands, native, local, neighborly!
O line of the horizons, frozen in my eyes,
What close tumultuous wind remains for ever distant,
And how you shimmer before me here!

To hell with life!
Having a profession weighs on the shoulders like a bought bundle,
Having obligations stagnates,
Having a morality dulls,
Rebelling against obligations and rebelling against morality
Lives in the street of illogic.

24 [28 October 1924]

When will we go away, ah, when will we go away from here?
When, away from these friends I don't even know,
From these ways of understanding I don't understand,
From these wills so unwillingly
Contrary to mine, so contrary to me?!

Ah, ship setting off, with every intention of setting off,
Ship with sails, ship with engine, ship with oars,
Ship with something-or-other with which to carry us off,
Ship somehow-or-other leaving behind it this coast,
This, this always-this-coast, this always-these-people,
Only validates emotion through a future nostalgia,
Nostalgia, a forgetting remembered,
Nostalgia, an illusion that unremembers reality,
Nostalgia, a remote sense of the uncertain
Vague mysterious ancestor we once were,
A renewal of prenatal life, a slow milky way
Absurdly emerging, static and constellated,
Out of the dynamic vacuum of the world.

I am one of those who suffer without suffering,
Who carries reality in his soul,
Who is not a myth, but reality,
Who feels no joy in body or soul, the kind
Who spends his life begging for alms and hoping to lose them ...
I want to leave, like someone actually leaving.
Why must I be where I am if it is only where I am?
Why must I always be I if I cannot be who I am?
But all this is like the distant contentment
Of those who did not leave or those
Whose home is no-home and is many.
When, shipwrecked ship, will we leave the home we do not have?

Come, ship, come!
O lugger, corvette, barge, cargo ship, steamboat,
Collier, schooner, tramp steamer,
Passenger ship for all the many nations,
Ship that is all ships,
Ship-possibility to travel in every ship
Indefinitely, incoherently
In search of nothing, in search of not searching,
In search simply of leaving,
In search simply of not being
Of the first possible death-in-life—
Departure, distance, separating ourselves from ourselves.

For we always separate ourselves from ourselves when we leave
        someone else,
It's always we whom we leave behind when we leave coast,
House, field, bank, station, or quay.
Everything we've ever seen is us, we alone experience the world.
We have only ourselves inside and outside,
We have nothing, we have nothing, we have nothing ...

Only the fleeting shadow on the floor of the cave, the dumping
        ground for souls,
Only the brief breeze caused by the passing of a consciousness,
Only the drop of water on the dry leaf, futile dew,
Only the multicolored wheel spinning white before the eyes
Of the inner phantom that we are,
A tear from beneath the closed lids
Of the divine, veiled eyes.

Ship, whoever I am, I don't want to be me! Take away
The oar or sail or engine, take them away!
Go. Let me see the abyss open up between me and the coast,
The river between me and the bank,
The sea between me and the quay,
The death, the death, the death, between me and life!

25   [c. 1924]

I leaned back in the chair on deck and closed my eyes,
And my destiny appeared in my soul like a precipice.
My past life mingled with my future life,
And somewhere in the middle a noise like that in a smoking room,
Where, to my ears, they had just finished playing a game of chess.

Ah, rocked
By the sensation of the waves,
Ah, lulled
By the very cozy idea of today not yet being tomorrow,
Of at least not for the moment having any responsibilities
        whatsoever,
Of having no personality of my own, but still feeling that I'm there,
Sitting on the chair with a book left behind by the Swedish woman.
Ah, plunged

Into an imaginative torpor, doubtless a light sleep,
So peacefully restless,
So analogous suddenly with the child I once was
When I played in the garden and knew no algebra,
Nor the other algebras with the x's and y's of feeling.

Ah, all I want
In this moment devoid of importance
In my life,
All I want in this moment, as in other analogous moments—
Those moments when I was of no importance at all,
When I understood the vacuousness of existence but lacked the
        intelligence to understand it
And when there was moonlight and sea and solitude, O Álvaro.

26   [26 April 1926*]

If you want to kill yourself, why then don't you want to kill yourself?
Seize the moment! I, who so love death and life,
If I dared to kill myself, I would ...
Ah, if you dare, then be daring!
What is the point of the endless round of external images
That we call the world?
The cinematography of the hours represented
By actors with certain conventions and poses,
The polychrome circus of our endless dynamism?
What is the point of that inner world of yours of which you know
        nothing?
Perhaps by killing yourself, you would finally get to know it ...
Perhaps by ending you could begin ...
Besides, if existing wearies you,

* If this date is real, it coincides with the tenth anniversary of the death of
Pessoa's closest friend and literary confidante, the Lisbon-born poet Mario de
Sá-Carneiro (1890–1916).

Then be nobly weary,
And don't, like me, sing of life just because you're drunk,
Don't, like me, salute death in literature!

Are you necessary? O futile shadow called person!
No one is necessary; you're not necessary to anyone ...
Without you everything will simply carry on without you.
Perhaps it's worse for others if you exist rather than if you kill your-
      self ...
Perhaps you're more of a burden remaining than ceasing to remain ...

The grief of others? ... Are you filled with premature remorse
Because others will mourn you?
Don't worry: they won't mourn you for long ...
The vital impulse gradually dries any tears
When shed for something not ours,
When shed for something that happens to the others, especially
      death,
Because after death nothing happens to the others ...

First, there's the anguish, the surprise at the arrival
Of the mystery and the absence of your failed life ...
Then the horror of the visible, material coffin,
And the men in black whose profession is to be there.
Then the family keeping vigil, inconsolable and telling anecdotes,
Grieving and commenting on the latest news in the evening papers,
Interweaving the sorrow at your death with the latest murder ...
And you are only occasionally the cause of that weeping,
You are truly dead, far deader than you think ...
Far deader here than you think,
Even if you're far more alive in the beyond ...

Then the black procession to the tomb or the grave,
After which begins the death of your memory.
Initially everyone feels a slight relief

From the rather tedious tragedy of your death ...
Then, day by day, the conversation grows lighter,
And everyday life resumes ...

Then, slowly, you're forgotten.
You're only remembered anniversarily on two dates:
When you were born and when you died.
Nothing more, nothing more, absolutely nothing more.
Twice a year they think about you.
Twice a year those who loved you sigh for you,
And they occasionally sigh, too, if they happen to speak of you.

Take a long cool look at yourself, take a cool look at what we are ...
If you want to kill yourself, then go ahead and kill yourself ...
Forget any moral scruples, any intellectual doubts! ...
Does the mechanism of life have scruples or doubts?
Does the impulse that generates sap, the circulation of the blood,
            and love
Have any chemical scruples?
Does the joyful rhythm of life retain any memory of other people?

Ah, poor flesh-and-bone vanity called man,
Don't you see that you're of absolutely zero importance?

You're important to you, because you are you.
You are everything to yourself, because for you, you are the universe,
And the actual universe and everyone else are
Merely satellites of your objective subjectivity.
You're important to you because you alone are important to you.
And if you're like that, O myth, won't the others be the same?

Do you, like Hamlet, have a fear of the unknown?
But what is known? What do you know
That you can describe one particular thing as unknown?

Do you, like Falstaff, love lubricious life?
If you love it materially, then love it still more materially:
Become a carnal part of the earth and things!
Scatter yourself, you physico-chemical system
Of cells nocturnally conscious,
Over the nocturnal consciousness of the unconsciousness of bodies,
Over the great blanket of appearances that covers nothing,
Over the grass and weeds of proliferating beings,
Over the atomic fog of things,
Over the whirling walls
Of the dynamic vacuum of the world ...

27   [26 April 1926]
Lisbon Revisited (1926)
Nothing binds me to anything.
I want fifty things at the same time.
With the anguish of someone hungry for flesh I yearn,
But for quite what I don't know—
Although definitely for something indefinite ...

I sleep restlessly, and I live in the restless dream state
Of someone who sleeps restlessly, half asleep.

All the necessary abstract doors have been closed to me.
As have all the curtains inside all the hypotheses I could see from
        the street.
And in the alleyway I can't find the number of the house I was given.

I woke to the same life I fell asleep in.
Even my dreamed armies were defeated.
Even my dreams felt false when I dreamed them.
Even the life I wanted bores me—yes, even that life ...

I understand at disconnected intervals;
I write in brief flashes of tiredness;
And a boredom with boredom itself casts me up on the beach.

I don't know what destiny or future would suit my rudderless anguish;
I don't know what islands in the impossible South await my ship-
        wrecked self;
Or which literary palm groves will grant me at least one line of
        poetry.

No, I don't know this, or that, or anything else ...
And in the depths of my mind, where I dream what I dreamed,
In the far-flung fields of the soul, where I pointlessly remember
(and the past is a natural fog of false tears),
Along the roads and paths in distant forests
Where I imagined my being,
Along them flee the last scattered remnants
Of the final illusion,
My dreamed armies, defeated before they ever were,
My cohorts-to-be, dispersed and destroyed in God.

Again I see you,
City of my childhood so painfully lost ...
Sad, joyful city, again I dream you here ...
Me? But am I the same Me who lived here, and returned here,
And who returned here again, and again,
And who returned here again?
Or are we, all the Mes that I or they were here,
Just a series of stories-cum-beings linked by a thread of memory,
A series of dreams of me dreamed by someone outside of me?

Again I see you,
With my more distant heart, with my less-than-mine soul.

Again I see you—Lisbon and the Tejo and everything—
A random passerby in you and in me,
A foreigner here as everywhere,
As incidental in my life as in my soul,
A phantom wandering rooms of recollections,
To the sounds of the mice gnawing and the floorboards creaking
In the accursed castle of having to live ...

Again I see you,
A shadow that passes through other shadows, and shines
For a moment in a gloomy, unfamiliar light,
Then enters the night like the wake of a ship disappearing
Off over waters that can no longer be heard ...

Again I see you,
But, alas, not myself!
The magic mirror reflecting my old identical self has shattered,
And in each fateful fragment I see only a mite of me—
A mite of you and of me!...

28   [30 April 1926]
Distant lighthouses,
Their lights suddenly so bright,
With night and absence so swiftly restored,
At night, on deck, how troubling this seems!
The final pain of farewells,
The fiction of thinking ...

Distant lighthouses ...
The uncertainty of life ...
The bright light returning even brighter
In my lost, drifting gaze ...

Distant lighthouses ...
The pointlessness of life ...
The pointlessness of thinking about life ...
The pointlessness of thinking about thinking about life ...

We are going far away, and the light that seems so big grows smaller,
Distant lighthouses ...

29   [30 April 1926]

The flowering of a chance encounter
With those who will always be strangers ...

The only disinterested gaze received at random
From some fast foreign woman ...

The interested look of a child holding hands
With his distracted mother ...

The incidental words exchanged
With the incidental traveler
On this incidental voyage ....

The great pain of all things fragmented ...
An endless journey ...

30   [c. 1926]

News Section
Of the Lloyd Georges of Babylon
History has nothing to say.
Of the Briands of Assyria or Egypt,
Of the Trotskys of some long gone

Greek or Roman colony,
Their names, even if written down, are dead.

Only the occasional foolish poet,
Or some mad philosopher,
Or an ancient geometer,
Survive all the nonentities
Who lie lurking in the darkness
And whom not even history bothers to record.

O great men of the Moment!
O the great, fiery glories
Of those in flight from obscurity!
Make the most of it and don't think!
Enjoy the fame and the feasting,
For tomorrow belongs to today's madmen!

31 [c. 1926]

The strange, silent thing inhabiting the whole body
Lying there, like ivory, in the coffin,
The human body no longer a human body,
Silencing the entire room;
The deserted quay awaiting the departed,
Cold disbelief pushing open
The supreme, invisible door;
The incomprehensible nexus
Between energy and life,
A window onto the unknowable night ...
He—that other man's corpse—
Evokes the future me,
Yes, me, my own self, yes, even me ...
And my hopes don mourning clothes,

My faith shudders like a drunken landscape,
My plans meet an infinitely infinite wall.

32   [12 January 1927]
Mortal Ode
You, Caeiro, my master, whatever clothes
You are wearing now, near or far, the essence
Of your universal local soul,
Of your divine intellectual body ...

With your perfect blindness you saw beyond not seeing ...
Because what you saw with your physical, admirable fingers
Was the sensitive face of things, not the physiognomical face,
It was reality, not the real,
And reality becomes visible in the light
And is only visible because there is light,
Because the truth, which is everything, is only the truth that lies in
        everything,
And the truth that is there in everything is the truth that reveals
        everything!

No fear
No anguish
No anticipated weariness before the departure
No corpse watched over by the mind's own corpse
On nights when the wind whistles in the deserted world
And the house where I sleep is a tomb of everything,
No feeling of self-importance because I am a corpse,
No consciousness of having no consciousness inside the planks and
        the lead,
No anything ...
I look up at the daytime sky, and I look up at the nighttime sky,
And I see this spherical, concave universe

Like a sphere inside which we live,
Limited because it is the inside
But with stars and the sun tearing away at the visible
World outside, to reveal the convex, infinite sky.

And there, in the Real Reality,
I will take the stars and life out of my pocket as a present for the Truth,
I will read Life again, like a letter I had stashed away
And then, in a better light, I will see the writing and I will know.

The quay is full of people waiting to see me off.
But the quay is all around me, and I fill the entire ship—
And the ship is bed, coffin, grave—
And I don't know what I am because I'm no longer there ...

And I who sang the praises
Of modern civilization, which was, besides, identical to the old one,
As well as all the things of my day simply because that day was mine,
The machines, the engines,
[...]
I travel diagonally over everything.
I pass through the interstices of everything,
And, like dust, my shell remains intact
And I will set off, *globe-trotter* of the Divine,
Who knows how many times? Returning to the same point
(What does any night walker know of walking or the night?)
I will carry in my satchel everything I have seen—
The sky and the stars, and the sun in all its aspects,
And all the seasons and their ways with color,
And the fields, and the mountains, and the land that ends in beaches
And the sea beyond, and beyond the sea that lies beyond.

And suddenly the Final Door of all things will open,
And God, like a Man, will finally appear to me

And he will be the Unexpected that I expected—
The Unknown I have always known—
The one and only that I always knew.
And […]

Shout with joy, shout with me, shout,
You, things overflowing, more than overflowing,
That make up my whirlwind life …
I will leave the hollow sphere
Not through a star, but through the light of a star—
I will enter real space …
Because the space inside here is an enclosed space
And only seems infinite because the enclosure is far away—
Very far when I think about it.

My hand is already on the light switch.
I'm going to open with a sweeping gesture,
With an authentic, magical gesture,
The Door into the Convex,
The Window into the Formless,
The Reason into the definitively marvelous.

I will be able to circumnavigate from outside the inside
That exists in stars, I will have a sky
Beneath the curved attic—
The roof of the cellar of real things,
Of the nocturnal vault of death and life …

I am going to leave for OUT THERE,
For the Infinite Outskirts,
For the exterior metaphysical circumference,
For the light outside the night,
For the Life-death outside death-Life.

33

In future markets—perhaps the same as ours—
Will elixirs be touted abroad?
With different labels, just as in the Egypt of the Pharaohs;
With different ways of persuading people to buy them, different
        from our ways.

And the metaphysics lost in the corners of cafés everywhere,
The solitary philosophies from the attic rooms of losers,
The chance ideas of so many chancers, the intuitions of so many
        nobodies—
One day perhaps, abstractly fluid, implausibly substantial,
They will form a God and occupy the world.
For me, today, for me
There is no peace in thinking about the properties of things,
About destinies I cannot reveal,
About my own metaphysics, which I have because I think and feel.
There is no peace,
And yet the great sunlit hills abound in it!

Do they? The sunlit hills have no mind to think with.
They wouldn't be hills, they wouldn't be sunlit if they did.

The weariness of thinking, going down into the depths of existence,
Makes me feel old, even my body feels cold, and has done since the
        day before yesterday.

What has become of lost intentions, and impossible dreams?
And why are there dead intentions and irrational dreams?
On days of slow, continuous, monotonous, singular rain,
I find it hard to get up from the chair I hadn't even realized I'd sat
        down on,
And the universe around me is utterly hollow.

The tedium that ends up becoming our very bones has drenched
    my being,
And the memory of something I can't remember chills my soul.

South Sea islands are probably capable of dreaming,
And the sands of deserts doubtless enjoy some compensatory
    imagination;
But in my heart without seas or deserts or islands I feel
That my soul is empty,
And I tell my own story longwindedly, meaninglessly, like a fool
    with a fever.

Cold fury of destiny,
Intersection of everything,
Confusion of things with their causes and their effects,
Consequence of having body and soul,
And the sound of the rain reaches my very being, and it grows dark.

34   [1 October 1927]

Ah, Margarida,
If I were to give you my life,
What would you do with it?
—I'd get my earrings out of hock
Find a blind man to marry me
Then go and live high on the hog.

But Margarida,
If I were to give you my life,
What would your mother say?
—(She knows me inside out.)
That of fools there is no shortage,
And a fool, my friend, art thou.

And Margarida,
If I were to give you my life
In the sense that I died?
—Well, I'd certainly go to your wake,
But thinking it was a big mistake
To want to love but not live.

But Margarida,
What if giving you my life
Was just a bit of poetry?
—Then, my boy, forget it.
That wouldn't work at all.
No credit given here.

Written by the Naval Engineer
Senhor Álvaro de Campos
in a state of alcoholic
unconsciousness

35   [c. 1 October 1927]

Episodes

... The tedium of radioidiots and aerobores,
Of all the quantitative achievements of this life without qualities,
The nausea of being contemporary with myself—
And the longing for the new new, the true true,
For the source, the beginning, the origin.

The stone in the wrong ring on your finger
How it glows in my memory,
O poor sphinx of the bourgeois aristocracy I chatted to on the
        voyage!
What vague love affairs were you hiding in your real-but-Oh-so-false

Elegance, poor lucidly deluded lady,
Met on board this ship, as happens on all ships!

You were taking cocaine as your betters had taught you,
You would laugh at the old bores only slightly less boring than you,
Poor orphan child of more than just father and mother,
Poor deranged wretch, poor almost-*flapper*!
And I, being the modern man I am, I who allow
Gypsies to pitch camp in the suburbs of my sensibility,
I the paper money of all modernity;
I, incongruent and hopeless,
I, in transit on this ship like you, but more transitory than you,
Because where you are certain, I am uncertain,
Where you know who you are I don't know who I am and know that
        you don't know who you are,
And in between the dances played *ad nauseam* by the ship's band
I lean out over the night sea and feel a nostalgia for myself.

What have I made of my life?
What have I made of what I wanted to make of life?
What have I made of what I could have made of life?
Am I like you, O traveler with the Anaphrodisiac Ring?
I look at you and can barely distinguish you from the amorphous
        matter of things,
And I laugh in the depths of my empty, oceanic thoughts.

In the garden of my small, provincial house—
A house like the one owned by millions unlike me in the world—
At this hour, there ought to be peace, without me.
But there will never be peace in me,
Nor anything with which to make peace,
Nor anything with which to imagine peace …
So why, then, do I laugh at you, the superior traveler?

O poor eau-de-Cologne of the finest quality,
O modern perfume in the best possible taste and in a fancy bottle,
My poor unloved love, like some pretty caricature!
What an excellent text for a sermon you wouldn't make!
What poems a real poet would write without a thought for you!

But the ship's band roars and then stops ...
And the rhythm of the Homeric sea climbs into my brain—
The old Homeric sea, O savage from the Greek world,
With a feather headdress on his soul,
With rings in the nose of his sensuality,
With the consciousness of a half mannequin who thinks the world
        is looking at him.

But the fact is that the ship's band has stopped playing,
And I can honestly say
That I thought of you while the ship's band played.
Deep down we are all
Romantics,
Shamefully romantic,
And the sea continues, rough and calm,
The eternal slave of the stern attentions of the moon,

As, too, is the smile with which I interrogate myself
And gaze up at the sky without metaphysics and without you ...
A cuckold's grief ...

36   [c. 9 October 1927]
The special chill of mornings before a voyage,
The anguish of leaving, almost carnal in the shiver
That runs from heart to skin,
That almost weeps although happy.

37

I lost hope the way you might lose an empty wallet ...
Fate made mock of me; I crossed my fingers while its back was turned,
And my rebellion might just as well have been a piece of beadwork
     made by my grandmother
And a relic in the living room of the old house I don't own.

(We used to dine early, in another time that already seems part of
     another incarnation,
And then we would take tea in those quiet nights that will never
     return.
My childhood, my past life bypassing adolescence, have passed,
I felt sad, as if someone had told me the truth,
But the only truth anyone ever told me was to feel the past.)

38

I know: someone told the truth—
Even the washing line seems upset
Objectivity entered the house
And we were all left outside, like a sheet on the washing line
Left out in the rain on a night of closed windows.

39

Ah, the sound of the maid doing the ironing
At the window through which my childhood peeps in!
The sound of clothes being washed in the basin!
All those things are, in a way,
Part of what I am.
(O dead nursemaid, what became of your gray-haired love?)
My childhood at just above table height ...
My chubby hand resting on the tablecloth being rolled up.
And me, on tiptoe, peering over my plate.

(Now if I stand on tiptoe, it's only intellectually.)
And here, my table has no tablecloth and no one to lay the table ...
I studied the ferment of failure
In the demonology of the imagination ...

40   [c. 1927]
Almost unwittingly (if we only knew!) the great men emerge from
    the vulgar.
The sergeant becomes emperor through imperceptible changes
In which achievement
Is mingled with the dream of what is to be achieved
And the path rises up quickly by invisible steps,
Alas for those who, right from the start, see the end!
Alas for those who aspire to leaping over the stairs!
The conquistador of all the empires is still a mere assistant
    bookkeeper.
The mistress of all the kings—even the dead ones—is a sensible,
    affectionate mother.
If only I could see the souls inside as clearly as I see the bodies from
    outside.

Ah, how penitentiary are our desires!
What a lunatic asylum the meaning of life!

41   [c. 1927]
To have no duties, no fixed hours, no realities ...
To be a different bird
Flying kingfisher-like above the intransigence of the world—
Earning his nightly bread from the sweat of other people's brows—
A sad factotum
At a tearful circus,
An old compère, rather plumper than the Venus de Milo,

In the transience of chance events.
And a little sun at least, for the dreams in which I do not live.

42   [c. 1927]
Life is for the unthinking (O Lydia, Célimène, Daisy)
And thinking is for the others—thinking minus life.
I smoke a cigarette which smells strongly of other people's pain,
And I seem ridiculous to them because I'm observing them and
        they're observing me.
Not that I care.
I divide myself into Caeiro and engineer—
An engineer of machines, an engineer of people, an engineer of
        fashion.
And I am not responsible for what I see around me, not even in
        verse,
The tattered flag, darned with silk, from the empires of Maple & Co.
Stick it in the drawer for posthumous things and be done with it …

43   [15 January 1928]
Tobacconist's Shop
I'm nothing.
I'll always be nothing.
I can't even hope to be nothing.
That said, I have inside me all the dreams of the world.

O windows in my room,
A room inhabited by one of the many millions in the world unknown
        to anyone
(And if I was known to someone, what would that someone know?),
You look out onto the mystery of a street constantly crisscrossed by
        people,

Onto a street inaccessible to all thoughts,
Real, impossibly real, true, unknowably true,
Along with the mystery of the things underneath the cobblestones
        and the passing humans,
With death leaving damp stains on the walls and white hairs on
        men's heads,
With Fate driving the cart of everything along the street of nothing.

Today I am defeated, as if I knew the truth.
Today I am lucid, as if I were about to die,
And as if my only fellow feeling with things
Were a long farewell, with this house and this side of the street
Turning into a line of train carriages, and a parting whistle
Inside my head,
And a jolt to my nerves and a creaking of bones as we set off.

Today I feel perplexed, like someone who had thought and found
        and forgotten.
Today I feel divided between the loyalty I owe
To the Tobacconist's on the other side of the street, which is a real
        thing out there,
And the feeling that everything is a dream, which is a real thing
        inside me.

I've failed in everything.
Since I never had any ambition, perhaps it was all simply nothing.
They gave me an education,
But I climbed out of the back window of the house.
I went into the countryside full of grand ambitions,
But there I found only grass and trees,
And when I did meet people they were just the same as all the others.
I climb back in through the window and sit down on a chair. What
        shall I think about?

How should I know what I will be, since I don't even know who I am?
Should I be what I think? But I think of being so many things!
And there are so many thinking they'll be the same thing that we
    can't all be that thing!
A genius? At this very moment
A hundred thousand brains are dreaming that they, too, are geniuses
    like me,
And history will not record, who knows, even one,
There won't even be any dung left behind from all those future
    conquests.
No, I don't believe in me.
The lunatic asylums are full of madmen brimming with certainties!
And since I have no certainty, am I more right than them or less?
No, I don't even believe in me ...
At this very moment, how many self-proclaimed geniuses
Will be dreaming in the world's many garrets and non-garrets?
How many lofty, noble, lucid aspirations—
Yes, genuinely lofty, noble and lucid—
And possibly even achievable,
Will never see the light of day or reach the ears of others?
The world is for those born to conquer it
And not for those who dream they might conquer it, even if they're
    right.
I've dreamed far more than Napoleon ever did.
I've clutched to my hypothetical bosom more humanities than
    Christ ever did.
I've secretly written philosophies that no Kant ever wrote.
But I am, and perhaps always will be, a tenant in one of those garrets,
Even if I don't live in one;
I will always be one of those not born to do this;
I will always be one of those who only ever showed potential;
I will always be one of those who waited for someone to open the
    door in a wall that had no door,
And sang the song of the Infinite in a chicken run,
And heard the voice of God in a sealed well.

Believe in me? No, nor in anything else.
Let Nature pour down onto my burning head
Its sun, its rain, the wind tousling my hair,
And let everything else happen if it happens or has to happen or
        doesn't.
We cardiac slaves of the stars,
We have conquered the whole world before even getting out of bed;
But we wake and the world is a blur,
We get up and the world belongs to others,
We leave the house and the world is the entire earth,
Plus the Solar System and the Milky Way and the Indefinite.

(Eat your chocolates, little girl;
Eat your chocolates!
Because chocolates are the only metaphysics in the world.
Because confectionery teaches us far more than all the religions put
        together.
So eat, you grubby little thing, eat!
I wish I could eat chocolates as genuinely as you do!
But I think and, when I throw down the silver paper, which is actu-
        ally tinfoil,
I throw down everything, just as I have thrown down my life.)

At least, though, the lingering bitterness of what I will never be
Remains here in these rapidly scribbled lines,
A broken portico into the Impossible.

At least I treat myself with unsentimental scorn,
Noble at least in the generous gesture with which I cast off
The dirty laundry that is me—minus laundry list—into the stream
        of things,
And stay at home shirtless.

(You, who console, and can console because you don't exist,
Whether a Greek goddess conceived as a living statue,

Or a Roman patrician, impossibly noble and doomed,
Or a troubador's princess, terribly elegant and colorful,
Or an eighteenth-century marchioness, *décolletée* and distant,
Or a famous *cocotte* from the time of our fathers,
Or some modern type—I can't quite think who—
Whatever you might be, if you can inspire, then inspire me!
My soul is an empty bucket.
Just as those who summon up spirits summon up spirits, I summon
        up
Myself and find nothing.
I go over to the window and see the street with absolute clarity.
I see the shops, I see the sidewalks, I see the passing cars,
I see the clothed living beings coming and going,
I see the dogs who also exist,
And all of this weighs on me like a sentence of exile,
And all of this is foreign, like everything else.)

I lived, I studied, I loved, and I even believed,
And now there isn't a beggar I don't envy simply because he's not me.
I study the rags and sores and delusions of each and every one,
And I think: you may never have lived or studied or loved or believed
(Because it's possible to have done all those things without ever hav-
        ing done them);
Perhaps you merely existed, like a lizard whose tail was cut off,
But whose tail continues to twitch without said lizard.

I made of myself something I didn't know how to make
And what I could have made of myself I didn't.
I chose the wrong carnival costume.
People mistook me for someone I wasn't, and since I didn't deny it,
        I was lost.
When I tried to take off my mask,
It was stuck to my face.
And when I did pull it off and saw myself in the mirror,

I had grown old.
I was drunk, and no longer knew how to wear the costume I was still
        wearing.
I threw away the mask and slept in the cloakroom
Like a harmless dog the management puts up with,
And I'm going to write this story to prove that I'm sublime.

Musical essence of my futile verses,
If only I could think of you as something I had made,
If only I wasn't always facing the Tobacconist's shop facing me,
Trampling underfoot my awareness that I exist,
Like a rug a drunkard stumbles over
Or a worthless doormat stolen by gypsies.

But the Owner of the Tobacconist's has now come to the door and is
        standing there.
I look at him as awkwardly as if I had a crick in my neck,
I look at him with my awkwardly uncomprehending soul.
He will die and I will die.
He will leave a signboard and I will leave these verses.
At a certain point, the signboard will die too, as will my verses.
After a certain point, the street in which the signboard stood will die,
Along with the language in which these verses were written.
Then the turning planet where all this took place will die.
On other satellites of other systems something like people
Will continue making things like verses and living under things like
        signboards,
One thing always facing another,
One thing always as futile as another,
The impossible always as stupid as the real.
The mystery of the deep always as true as the mystery drowsing on the
        surface,
Always this or always something else, or neither one thing nor the other.

Then a man went into the Tobacconist's (to buy tobacco?),
And suddenly plausible reality fell upon me.
I half get up, enlivened, convinced, human,
And fully intending to write these lines in which I say the complete
        opposite.
I light a cigarette as I think about writing them
And in that cigarette I savor a liberation from all thought.
I follow the smoke as if following my own path,
And for one sensitive, seemly moment, I enjoy
A liberation from all speculation
And an awareness that metaphysics is merely a consequence of feel-
        ing slightly indisposed.

Then I sit back in my chair
And continue smoking.
As long as Fate allows, I will continue smoking.

(If I were to marry my washerwoman's daughter,
I might perhaps be happy.)

And so I get up from my chair. I walk over to the window.
The man has come out of the Tobacconist's (putting some change in
        his trouser pocket?).
Ah, I know him: it's the entirely unmetaphysical Esteves.
(The Owner of the Tobacconist's has come to the door again.)
As if by some divine instinct, Esteves turned and saw me.
He waved, I called out *Hello, Esteves!*, and the universe
Was restored to me without ideals or hopes, and the Owner of the
        Tobacconist's smiled.

44   [25 January 1928]
Written in a Book Left Behind on a Journey
I've come from the outskirts of Beja.
I'm heading for the center of Lisbon.

I bring nothing and will find nothing.
I feel the anticipated weariness of what I won't find,
And the nostalgia I feel is neither for the past nor the future.
I leave inscribed in this book the image of my dead motto:
I grew like a weed that no one pulled up.

45

Postscript
Make the most of time!
But what is time that I should make the most of it?
Make the most of time!
Not a day without a line written ...
Honest, superior work ...
Work à la Virgil, à la Milton ...
But it's so difficult to be honest or superior!
And so unlikely that I'll ever be another Milton or Virgil!

Make the most of time!
Take from my soul just the right pieces—neither more nor less—
And fit them together to make a jigsaw
Forming the appropriate illustrations for my story
(On the underside too, the part you can't see) ...
Make a house of cards out of my sensations, a very dull soirée,
Arrange my thoughts dominoes-fashion, matching like with like,
And treat my will as if it were a difficult cannon shot in billiards ...
Images of games of patience or solitaire or other pastimes—
Images of life, images of lives, Image of Life ...

Mere words ...
Words, words ...
Make the most of time!
Never let a minute pass unexamined by my consciousness ...
Never commit a single undefined or factitious act ...
Never make a move that does not perfectly fit my aims ...

The good manners of the soul …
The elegance of persevering …

Make the most of time!
My heart is as weary as a veritable beggar.
My brain stands ready like a parcel left lying in a corner.
My corner (words, words, words!) is simply the way it is and it's sad.
Make the most of time!
Five minutes have passed since I began writing this.
Did I make the most of them or not?
If I don't know, how will I know about all the other minutes?

(You, the lady who has so often traveled in the same compartment as
    me
On the local train,
Did you ever feel intrigued by me?
Did I make the most of time by looking at you?
What was the rhythm of our stillness on that moving train?
What was the understanding that we never reached?
What life was there in all this? What meaning did it have for life?)

Make the most of time! …
Oh, please, let me not make the most of anything at all!
Neither time, nor existence, nor memories of time or existence!
Let me be a leaf on a tree, tickled by the breeze,
The dust on a road, will-less and alone,
The chance stream left by the rain now gradually stopping,
The furrow left on the road by the wheels until other wheels come
    along,
The boy's top, about to stop spinning,
And which wobbles, just like the earth,
And trembles, just like the soul,
And falls, as gods fall, onto the pavement of Fate.

Demogorgon

In the sun-filled street houses stand still and people walk.
A horror-filled sadness chills me.
I sense something is about to happen beyond the façades and the
        movement.

No, no, not that!
Anything but having to learn the true nature of the Mystery!
Surface of the Universe, O Lowered Eyelids,
Never ever open!
The gaze of the Final Truth must be quite unbearable!

Let me live without knowing anything, and die with no prospect of
        knowing anything!
The reason for being to exist, the reason for beings to exist, for
        everything,
Must bring on a madness far greater than the spaces
Between souls and between the stars.

No, no, not the truth! Just leave me with these houses and these
        people;
Just that, nothing more, just these houses and these people ...
What vile, icy breath touches my closed lids?
I don't want to open them to life! O Truth, just forget all about me!

47   [14 April 1928]

Procrastination

The day after tomorrow, yes, the day after tomorrow ...
I'll spend tomorrow thinking about the day after tomorrow,
I can manage that, but not today ...
No, today is impossible; today, I can't do it.

The fuddled persistence of my objective subjectivity,
Interspersed with my drowsing real life,
With the thought of an infinite weariness.
A weariness so vast I can't even run for a tram …
This sort-of-soul …
No, the day after tomorrow …
Today I want to prepare myself,
I want to prepare myself to think about the next day tomorrow …
That is crucial.
I've already drawn up a plan; but no, I'm not drawing up any plans
        today …
Tomorrow is the day for plans.
Tomorrow I will sit at the desk ready to conquer the world;
But I'll only conquer the world the day after tomorrow …
I feel like crying,
I suddenly feel like crying a lot—from inside …
No, you don't want to know any more, it's a secret, I'm saying nothing.
Only the day after tomorrow …
When I was a child, the circus on Sunday would keep me amused
        for the rest of the week.
Now the circus on Sunday only keeps me amused for a whole week
        of my childhood …
The day after tomorrow I'll be different.
My life will triumph,
All my real qualities as an intelligent, well-read, practical fellow
Will be summoned by decree …
But by tomorrow's decree …
Today I want to sleep, I'll write it tomorrow …
Today, though, what entertainment would bring back my
        childhood?
One that I could buy tickets for tomorrow,
Because the day after tomorrow would be a good day to see a show …
Not before …
The day after tomorrow I'll have the public pose that I'll perfect
        tomorrow.

The day after tomorrow I will finally be what I could never be today.
Only the day after tomorrow ...
I feel sleepy like a stray dog left out in the cold.
I feel so sleepy.
Tomorrow I'll tell you the words, or the day after tomorrow ...
Yes, perhaps the day after tomorrow ...

The future ...
Yes, the future ...

48   [15 April 1928]

Master, my dear master!
The heart of my entire intellectual body!
The original source of my inspiration!
Master, what has become of you in this life of ours?

You didn't care if you lived or died, nor about yourself or about
        anything,
A visual, abstract soul down to your very bones,
Marvelous alertness to the always multiple outside world,
Refuge for all nostalgias—ah, the old gods,
Human spirit of mother earth,
Flower blooming above the deluge of subjective intelligence ...

Master, my master!
In the sensationist anguish of everyday experience,
In the quotidian pain of the mathematics of being,
I, the slave of everything as dust is to every wind,
I raise my hands to you, who are far, so very far from me!

My master and guide!
Whom nothing wounded, pained, or troubled,
Certain as a sun unwittingly doing its daily round,
Natural as a day revealing everything,

My master, my heart never learned your serenity.
My heart learned nothing.
My heart is nothing.
My heart is lost.

Master, I could only be like you if I had been you.
How sad the great joyful moment when I first heard you speak!
Since then, everything has been weariness in this subjectivized
    world,
Everything has been effort in this world of wanting things,
Everything has been lies in this world where things are thought,
Everything has been something else in this world where everything
    is felt.
Since then, I have been like a beggar left out in the damp night air
By the indifference of the whole town.
Since then, I have been like uprooted weeds
Left in neatly lined up sheaves scattered by the wind.
Since then, I have been me, yes, me, unfortunately,
And I, unfortunately, am neither me nor anyone else, not even
    nobody.
Since then ... but why did you teach me your clarity of vision,
If you couldn't teach me to have the necessary soul to see clearly?
Why did you call me to the top of the mountains
If I, a child of the cities of the plain, couldn't breathe the air?
Why did you give me your soul when I didn't know what to do with it,
Like someone laden down with gold in a desert,
Or singing in a divine voice amidst ruins?
Why did you awaken me to sensation and a new soul
If I don't know how to feel, and if my soul is still always my soul?

If only that ignoramus God had left me as I was,
A foolishly pretentious, decadent poet,
Who might perhaps at least entertain,

And not instilled me with the terrifying science of seeing.
Why did you make me me? You should have left me to be human!

Happy the junior clerk,
Who has his normal daily workload, light even when it's heavy,
Who has his usual life,
For whom pleasure is pleasure and leisure is leisure,
Who sleeps sleep,
Who eats food,
Who drinks drink, and is, therefore, happy.

You gave me your calm, which for me became disquiet.
You freed me, but the human fate is to be a slave.
You woke me up, but the meaning of being human is to sleep.

49 [29 April 1928]

Sometimes I meditate,
Sometimes I meditate, and I meditate so deeply, and still more deeply
And the whole mystery of things appears to me like oil floating on
      the surface,
And the whole universe is a sea of faces with wide eyes looking at me.
Each thing—a streetlamp on the corner, a stone, a tree—
Is an eye staring at me from some incomprehensible abyss,
And parading through my heart go all the gods, and the idea of gods.
Ah, that there should be things!
Ah, that there should be beings!
Ah, that there should be a way of there being beings,
That there should be a should be,
That there should be a way of there being a should be ...
That there should be ...
Ah, that the phenomenon of abstraction should exist—exist,
That there should be consciousness and reality,

Whatever that is …
How can I express the horror all this arouses in me?
How can I put into words what this feels like?
Where is the soul of that should-be?

Ah, the terrifying mystery of the existence of the tiniest thing
Because it is a terrifying mystery that there should be anything
Because it is a terrifying mystery that there should be …

50   [1 May 1928]

On the Last Page of a New Anthology
So many good poets!
So many good poems!
They really are good, very good.
With such competition no one can possibly last,
Or they'll do so only by chance, in the lottery of posterity,
Winning a place on the whim of the Impresario …
So many good poets!
Why do I write poems?
When I write them it seems to me
Just as my emotions when I wrote them seem to me—
The one great thing in the world …
My fear of myself fills the whole universe with cold.
Then, written down, visible, legible …
And what about this anthology of minor poets?
So many good poets!
What is genius, after all, or how do we distinguish
Genius from mere skill, and the good poets from the bad poets?
I don't really know if we can …
Best just to sleep …
I close the anthology feeling more tired than I am of the world—
Am I being trite?
There are so many good poets!
Good grief!…

51   [c. 1 May 1928]

In the sunset over Lisbon, in the tedium of the passing days,
Transfixed by the tedium of the permanently passing day
I live in that state of involuntary watchfulness like a lock on a door
That locks nothing at all.
My involuntary, impulsive heart
Shipwrecking idle sphinxes
On the rocks of consequences and intentions, waking up in the
        beyond …

52   [11 May 1928]

At the wheel of the Chevrolet driving along the Sintra road,
In the moonlight and in dreams, along the deserted road,
Alone, I'm driving, driving almost slowly, and it almost
Seems to me, or I almost try to make it seem,
That I'm driving down another road, through another dream,
        another world,
That I'm driving with no Lisbon to leave behind or Sintra to
        arrive in,
That I'm driving, and what is the point of driving except not
        stopping but driving on?

I'm going to spend the night in Sintra so as not to spend it in Lisbon,
But when I reach Sintra, I will regret not having stayed in Lisbon.
Always this aimless restlessness, pointless, inconsequential,
Always, always, always,
This excessive mental anxiety about nothing at all,
On the road to Sintra, on the road of dreams or on the road of life …

Responsive to my subconscious movements at the wheel,
The borrowed car races along beneath me, with me.
I smile at this symbol, as I think of it, as I make a right turn,
Thinking how, thanks to so many other borrowed things, I continue
        in the world!

How many of those borrowed things do I drive as if they were mine!
And alas, how much of me is those borrowed things!

To the left there's the little house—yes, the little house—beside the
    road.
To the right open countryside, with the moon in the distance.
The car, which, moments before, seemed to have given me freedom,
Is now a thing in which I am enclosed,
That I can only drive if I'm enclosed within it,
That I can only master if I'm included in it, if it includes me.

To the left, behind me now, the modest, more than modest house.
Life there must be a happy one, simply because it's not my life.
If someone saw me through the window, they would think: There's
    a happy man.
Perhaps the child peering through the window on the upper floor
Will see me (in my borrowed car) like a dream, like some magical
    creature.
Perhaps the girl who, hearing the engine, looked out of the kitchen
    window
On the ground floor,
Will see me as the kind of prince for which every young girl's heart
    yearns,
And she'll gaze after me, through the window, until I disappear
    round the corner.
I'll leave dreams behind me, or would it be the car doing that?
I, the driver of that borrowed car, or the borrowed car that I am
    driving?

On the road to Sintra in the moonlight, in this sad mood, surrounded
    by countryside and night,
Disconsolately driving this borrowed Chevrolet,
I lose myself on the future road, vanish into the distance I keep
    reaching,

And filled by a terrible, sudden, violent, inconceivable desire,
I accelerate ...
But my heart was left behind on the pile of rocks that I avoided
        when I saw it or didn't see it,
At the door to the little house,
My empty heart,
My dissatisfied heart,
My heart more human than I am, more precise than life.

On the road to Sintra, close to midnight, in the moonlight, at the
        wheel,
On the road to Sintra, feeling so weary of my own imagination,
On the road to Sintra, ever closer to Sintra,
On the road to Sintra, ever farther from me ...

53   [11 May 1928]

In the awful night, the natural stuff of all nights,
In the insomniac night, the natural stuff of all my nights,
I ponder, as I lie awake, drowsy, uncomfortable,
I ponder what I did or could have done in life.
I ponder, and an anguish
Spreads through me like a cold shiver or a shudder of fear.
The irreparable nature of my past—that is the real corpse!
All the other corpses might be mere illusions.
All the other dead might be alive somewhere else.
All my own past moments might exist elsewhere,
In the illusion of space and time,
In the falsity of the flow of time.

But what I was not, what I did not do, what I did not even dream;
What I only now see I should have done,
What I only now clearly see should have been—
That is the real death far beyond all the Gods,

That—which today is perhaps the best of me—is something not
   even the Gods can revive ...

If, at a certain moment,
I had turned to the left instead of to the right;
If, at a certain moment,
I had said yes instead of no, or no instead of yes;
If, during a certain conversation,
I could have spoken the sentences that only now, in my half sleep, I
   compose—
If all these things had happened,
I would be a different person today, and perhaps the whole universe
Would, imperceptibly, have turned out differently too.

But I did not turn to that side now irreparably lost,
I did not turn or think of turning, and only now do I grasp that;
But I did not say no or did not say yes, and only now do I see what I
   did not say;
But all the sentences I should have said then rise up inside me,
Clear, inevitable, natural,
The conversation drawn to a firm conclusion,
The matter entirely resolved ...
But only now does what never was, nor ever can be, hurt me.

What I failed to do really has no hope at all,
In any metaphysical system.
It may be that I can carry what I dreamed into another world,
But will I be able to carry into another world what I forgot to dream?
It is those dreams-to-be that are the corpse.
I bury it in my heart for ever, for all time, for all universes,
On this night when I cannot sleep, and the quietness surrounds me
Like a truth I do not share,
And outside, the moonlight, like the hope I do not have, is invisible
   to me.

Clouds

On this sad day my heart even sadder than the day ...
Moral and civic obligations?
Complicated duties and consequences?
No, nothing ...
A sad day, a disinclination to do anything ...
Nothing ...

Others travel (I once traveled too), others lie in the sun
(I lay in the sun too, or imagined I did),
They all have their reasons, or else life or a symmetrical ignorance,
Vanity, cheerfulness, and sociability,
And they emigrate in order to return or not to return,
On ships that simply transport them.
They don't feel the death in every departure,
The mystery in every arrival,
The horror in everything new ...
They don't feel: which is why they are politicians and financiers,
Go to dances and work in offices,
Go to all the theaters and know people ...
They don't feel: why would they?

Let these cattle in clothes from the corrals of the Gods
Go garlanded to the sacrifice
Beneath the sun, gaily, brightly, content to be feeling ...
Let them go, but, alas, I go with them to the same fate,
But without a garland!
I go with them without the sun I can feel, without the life that I have,
I go with them without their ignorance ...

On this sad day my heart sadder than the day ...
On this sad day every day ...
On this very sad day ...

55 [16 June 1928]

Daytime Nocturne

... No: I'm just sleepy.
Really? Are you tired because you have so many responsibilities,
Are you bitter perhaps because you're not famous,
Do all your highly developed views on immortality come from ...
Look, my friends, I'm just sleepy ...
At least allow me to be sleepy; who knows what else I might be?

56 [1 December 1928]

Song in the English Style

I've cut off all relations with the sun and the stars, I've had it with
    the world.
I carried my knapsack of my familiar longings far and wide.
I traveled, I bought the useless, found the uncertain,
And my heart is the same as it always was, a sky and a desert.
I failed in what I was, I failed in what I wanted, I failed in what I knew.
I no longer have a soul that the light can awaken or the darkness steal.
All I am is nausea, all I am is schism, all I am is longing,
I am a thing left somewhere a long way off.
And I keep going, only because my being feels comfortable and
    profound,
Stuck like a gobbet of spit to one of the world's wheels.

57 [c. 1928]

Ah, faced by this one reality, which is the mystery,
Faced by this one terrible reality—that there is a reality,
Faced by this horrible existence, namely that there is existence,
Faced by this abyss of the existence of an abyss,
The abyss of the existence of everything being an abyss,
Being an abyss simply by virtue of being,
Of being able to be,

180

For being itself to exist!
—Faced by this, everything, as with everything men do,
That men say,
That they build or undo or that is built or undone through them,
Everything shrinks!
No, it doesn't shrink … it becomes something else—
A single formidable, impossible, black thing,
A thing that exists beyond the gods, God, Fate—
The thing that causes gods, God, and Fate to exist,
That causes there to be being so that beings can exist,
That subsists through all forms
Of all lives, abstract or concrete,
Eternal or contingent,
True or false!
The thing that when it embraced everything still remained outside,
Because when it embraced everything, it did not embrace an expla-
        nation as to why it is an everything,
Or why there is anything, why there is anything, why there is
        anything!

My intelligence became a heart filled with horror,
And it's my ideas that set me trembling, my consciousness of myself,
The essential substance of my abstract being
Which I try to stifle because it's incomprehensible,
Which I suppress inside me because it's so ultratranscendent,
And from this fear, from this anguish, from this danger of that
        ultraexistence,
There is no running away, no running away, no running away!

Prison of Being, is there no escape from you?
Prison of thinking, is there no escape from you?
Ah, no, none—neither death, nor life, nor God!
We, twin brothers of the Fate in which we both exist,
We, twin brothers of all the Gods, of all species,

Sharing the same abyss, the same shadow,
Then, whether we are shadow or whether we are light, it is always
    the same night.

Ah, if I confidently confront life, the uncertainty of fate,
Smilingly, heedlessly, the quotidian possibility of all possible ills,
Unthinkingly confront the mystery of all things and all gestures,
Why should I not face Death too equally smilingly and heedlessly?
I don't know? But then is there anything I do know?
The pen I pick up, the words I write, the paper on which I write,
Are they any less mysterious than Death? As if everything were the
    same mystery?
And I write, I am writing, out of an unnecessary necessity.

Ah, let me face death like an animal that doesn't even know death
    exists!
Let me have the profound lack of consciousness of all natural things,
Because, however conscious I may be, everything is unconsciousness,
Unless, that is, someone had created everything, but to have created
    everything is also unconsciousness,
Because to create everything one would need to exist,
And to exist is to be unconscious, because to exist means that exis-
    tence is possible,
And the possible existence of existence is greater than all the Gods.

58   [25 January 1929]
Perhaps it's only a dream ...
That smile must be for someone else, or about someone else,
A frail blonde ...
The way she glanced at me, casual as a calendar ...
The way she thanked me when I helped her off the tram,
A thank you ...
Yes ...
I like to hear in dreams what she didn't say next,

The things that never took place.
Some people are never grown-up or practical!
I actually think very few people become grown-up and practical—
And anyone who does become grown-up and practical dies without
        noticing they are.
A frail blonde, an English figure, yet absolutely Portuguese,
Whenever I meet you, I remember poems I've forgotten—
Obviously you mean nothing to me,
And I only remember having forgotten you when I see you,
But meeting you lends sound to the day and to my indolence,
A poetry of the surface,
Too much in the too little of life's fruitlessness ...
Frail blonde, happy because you're not entirely real,
Because nothing worth remembering is entirely real,
And nothing worth being real is worth it.

59   27 March 1929
Insomnia
I can't sleep, nor do I expect to sleep.
Not even in death do I expect to sleep.

What awaits me is an insomnia the breadth of the stars,
And a pointless yawn the entire length of the world.

I can't sleep; I can't read when I wake in the night,
I can't write when I wake in the night,
I can't think when I wake in the night—
Good grief, I can't even dream when I wake in the night!

Ah, for the opium of being someone else!

I can't sleep, I lie there, a waking, feeling corpse,
And any feeling is just an empty thought.
A jumble of things that happened to me pass through me

—All the things I regret or feel guilty about—;
A jumble of things that didn't happen to me pass through me
—All the things I regret or feel guilty about—;
A jumble of utterly inconsequential things pass through me
Even those I regret and feel guilty about, and I can't sleep.

I don't have the strength to have the energy to light a cigarette.
I stare at the opposite wall of my room as if it were the universe.
Outside lies the silence of this whole thing.
A vast, terrifying silence from some other occasion,
Some other occasion when I was able to feel.

I am writing truly sympathetic poems—
Poems saying that I have nothing to say,
Poems insisting on saying the same thing over and over,
Poems, poems, poems, poems, poems …
So many poems …
And the whole truth and the whole of life exist outside of them and me!

I'm sleepy, but I can't sleep, I feel and don't know what to feel.
I am a sensation without a corresponding person,
An abstraction of self-consciousness barren of everything,
Apart from the bare essentials for feeling consciousness,
Apart from—apart from who knows what? …

 I can't sleep. I can't sleep. I can't sleep.
And yet my head, my eyes, my soul are so sleepy!
Sleepy in every way except in my ability to actually sleep!

O dawn, so slow to arrive … Come …
Come, however pointlessly,
Bring me another day the same as this one, to be followed by another
        night the same as this one …
Come and bring me the joy of that sad hope,

Because you are always joyful and always bring hope.
According to the old literature of sensations.
Come, bring hope, come, bring hope.
My tiredness seeps into the mattress.
My back aches from not lying on my side.
Although if I were lying on my side, my back would ache from lying
      on my side
Come, dawn, come soon!

What time is it? I don't know.
I don't have the energy to reach out to pick up my watch …
I don't have the energy to do anything, or for anything else …
Only to write these lines, written the following day,
All lines are always written the following day.

Absolute night, absolute quiet, outside.
The whole of Nature is at peace.
Humankind is resting, oblivious to its griefs.
Exactly.
Humankind forgets its joys and griefs.
That's what people usually say.
Humankind forgets, yes, humankind forgets,
But even when awake humankind forgets.
Exactly. But I can't sleep.

60   [27 March 1929]

Chance
By mere chance, a street, and in it, by chance, a sighting of a fair-
      haired girl.
But no, it isn't her.

The other girl was in another street, in another city, and I was another I.

I suddenly forget about the present sighting,
And am once again in that other city, that other street,
And that other girl is passing.

What a huge advantage it is to remember so intransigently!
Now I regret not having seen that other girl again,
And I regret, too, not even having looked at this one.

What a huge advantage it is to wear one's soul inside out!
At least I write poems.
Write poems, have people think me mad, and later, possibly, a genius,
Possibly, or perhaps impossibly.
The marvel of celebrity!

I was saying that at least I write poems …
But that was vis-à-vis a girl,
A fair-haired girl,
But which one?
There was the one I saw a long time ago in another city,
In another kind of street;
And there was this one I saw a long time ago in another city
In another kind of street;
Because all memories are the same memory,
Everything that was is the same death,
Yesterday, today, perhaps tomorrow too?

A passerby looks at me with random curiosity.
Could I have been writing poems in gestures and grimaces?
Maybe … And the fair-haired girl?
She was, in the end, the same one …
In the end, everything is the same …

Only I in some way am not the same, but that, in the end, is the same.

61 [4 April 1929]

Ah, open up another reality for me!
Like Blake, I want the close companionship of angels
And to have visions for lunch.
I want to encounter fairies in the street!
I want to unimagine myself from this world made of claws,
From this civilization made of nails.
I want to live, with a flag flapping in the breeze,
A symbol of something or other on the top of some other thing!
Then bury me wherever you want,
My true heart will continue to keep watch,
A piece of cloth emblazoned with sphinxes,
Atop the mast of Vision
Buffeted by the four winds of the Mystery.
The North—which everyone wants
The South—which everyone desires
The East—from which everything comes
The West—where everything went
—The four winds of the mystical air of civilization
—The four ways of not being right and of understanding the world.

62 [7 April 1929]

Marinetti, Academician
It's where everyone ends up, everyone ...
One day, subject to prior sale, I'll end up there too ...
After all, that's what we were born for ...

I have no alternative but to die first,
I have no alternative but to scale the Great Wall ...
If I stay here, they'll force me to be sociable ...
It's where everyone ends up, because that's what they were born for,
And you only end up where you were born to be ...

It's where everyone ends up …
Marinetti, academician …

The Muses took their revenge with electric lights, my friend,
And finally put you in their old cellar with a spotlight on you,
And your dynamics, always slightly Italian,
        f-f-f-f-f-f-f- …

63   [c. 7 April 1929]

For Fernando Pessoa
After Reading his Static Drama "The Sailor" in Orpheu I*
After twelve minutes
Of your drama *The Sailor*,
In which the most agile and astute
Sit there sleepy and brutish,
And make not a whiff of sense,
One of the women keeping vigil
Says with languorous magic:

Only the dream is eternal and beautiful. Why are we still speaking?

Now that is precisely what I was going
To ask those ladies …

64   [10 April 1929]

The raw light of premature summer
Emerges like a shout into the spring air …
My eyes sting as if it came from the Night …

* Published in Lisbon in *Orpheu* in 1929. It was published with the fictitious
date 1915, so the public wouldn't think Campos had read the play in 1929.

My brain is dizzy, as if I wanted justice …
In the raw light all shapes are silhouettes.

65   [10 May 1929]
My heart, a mystery battered by the specters of the winds …
A flag flapping wildly up high,
A tree buffeted, bent, shaken by the storm,
Trembling like green foam firmly attached to itself,
[…]
Forever condemned for my inability to express myself!

I'd like to cry out with a voice that could speak!
I'd like to bring to at least one other heart an awareness of mine!
I'd like to be out there, […]
But what am I? The rag that was once a flag,
The leaves, now branchless, swept into a corner,
The words endlessly misunderstood, even by those who value them,
Words into which I tried to pour my whole soul,
And all that remained was the beggar's hat under the car,
The spoiled spoiled,
And the laughter of the speedsters rang out behind on the road of
        the happy …

66   [15 May 1929]
Quasi
To sort out my life, put up shelves in my will and my actions …
I want to do this now, as I always have, with the same result;
But how good it is to have the clear intention, firm only in its clarity,
        to do something!

I'm going to pack my bags for the Definitive,

Organize Álvaro de Campos,
And tomorrow be in exactly the same place as the day before yester-
    day—an eternal day before yesterday ...

I smile in anticipatory knowledge of the nothing I will be ...
At least I can smile; smiling is something after all.

We are all the products of romanticism ...
And if we weren't the products of romanticism, we might well be
    nothing.

That is how literature is made ...
Yes, Gods, poor things, that's how life is made too!

The others are also romantics,
The others also achieve nothing, and are rich and poor,
The others also spend their lives looking at the cases waiting to be
    packed,
The others also sit dozing next to a jumble of papers,
The others are also me.

Streetseller crying out your wares as if singing an unintentional
    hymn,
Tiny cogwheel in the clockwork of political economy,
Mother, present or future, of those who die as Empires crumble,
Your voice reaches me like a summons to nowhere at all, like the
    silence of life itself ...

I look up from the papers I'm now thinking of not sorting out
At the window through which I heard but did not see the
    streetseller,
And my smile, which had not yet ended, ends up in my brain as
    metaphysics.

I lost faith in all the gods while sitting at a desk that needs tidying,
I faced down all the fates while distracted by that shouting
     streetseller,
And my weariness is an old boat rotting on a deserted beach,
And with an image that any poet could have come up with I close
     my desk and this poem.

Like a god, I have sorted out neither the truth nor life.

67   [before 17 May 1929]
Note
My soul shattered like an empty vase.
It fell an excessively long way down the stairs.
It fell from the hands of the careless maid.
It fell, breaking into more pieces than there was china in the vase.

Nonsense? Impossible? Who knows!
I have more sensations than I had when I felt I was me.
I'm a scattering of shards on a doormat that needs shaking.

I made a noise when I fell like a vase breaking.
What gods there are lean over the banister.
And they stare down at the shards their maid made of me.

They're not angry with her.
They're very sympathetic.
What was I, after all, but an empty vase?

They look at the absurdly conscious shards,
Conscious of themselves, not of them.

They look and they smile.

They smile sympathetically at the heedless maid.

The grand staircase stretches upwards, carpeted with stars.
Among the stars, a shard gleams, its glazed surface uppermost.
My work? My principal soul? My life?
A shard.
And the gods pay it special attention, because they don't know what
    it's doing there.

68   [17 June 1929]
Poem-song about Hope

I
Give me lilies, lilies,
And roses too.
But if you have no lilies
Or roses to give me,
At least be willing
To give me the lilies
And the roses too.
It's enough that you should be willing,
If, of course, you are,
To give me the lilies
And the roses too,
And I will have the lilies—
The finest lilies—
And the finest roses
Yet receive nothing,
Apart from the gift
Of your willingness
To give me lilies
And roses too.

II
You're wearing a dress
That acts as a reminder
To my heart.
It was worn once
By someone who,
Even though unseen,
Remained in my memory.
Everything in life
Is done by remembrance.
We love by memory.
A certain woman moves us
With a gesture that reminds us of our mother.
A certain girl fills us with joy
Because she speaks like our sister.
A certain child draws us out of our distraction
Because we loved a woman who resembled her
When we were young and never spoke to her.
That's pretty much how everything is,
The heart stumbles on.
To live is to miss meeting yourself.
In the end, if I were sleepy, I would sleep,
But I would like to meet you and to talk.
I'm sure we'd get on well together,
But if we don't meet, I will keep the moment
When I thought we might meet.
I keep everything,
I keep the letters people write to me—
I even keep the letters they don't write—
Good grief, we keep everything even if we don't want to.
And that little blue dress of yours, goodness, if only I could draw
You to me through that dress!
Well, anything's possible ...

You're still green—so young, as Ricardo Reis would say—
And my vision of you explodes literarily,
And I lie back on the beach and laugh like some inferior elemental
      spirit,
After all, feeling is very tiring, and life is hot when the sun is high.
Goodnight in Australia!

69 [17 June 1929]

Ah, how refreshing it is when we fail to do our duty!
It's like being in the countryside!
Unreliability becomes a refuge!
I breathe more easily now that I've missed all my appointments.
Yes, I missed them all, with the deliberateness of neglect,
I waited to feel the desire to go there, a desire I knew wouldn't
      come.
I am free, the enemy of organized, clothed society.
I am naked, and I plunge into the waters of my imagination.
It's too late for me to be in either of the two places where I should
      be at this hour,
Deliberately arranged for the same hour ...
It's fine, I'll stay here dreaming poems and smiling in italics.
It's so amusing this bystanding part of life!
I can't even manage to light my next cigarette ... That would be a
      gesture,
And it can stay there with the others that await me in the missed
      meeting that is life.

70 [18 June 1929]

Don't worry about me: I, too, have the truth.
I can pluck it out of my pocket
Like a conjurer.
I, too, belong ...

No one can conclude without me, that's clear.
And being sad is having such ideas.
Ah, my caprice found on aristocratic terraces,
My heart in shirtsleeves eating bread soup.

71   [29 August 1929]
Solvent
My neighbor at number fourteen is laughing today at her door
Through which, a month earlier, her small son's coffin was carried.
She's laughing quite naturally, wholeheartedly.
She's right: that's life.
Grief doesn't last because grief doesn't last.
She's right.
I repeat: she's right.
But my heart doesn't feel right.
My romantic heart makes enigmas out of life's egotism.

Here is the lesson, O soul of the people!
If the mother forgets the son who was born of her and died,
Who will ever go to the trouble of remembering me?
I'm as alone in the world as a broken brick.
I can die like the evaporated dew.
Thanks to a natural talent of solar nature,
I can die at the whim of someone's forgetfulness,
I can die just like anyone else …
But that hurts,
That's indecent for anyone with a heart …
That's …
Yes, that sticks in my gullet like a *sandwich* of tears …
Glory? Love? The yearning of a human soul?
Apotheosis turned on its head …
Give me water from Vidago, I want to forget about Life! …

72   [17 September 1929]
De la musique …
Ah, little by little, from among the ancient trees,
Her silhouette emerges, and I leave off thinking …

Little by little I, too, emerge from my anguish …

The two figures meet in the clearing by the lake …

… The two dreamed figures,
Because this was just a shaft of moonlight and a sadness of mine,
And a supposition of something else,
And the result of existing …

Did those two figures actually meet
In the clearing by the lake?

                    (… But what if they don't exist? …)

… In the clearing by the lake … … … …

73   [2 December 1929]
Pop!
Today, feeling ill at ease, and not knowing what to say,
Today, though feeling intelligent enough, I don't know what I crave,
I'd like to write my epitaph: Here lies Álvaro de Campos, dead,
Here lies what remains of the Greek Anthology half-read …
And why all of a sudden this deluge of rhymes?
No reason … A friend of mine, called (let's say) Symes,
Asked me in the the street what I was doing there,
And these lines are instead of saying I have no idea.
I only very rarely rhyme, and very rarely does rhyme chime.
But then again one must rhyme sometimes.

My heart, like a paper bag blown full of air
Then slammed against a wall, goes *pop*, and, caught unawares,
A chance passerby jumps, then spins round to look,
And thus I end this poem inconclusively and close my book.

74   [31 December 1929*]

However much I travel, however familiar I am
With leaving a place, arriving at a place, known or unknown,
I never lose, on leaving, on arriving, and on the shifting line that
     connects the two,
The shiver of horror, the fear of the new, the nausea—
That nausea which is the feeling that knows the body has a soul.
Thirty days traveling, three days traveling, three hours traveling—
Always the same sense of oppression seeping into the depths of my
     heart.

75   [c. 1929]

And I, drunk on all the injustice in the world
—God's flood and the fair-haired baby bobbing dead upon the
     waters—
I, in whose heart the anguish of others is rage,
I, the vast humiliation of the existence of an unspoken love—
I, the madman who makes sentences because he cannot make fate,
I, the ghost of my redemptive desire, a cold mist—
I don't know where to make poems from, how to write words,
     because the soul—
The numberless souls of others are always suffering somewhere
     outside of me.

* Atop the manuscript are Campos's initials, the date, and the location "Évora,"
which indicates that Campos welcomed the New Year in this town some eighty-
five miles southwest of Lisbon.

My verses are my own impotence.
What I cannot achieve, I write,
And the diverse rhythms that I create alleviate my cowardice.

The naive seamstress seduced into rape.
The junior clerk a rat always caught by the tail,
The prosperous businessman a slave to his own prosperity
—I make no distinctions, I hand out no praise, I don't [...]–
Ah, poor human creatures, stupidly suffering.

When I feel all this, when I think all this, when I rage at all this,
I tragically break my heart like a mirror,
And all the injustice of the world is heartfelt inside me.

My skiff-heart, my [...] heart, my gallows-heart—
All crimes happened and were paid for inside me.

Futile lacrimosity, human mawkishness of the nerves,
Drunkenness of altruistic servility,
The voice of the archivist crying out in the desert of a fourth-floor
        apartment ...

76   [c. 1929]
I know it's all perfectly natural
But I still have a heart ...
Oh, to hell with it all! ...
(Break, my heart!)
(To hell with the whole of humanity!)

In the house of the mother of the boy who was run over,
It's all laughter and fun.
And there's a great clamor of party horns, and the dead forgotten.

They received compensation:
Baby equals X amount of money,
They're enjoying X at this very moment,
They're eating and drinking their dead baby,
Bravo! That's what people are like!
Bravo! That's what humanity is like!
Bravo! That's what all fathers and mothers are like,
Those who have run-over-able children!
How easily everything is forgotten when there's money available.
Baby equals X.

They repapered the whole house with that.
They paid off the final installment on the furniture.
Poor little Baby.
But if he hadn't been run over and killed, how would they have paid
  the bills?

Yes, he was loved.
Yes, he was wanted.
But he died.
Too bad, he died!
What a shame, he died!
But because of him we could afford to pay the bills
And that's worth something.
(Of course it was a terrible misfortune)
But now we can pay the bills.
(Of course his poor little body
Did get crushed)
But now, at least, we don't owe the grocer.
(It's a shame, yes, but every cloud, etc., etc.)

The baby died, but what survives are those ten *contos*.
Yes, ten *contos*.

You can do a lot (poor baby) with all that money.
Pay off a lot of debts (poor dear little baby)
With ten *contos*.
Put a lot of things in order
(You sweet little thing, now dead) with ten *contos*.
We know, it's very sad
(Ten *contos*)
Our little child run over and killed
(Ten *contos*)
But the thought of having the house refurbished
(Ten *contos*)
Our home restored
(Ten *contos*)
Helps you forget a lot of things (how we mourned him!)
Ten *contos*!
It's as if God himself had given them to us
(Those ten *contos*).
Poor baby crushed to death!
Ten *contos*.

77   [6 January 1930]

I'm walking down a suburban street at night,
Coming home after listening to lectures by experts like me.
Coming home alone, a poet now, stripped of expertise and
        engineering,
Human even in the sound my lone footsteps make in the early
        evening,
Where, in the distance, a shop door is belatedly lowering its
        shutters,
Ah, the sound of supper in happy houses!
I walk past, and my ears see inside the houses.

My natural state of exile eases in the darkness

Of the street-my-home, the street-my-being, the street-my-blood.
Being a child with no need to worry about money,
With a soft bed and the deep sleep of childhood, as well as a maid!
O my unprivileged heart!
My excluded sensibility!
My grief external to my self!

Who made firewood out of the entire cradle of my childhood?
Who made floor cloths out of my childhood sheets?
Who discarded in the world's trash cans,
Among the peelings and the dust,
The lace from the christening robe made especially for me?
Who auctioned me off to Fate?
Who exchanged me for me?

I have just been speaking very precisely and positively.
I set out concrete points, like an automatic calculator.
I was right in the way that a pair of scales is right.
I spoke as I knew how.

Now, on my way to the terminus to get the tram back into the city,
I, a bandit, I, metaphysical, walk beneath the light of the few
        streetlamps,
And in the shadows between two streetlamps I feel like not going
        on ...
But I will catch the tram.
It'll ring twice, the bell at the invisible end of the strap pulled
By the fat-fingered hand of the unshaven conductor.
I will catch the tram.
Alas, despite everything, I will catch the tram.
Always, always, always ...
I've always gone back to the city,
I've always gone back to the city, after speculations and diversions,
I've always gone back in the mood for supper,

But I never had the kind of supper I can hear behind the shutters
Of the happy households in the suburbs whence I return in the tram,
The conjugal households of the normality of life!
I buy my ticket through the interstices,
And the conductor walks past me as if I were the Critique of Pure
        Reason ...
I bought my ticket. I did my duty. I am just like anyone else.
And not even suicide can cure any of these things.

78   [9 March 1930]

Today when everything slips away from me, like the ground be-
        neath my feet,
When I barely, painfully know myself, when all the literature
I write for myself alone, so as to have some awareness of myself,
Falls away, like the wrapper on a bad boiled sweet—
Today my soul resembles the death of the nerves—
Necrosis of the soul,
Putrefaction of the senses,
Everything I've done, I see now, is nothing.
Everything I dreamed could have been dreamed by an errand boy.
Everything I loved, if I could remember what I loved, died long ago.
O Lost Paradise of my bourgeois childhood,
My Eden warming my hands on my nighttime cup of tea,
My bedspread when I was a boy!
Fate set me aside like an interrupted manuscript.
No highs or lows—a consciousness of not even having a conscious-
        ness ...
An old maid's curling papers—that sums up my life.
I feel a nausea in my lungs.
I find it hard to breathe enough to sustain my soul.
I have many sad aches in the joints of my will.
My poet's garland—you were made of paper flowers,

Your presumed immortality lay in not having lived.
My poet's crown of laurels—dreamed petrarchanly,
No cape, just fame,
No dice, just God—
A sign selling adulterated wine in the last corner tavern!

79   [9 March 1930]

There are so many gods!
They're like books—you can't read them all, you really don't know
        anything.
Blessed is he who knows only one god, and tells no one.
I have different beliefs every day—
Sometimes I have several different beliefs on the same day—
And I would like to be the child whose image catches my eye
In the downstairs window—
Eating a cheap cake (she's a poor child) with no effective cause or aim,
An animal pointlessly elevated above the other vertebrates
And singing to herself an obscene song from a review …
Yes, there are many gods …
But I'd give everything to the god who could kill that child for me.

80   [6 April 1930]

Cesário, who succeeded
In seeing clearly, seeing simply, seeing purely,
Seeing the world in its objects,
Being a gaze with a soul behind it, and he had such a brief life!
A Lisbon child of the Universe,
May everything that can be seen heap blessings upon you!
In my heart, I adorn the whole of Praça da Figueira just for you,
And there isn't a corner that I don't see through your eyes, even the
        corner of a corner.

81   [8 April 1930]

*Carry Nation**

My Joan of Arc with no motherland!
My human St. Theresa!
Stupid in the way all saints are
And as militant as the soul that hopes to conquer the world!
You should be toasted with the wine you hated!
We will canonize you by raising our glasses and weeping!

A salutation from enemy to enemy!
I, who so often got falling-down drunk simply because I didn't want
          to feel,
I, who was so often the worse for wear because I didn't have soul
          enough,
I, your opponent,
I snatch the sword from the angels, the angels guarding Eden,
And raise it up in ecstasy and call out your name.

82   [c. 8 April 1930]

Carry Nation

Not an aesthetic saint like St. Theresa,
Not a dogmatic saint,
Not a saint at all
But a human saint, crazy and divine,
Maternal, aggressively maternal,
Odious, like all saints,
Persistent, with the insanity of sainthood.
I hate her, and yet I take my hat off to her

---

* Caroline Amelia Nation (1846–1911), often referred to as Carrie or Carry Na-
tion, was a radical member of the temperance movement. She became known
as Hatchet Granny because of her habit of attacking alcohol-serving establish-
ments with a hatchet.

And for reasons unknown, I cheer her!
American stupor haloed with stars!
A witch with good intentions …
Don't throw rose petals on her grave,
But laurels, the laurels of glory.
Let us both glorify and insult her!
Let us drink to the health of her immortality
With the strong wine of hardened drinkers.

I, who never did anything in the world,
I, who never knew how to love or to know,
I, who was always an absence of will,
I toast you, mad little mother, sentimental system!
Exemplar of human aspiration!
Marvel of the kind gesture and the iron will!

83   [21 April 1930]

With this misty day comes a kind of forgetting.
Wafting gently in on the evening comes the opportunity for loss.
In the damp air of life I fall asleep without sleeping.

It's useless telling me that all actions have consequences.
It's useless my knowing that all actions use consequences.
Everything is useless, everything is useless, everything is useless.

With this misty day comes nothing at all.

Just now I felt
Like going to wait for the promised traveler to arrive on the Europe train,
To go to the quay and see the ship come in and feel sad about
        everything.

Wafting in on the evening comes no opportunity at all.

84 [28 May 1930]

Stop. Zone

Bring me oblivion on a platter!
I want to devour the leaving of life!
I want to lose the habit of shouting inside myself.
Stop it, that's enough. I don't know what, but that's enough …
You're living tomorrow, are you? … And what about today?
Are you living tomorrow by postponing today?
Did I realize I was buying a ticket for this show?
Anyone capable of laughter must be splitting his sides!
And now the tram has arrived—the one I was waiting for—
I wish it was another one … And I have to get on!
No one is forcing me to, but then why let it go?
Just let them all go, along with myself, and life …
What a feeling of nausea in the real stomach that is the conscious soul!
What a dream to be someone else, anyone else …
I understand now why boys want to be brakemen …
No, I don't understand anything …
Evening of blue and gold, the joy of ordinary people, the clear eyes
    of life …

85 [13 June 1930*]

Birthday

In the days when they used to celebrate my birthday,
I was happy and no one had died.
In the old house, even celebrating my birthday was a centuries-old
    tradition,
And the happiness of everyone, including me, was as certain as any
    religion.

---

* This poem was published with the fictitious date October 15, 1929, to coincide
with Campos's birthday instead of Pessoa's on June 13.

In the days when they used to celebrate my birthday,
I was brimming with the kind of health that understands nothing,
That enjoys being considered the intelligent one in the family,
And not sharing the same hopes others had for me.
When I did eventually have hopes, I no longer knew how to have
    them.
When I did eventually look at life, life had lost all meaning.

Yes, what I supposedly was to myself,
What I was in heart and kinship,
What I was during those semiprovincial evenings,
What I was when I was loved and a little boy,
What I was—ah, dear God, what I only now know that I was ...
And it's all so far away!
(Not even an echo ...)
The days when they used to celebrate my birthday!

What I am today is like the damp stain in the corridor at the far end
    of the house,
Spreading over the walls ...
What I am today (and the house of those who loved me trembles
    through my tears),
What I am today is the house being sold,
It's everyone having died,
It's me, this remnant of myself like a spent match ...

In the days when they used to celebrate my birthday ...
How I love that time as if it were a person!
I feel a physical desire in my soul to be there again,
Making a journey both carnal and metaphysical,
Like a duality between me and myself ...
Eating the past like a starving man's dry crust, with no buttery time
    on my teeth!

I see everything again with a clarity that blinds me to what is here ...
The table set with more places, with prettier patterns on the china,
    with more glasses,
The sideboard crammed with more treats—desserts, fruit, and other
    things on the shelf underneath—
The old aunts, the various cousins, and all because of me,
In the days when they used to celebrate my birthday ...

Stop it, my heart!
Don't think! Leave thinking to my head!
Oh dear God, dear God, dear God!
I don't have birthdays anymore.
I simply endure.
The days accumulate.
I will be old when I am old.
Nothing more.
Only anger that I did not steal the past and put it in my pocket! ...

The days when they used to celebrate my birthday! ...

86   [18 June 1930]
I'm weary of the intellect.
Thinking is bad for the emotions.
There's always an overreaction.
You suddenly burst into tears, and there are all your dead aunts
    making tea
In the old house on the old estate.
Heart, stop it!
Factitious hope, calm down!
If only I could never have been anything but the child I was ...
Sleeping soundly simply because I was sleepy and had no troubling
    thoughts to forget!

My horizon of garden and sea!
My end before my beginning!

I am weary of the intellect.
If only it could be used to know something!
But all I know is this deep-seated weariness, like the dregs
That float around in a glass of wine and weary the wine.

87   [18 June 1930]
Diagnosis
Just a pinch of truth! Just a pinch!
I am quite right as long as I don't think.
Just a pinch of truth …
Slowly …
Someone might come to the windowpane …
Keep a lid on your emotions!
Careful!
If they gave it to me I would accept …
No need to insist, I would accept …
Why?
What a question! I would accept …

88   [26 June 1930]
Bicarbonate of Soda
A sudden anguish …
Ah, what anguish, what nausea in the soul!
What so-called friends I've had!
How utterly empty every city I've visited!
What metaphysical garbage all my plans!

An anguish,

A despondency in my soul's epidermis,
A despair at the setting sun of all effort ...
I renounce.
I renounce everything.
I renounce more than just everything.
I renounce by the sword all the Gods and those who deny them.

But what is it that I lack, what is it that I feel I lack in my stomach
    and my circulation?
What vapid befuddlement stultifies my brain?

Should I take something or kill myself?
No: I am going to exist. Damn it! I am going to exist.
E-x-ist ...
E—x—ist ...

Dear God, what buddhism chills my blood!
A renunciation of all open doors,
Faced by the landscape of all landscapes,
Without hope, free,
Without ties,
An accident of the inconsequentiality of the surface of things,
Monotonous but sleepy,
And what breezes waft in when all the doors and windows are open!
What a delightful summer other people enjoy!

I'm not thirsty, but give me a drink!

89   [29 June 1930]
That English girl, so fair, so young, so kind,
Who wanted to marry me ...
What a shame I didn't marry her ...
I would have been happy,

But how do I know I would have been happy?
How do I know anything about how it would have been,
The what-would-have-happened-and-never-was?
Today I regret not having married her,
Or, rather, the mere hypothesis of being able to regret not having
        married her.
And so everything is regret.
And regret is a pure abstraction
That brings with it a certain discomfort
But also a desire to sleep ...

Yes, that girl was an opportunity for my soul.
Today, it's my regret that feels far from my soul.
Good grief, what complications, and all because I didn't marry an
        English girl who has probably forgotten me by now! ...
But what if she hasn't forgotten me?
What if (because it's possible) she still remembers me and has re-
        mained constant
(And whether I'm ugly or not is beside the point, ugly men are also
        loved
And sometimes by women!)
If she hasn't forgotten me, then she'll still remember me.
That is really another sort of regret.
And there's no forgetting someone who caused us pain.

Anyway, these conjectures are just my vanity speaking.
She's hardly likely to remember me, with her fourth child in her arms,
Leafing through the *Daily Mirror* for photos of Princess Mary.

At least it's best to think that's so.
It's a picture of a suburban English house,
It's a nice interior landscape of fair heads,
And any remorse lies in the shadows ...
If that's the case, then there's still a shred of jealousy.

The fourth child is another man's child, the *Daily Mirror* is in their
    house.
What might have been ...
They eat marmalade for breakfast in England ...
I have my revenge on all the English bourgeoisie by being a Portuguese
    fool.

Ah, but I can still see
Your eyes—as genuinely sincere as they were blue—
Looking at me just like another child ...
And it's not with witty salty lines that I can erase you from the image
You have in my heart,
I won't disguise you, my only love, and I want nothing from life.

90   [2 July 1930]
Cul-de-lampe
Little by little,
Without lacking anything,
Without having too much of anything,
Without anything being in any particular position,
I walk while standing still,
I live while dying,
I exist through a number of people who do not exist.
I am everything except myself.
I have finished.

Little by little,
Without anyone speaking to me
(What does it matter what has been said to me in my life?)
Without anyone listening to me
(What does it matter what I said or was heard to say?)
Without anyone loving me
(What does it matter what was said by someone who said they loved
    me?)

Fine ...
Little by little,
Without any of that,
With only that,
I am slowly stopping,
I will stop,
I have finished.

Finished!
I'm fed up with feeling and pretending to think,
And I haven't finished yet.
I am still writing poems.
I am still writing.
I am still

(No, I'm not going to finish ...
Yet ...
I'm not going to finish.
I have finished.)

. . . .

Suddenly, in the side street, a figure appears in a high window, but
          who is it?
And the horror of having lost the childhood I never had there
And the vagabond path taken by my unachievable consciousness.

What more do you want? I have finished.
No need for the neighbor's canary, O morning of another age,
Or the (baskety) sound of the baker on the stairs
Or the streetsellers' cries gone who knows where
Or the funeral (I hear voices) out in the street,
Or the sudden thunder of the shutters opposite in the summer air,
Or ... so many things, so much soul, so much that is irreparable!
Now it's all cocaine ...

My love a lost childhood!
My past a pinafore!
My rest a slice of bread spread with good butter and eaten at the
     window!
Enough, I'm already blind to what I can see!
Dammit, I have finished!
Enough!

91   [3 July 1930]

Yes, it's clear,
The universe is black, especially at night.
But I, like everyone else,
Suffer from toothaches and corns, and the other pains pass.
Poems can be made of those other pains,
The painful pains are just annoying.

The inner constitution of poetry
Helps a lot ...
(It serves as an analgesic for the not very painful pains of the soul ...)
Now let me sleep.

92   [9 July 1930]

My poor friend, I have no compassion to offer you.
Compassion requires effort, especially the genuine sort, and on
     rainy days.
I mean: it requires effort to feel on rainy days.
Let us feel the rain and leave psychology for another kind of sky.
Some sexual problem, then?
But after the age of fifteen that's indecent.
Preoccupation with the opposite sex (let's assume) and their
     psychology—

But that's ridiculous, boy.
The opposite sex exists to be sought after, not discussed.
The problem exists in order to be resolved, and not as a source of worry.
To worry is to be impotent.
And you should be less frank about yourself.
Do you know "La Colère de Samson?"
"*La femme, enfant malade et douze fois impure.*"
But that's not it.
Don't pester me, don't force me to feel sorry for you!
Look: everything is literature.
Everything comes to us from outside, like the rain.
Most of us are pages that read like something out of a novel.
Translations, my friend.
Do you know why you are so sad? It's because of Plato,
Whom you've never read.
Your Petrarchan sonnet, another writer you've not read, came out all
    wrong.
And that's how life is too.
Roll up your civilized shirt sleeves
And dig in exact fields!
Better that than have other people's souls.
We are merely the ghosts of ghosts,
And today's landscape is of little help.
Everything is geographically external.
The rain falls according to a natural law
And humanity loves because it has heard others speak of love.

93   [19 July 1930]
I sold myself for a song to the fortuitous nature of the encounter.
I loved wherever I found love, almost without thinking.
I jumped from interval to interval
And so I arrived where I arrived in life.

Today, remembering the past,
I find in it only the person I wasn't ...
The thoughtless child in the house he would one day leave,
The older and more errant child in the house of some aunts now dead,
The thoughtless adolescent left in the charge of a priest cousin I
     called uncle,
The older adolescent sent abroad (the new tutor's idea),
The thoughtless youth studying in Scotland, studying in Scotland ...
The thoughtless youth now a man weary of studying in Scotland,
The thoughtless man he became, so different and so stupid ...
Having nothing in common with the person I was,
Having nothing that chimed with what I think,
Having nothing even resembling what I could have been,
I [...].

I sold myself for a song and in exchange they gave me beans—
The beans we used in the board games from my childhood long
     since swept away.

94   [11 August 1930]

No! All I want is freedom!
Love, glory, and money are all prisons.
Beautiful rooms? Fine upholstery? Soft carpets?
No, let me out so that I can find myself.
I want to breathe the air alone,
My pulse doesn't keep time with anyone else's,
I'm unmoved by company shares,
I am me, only me, I was born only as me, I am full to the brim with me,
Where would I like to sleep? In the garden ...
I don't want any walls—only the great understanding—
Me and the universe,
And what quiet, what peace to fall asleep not before the specter of
     the wardrobe,

But before the great splendor, black and cool, of all the stars together,
The great infinite abyss above
Sending breezes and bounty down from above onto the flesh-covered
    skull that is my face,
Where only my eyes—that other sky—reveal the great subjective sky.

No, I want only freedom!
I want to be equal to myself.
Don't geld me with ideas!
Don't strap me into the straitjacket of manners!
Don't make me praiseworthy or intelligible!
Don't kill me alive!
I want to be able to throw a ball high up at the moon
And hear it drop into the garden next door!
I want to lie on the grass thinking: "Tomorrow I'll go and fetch it …
Tomorrow I'll go and fetch it from the garden next door …
Tomorrow I'll go and fetch it from the garden next door …
Tomorrow I'll go and fetch it from the garden …
Fetch it from the garden
From the garden
Next door … "

95   [17 August 1930]

Freedom, yes, freedom!
Real freedom!
To think without desires or convictions.
To be master of oneself untainted by novels!
To exist without Freud or airplanes,
Without cabarets, not even in my soul, without velocities, even in
    my weariness!
The freedom of leisure, of healthy thoughts, of a love for natural
    things,
The freedom to love the morality we should give to life!

Like moonlight when the clouds open,
The great Christian freedom of my prayerful childhood
That suddenly, kindly, spreads its silver blanket over the whole
     earth ...
Freedom, lucidity, coherent reasoning,
The juridical notion of other people's souls as human,
The joy of having these things, and being once again able to
Enjoy the fields without reference to anything
And to drink water as if it were all the wines of the world!

Every step the scampering steps of a child ...
The smile of a kind old woman ...
The handshake of a good friend ...
What a life mine has been!
How long have I been waiting at this country station!
How long have I lived merely in life's printed form!

Ah, I have such a healthy thirst on me. Give me freedom,
Give it to me in the old jug that stood next to the barrel
At the house in the country, home of my old childhood ...
I would drink and it would fizz in the jug,
I was cool and the jug was cool too,
And because I had nothing to worry about, I was free.
What became of that jug and that innocence?
What became of the person I should have been?
And apart from that desire for freedom and goodness and air, what
     became of me?

96   [4 September 1930]
The deserts are vast, and everything is a desert.
The deserts are not a few tons of stones and bricks piled high
Disguising the soil, the soil which is everything.
The deserts are vast and souls, too, are vast and deserted—
Deserted because only the souls themselves pass through them,

Vast because from there you can see everything, and everything has
     died.

The deserts are vast, O soul of mine!
The deserts are vast.

I didn't buy a ticket for life,
I missed the door to feeling,
There wasn't a desire or an occasion I didn't miss.
Today all that's left to me, on the eve of the voyage,
With my suitcase open waiting for me to stop putting off doing my
     packing,
Sitting on the chair along with the shirts that won't fit in,
Today all that's left to me (apart from the discomfort of sitting here)
Is the knowledge that:
The deserts are vast and everything is a desert.
Life is vast, and there's no point in there being life.

I'm better at packing my suitcase with my eyes thinking about packing
Than actually packing it with my factitious hands (and factitious is
     the right word, I think).
I light a cigarette to postpone the voyage,
To postpone all voyages,
To postpone the entire universe.

Come back tomorrow, reality!
That's enough for today, people!
Postpone yourself, absolute present!
Better not to have a present than to be like this.

Buy some chocolates for the child I mistakenly replaced,
And take down the sign, because tomorrow is infinite.

But I really must pack my suitcase.
I absolutely must pack my suitcase,

Yes, my suitcase

I can't possibly carry my shirts in a hypothesis or my suitcase in my
    reason.

Yes, all my life I've been having to pack my suitcase.

But all my life I've sat in the corner along with the pile of shirts,

Ruminating, like an ox that never fulfilled its destiny as the god Apis.

I have to pack my suitcase of being.

I have to exist packing suitcases.

The ash from my cigarette falls on the shirt on top of the pile.

I glance to the side and realize I'm sleeping.

I know only that I have to pack my suitcase,

And that the deserts are vast and that everything is a desert,

And some other parable along the same lines, and which I've
    forgotten.

I suddenly leap to my feet like all the Caesars rolled into one.

I'm definitely going to pack my suitcase.

Dammit, I must pack it and close it;

I must watch it leave this place,

I must exist independently of my suitcase.

The deserts are vast and everything is a desert,

Always assuming I'm right, of course.

Poor human soul whose only oasis is in the desert next door!

I'd better pack my suitcase.

End.

97   [10 September 1930]

Rag

The day has turned out rainy.

And yet the sky this morning was quite blue.

The day has turned out rainy.

I've been feeling a bit sad all morning.
Anticipation? Sadness? Nothing at all?
I don't know, but I felt sad the moment I woke up.
The day has turned out rainy.

I know: the penumbra of the rain is elegant.
I know: the sun is vulgar and displeases the elegant.
I know: being susceptible to changes in the light is not elegant.
But who told the sun or the others that I wanted to be elegant?
Give me the blue sky and the visible sun.
Mist, rain, overcast skies—I have all that inside me.
Today I just want peace and quiet.
I would even like a home, as long as I didn't actually have one.
I feel almost sleepy in my desire for peace.
No, let's not exaggerate!
I do actually feel sleepy, and for no reason.
The day has turned out rainy.

Friendships? Affections? They are mere memories …
You need to be a child to feel such things …
My lost dawn, my true blue sky!
The day has turned out rainy.

The caretaker's daughter's pretty mouth,
Like the soft fruit of a heart yet to be eaten …
When was that? I don't know …
In the blue of the morning …

The day has turned out rainy.

98   [c. 15 October 1930]
I have written more verses than I have truth.
I have written largely
Because others have written.

If there had never been any poets in the world,
Would I be capable of being the first?
Never!
I would be a perfectly biddable individual,
I would have my own house and a morality.
Senhora Gertrudes!
You haven't cleaned this room properly:
Remove these ideas from me this instant!

99 [c. 1930]

I would love to love loving.
Just a moment … Hand me a cigarette, will you,
From the pack on my bedside table.
Go on … You were saying
That in the development of metaphysics
From Kant to Hegel
Something had been lost.
I agree absolutely.
No, I was listening, really I was.
Nondum amabam et amare amabam (St Augustine).*
How odd these associations of ideas can be!
I'm tired from thinking about feeling something else.
Thank you. Let me just light my cigarette. Go on. Hegel …

100 [c. 1930]

Mists of all my memories together
(The fair-haired primary school teacher in her peaceful garden)
I remember everything wrapped in golden sun and tissue paper …
And the little boy's hoop almost brushes me as it passes …

---

* "I was not yet in love, and I loved to be loved." The Latin words appear in the
epigraph of Shelley's "Alastor; or, The Spirit of Solitude" (1816).

101 [c. 1930]

The placid, anonymous face of a dead man.

Just as the ancient Portuguese mariners,
Who lived in dread of the great Final Sea, but carried on regardless,
Saw, at last, not monsters or great abysses,
But marvelous beaches and stars as yet unseen.

What do the fences of the world conceal of God's storefront?

102 [14 March 1931]

I have a really terrible cold,
And as everyone knows, terrible colds
Alter the whole system of the universe,
They make us angry with life,
And even make metaphysics sneeze.
I have wasted the whole day blowing my nose.
I have a slight headache.
A sorry condition for a minor poet!
Today I truly am a minor poet.
What I was before was a mere wish; it broke in two.

Farewell forever, fairy queen!
Your wings were made of sunlight, and here I am just plodding along.
I won't feel all right until I lie down in bed.
I never did feel right except when I was lying in bed in the universe.
Excusez un peu ... What a terrible physical cold!
What I need is truth and some aspirin.

103 [9 June 1931]

Oxfordshire
I want the good and I want the bad, and in the end I want nothing
      at all.

I'm uncomfortable lying on my right side and uncomfortable lying
        on my left side,
And uncomfortable lying on my awareness that I exist.
I am universally uncomfortable, metaphysically uncomfortable,
But the worst thing is that my head aches.
This is far more serious than the meaning of the universe.

Once, near Oxford, on a country walk,
I saw, around a bend in the path, not far off,
The old church steeple rising up above the houses of the village or
        hamlet.
This utterly insignificant incident stayed with me with photo-
        graphic clarity,
Like a transversal fold ruining the crease in my trousers.
Now it's relevant though …
From the path I saw spirituality in that church tower,
The faith of all ages, and Christian hope.
Seen from the village, though, the steeple was just the steeple,
And what's more, there it was.

You can be happy in Australia, so long as you don't actually go there.

104   [6 August 1931]
Yes, when all's said and done, I am I, me,
A kind of accessory or spare part of myself,
The rough-and-ready outskirts of my genuine emotion,
I am me here inside me, I am I.

Everything I was, everything I wasn't, I am all those things.
Everything I wanted, everything I didn't want, I was shaped by all
        those things.
Everything I loved or ceased to love provokes the same longing in me.

And, at the same time, I have the slightly contradictory feeling,
Like a dream based on a mixture of realities,
That I left me, myself, on a seat in a tram,
To be found by chance by whoever happened to sit down on top of
      me.

And, at the same time, there's a slightly distant feeling,
Like a dream you try to remember in the half darkness to which you
      wake,
That there is something better in me than me.

Yes, the simultaneous, almost painful feeling,
Like waking from a dreamless sleep to a day full of creditors,
That I have bungled everything, like tripping over the doormat,
That I have ruined everything, like forgetting to pack a hairbrush,
That somewhere in life I have replaced myself with something else.

Enough! That's a rather or, rather, a very metaphysical feeling,
Like the sun shining in for the last time through the window of the
        house you're about to leave,
The feeling that it's better to be a child than to try and understand
        the world—
A bread-and-butter-and-toys feeling
Of great peace without Proserpine's Gardens,
Of being at ease with life, your head resting on the window pane,
Watching the rain pattering down outside
And not the grown-up tears that are so hard to swallow.

Enough, yes, enough! I am I, the changeling,
The emissary without a letter and without credentials,
The sad clown, the fool wearing someone else's baggy suit,
With other people making the bells on my hat jingle
Like the small cowbells of an oppressive servitude.

I am I, the syncopated charade,
Which, at provincial parties, no one in the circle can guess.

I am I, and there's nothing to be done about it!...

105 [12 October 1931]

Ah, a Sonnet...
My heart is a completely crazy admiral
Who, having abandoned the life naval,
Now summons it up for hours and hours
As he paces and paces through the house...

As he paces (I even shift in my chair
Simply to imagine him over there)
The seas he abandoned come into focus
In those muscles grown weary of idleness.

There is much longing in his legs and arms.
His brain brims with longing for the past,
As he rages wearily at those lost charms.

Come now! Having begun with the heart...
How the devil did I end up here,
With an admiral rather than something more sincere?...

106 [21 October 1931]

Keep your voice down, for this is life—
Life and our awareness of it,
Because night is coming on, and though I'm tired, I can't sleep,
And, if I go over to the window,
I see, from beneath my brute eyelids, the many places of the stars...
I wore out the day hoping that I would sleep tonight,

And now it's night, almost tomorrow. I'm sleepy, but I can't sleep.
I feel I am the whole of humanity and through my tiredness—
A tiredness that almost turns my bones to foam …
That is what we all are …
Like flies, winged and trapped, we bumble about
In the world, a spider's web over the abyss.

107 [22 November 1931]

No, you're right, I'm wrong …
Allow me to drift off from this pointless argument,
I'm wrong in my opinion, that's fine, I'm not deeply attached to that
    opinion anyway …

I'm not even listening, you say? I don't know.
I think I am. But repeat what you just said.
Love should be constant?
Yes, it should be constant.
But only in love, of course.
Say it again, will you? …

People make life so very complicated!
Yes, fine, I'll bring the money tomorrow.

O great sun, you know nothing of this,
A joy we cannot even contemplate in the serene blue unreachable sky.

108 [22 November 1931]

There's no point prolonging this conversation of silences … .
You're sitting, smoking, at the end of the big sofa—
I'm sitting, smoking, on the sofa with the very deep seats.
For nearly an hour now, nothing has passed between us
Apart from a few glances expressive of a desire to speak.

The only thing that's changed are our cigarettes—the new replacing
    the old,
And then we continued our silent conversation,
Interrupted only by the glanced desire to speak ...

Yes, it's pointless,
But everything, even life in the open air, is equally pointless.
There are some things that are hard to say ...
This problem, for example.
Which of us does she like? How can we possibly talk about that?
Or even talk about her, isn't that right?
And certainly not be the first to think about talking about her!
To talk about her to the impassive other man and friend ...
You've just dropped ash on your black jacket—
I was going to warn you, but that would have meant speaking ...

We look at each other again, like two people passing in the street.
And the mutual crime we have not committed
Surfaces simultaneously in the depths of those two glances,
You suddenly yawn and stretch and half get up. No need to speak ...
"Time for bed!" you said, just to say something.
And all this, so psychological, so involuntary,
And all because of a pleasant, solemn young woman in the office.
Yes, time for bed!
The very fact that I'm writing a poem about this is, just so you know,
    pure contempt!

109   [25 November 1931, a.m.]
I wake in the night, deep in the night, to total silence.
It is—the clock's visible ticktock—four hours until day comes.
I fling open the window in my insomniac despair.
And suddenly, human,
The crisscross rectangle of a lighted window!
The fraternity of the night!

228

An anonymous, unwitting fraternity in the night!
We are both awake and the rest of humanity oblivious.
They're sleeping. We have light.

Who are you? Ill, a counterfeiter, a simple insomniac like me?
No matter. In this place, the eternal, formless, infinite night
Has only the humanity of our two windows,
The beating heart of our two lights,
In this moment and place, we, strangers, are all of life.

Leaning on the sill of the window at the back of the house,
Feeling the wood beneath my hands damp with night,
I peer out at the infinite and, just a little, at myself.

There aren't even any cockerels crowing in this definitive silence!
What's wrong, O comrade of the lighted window?
A dream, lack of sleep, life?
The warm yellow of your anonymous window …
It's funny: you don't seem to have electric light.
O kerosene lamps of my lost childhood!

110   [8 December 1931]
Notes in Tavira
I finally reached my childhood village.
I got off the train, I remember, I looked, saw, compared.
(All this took as long as a rather weary glance.)
Everything is old where I was young and new.
For a start—different shops, and different colored frontages on the
          same buildings—
A car I'd never seen before (there weren't any then)
Stagnating darkly yellow outside a half-open door.
Everything is old where I was young and new.
Yes, because even things younger than me make the rest look old.
The newly painted house seems older because it's newly painted.

I stop to look around, and what I see is me.
When I lived here I had a vision of myself in the splendor of my
    forty years—
Master of the universe—
And it's at forty-one that I unwittingly step off the train.
What did I conquer? Nothing.
No, I haven't really conquered anything.
I carry my tedium and the physical weight of my failure in the way
    my suitcase weighs on me ...
Suddenly I step forward, firmly, resolutely.
All my hesitation gone.
My childhood village is, after all, a foreign place.
(I am at ease, as always, before the unknown, which means nothing
    to me.)
I am a foreigner, a *tourist*, a passerby.
Of course: that's what I am,
Even to myself, dear God, even to myself.

111   [8 December 1931]
I want to die among roses, because I loved them as a child.
As for the chrysanthemums that came later, I coolly plucked their
    petals.
Don't say much, speak slowly.
So that I won't hear, especially with my thoughts.
What did I want? My hands are empty,
Feebly scrabbling at the distant bedspread.
What did I think? My mouth is dry, abstract.
What did I live? Ah, it would be so good to sleep!

112   [c. 1931]
In the dark and foolish fight
Between mere light and trade,

Let us at least shed some light
On the truth, which is this:

Since the average shopkeeper tends
To make a profit of one hundred percent
But protests at any increase
That he perceives as too scant.

And he will then loudly object
When the grandees turn thief,
And have the cheek to neglect
The retailers' customary deceit.

O Enlightened ones, why not then
Slap on two hundred percent!?
And thus bring to a swift, conclusive end
The quarrel between Mafia and Camorra ...

113   [c. 1931]

And yet, and yet,
There were swords and even colored flags
In my springtime dream of myself.
As well as hope
Bedewing the fields of my involuntary vision,
And there was even someone who smiled at me too.

Now I feel as if that someone had been someone else.
The person I was remembers me only as an add-on story.
The person I will be is, like the future of the world, of no interest to
        me.

I suddenly fell down the stairs,
And even the sound of me falling was the fall laughing.

Every step a harsh, importunate witness
To the ridiculous figure I cut.

Pity the poor fellow who lost the post offered to him because he
         didn't have a clean jacket to wear,
But pity, too, the fellow who, though rich and noble,
Lost the post offered by love because he wasn't wearing a decent
         jacket inside his affections.
I am as impartial as the snow.
I've never favored the poor over the rich,
Just as, in myself, I've never preferred one thing over another.

I always saw the world as being quite independent of me.
Behind this lay my own vivid feelings,
But that was another world.
And yet my grief never made me see what was orange as black.
First and foremost, the external world!
I just have to put up with myself and myselves.

114 [c. 1931]

The concentrated tumult of my intellectual imagination ...

Begetting children from practical reason, like vigorous believers ...

My perpetual youth
Of experiencing things as sensations rather than responsibilities,
Of [...]

(Álvaro de Campos, born in the Algarve, brought up by a great-uncle
         priest who instilled in him a certain love for things classical ...)
         (Came to Lisbon when he was very young ...)

The capacity to think what I feel, which distinguishes me from the
     ordinary man
More clearly than it distinguishes the ordinary man from the monkey.
(Yes, tomorrow the ordinary man might read my verses and under-
     stand the substance of my being,
Yes, I admit that,
But the monkey already knows how to read the ordinary man and to
     understand the substance of his being.)

If something once was why is it not still?
Isn't being being?

Will I not have the flowers of the field of my childhood eternally
But in a different way of being?
Will I lose for ever the affections I had, and even the affections I
     thought I had?
Is there someone who holds the key to the door of being, which has
     no door,
And who can unlock with pure reason the intelligence of the world?

115 [5 February 1932]

There are so few moments of pleasure in life ...
We must enjoy it while we can ... Yes, I've often heard this said;
I myself have said it. (To repeat is to live.)
Yes, we must enjoy it while we can, mustn't we?

Let's enjoy it, peroxide blonde, let's enjoy it, casual strangers,
You, with your movie-star gestures,
With your sideways glances at nothing at all,
Fulfilling your function as complicated animal,
I on the inclined plane between consciousness and indifference;
Let's love each other here and now. Time is only a day.

Let's savor the romanticism of it all!

Behind me, I am keeping watch, involuntarily.

I am someone or other in the words I say to you, and they are sweet words—the words you were hoping to hear.

On this side of my Alps, and what Alps they are! We belong to the body.

There's nothing to prevent this present brief encounter from becoming a future connection,

And everything trips along elegantly, like in Paris, London, Berlin.

"I can tell," you say, "that you've spent a lot of time abroad,"

And I feel rather proud to hear this!

My only fear is that you're going to talk to me about your life …

A cabaret in Lisbon? If so, then so be it.

I suddenly, visually, remember an ad in the paper

"Elegant society rendezvous,"

That's it.

But none of these bold, future thoughts

Interrupt the involuntary conversation in which I could be just anyone,

I'm talking averages and imitations

And I see and feel that you are beginning to like me more and more today.

It's at this point that, suddenly, leaning across the table,

I indiscreetly whisper in your ear precisely the right words.

You laugh, all meaningful glances and part effusive, available mouth.

And I really do like you.

There rings out in us the sexual signal that we should leave.

I turn my head to ask for the bill …

Joyful, jubilant, I touch you, and you speak …

I smile.

Behind the smile,

I am not me, […]

116

*Costa do Sol**

I

So many impressive things in the world.
As long as there are roses and blood,
Certain good moments are sure to occur
When things that are not-things happen.

My heart, a sudden jolt, or, rather,
A conscious interval. Slates now cover
Those who, like me, acted on impulse
And set off to vanquish the stubborn.

But the sky rocket is a symbol that rises
Only to fall, a stick-cadaver—
Having first made a racket up above—on the very person

Who launched it ... What the boy picks up
In the street—a charred stick—is all that's left of me ...
What absurd pyrotechnics propel it skywards?

II

O gods, I leave behind my former lady
(And I set down in a different hand
The absurdity of it all, and laugh because I suffer)
As I say: I drop the person I once loved, like a prefix ...

Once, when I was anonymous and prolix

* "Costa do Sol" here refers to the coastline to the west of Lisbon and the
seaside resorts of Cascais and Estoril.

(Two adjectives I've clung to for a long time)
I loved only so as to find a fellow loving heart,
Now I love what I love only because I pursue it.

Give me wine that Horace might have praised!
I want to forget the myness of mine ...
I want to advance without actually having to move.

I'm in Estoril looking up at the sky ...
Ah, it's still there, that triumphant blue
That once shone down on the Aegean sea.

III
We are the children of a springtime
Someone built out of bricks. When I think
I remove from my cigarette case a mysticism
That I light and smoke as if it wasn't mine.

In your air of being asleep in your chair
(I realize now, having performed the exorcism,
That this third sonnet rises up from the abyss)
You're always the same, anonymous—third ...

O great Atlantic Ocean, forgive me!
I spat out three sonnets on your shores.
Yes, but I spat them out on my own guilt.

Woman, love, chance—you are our shelter!
Only you, the sea and the sky, set us free,
For you blithely adorn any odd scrap of cloth.

———————————

Peace? That was long ago, never to return!
Dirceu's Marília was written in prison.

The only thing I have that is truly mine is me.
If only I could build a wall against the spy inside

(In its pale imperfect profile,
A dead silhouette against a living sky,
[...]

117   [15 December 1932]
Reality
Yes, twenty years ago, I often used to come here ...
Nothing has changed—not at least that I've noticed—
In this part of the city ...

Twenty years ago! ...
How different I was then! I was another person ...
Twenty years ago, and the houses know nothing of that ...

Twenty useless years (if they were useless!
What do I know about what's useful or useless?) ...
Twenty wasted years (but what would well-spent years be like?)

I try to reconstruct in my imagination
The person I was and what I was like when I used to pass by here
Twenty years ago ...
I don't remember, I can't remember.
If he existed now, that other person who came here then,
Perhaps he would remember ...
There are so many characters in novels that I know far better inside
Than I do the me who used to come here twenty years ago!

Yes, the mystery of time.
Yes, our not knowing anything,
Yes, our having all been born on board ship.
Yes, yes, all those things, or some other way of saying it ...

A girl slightly older than me—I distinctly remember she wore
    blue—used to lean out
From that second-floor window, which is still identical to itself,
What will be there now?
We can imagine everything of which we know nothing.
I am frozen physically and morally: I don't want to imagine any-
    thing ...

There was a day when I walked up this street thinking happily
    about the future,
Because God sheds a particularly bright light on what doesn't exist.
Today, walking down this same street I'm not even thinking happily
    about the past.
At best, I don't even think ...
I have the impression that those two people passed in the street, not
    then or now,
But right here, with no time to trouble their passing.
We eye each other indifferently.
And the former me walked up the street imagining a sunflower
    future.
And the modern me walked down the street not imagining anything.

Perhaps that really happened ...
Truly happened ...
Yes, carnally happened ...

Yes, perhaps ...

118   [c. 1932]

After all is done, sleep.
After all what is done?
After all that appears to be ...
This small provincial universe among the stars,

This little village in space,
And not just in visible space, but in all of space.

119 [c. 1932]

The Emigrés

Alone in the big unfriendly cities,
Unable to speak the language people speak in, let alone the one they
      think in,
Cut off from all relation with others,
They will later return home full of the triumphs of their visit.
Poor wretches who conquer London and Paris!
They return home with no better manners and no better faces,
They merely dreamed from close to what they saw—
Permanently foreign.
I'm not making fun of them though. Haven't I done just the same
      with the ideal?

And what about the plan I once drew up in a hotel, so seamless and
      coherent?
That is one of the stumbling blocks in the biography I did not have.

120 [c. 1932]

Poem in a Straight Line

I've never met anyone who took a beating.
All my acquaintances have been champions in everything.

And I, so often worthless, so often filthy, so often base,
I, so often unquestionably a parasite,
Inexcusably grubby,
I, who have so often lacked the patience to take a bath,
I, who have so often been ridiculous, absurd,
Who have publicly tripped over the carpets of etiquette,

Have been grotesque, mean-spirited, submissive, and arrogant,
Have been insulted and said nothing,
And whenever I did say something, have been even more ridiculous;
I, who have been the laughingstock of chambermaids,
I, who have felt errand boys exchanging mocking glances behind
      my back,
I, who have made shameful financial blunders, have borrowed
      money and never paid it back,
I, who, when a punch was coming, have crouched down
Out of range of that punch;
I, who have worried myself sick about tiny ridiculous things,
I can say that not a soul in the world can match me in this.

No one I know and no one I speak to
Has ever committed a single ridiculous act, has ever been insulted,
Was ever anything less than a prince—yes, they're all princes—in
      life ...

I just wish I could hear from someone the human voice
Confessing not to a sin, but to an infamous act;
Who would describe not an embarrassment, but an act of cowardice!
No, they are all the Ideal, according to what they say.
Is there anyone in this wide world who would admit he had ever
      behaved vilely?
My brothers are such princes.

Dammit, I've had enough of demigods!
Where are the real people in this world?

Am I then the only base, wrongheaded creature on the earth?

Women might not have loved them,
They might even have betrayed them—but ridiculous? Never!
And I, who have been ridiculous but never betrayed,

How can I speak to my superiors without trembling?
I, who have been base, literally base,
Base in the mean-spirited, despicable sense of baseness.

121 [c. 1932]

The human soul is as filthy as an asshole
And the Advantage of having a dick weighs in many imaginations.

————————————

My heart feels a distaste for everything, like an upset stomach.
The Round Table was sold off cheap,
And the biography of King Arthur was written by some gallant.
But the rust of chivalry
Still reigns in those souls, like a distant profile.

————————————

It's cold.
I put on the cape that reminds me of a shawl—
The shawl my aunt would put around my shoulders when I was a child.
But the shoulders of my childhood have vanished inside my present
        shoulders,
And my childhood heart has burrowed deep inside my present heart.

Yes, it's cold ...
It's cold in everything that I am, it's cold ...
Even my ideas are cold, like old people ...
And the cold I feel at the thought that my ideas are cold is even
        colder than them.
I wrap my cape closer about me ...
The Universe of people ... people ... everyone! ...
The multiplicity of motley humanity,
Yes, what we call life, as if there were no stars and planets ...
Yes, life ...

My shoulders droop so much that my cape slips off...
You want to help? Then put my cape straight, will you?

Ah, punch life in the face!
Free yourself and set your own quiet depths booming!

122   [c. 1932]
Scrap iron of the soul sold by the weight of the body,
If a crane lifts you up it is only in order to dump you...
No crane will lift you up except to cast you down.

Unwittingly I gaze analytically at what I unwittingly romanticize...

123   [c. 1932]
We all believe we will live after we are dead.
Our fear of death is the fear of being buried alive.
We want to keep close to us the corpses of those we loved
As if those corpses were still them
And not the great inner *maillot* given to us at birth.

124   [c. 1932]
What are we? Ships that pass one another in the night,
Each of us the life of those lines of brightly lit portholes
And each of us knowing of the other only that there is life within,
          nothing more.
Ships moving off, pinpointed with lights, into the darkness,
Each of us hesitantly, slowly disappearing into either side of the
          blackness,
Leaving only the silent night and the cold rising up from the waters.

125 [14 January 1933]

And the splendor of the maps, abstract paths into the concrete
    imagination,
Letters and irregular lines opening into the marvelous.

What dreams lie within those ancient bindings,
In the complicated (or else lean and simple) signatures on those old
    books.
(Remote, faded ink present here and now beyond death,
O visible enigma of time, the living void in which we exist!)
What a rebuttal to our daily lives is there in those illustrations,
How certain advertisements unwittingly advert.

Everything that suggests, or expresses what it does not express,
Everything that says what it does not say,
And the soul dreams on, different and distracted.

126 [c. 29 January 1933]

In my old aunts' spacious dining room
The clock ticktocked away the time more slowly.
Ah, the horror of the happiness you didn't know
Because you knew it without knowing it,
The horror of what was, because what is here is here.
Tea and toast in the provinces of another time
In how many cities have I thought of you and wept!
Eternally a child,
Eternally abandoned,
Ever since my heart lacked that tea and toast.

Warm yourself, my heart!
Warm yourself on the past,
Because the present is only a street walked by those who forget me ...

127   [c. 15 March 1933]

I think of you in the silence of the night, when everything is nothing,
And out of the sounds that exist in the silence comes the silence,
Then, alone in myself, a passenger failing to depart
On a journey in God, I pointlessly think of you.

The whole past, when you were an eternal moment,
Is like this silence of everything.
All that is lost, when you were what I most lost,
Is like those sounds,
All that is futile, when you were what was not to be,
Is like the nothing to come in this nocturnal silence.

I have seen die, or else heard that they are dying,
All those I loved or knew,
I have seen and heard nothing more from all the many who were once
With me, and it matters little if they were a person or a conversation,
Or a whole race omitted from the world,
And for me today the world is a cemetery at night
The white and black of graves and trees and of a strange moonlight
And this absurd peace inside me and inside all my thoughts of you.

128   [2 May 1933]

Pack your bags for Nowhere!
Set off for the negative universality of everything
With all flags flying on those pretend ships—
The small, multicolored ships of childhood!
Pack your bags for the Great Leaving Behind!
And don't forget, among the brushes and the scissors,
The polychrome distance of what cannot be had.
Pack your bags once and for all!
What are you doing here, where you live a useless, gregarious life—
The more useful the more useless—
And the truer the more false—

244

What are you doing here? What are you doing here? What are you
    doing here?
Set off, even without your bags, for your diverse self!
Isn't the only inhabited land the land that isn't where you are?

129   [7 November 1933]

Psychetypia
Symbols. Everything is symbols ...
Yes, perhaps everything is symbols ...
Are you a symbol too?

Exiled from you, I look at your white hands
Placed, with good English manners, on the tablecloth,
Like people quite independent of you ...
I look at them: are they symbols too?
So is the whole world just symbol and magic?
Perhaps it is ...
And why not?

Symbols ...
I'm tired of thinking ...
I finally raise my eyes to your eyes, which are looking at me.
You smile, knowing full well what I'm thinking ...
Good grief, and yet you don't know ...
I was thinking about symbols ...
I reply frankly to your conversation over the table ...
"It was very strange, wasn't it?"
"Awfully strange. And how did it end?"
"Well, it didn't end. It never does, you know."
Yes, *you know* ... I know ...
Yes, I know ...
That's the problem with symbols, *you know.*
Yes, I know.
A perfectly normal conversation ... But what about the symbols?

MAGNIFICAT

Quando e´que passará esta noite interna, o universo,
E eu, a minha alma, terei o meu dia?
Quando é que dispertarei de estar accordado?
Não sei. O sol brilha alto,
Impossivel de fitar.
As estrellas pestanejam frio,
Impossiveis de contar.
O coração pulsa alheio,
Impossivel de escutar.
Quando é que passará este drama sem theatro,
Ou este theatro sem drama,
E recolherei a casa?
Onde? Como? Quando?
Gato que me fitas com olhos de vida, Quem tens lá no fundo?
É Esse! É esse!
Esse mandará como Jesué parar o sol e eu accordarei;
E então será dia.
Sorri, dormindo, minha alma!
Sorri, minha alma, será dia!

                                        Alvaro de Campos

7-11-1933.

"Magnificat"

I can't take my eyes off your hands ... Who are they?
Good grief! Symbols ... Symbols ...

130   [7 November 1933]

Magnificat
When will this inner night, the universe, pass,
And when will I, my soul, have my day?
When will I wake from being awake?
I don't know. The sun is shining on high,
Impossible to look at.
The stars blink coldly,
Impossible to count.
My heart beats on obliviously,
Impossible to hear.
When will this drama-without-theater pass,
Or this theater-sans-drama,
And when will I go home?
Where? How? When?
Cat looking at me with the eyes of life,
What lies deep inside you?
That's the One! That's the One!
That's the One who, like Joshua, will order the sun to stop, and I
        will wake up:
And then it will be day.
Smile, my sleeping soul!
Smile, my soul; it will be day!

131   [7 December 1933]

Original Sin
Ah, who will write the history of what might have been?
If anyone does write it, that will be
The true history of humanity.

Only the real world exists, not us, but the world;
We are what does not exist, and that is the truth.

I am who I failed to be.
We are all who we supposed ourselves to be.
Our reality is what we never achieved.

What has become of our truth—the dream at the window of
    childhood?
What has become of our certainty—the plan drawn up at the desk
    of later on?

Sitting sideways on a chair, after supper,
I'm thinking, my head resting on my hands
On the high sill of the balcony window.

What became of my reality if I only have life?
What became of me, if all I am is this person who exists?

How many Caesars I was!

In my soul, and with a little truth;
In my imagination, and with some justice;
In my intelligence, and with some reason—
My God! my God! my God!—
How many Caesars I was!
How many Caesars I was!
How many Caesars I was!

132   [19 December 1933]
Typewriting
Alone in my cramped engineer's office, I am drawing up the plan,
I am devising the project, here, cut off,
Remote even from who I am.

Beside me, a banally sinister accompaniment,
The staccato tic-tac of the typewriters.

How repugnant life is!
How abject this regularity!
How sleep-inducing just being like this!

Once, when I was another person, it was all castles and knights
(Illustrations, perhaps, from some childhood book),
Once, when I was true to my dream,
It was vast landscapes from the North, explicit beneath the snow,
It was vast palm trees in the south, opulent in their greenness.

Once ...

Beside me, a banally sinister accompaniment,
The staccato tic-tac of the typewriters.

We all have two lives:
The real one, which is the one we dreamed when we were children,
And which we continue to dream as adults, in a substratum of mist;
The false one is the life we live in the company of others,
Which is the practical, the useful life,
The one where they end up putting us in a coffin.

In the other life there are no coffins, no deaths.
There are only illustrations from childhood:
Big colored books, to look at rather than read;
Big colorful pages to remember later on.
In that other life, we are us,
In that other life, we live;
In this one we die, which is what living means.
In this moment, out of sheer disgust, I am living only in that other
        life ...

249

But beside me, a banally sinister accompaniment,
If I stop meditating and wake up,
The staccato tic-tac of the typewriters raises its voice.

133 [c. 1933]
And the solitary sound of the clock seems louder
In the evening with no one here from a provincial dining room,
All of time sits perched on top of my soul,
And as long as I sit here waiting for my old aunts to serve tea
My heart hears time passing and suffers with me.

It's a more somnolent tick-tock than that of other clocks—
A wooden wall clock, this one has a pendulum that swings.
My heart yearns for quite what I don't know.
I will die.—
A firm, mechanical tick-tock—yes, even clocks in the provinces …

134 [c. 1933]
But it isn't just the corpse
This horrible person who is now no one,
This abyssal contrast with their usual body,
This stranger who appears through absence in the person we knew,
This abyss that exists between seeing and believing—
It isn't only the corpse that pierces the soul with fear,
That imposes silence deep in the heart,
The usual external belongings of the person who died
Also trouble the soul, but there's more tenderness in the fear.
Even if those things belonged to an enemy,
Who can look, unmoved, at the desk where he used to sit,
The pen he used to write with?
Who can see without a twinge of anguish

The rifle of the hunter who has vanished without it, to the great
    relief of all the surrounding hills?
The dead beggar's jacket, into whose pockets he would once plunge
    his hands (now for ever absent).
The dead child's toys, horribly tidied away,
All this weighs on me suddenly in my estranged mind
And a yearning the size of death strikes fear into my whole soul …

135   [c. 1933]
Let us enter death gaily! To hell
With having to wear a suit, having to wash our body,
Having to display reason, opinions, manners, and mores;
Having kidney, liver, lungs, bronchial tubes, teeth,
Things that bring pain and blood and problems
(To hell with all of that!)

I'm dead anyway, of sheer tedium,
I bump my head on the stars, laughing,
As if I'd bumped it on the carnival bunting
Strung from one side of the corridor to the other,
I will depart clothed in stars; with the sun instead of a bowler hat
In the great Carnival of the space between God and life.

My body is my underwear; what do I care
If its trashy nature should become earth in the tomb,
If the organic moth nibbles away at it all?
I am I.
Long live me because I am dead. Hurrah!
I am I.
What do I care about the clothes-corpse I leave behind?
What does our ass have to do with our trousers?
After all, won't we have underpants in infinity?

Won't the world beyond the stars give me another shirt?
Nonsense, there must be shops in God's broad streets.

I, amazing and unhuman,
Indistinguishable from the bright sphinxes.

I'm going to wrap myself in stars
And wear the Sun like a bowler hat
In the great postmortem carnival.
I will climb, like a fly or a monkey, up the solid wall
Of the vast arching sky of the world,
Enlivening the monotony of those abstract spaces
With the sheer subtlety of my presence.

136   [12 April 1934]

Wouldn't it be better
Not to do anything?
To let everything go tumbling down the hill of life
To a waterless shipwreck?

Wouldn't it be better
To pick not a single rose
From our dreamed-of rosebushes,
And lie quietly, thinking about the exile of others,
Of the springtimes to come?

Wouldn't it be better
To renounce, like the bursting of a popular balloon
In a party atmosphere,
Everything,
Yes, everything,
Absolutely everything?

137   [12 April 1934]
They put a lid on me—
The whole sky.
They put a lid on me.

What great aspirations!
What magnificent triumphs!
Some of them real …
But they put a lid
On all of them.
As they used to do on one of those old-fashioned chamberpots—
In the remote traditions of the provinces …
A lid.

138   [11 May 1934]
Lisbon with its houses
Of various colors,
Lisbon with its houses
Of various colors,
Lisbon with its houses
Of various colors …
By trying to be different, it succeeds only in being monotonous,
Just as by trying to feel, I do nothing but think.

If, at night, lying in bed but awake
In the futile lucidity of being unable to sleep,
I try to imagine one particular thing,
Something else always surfaces (because I'm sleepy,
And because I'm sleepy, a bit of dream slips in),
I may want to gaze in my imagination
Upon vast fantastical groves of palm trees,
But all I can see,

In a kind of inside-eyelids view,
Is Lisbon with its houses
Of various colors.

I smile, because here, lying down, it's quite different.
By trying to be monotonous, it succeeds in being different.
And by trying to be me, I fall asleep and forget that I exist.

All that remains, without the me I forgot because I fell asleep,
Is Lisbon and its houses
Of various colors.

139 [16 June 1934]

This old anxiety,
The anxiety I've carried around inside me for ages now,
Has overflowed the glass,
In tears, in great imaginings,
In dreams like nightmares without the fear,
In great sudden emotions that make no sense at all.

It overflowed.
I barely know how to behave in life
With this malaise making creases in my soul!
If only I could at least go properly mad!
But no: I'm stuck in this state of in-betweenness,
This almost,
This might-be … ,
This.

A patient in a lunatic asylum is at least someone.
I'm a patient in a lunatic asylum but without the lunatic asylum.
I'm rationally mad,
I'm both lucid and loony,
I'm indifferent to everything and the same as everyone:

I'm asleep wide awake with dreams that are utter madness
Because they're not dreams at all.
That's what I'm like ...

Alas, poor old house of my lost childhood!
Who would have thought you could so cast me out!
What became of your little boy? He's mad.
What became of the child who slept peacefully beneath your pro-
     vincial roof?
He's mad.
What became of the person I was? He's mad. He's now the person I
     am.
If I at least had some religion!
Could believe, for example, in that wooden idol
We had in the house, that house, brought from Africa.
It was incredibly ugly, grotesque.
But it was divine in the way all things are if someone believes in them.
If I could believe in such an idol—
Jupiter, Jehovah, Humanity—
Anything would do,
After all what is everything but what we think of it?

Shatter, O my stained-glass heart!

140   [16 June 1934]
There's always such happiness
In the house opposite mine and my dreams!

I don't know the people there, well, I've both seen and not seen them.
They're happy because they're not me.

The children who play on the high balconies
Live among pots of flowers,
Doubtless eternally.

The voices that emerge from that domestic interior
Are doubtless always singing,
Yes, they must be.

When there's a celebration out in the street, there's a celebration
        inside.
That's how it should be when all is in place—
Man to Nature, because the city is Nature.

What a joy not to be me!

Won't the others feel the same?
What others? There are no others.
What others feel is a house with the windows closed.
Or, when the windows open,
It's so that the children can play behind the balcony railings,
Among pots of flowers too far away for me to identify.

The others never feel.
We are the only ones who feel,
Yes, all of us,
Even I, who, at this moment, feel nothing.

Nothing? I'm not so sure …
A nothing that hurts …

141   [4 July 1934]
I got off the train,
Said goodbye to my traveling companion,
After spending eighteen hours together.
A pleasant conversation,
The fraternity of travel,
I was sorry to get off the train, to leave him.
A chance friend whose name I never knew.

I felt my eyes well up with tears …
Yes, every goodbye is a death.
We, in the train we call life,
Are all chance acquaintances,
And are all sad when we must finally get off.
Everything human moves me, because I am human.
Everything moves me, because I have,
Not shared ideas or doctrines,
But a vast fraternity with real humanity.

———————

The maid who was sorry to leave,
And wept nostalgically
For the house where she'd been rather shabbily treated …

All of this is there in my heart, the death and the sadness of leaving,
All of this lives, because it dies, inside my heart.

And my heart is a little larger than the entire universe.

142 [19 July 1934]

Music, yes, music …
The banal sounds of a piano coming from upstairs …
It's still music, though, music … .
The kind that comes in search of the immanent tears
Of any human creature,
That comes to trouble our calm,
Wanting to achieve a better calm …
Music … a piano being played upstairs
By someone who plays badly …
But it's still music …

Ah, how many childhoods I had!
How many good sorrows!

Music …
How many more good sorrows!
Always music …
The poor piano played by someone who can't play.
And yet despite all, it's still music.

Ah, she finally managed a whole tune—
A rational melody—
Rational, dear God!
As if anything were rational!
What new landscapes emerge from a badly played piano!
Music! … Music!

143   [9 August 1934]

It's beginning to be midnight, all is almost quiet,
In the various households piled one on top of the other,
The various stories of accumulated life …

The piano on the third floor has fallen silent …
I can no longer hear footsteps on the second floor …
On the ground floor, the radio has gone silent …

Everything is falling asleep …

I'm left alone with the entire universe.
I don't even want to go over to the window:
If I look out, what a multitude of stars!
What still greater silences exist up above!
What a very un-urban sky! …

Instead, closeted away
In a desire not to be closeted away,

I listen eagerly for the noises from the street ...
An automobile—driving much too fast!—

Two pairs of footsteps talking fill me with life ...
The sound of a door slamming hurts me ...

Everything is falling asleep ...

Only I am watching, sleepily listening ...
Waiting
For something before I drift off ...
Something ...

144   [9 August 1934]

On Sunday I will go to the vegetable gardens in the person of others,
Content in my anonymity.
On Sunday I will be happy—they, they ...
Sunday ...
Today is the Thursday of the week that has no Sunday ...
No Sunday ...
Never Sunday ...
But there will always be someone in the vegetable gardens this
        Sunday.
That's life,
Especially for anyone who feels,
More or less for anyone who thinks:
There will always be someone in the vegetable gardens on Sunday ...
Not on our Sunday,
Not on my Sunday,
Not on Sunday ...
But there will always be someone clse in the vegetable gardens next
        Sunday ...

145

For ages now, I've felt unable
To write a long poem!...
Years...

I've lost the gift of the rhythmic development
That allows the idea and the form,
In a union of body and soul,
To move as one.

I've lost everything that made me conscious...
What remains to me today
Of some kind of certainty in my being?...
The sun that appears without being summoned by me...
The day that required no effort on my part...
A breeze, or the lack of one,
That makes me conscious of the air...
And the domestic egotism of wanting nothing more than that.

Ah, my *Triumphal Ode*,
Your rectilinear movement!
Ah, my *Maritime Ode*,
Your general structure in strophe, antistrophe, and epode!
And the plans I had, the plans—
Those were the truly great odes!
And that last one, the final, supreme, impossible ode!

146

Patiently,
Incuriously,
Inattentively,
I see the crochet that with your two hands you are
Making.

I see it from the top of a nonexistent hill,
Stitch after stitch creating the fabric ...

What lies behind the impulse to keep
Hands and soul busy, the soul, that insubstantial thing
Through which you could poke a spent match?

Then again
What lies behind my impulse to criticize you?

Nothing.
I have my own *crochet*.
It dates back to when I began to think ...
Stitch after stitch forming a whole that's never whole ...
A piece of fabric that might be for a dress or for nothing at all, I
        don't know ...
A soul that might be for feeling with or for living, I don't know ...
I'm looking at you so intently
That I don't even notice you .....

Crochet, souls, philosophies ...
All the religions of the world ...
Anything that helps fill the evening of being ourselves ...
Two pieces of ivory, a stitch, silence ...

147   [16 August 1934]
I took off the mask and saw myself in the mirror ...
I was the child I'd been years ago ...
I hadn't changed at all ...

That's the advantage of being able to remove the mask.
One is always the child,
The past that remains,
The child.

I took off the mask, then put it on again.
It's better like that.
That way I am the mask.

And I return to *normality* as if to a tram terminus.

148 [16 August 1934]

... Just as, on days when important events are going on in the city
    center,
In the near-outskirts conversations in doorways fall silent ...
Groups stand round expectantly ...
No one knows anything.
The slightest trace of a breeze ...
Nothing real
And which, like a caress or a breath,
Touches what is there, brings it to life ...
The magnificence of spontaneity
Heart ...
What extraordinary Africas lie in each and every desire!
What far better things lie in the here and now!

My elbow touches that of the woman sitting next to me on the tram
Clumsily, unwittingly,
A short circuit of proximity ...
Chance ideas
Like an overturned bucket ...

I stare at it: it is an overturned bucket ...

It lies there: I lie there ...

149   [5 September 1934]

After not having slept,
After no longer feeling sleepy,
An interminable dawn when one always thinks without thinking,
I watched the day come
Like the most dreadful of curses—
A condemnation to still more of the same.
And yet what a wealth of blue, green, and yellow gilded with red
In the eternally distant sky—
In that orient others have spoiled
By saying it was the birthplace of civilizations;
In that orient stolen from us
By some shaggy-dog story of solar myths.
The marvelous orient with no civilizations or myths,
Simply sky and light,
Immaterial matter …
All light, and yet
The shadow, which is the light night gives to day,
Sometimes fills, with unmatched spontaneity,
The great silence of the wheat field when no wind is blowing,
The faded greenery of the fields far off,
Life and the feeling of life.
The morning inundates the whole city.
O my eyes heavy with the sleep you did not enjoy,
What morning will inundate what lies behind you,
What are you,
What am I?

150   [27 September 1934]

On the eve of never leaving
At least there's no need to pack your bags
Or draw up any plans,

With the unconscious accompaniment of things forgotten,
For what has become the free time of the following day.

There's nothing to do
On the eve of never leaving.

Ah, the relief of not even having anything
To feel relieved about!
Ah, the peace of mind of not even needing to shrug your shoulders
Because you have passed through tedium, poor tedium,
And deliberately arrived at nothing at all.
Ah, the joy of not needing to be joyful,
Like an opportunity turned inside out.

For months now I've been living
The vegetative life of the mind!
Every day lived *sine linea* ...

Such a relief, yes, relief ...
Such peace of mind ...
Such repose after so many journeys, physical and psychical!
Such power being able to look at my packed suitcases as if they were
        nothing!
Go to sleep, soul, sleep!
Make the most of it and sleep!
Sleep!

And you have so little time! Sleep.
It's the eve of never leaving ...

151   [9 October 1934]
What I feel above all is weariness—
Not about this or that,

Nor even about everything or nothing:
Just weariness itself,
Weariness.

The subtlety of futile feelings,
Violent passions about nothing at all,
Intense love for some imagined quality in someone,
All those things—
Those things and what is eternally absent from them—;
All this makes for weariness,
This weariness,
Weariness.

There are doubtless those who love the infinite,
There are doubtless those who desire the impossible,
There are doubtless those who want nothing—
Three types of idealist, and I am none of them:
Because I feel infinite love for the finite,
Because I feel impossible desire for the possible,
Because I love everything, or even a little more than everything
        were that feasible,
Or even if it wasn't …
And the result?
They have the life lived or dreamed.
They have the dream dreamed or lived,
They have the halfway point between everything and nothing,
        namely, life …
All I have is a great, profound,
And, ah, happily infecund weariness,
The supremissimo of all wearinesses,
Issimo, issimo, issimo,
Weariness …

152

So many contemporary poems!
So many bang-up-to-date poets—
All interesting, all of them interesting ...
Ah, but it's all only almost ...
It's all vestibule
It's all just so as to write something ...
Without art
Without science
Without genuine nostalgia ...
This one closely observed the silence of that cypress tree ...
That one clearly saw the sunset behind the cypress ...
That other one was keenly aware of the emotion aroused by all this
     ...
But then? ...
Ah, my poets, my poets—but then?
The worst is always that "but then" ...
Because in order to speak you have to think—
To think with your second thought—
And you, my friends, poets, and poems,
Think only with the rudimentary rapidity of desire—that of the
     pen—
Better the guaranteed classic,
Better the constant sonnet,
Better anything, however bad,
Than the as yet unbuilt suburbs of something really good ...
"But I have my soul!"
No, no you don't: you have the feeling of having a soul.
Beware of sensation!
It often belongs to others,
And is often only ours
By the dizzying accident of us feeling it ...

153
You rose to glory by going down the stairs.
A paradox? No: reality.
Words are the real paradox.
The reality is what you are!
You rose by going downwards.
That's fine.
Perhaps I'll do the same tomorrow.
For now, maybe I envy you,
I don't know if I envy you the victory,
I don't know if I envy you for achieving victory,
But I genuinely believe that I do envy you ...
Victory is victory after all ...
Wrap me up in a parcel
Then throw me in the river.
And don't forget that "maybe" when you do so.
That's important.
Don't forget that "maybe."
That's the important thing.
Because everything is maybe ...

154   [18 December 1934]
Symbols? I'm fed up with symbols ...
Some tell me everything is a symbol.
None of them tell me anything.

What symbols! Dreams ....
Let's say the sun is a symbol, fine ...
Let's say the moon is a symbol, fine ...
Let's say the earth is a symbol, fine ...
But who notices the sun except when the rain stops
And the sun breaks through the clouds and points behind it

To the blue of the sky?
Who notices the moon except to admire
The light it sheds, rather than the moon itself?
Who notices the earth beneath their feet?
They call earth the fields, the trees, the hills
Out of an instinctively reductive tendency,
Because the sea is also the earth ...

All right, fine, let's say all those things are symbols ...
But what is symbolic about, not the sun, not the moon, not the earth,
But this precocious sunset, gradually unblueing itself,
The sun among the fading scraps of clouds,
While the moon can already be seen, mystical, on the other side,
And what remains of the light of day
Gilds the head of a seamstress who happens to pause vaguely on the
    corner
Where she once used to linger (she lives close by) with the lover
    who left her?

Symbols? ... I don't want symbols ...
All I want—poor thin, helpless figure!—
Is for the seamstress's lover to come back.

155   [18 December 1934]
I sometimes have really good ideas,
Really good ideas out of nowhere, in the form of ideas
And the words in which they naturally express themselves ...

After writing, I read what I wrote ...
Why did I write this?
How did I think of that?
Where did that come from? This is better than me ...

In this world, are we merely pens full of ink
With which someone actually writes what we set down on paper?*

156   [20 December 1934]
The house had no electricity.
That's why it was by the light of a flickering candle
That I used to read, tucked up in bed,
Whatever there was to read—
The Bible in Portuguese because (oddly enough) they were
        Protestants.
And I reread the First Epistle to the Corinthians.
All around me the excessive peace and quiet of provincial nights
Would, on the contrary, be making a tremendous racket,
And I would feel like weeping out of sheer desolation.
The First Epistle to the Corinthians ...
I reread it by the light of a candle grown suddenly very ancient,
And a great sea of emotion would be weeping inside me ...

I'm nothing ...
I'm a fiction ...

What do I want of myself or of anything else in the world?
"If I have not charity" ...
And the sovereign voice sends down through all the centuries
The great message that will set the soul free ...
"If I have not charity" ...
Dear God, and what will become of me, for I have no charity! ...

* In the top lefthand corner, the author added this note in Portuguese: "To the
memory of Soame Jenyns, whom I thought of after writing this poem."

157

No: slowly.
Slowly, because I don't know
Where I want to go.
There is between myself and my steps
An instinctive divergence.

There is between who I am and what I am
A grammatical difference
That corresponds to reality.

Slowly …
Yes, slowly …
I want to think about what
That slowly means …

Maybe the outside world is in too much of a hurry.
Maybe the ordinary soul wants to get there too early.
Maybe the impression left by the moments is too close …
Maybe all of those things …
But what preoccupies me is that word: slowly …
What is it that must be slow?
Perhaps it's the universe …
God commands that the truth be told.
But has anyone ever heard such a thing from God?

158

"Don't you know that song, Mr. Engineer?"
"What song, woman? … "
"That really old one. So you don't know it?
The one that goes—
              All night long the rain kept falling"
"Yes, I remember it now, but go away, will you?"

"Yes, I remember."
Do I remember?
I know that I remember now.
I know that now I remember all possible life
The real one, the essential one
The one in which
        All night long the rain kept falling
        On the little gargoyles in the square ...
How should I know (O my heart) what "little gargoyles in the square"
      means!
But what did that universal *musique de fond*
Mean to me?
And so
        All night long the rain kept falling
        On the little gargoyles in the square ...

And here I am, here, here,
Definitively here!
Irremediably here!

Where is that square?
Where is that night?
Where is that rain?
And you, Senhora Dona Maria,
And you, and you, and your small carnation-red mouth?

I've suffered many bouts of weariness
Full of vague hopes for some kind of future.
I've often slept out in the open,
Exposed to all dreams ...
I've been useless, coarse, inconsistent—
Just like everything else out there, namely life.
I have been all those futile nothings.

Senhora Dona Maria,
Were I to meet you one day,
Ah, how I would love you!
And with all the love of those who loved without a future!
But when does it rain all night
On the little gargoyles in the square?
When? And where? Where?
Small carnation-red mouth?

It was you, it was you, the one I always loved!
But I didn't know your name—I know now.
I didn't know what you were like—I know now …
Senhora Dona Maria
Small carnation-red mouth
I know you better now, but I'm no nearer to you.
I lose you all the more because I met you.

159   [3 January 1935 *first this year**]

The ancients used to invoke the Muses.
We invoke ourselves.
I don't know if the Muses ever appeared—
That would presumably depend on who was invoked and on the
      invocation—
But I do know that we do not appear.

How often have I leaned over the edge
Of the well I imagine myself to be
And hollered "Ho!" just to hear an echo,
And heard nothing, only seen what I could see—
The vague, darkly bright glow of the water
Down in the pointless depths.
No echo for me …

* The note following the date was written in English.

Only very vaguely a face, which must be mine because it can't be
    anyone else's.
Almost invisible,
Except as it rises luminously up
From below ...
In the silence and the false light of the deep ...

Some Muse!...

160   [5 January 1935]
I've been sitting at my desk
For more than half an hour
With the sole aim
Of looking at it.

(These verses are out of my usual rhythm.
I, too, am out of my usual rhythm.)

An inkwell (large) before me.
Pencils with shavings further off.
Closer to me some very clean paper.
To the left a volume of the Encyclopaedia Britannica.
To the right—
Ah, to the right!—
The paper knife that I couldn't be bothered to use
Yesterday to cut all the pages
Of the book I'm interested in, but won't read.

If only someone could hypnotize all this!

161   [3 January 1935]
After I had stopped thinking about afterwards
My life became much calmer—

273

That is, less life.
I became instead my own muted accompaniment.

I look out, from the height of my low window,
At the girls playing and dancing in the street.
Their inevitable fate
Pains me.
I can see it in the dress that's come unbuttoned at the back, and it
    pains me.

O great steamroller, who told you to steamroll this street
Which is paved with souls?

(But your voice interrupts me
—A loud voice, coming from outside in the park, a girl's voice—
And it's as if I'd
Irresolutely dropped a book on the floor.)

In this dance of life, my love,
Which we perform spontaneously, just for fun,
Do we not wear the same unbuttoned dresses
And the same neckline revealing the skin beneath the grubby shirt?

162   [4 January 1935]

I, I myself …
I, full of all the wearinesses
The world can offer …
I …

Everything, in short, since everything is I,
And even the stars, it seems,
I plucked from my pocket to dazzle children …
Which children I don't know …

I...

Imperfect? Unknown? Divine?
I don't know.
I...

Did I have a past? Of course ...
Do I have a present? Of course ...
Will I have a future? Of course,
Even though it might stop shortly ...
But I, I ...
I am I,
I remain I ...
I...

163 [5 January 1935]

I don't know if the stars dictate what happens in this world,
Nor if the cards—
Playing cards or Tarot cards—
Can reveal anything.

I don't know if throwing the dice
Helps you arrive at some conclusion.
Nor do I know
If anything is achieved
by living like most ordinary men.

No, I don't know
If I should believe in this everyday sun,
Whose authenticity no one can guarantee,
Or if it would be better, better or more comfortable,
To believe in some other sun—
One that sheds its light even at night,

Or in the luminous profundity of things
Of which I understand nothing ...

Meanwhile ...
(Let's go slowly)
Meanwhile
The banister on the stairs is absolutely solid,
I grip it firmly with my hand—
The banister that does not belong to me
And on which I lean as I ascend ...
Yes ... ascend ...
I ascend to this thought:
I don't know if the stars dictate what happens in this world ...

164   [12 January 1935]
Ah! To be indifferent!
For it's from the lofty power of their indifference
That the bosses of the bosses rule the world.

Oh to be oblivious even to oneself!
It's from that lofty sense of obliviousness
That the teachers of saints rule the world.

Oh to forget that one even exists!
It's from the lofty idea of that forgetting
That the gods of the gods rule the world.

(I didn't hear what you were saying ...
I could hear only the music, and I didn't even hear that ...
Were you playing and speaking at the same time?
Yes, I think you were playing and speaking at the same time ...
Who with?
With someone in whom everything ended with the world falling
     asleep ...)

165 [c. March 1935]

My heart, that deluded admiral,
Commander of an imaginary fleet,
Attempted a route denied him by Fate,
Wanting to be happy when he could not.

And thus, prolix, absurd, permanently postponed,
Resigned to the results of a life of abstention,
No, not resigned, not resigned, not resigned,
As that repetitive line attests.

For in the shadow and silence of defeat
There are compensations that absolve,
Heaping more roses on the soul than victories.

Thus the fleet emerged, imperial,
Laden with yearnings and glories,
And allowed the admiral to follow his chosen route.

166 [5 March 1935]

Yes, everything's just fine.
Everything is perfectly fine.
The trouble is that it's not.
I know this house is painted gray
I know the number of this house—
I don't know what it's worth, although I could find out
From those tax offices that exist for that purpose—
I know, I know …
But the trouble is there are souls inside
And the Treasury completely failed to exempt
My next-door neighbor from losing her son.
The Department-of-something-or-other couldn't avoid
The husband of my upstairs neighbor running off with his sister-in-
    law …

But, needless to say, everything's fine ...
And, except for the fact that it's not, it is: it's perfectly fine ...

167   [24 June 1935]

I'm tired, of course,
Because there comes a point when we do feel tired.
I'm not sure what it is I'm tired of.
And there'd be no point in knowing
Because the tiredness would be just the same,
The wound hurts the way it hurts
And not according to the thing that caused it.

Yes, I'm tired,
And rather cheered
That this is all that tiredness is—
A desire for sleep in the body,
A desire not to think in the soul,
And above all a lucid tranquility
Of retrospective understanding ...

And the silent luxury of abandoning all hopes?

I'm intelligent, that's all.
I've seen a lot and I've really understood what I've seen,
And there is a certain pleasure even in the tiredness that this brings,
Because at least the head serves some purpose in life.

168   [6 July 1935]

I'm not thinking about anything
And that central thing, which is nothing at all,
Is as pleasing to me as the night air,
Cool in contrast to the hot summer of the day.

I'm not thinking about anything, how nice!

Thinking about nothing
Means having your entire soul to yourself.
Thinking about nothing
Means living intensely
The ebb and flow of life ...

I'm not thinking about anything.
Or only, as if I'd slept in the wrong position,
A pain in my back, or one side of my back,
There's a bitter taste in my soul:
But, when all's said and done,
I'm not thinking about anything,
Really nothing,
Nothing ...

169 [28 August 1935]

The sleep descending on me,
The mental sleep descending physically on me,
The universal sleep descending individually on me—
This sleep
Might seem to others to be the sleep of sleeping,
The sleep of wanting to sleep,
The sleep of being sleep.
But it's more than that, it comes more from inside, more from above:
It's the sleep of the sum of all disillusionments,
It's the sleep of the synthesis of all despairs,
It's the sleep of there being a whole world inside me
Without my having contributed to it at all.

And yet the sleep descending on me
Is like all sleep.

The tiredness is at least gentle,
The exhaustion is at least restful,
The surrender is at least an end to effort,
The end is at least no longer having to hope.

There's the sound of a window opening,
I look indifferently to the left
Over the shoulder that's hearing the sound,
I look out of the half-open window:
The girl who lives on the second floor of the house opposite
Is leaning out, her blue eyes looking for someone.
Who?
Asks my indifference.
And all of this is sleep.

Good God, so much sleep! ...

170   [c. September 1935]

Good health to all those who want to be happy:
Health and stupidity!

––––––––––––––––

This business of having nerves
Or having intelligence
Or even thinking that we have one or the other
Will come to an end one day ...
Will definitely come to an end
If authoritarian governments have their way.

171   [12 September 1935]

I feel dizzy,
Dizzy from sleeping so much and thinking so much,

Or from both those things.
All I know is that I feel dizzy
And I don't quite know whether I should get up from my chair
Or how I could get up.
Let's settle for this: I feel dizzy.

After all
What life did I make of life?
Nothing.
Only interstices,
Only approximations,
Only what emerged from the irregular and the absurd,
Only nothing …
That's why I'm feeling dizzy …

Now
Every morning I wake up
Feeling dizzy …
Yes, really dizzy …
Not even knowing my own name,
Not even knowing where I am,
Not even knowing what I was,
Not knowing anything.

But if that's the way it is, so be it.
Let me stay in my chair.

I feel dizzy.
Fine, I feel dizzy.
I'll just sit here
And feel dizzy,
Yes, dizzy,
Dizzy …
Dizzy …

All love letters are
Ridiculous.
They wouldn't be love letters if they weren't
Ridiculous.

I've also written love letters in my time,
Equally
Ridiculous.

Love letters, where love exists,
Are inevitably
Ridiculous.

In the end, though,
It's the creatures who've never written
Love letters
Who are truly
Ridiculous.

If only I'd known this
In the days when I wrote
Love letters that were
Of course
Ridiculous.

The truth is that today,
It's my memories
Of those love letters
That are
Ridiculous.

(All eccentric words

Like all eccentric sentiments,*
Are naturally
Ridiculous.)

173   [3 February 1935†]

Homecoming
It's been ages since I wrote a sonnet.
No matter: I'm writing one now.
Sonnets are childhood and, at this hour,
My childhood is a mere black dot,

Which throws me off the train-that-I-am,
As it follows its fatal, frozen course.
And the sonnet is like some strange man
Who's spent the last two days inside my thoughts.

Fortunately, I do still know that I have
Fourteen lines, neither more nor less,
So that people will know where they are ...

Where they are, or I am, I don't know ...
I don't wish to know that or anything else,
And don't give a damn for what I will one day know.

* The word *exdrúxulo* (*esdrúxulo* in modern spelling) refers to words with
the stress on the penultimate syllable, but it is also used colloquially to mean
strange, eccentric. —Trs.
† Next to the title, written in English: "(End of Book)." This poem was likely
projected as the last poem for *Álvaro de Campos's Book of Verses*.

A. de Campos

Repom os dois. (and the text)

Ha quanto tempo não escrevo um soneto...
Mas não importa: escrevo-o agora.
Sonetos são infâmia, e, nesta hora,
...

3/2/35

"Homecoming"

Undated Poems

174
Barrow-on-Furness*

I

I am low and base, like everyone else,
I have no ideals, but, tell me, who does?
Anyone claiming he has is the same as me, but a liar.
Any seeker after ideals clearly has none either.

I love goodness with my imagination.
My worthless self, however, won't allow it.
I drift, a mere ghost of my present self,
Intermittently drunk on some kind of Beyond.

Like all men, I don't believe what I believe.
Perhaps that's an ideal I could die for.
Until I do die, though, I talk and read.

Justify myself? I am what all men are ...
Change myself? What, so as to be like my equal? ...
—Enough of this, my foolish heart!

---

* This should, of course, be Barrow-in-Furness, a city in the north of England
famous for its shipbuilding. This said, there is no river with the name of Furness.

II

Deities, forces, souls of science or of faith,
Why so much explanation explaining nothing!
I'm sitting on the quayside, on a barrel,
And I understand no more than if I were on my feet.

But then again why should I?
True, but then again why not?
Cold, grubby waters flowing past,
I pass just as you do, and am no more useful ...

The universe, a tangled skein,
Whose patient fingers could idly pick you apart
With his mind on other matters?

What's left is no longer a skein ...
What should we play at? Love? Indifference?
I'll make do with getting up from this barrel.

III

Flow, wretched river, carry down with you to the sea
This my entirely subjective indifference!
"To the sea!" What does your elusive presence
Have to do with my thoughts or with me?

O indolent fate! I ride through life astride
The shadow of a donkey. Life itself
Lives by naming what has no life,
And dies affixing labels to the open skies ...

Bland, brazen Furness, just three more days
Must I stay here with you, me, poor engineer,
Kept prisoner here by inspection upon inspection ...

Then I will leave, well, me and my disdain
(While you will carry on precisely as before)
Anonymous, cigarette lit, waiting for a train.

IV
Conclusion by weight! I did the sums,
They came out right, and I was highly praised ...
My heart is a vast dais, an enormous stage
On which a tiny creature is displayed.

Using the microscope of disillusion
And lingering long over futile details ...
I reached my practical, pointless conclusions ...
My theoretical conclusions and confusions ...

What theories are there for one who feels
His brain snap in two, like the tooth of a comb
That once belonged to some poor emigré?

I carefully close my notebook and
Sit doodling faint gray lines at random
On the back of the envelope of who I am ...

V
We've been living apart, Portugal,
For such a long time now! Ah, but my soul,
This hesitant soul, never calm or strong,
Can't forget you, not entirely, not for long.

I, a closet hysteric, dream of some safe nook ...
The river Furness, which flows through here,
Accompanies me but in a way so ironic,
With me stopped still and him flowing fast ...

Fast? Yes, relatively fast …
But let's have no more distinctions,
No subtleties, no interstices, no in-betweens,
The metaphysics of sensations—

Let us be done now with everything of that sort …
Ah, the human longing to be river or port!

175

The quayside is full of the hubbub of an imminent arrival,
The early meeters and greeters are beginning to arrive,
The steamship from Africa is already hoving into view, growing in
        size and clarity.
I came here in order to wait for no one,
To see the others waiting,
To be all the others waiting,
To be the hope of all the others.

I carry with me the great weariness of being so many things.
The first latecomers are arriving,
And suddenly I grow impatient with waiting, with existing, with being,
I leave so abruptly that the porter notices and stares at me, but only
        briefly.
I return to the city as if to freedom.

It's worthwhile feeling even if only then to stop feeling.

176

But I, in whose soul are reflected
All the forces of the universe,
Whose emotive reflection is shaken,
Minute by minute, emotion by emotion,
By a succession of absurd, opposing things—

I the futile focus of all realities,
I the phantom born of all sensations,
I the abstract, I the projected image on the *écran*,
I the sad, legitimate wife of the Whole,
Through all this I must suffer being me like someone feeling thirsty
       for something other than water.

177

Night so serene!
Moonlight so lovely!
Lovely little boat
Bobbing on the sea!

Very gently, my whole past—my Lisbon past—rises up inside me …
My aunts' third-floor apartment, the peace of long ago,
Various kinds of peace,
Childhood with not a thought for the future,
The apparently continuous clatter of their sewing machines,
When all was well and timely,
A wellness and a timeliness now dead.

Good god, what have I made of my life?

Night so serene!
Moonlight so lovely!
Lovely little boat
Bobbing on the sea!

Who was it who used to sing that?
I know it was then.
I remember but forget.
And it hurts, hurts, hurts …

For the love of God, please stop playing that tune inside my head.

178

Having appointments to meet, what an endlessly tedious thing that is!
At five to one I have to be
At Rossio Station, upper floor—saying goodbye
To a friend traveling on the same "Sud Express" everyone travels on
And going where everyone goes to, Paris …

I have to be there,
And, believe me, the weariness I feel in advance is so vast
That if the "Sud Express" knew about it, it would come off the rails …

A childish joke?
No, it really would come off the rails …
Ah, if only it was carrying my life inside when it did derail!…

That is my strongest wish,
And my wish, because it is so strong, enters into the very substance
      of the world.

179

The pawnbroker's child has such lovely innocent blue eyes!
Goodness, what a crossroads life is!

For better or worse, I've always had a very humanized sensibility,
And all of death has always wounded me personally,
Yes, not just because of the mystery of remaining inexpressive and
      organic,
But very directly, here in my heart.

How the sun gilds the houses of reprobates!
Could I hate them without despising the sun?

What an odd thing to think with my distracted feelings
And all because of the childish eyes of a child …

180

Villeggiatura

The stillness of night, in this rural retreat up high;
The stillness, which only accentuates
The sparse barking of the guard dogs in the night;
The silence, which grows more emphatic,
Because it keeps humming or murmuring something or other in the
    darkness ...
Ah, how oppressive it all is!
As oppressive as being happy!
What an idyllic life if only it belonged to someone else
The monotonous hum or murmur of nothing
Beneath the sky freckled with stars,
And the dogs' barking sprinkling dust over the peace of everything!

I came here to rest,
But forgot to leave myself at home.
I brought with me the elemental thorn of being conscious.
The vague nausea, the nebulous malaise of feeling that I exist.
Always the same unease nibbled away at
Like a piece of thin, dark, crumbly bread.
Always the same discomfort drunk down in bitter gulps
Like a drunkard downing wine knowing he'll only throw it up again.
Always, always, always
The same faulty circulation in the soul itself,
This swooning of the sensations,
This ...

Your slender hands, slightly pale and slightly mine,
Lay quite still in your lap that day,
Just as and where the scissors or the thimble of another might lie.
You were thinking and looking at me as if I were mere empty space.
I remember this so as to have something to think about without
    actually thinking.
Then, with a half sigh, you suddenly stopped what you were being.

You consciously looked at me and said:
"I wish every day could be like this"—
Like this, like that day which had been nothing at all...

Ah, you didn't know,
Fortunately, you didn't know,
That the real sadness is that every day is like this, like this;
That the problem is that, for good or ill,
The soul savors or suffers the intimate tedium of everything,
Consciously and unconsciously,
Thinking or about to think—
That this is the real sadness...
I have a photographic memory of your still hands,
Lying there limply.
I have a clearer memory of your hands just then than I do of you.
What will have become of you?
I know that, in the vast somewhere of life,
You got married. I believe you are a mother. You must be happy.
Why wouldn't you be?

Only out of spite...
No, that would be unfair...
Unfair?

(It was a sunny day in the fields, and I was drowsing, smiling.)

....

Life...
White or red, it's all the same: enough to make you want to throw up.

181
Ah, wherever I am or have been, or wherever I'm not and have never
        been,

There's the same all-consuming banality of every face!
Ah, the unbearable anguish of other people!
The undeniable weariness of seeing and hearing!

(The long-lost murmur of my own streams, of my own woods.)

I'd like to vomit up everything I've seen, simply from the nausea of
    having seen it,
My soul's upset stomach at having to exist …

182

Our paths crossed in a downtown Lisbon street, and he came over to me,
That shabbily dressed man, with professional beggar written all over
    his face,
And he clearly felt drawn to me and I to him;
And reciprocally, in a generous, extravagant gesture, I gave him every-
    thing I had
(Except, of course, what was in the pocket where I keep most of my
    money:
I'm no fool, nor some earnest Russian novelist,
Romanticism's all very well, in small doses …).

I feel drawn to all such people,
Especially when they don't deserve my sympathy.
Yes, I, too, am a vagabond and a beggar,
And it's my own fault.
Being a vagabond and a beggar doesn't mean being a vagabond and a
    beggar:
It's being bumped off the social ladder,
It's being incapable of adapting to life's norms,
Life's real or sentimental norms—
Not being a Supreme Court judge, a reliable employee, a prostitute,
Not being desperately poor, an exploited worker,

Not being ill with some incurable disease,
Not being athirst for justice or a captain of cavalry,
Not being, in short, one of those social beings beloved of novelists
Who stuff themselves with words because they have a reason to shed
        tears,
And who rebel against society because they have a reason to rebel.
No, anything but having a reason for something!
Anything but caring about humanity!
Anything but succumbing to humanitarianism!
What is the point of a sensation if there's an external reason for it?

Yes, being a vagabond and a beggar, as I am,
Isn't being a vagabond and a beggar in the ordinary sense:
It's being isolated in one's soul, that's what being a vagabond means,
It's begging the days to pass by and leave us, that's what being a beg-
        gar means.

Anything else is just plain stupid like a Dostoyevsky or a Gorky.
Anything else is going hungry or having no clothes.
And even if that happens, it happens to so many people
That it's really not worth feeling sorry for the people it happens to.
I am a proper vagabond and beggar, that is, in the figurative sense,
And I'm positively brimming with charitable feelings for myself.

Poor Álvaro de Campos!
So cut off from life! So sensorially depressed!
Poor him, stuck in the armchair of his melancholy!
Poor him, who today, with (real) tears in his eyes,
Gave away, in a generous, liberal, Muscovite gesture,
Everything he had, from the pocket in which he had very little, to that
Poor man who wasn't poor, whose eyes were only sad for profes-
        sional purposes.
Pity poor Álvaro de Campos, whom nobody cares about!
Pity him for feeling such pity for himself!

And, yes, pity him!
Pity him more than the many who are vagabonds who actually go
     vagabonding,
Beggars who actually beg,
Because the human soul is a deep abyss.

And I should know. Pity him!

How satisfying to be able to rebel at a rally held inside my own soul!
Not that I'm a fool!
I don't even have the excuse of holding socialist views.
No, I have no excuse at all: I'm perfectly lucid.

Don't try to change my views: I'm lucid.
There, I've said it: I'm lucid.
Don't talk to me about aesthetics with heart: I'm lucid.
Goddammit! I'm lucid.

183
Ah, at last … excellent …
Here it is at last!
Madness has finally installed itself inside my head.

My heart exploded like a firecracker,
And my head felt the shock run up my spine …

Thank heavens for madness!
Because everything I've given has turned into trash,
And, like a gobbet of spit launched onto the wind,
Splattered my bare face!
Everything that I was has wound its way about my feet
Like a piece of sacking wrapped around nothing at all!
Everything I thought tickles the back of my throat,

Making me want to throw up even though I haven't eaten a thing!
Thank heavens for that, because, just as when you've drunk too much,
Throwing up is always a solution.
Good heavens! I've found a solution in my stomach of all places!
I've found a truth, I felt it in my intestines!

Oh, I, too, have written transcendental poetry in my time!
Great lyrical raptures have passed through this head of mine!
The organization of poems relative to the vastness of each subject
      resolved into several parts—
So there's nothing new about that.
I feel like throwing up, like throwing up my own self…
I feel so sick that if I could devour the whole universe in order to
      vomit it up into the sink, I would.
It would take an effort, but it would be for a good purpose.
At least it would have a purpose.
As it is, I have neither purpose nor life…

184

Even with *Teucro duce et auspice Teucro*
It's always *cras*—tomorrow—that we'll set out to sea.

Be still, my foolish heart, be still!
Be still, because there's nothing to hope for,
Which means there's no need to lose hope either…
Be still… The olive trees in the neighbor's garden
Peer distantly over the wall.
As a child, I saw another such grove, but not that one:
I don't know if the same eyes of the same soul saw it.
We postpone everything until death arrives.
We postpone everything and our understanding of everything,
With a sense of anticipated weariness about everything,
With a predictable, empty yearning.

185

Là-bas, je ne sais où ...
The eve of a journey, the alarm clock rings ...
There's no need for such a strident reminder!

I want to enjoy the peace of the train-station-soul that is mine,
Before seeing, heading towards me, the iron arrival
Of the final train,
Before feeling the actual departure in the pit of my stomach,
Before stepping on board with a foot
That's never learned not to feel excited when it's time to leave.

Right now, smoking a cigarette at the way station of today,
I still want to cling to a small piece of the old life.
A useless life, which it would be best to leave behind, a prison cell?
So what? The whole universe is a prison cell, and imprisonment has
        nothing to do with the size of the cell.
My cigarette tastes to me of an incipient nausea. The train has
        already left from the other station ...
Goodbye, goodbye, goodbye to all the people who didn't come to
        wave me off,
My abstract, impossible family ...
Goodbye to today, goodbye to the way station of today, goodbye
        life, goodbye life!
To stay here like a neatly labeled parcel
Forgotten in one corner of the shelter for passengers on the opposite
        platform.
To be found by the temporary guard once the train has gone—
"What's this? That fellow must have left it here."—

To stay and simply think about leaving,
To stay and be right,
To stay and die less ...

I'm heading off into the future as if it were a difficult exam.
What if the train never arrives and God takes pity on me?

I can see myself now at the station which, up until now, was a mere
    metaphor.
I'm a perfectly presentable individual.
People say they can tell that I've lived abroad.
I apparently have the manners of an educated man.
I pick up my suitcase, rejecting the porter as if he were some loath-
    some vice.
And the hand with which I pick it up sets both me and the case
    trembling.

To depart!
I will never return,
I will never return because there is no return.
The place you return to is always different,
The station you return to is a different one.
The people aren't the same, the light isn't the same, nor the
    philosophy.

To depart! My God, to leave! I'm afraid of leaving!...

186

A disaster composed of idleness and stars ...
Nothing more ...
Enough ...
Dammit ...
The whole mystery of the world has seeped into my economic life.
Basta!...
What I wanted to be and will never be ruins the streets for me.
Will this never end?

Is it fate?
Yes, it's my fate
Deposited by my achievements among the trash
And my plans at the side of the road—
My achievements torn up by children,
My plans peed on by beggars,
And my entire soul a dirty towel lying crumpled on the floor.
....

The horror of the sound of the clock at night in the dining room of
      a house in the country—
The monotony and the inevitability of time …
The sudden horror of a passing funeral cortège
That tears the mask off any hopes.
There …
There's the conclusion.
There, signed and sealed,
There, beneath the leaden seal and with a chalk-smeared face
Goes the thing that grieves like us,
Goes the thing that felt like us,
Go our selves!
There, beneath a thin piece of cloth as crude and horrific as the
      vault of a prison
There, there, there … And me?

187

Tripe Oporto-style
One day, in a restaurant, outside of space and time,
I was served up love in the form of cold tripe.
I said, very politely, to the missionary from the kitchen
That I preferred it hot,
That tripe (and this was tripe Oporto-style) is never eaten cold.

They got rather annoyed with me.
One is never right, not even in a restaurant.
I didn't eat it, nor did I order anything else, I paid the bill,
And went out into the street where I paced up and down.

Who knows what this means?
I don't know, and it happened to me ...

(I do know that in everyone's childhood there was a garden,
Private or public or a neighbor's.
I know that we played there as if we were the true owners,
And that this sadness belongs only to today.)

I know this perfectly well,
But, if I ordered love, why then did they bring me
Tripe Oporto-style served cold?
It's not a dish you can eat cold.
But they brought it to me cold.
I didn't complain, but it was cold,
And it's never eaten cold, yet it was served cold.

188

No, it's not tiredness ...
It's an accumulation of disillusionments
That gets under the skin of that way of thinking,
It's a Sunday completely at odds with
Feeling,
A holiday spent in the abyss ...

No, it's not tiredness ...
It's the fact of me continuing to exist
And the world too,

With everything that it contains,
With everything that proliferates within it
And which is, basically, the same thing in various identical forms.

No. Why should I feel tired?
It's an abstract sensation
Drawn from concrete life—
Something like a scream
As yet unuttered,
Something like an anguish
As yet unfelt,
Or only incompletely,
Or to be felt as …
Yes, or to be felt as …
That's it, as …

As what?
If I knew that, I wouldn't be feeling this false tiredness.

(Ah, a group of blind street singers,
What an amazing barrel organ
They make, with one man on the Portuguese *guitarra*, another on
        the guitar, and the woman singing!)
Because I hear, I see.
All right, I admit it: it is tiredness!…

189
Clearly not Campos!
I don't know what it is, the feeling, as yet unexpressed,
That, like a sudden sense of being suffocated, afflicts
My hcart which, abruptly,
In the midst of life, forgets itself.

I don't know what the feeling is
That throws me off course,
That fills me suddenly
With disgust for the path I was following,
A desire never to go home,
A desire for the indefinite,
A lucid desire for the indefinite.

The false seasons of the false year
Have changed four times in the immutable
Flow of consequential time;
Dry follows green and green follows dry;
And no one knows which came first
Or last, or how they end.

190
I'm beginning to know myself. I don't exist.
I'm the interval between what I want to be and what others made of
        me,
Or half of that interval, because there's life too …
This, ultimately, is what I am …
Turn out the light, close the door, and wait for the sound of those
        slippered footsteps in the corridor to go away.
Let me stay in my room alone with just the great peace and quiet of
        my self.
A cheap universe.

Prose

Ultimatum
1 [c. November 1917]

This is an eviction order issued to the mandarins of Europe. Get out!

Get out, Anatole France, Epicure of a homeopathic pharmocopeia,
      get out, Jaurès, tapeworm of the Ancien Régime, a Renan-
      Flaubert salad served up in fake seventeenth-century
      porcelain!

Get out, Maurice Barrès, you Action Française feminist, Chateau-
      briand of bare walls, stage pimp of populist nationalism,
      decrepit follower of the Maid of Lorraine, cut-price tailor of
      other people's deaths, dressed in his own clothes!

Get out, Paul Bourget of All Souls, lampbearer of alien particles,
      psychologist hiding behind a coat of arms, vile plebeian
      snob, underlining with a splintered ruler the Church's
      commandments!

Get out, Kipling you merchandizable, practical man of verse,
      scrap-iron imperialist, Homer of the battles of Majuba and
      Colenso, Empire Day of military slang, tramp steamer of base
      immortality!

Get out, get out!

Get out, George Bernard Shaw, paradoxical vegetarian, sincere
      charlatan, cold tumor of Ibsenism, contriver of unexpected
      intellectualism, Kilkenny-Cat of your own self, Calvinist *Irish
      Melody* with words from *The Origin of Species*!

303

Get out, H. G. Wells, clay-footed ideas man, cardboard stopper in the bottle of Complexity!

Get out, G. K. Chesterton, Christianity for conjurors, barrel of beer at the foot of the altar, adipose representative of the Cockney dialect with a horror of the influence of soap on cleansing all rational thinking.

Get out, Yeats of the Celtic mist encircling a signpost with no sign, sack of vices washed ashore after the shipwreck of English symbolism!

Get out, get out!

Get out, Rapagnetta-Annunzio, banality in Greek characters, "Don Juan in Patmos" (solo for trombone)!

And you, Maeterlinck, oven of Mystery with the fire burned out!

And you, Loti, cold, salty soup!

And finally, you, Rostand-tand-tand-tand-tand-tand-tand-tand!

Get out! Get out! Get out!

And if I've missed anyone, you'll find them hiding in a corner over there!

Remove them from my sight!

Out with them all, out!

And what are you doing being so famous, Wilhelm II of Germany, left-handed wizard with no left arm, Bismarck without a lid to douse the fire?!

And who are you, with your socialist mane, David Lloyd George, a fool in a Phrygian bonnet made of Union Jacks?!

And you, Venizelos, a slice of Pericles with butter, fallen on the floor buttered side down?!

And you, anyone, all of you, a Briand-Sato-Boselli soup of incompetence before the facts, all war-fodder statesmen who date from long before the war! All of you! All of you! Trash, dust, provincial rabble, intellectual dross!

And all the other heads of state, nakedly incompetent, trash cans emptied out at the door of the Age of Inadequacy!

Remove them from my sight!
Make bundles of straw and pretend they are people!
Get rid of everything! Everything!
This is an ultimatum to them all, and to all the others like them!
If you don't want to leave, then stay and wash yourself clean!

A general collapse of everything caused by everyone!
A general collapse of everyone caused by everything!
The collapse of peoples and of fates—total collapse!
The nations parade past my utter Scorn!
You, Italian ambition, a lapdog called Caesar!
You, the so-called "French Effort," a plucked cockerel with its skin
      painted with feathers! (Don't wind him up too much, he'll
      break!)
You, British organization, with Kitchener at the bottom of the sea
      right from the beginning of the war!
(It's a long, long way to Tipperary, and a jolly sight longer to Berlin!)
You, German culture, a Sparta rotten with the oil of Christism and
      the vinegar of Nietzscheism, a tin beehive, an imperialoid
      overspill of hamstrung servilism!
You, subject Austria, mixture of sub-races, doorjamb type K!
You, Von Belgium, forced to be heroic, wipe your hand on the wall
      that you once were!
You, Russian serfdom, Europe of Malays, liberated from the sprung
      spring, because it broke!
You, Spanish "imperialism," political *salero*, with matadors who
      could, at any moment , don the robe of a penitent, their war-
      like qualities buried in Morocco!
You, United States of America, bastard synthesis of Lower Europe,
      the garlic in the transatlantic soup, nasal twang of inesthetic
      modernism!
And you, five-cents Portugal, a remnant of Monarchy sliding into a
      Republic, last-rites-slurry of Disgrace, artificial collaboration
      in the no-balls war in Africa!

And you, Brazil, "our fellow republic," very funny, a joke invented by
    Pedro Álvares Cabral, who didn't even want to discover you!
Please, just throw a tablecloth over the whole lot of them!
Lock 'em all up and throw away the key!
Where are the ancients, the soldiers, the men, the guides, the guards?
Go to the cemetery, because today they're only names on
    gravestones!
Today, philosophy is Fouillée having died!
Today, art is Rodin still being here!
Today, literature is Barrès actually meaning something!
Today, criticism is having fools who don't call Bourget a fool!
Today, politics is the fat-laden degeneration of organized
    incompetence!
Today, religion is the militant catholicism of the innkeepers of
    the faith, the French-cuisine enthusiasm of the Maurras, of
    reason-unwrapped, it's the spectaculitis of Christian pragma-
    tists, of Catholic intuitionists, of Nirvanic ritualists, touting
    for business for God!
Today, it's war, a game of push and shove and slamming the door!
I'm suffocating surrounded by nothing but all this garbage.
Let me breathe!
Open all the windows!
Open more windows than there are windows in the world!

No more big ideas, or final plans or some born-to-be-emperor's
    imperial ambitions!
No more ideas for a structure, for a sense of a Building, no more
    yearning for the Created-Organic!
No miniature Pitt, no cardboard Goethe, no Napoleon of
    Nuremberg!
No literary trend that is only the noonday shadow cast by
    romanticism!
No military impulse that smells even faintly of Austerlitz!
No political current that sounds like the germ of an idea

rattling around, some Gaius Gracchus drumming on the
windowpane!
Vile era of the secondary, the almost, of lackeys with lackey ambi-
tions to be king-lackeys!
Lackeys who have no inkling of Aspiration, the bourgeoisie of
Desire, diverted from the shop counter behind which they
so rightly belong! Yes, all you who represent Europe, all you
politicians of the kind we see throughout the world, the mi-
nor literati of European trends, who are somebody-or-other
in this maelstrom of warm tea!

High-ups in Lilliputian Europe, pass by beneath my Contempt!
Pass by, those who long for quotidian luxury, for seamstresses of
both sexes, those whose "type" is the plebeian d'Annunzio,
aristocrat in a golden loincloth!
Pass by, those who are the creators of social trends, literary trends, ar-
tistic trends, the other side of the coin of the inability to create!
Pass by, you weaklings who feel the need to be the ists of some ism
or other!
Pass by, radicalists of the Little, ignoramuses of Progress, who be-
lieve ignorance is a pillar of boldness, impotence the main-
stay of neo-theories!
Pass by, giants of the anthill, drunk on your children-of-petit-bour-
geois personality obsessed with having been robbed of the
high life in the paternal pantry and with a long-buried legacy
of fragile nerves!
Pass by mongrels; pass by, you sissies singing the praises of weak-
ness; pass by, you ultra-sissies singing the praises of strength,
bourgeois fools gazing goggle-eyed at the fairground athlete
you hope to create out of your own febrile indecision!
Pass by, pathetic epileptoid dung, hysterical detritus of the circus,
social senility of the individual concept of youth!
Pass by, mildewed Novelty, shoddy merchandise of the brain that
produced it!

Pass by, on the left of my right-facing Scorn, you creators of "philosophical systems," the Boutroux, Bergsons, and Euckens of this world, hospitals for the incurably religious, pragmatists of metaphysical journalism, *lazzaroni* of considered construction!

Pass by, and don't come back, you bourgeois members of One-Europe, pariahs of the desire to appear big, Paris provincials!

Pass by, you decigrams of Ambition, great only in an age that counts greatness in centimilligrams!

Pass by, you provisional, pootling artists and politicians of the *lightning-lunch* variety, servants perched on the fleeting Hour, footmen of the Instant!

Pass by, spineless "delicate sensibilities"; pass by constructors of cafés and conferences, a heap of bricks with pretensions to being a house!

Pass by, suburban intellectuals, street-corner cognoscenti!

Futile luxury, pass by, vainglorious greatness within the reach of all, triumphant megalomania of the villager of village-Europe! You who confuse the human with the popular, and the aristocratic with nobility! You who confuse everything, who, when you're thinking absolutely nothing, always have something to say! You empty rattles, you mere splinters, pass by!

Pass by, pretenders to a little bit of a throne, lords of sawdust, feudal gentlemen of the Cardboard Castle!

Pass by, posthumous romanticism of lily-livered liberals, classicism preserved in alcohol like Racine's foetuses, Whitman's door-step dynamism, of those who must beg for inspirations, empty heads that only make a noise because they're about to bang them against the wall!

Pass by, cultivators of domestic hypnotism, dominators of the next-door neighbor, barrack-masters of a Discipline that neither costs nor creates!

Pass by, smug traditionalists, genuine anarchists, socialists proclaiming their workerly qualities while wishing they could stop work! Routine revolutionaries, pass by!

Pass by, eugenicists, organizers of a tin-can lifestyle, Prus-
    sians of applied biology, neo-Mendelians of sociological
    incomprehension!
Pass by, vegetarians, *teetotalers*, vicarious Calvinists, *killjoys* of redun-
    dant imperialism!
Pass by, amanuenses of corner-shop *vivre sa vie* philosophy, Ibsenoid
    Bernstein-Batailles, the strong men of the green room!
Tango danced by Blacks, if only you were a minuet!
Pass by, once and for all, pass by!

Come at last and feel my Disgust, prostrate yourself beneath the
    soles of my Scorn, the grand finale of the foolish, confla-
    gration-cum-disdain, a fire on a small dungheap, dynamic
    synthesis of the Era's innate inertia!
Come, hurl yourself, crawl, loudmouthed impotence!

Prostrate yourselves, cannons proclaiming bullets over ambition,
    bombs over intelligence!
For this is the muddy equation of the infamous cosmopolitanism of
    gunfire:

$$\frac{\text{VON BISSING}}{\text{BELGIUM}} = \frac{\text{JONNART}}{\text{GREECE}}$$

Declare to the four winds that no one is fighting for freedom or for
    Right! They are all fighting out of fear of the others! Their
    commands have no more meters than these millimeters!
Verborrheic warrior crap! Joffre-Hindenburgeresque dung! The
    European latrine of the Usual Suspects in flabby scission!
Who believes in them?
Who believes in the others?
Shave the beards off the *poilus*!
Knock the berets off the whole flock of them!
Send them all home to peel symbolic potatoes!

Wash out that bowl of unthinking mishmash!
Couple up a locomotive to that war!
Put a collar on it and go and exhibit it in Australia!

Men, nations, plans, all null and void!
The collapse of everything because of everyone!
The collapse of everyone because of everything!
Complete and utter and total:

SHIT!

Europe is thirsty for creativity, hungry for Future!
Europe wants great Poets, great Statesmen, great Generals!
It wants a Politician who can consciously build the unconscious
    fates of their People!
It wants a Poet searching passionately for Immortality, caring noth-
    ing for reputation, reputation is for actresses and pharmaceu-
    tical products!
It wants a General who will fight for a Constructive Triumph, not
    for a victory that merely involves defeating others!
Europe wants many such Politicians, many such Poets, many such
    Generals!
Europe wants the Big Idea inside those Strong Men—the idea that
    will give a Name to their nameless inner wealth!
Europe wants a New Intelligence that will give Form to its chaotic
    Matter!
It wants a New Will that will make a Building out of the random
    bricks of Life today!
It wants a New Sensibility that will bring together the egotisms of
    the lackeys of the moment!
Europe wants Masters! The World wants Europe!
Europe is fed up with not yet existing! It's fed up with being only a
    suburb of itself! The Machine Age is feeling its way towards
    the coming of Great Humanity!

Europe is longing for Theoreticians of What-will-be, for Singer-
Seers of its Future!
Give us some Homers for the Machine Age, O scientific Fates! Give us
Miltons for the Age of Electric Things, O Matter's inner Gods!
Give us the Self-Possessed, the Strong, give us Subtle Harmonics!
Europe wants to go from being a geographical designation to a
civilized person!
The thing eating away at Life can be manure for the Future!
What there is now cannot last, because it is nothing!
Coming as I do from a Race of Navigators, I declare that it cannot
last!
Coming as I do from a Race of Discoverers, I despise anything less
than discovering a New World!
Who in Europe does not suspect where that New World is? Who is
poised to set off from some new Sagres?
I, at least, am one huge Longing, the exact size of the Possible!
I, at least, am of the stature of Imperfect Ambition, an Ambition for
Gentlemen, not for slaves!
I rise up before the setting sun, and the shadow of my Scorn casts
black night over the whole lot of you!
I, at least, am enough to show the Way!
I will show the way!

BEWARE!

Firstly, I proclaim:

The Malthusian Law of Sensibility

*The stimuli to sensibility increase in a geometric progression; sensibility
itself increases only in an arithmetic progression.*

Understand the importance of this law. Sensibility—here used in
its widest possible sense—is the fount of all civilized creation. But
that creation can only happen fully when sensibility adapts itself to
the environment in which it functions; the quality and strength of

the resulting work is proportionate to the extent to which sensibility adapts to its environment.

Now sensibility, while it may vary a little under the insistent influence of its current environment, is, generally speaking, constant and fixed in each individual from birth, a matter of inherited temperament. Sensibility, therefore, progresses *by generations.*

Civilization's creations—civilization being sensibility's environment—are culture, scientific progress, changing political (in its broadest sense) conditions; now these creations—especially cultural and scientific progress—are not the work of generations, but rely on interaction with the work of *individuals*, and although any change is slow at first, these creations soon progress to the point where they change and grow from generation to generation thanks to the hundreds of subtle changes that occur in these new stimuli to sensibility, although, admittedly, there is only one advance per generation, because a father can only transmit to his child a small part of his own acquired qualities.

This means that, at a certain point in the evolution of civilization, sensibility will fail to adapt to the environment or to stimuli. This is happening in our own age, where the inability to create great values springs from that failure.

The failure to adapt was less pronounced in the early period of our civilization, from the Renaissance to the eighteenth century, when the stimuli were mainly of a cultural kind, because those stimuli were naturally slow to progress and initially reached only the upper echelons of society. The failure to adapt became more marked in the second period, from the French Revolution to the nineteenth century, when the stimuli were, above all, political, where progress was easier and the range of stimuli wider. The failure to adapt grew at a dizzying speed from the mid-nineteenth century to the present day, when stimuli, in the form of scientific creations, provoked a rate of development that left behind any progress made by sensibility, and in their practical applications, they affect all of society. Thence the enormous disparity between the geometric progression of the stimuli and the corresponding arithmetic progression of sensibility itself.

Therein lies the cause of our own age's failure to adapt and to create. We are, then, faced by a dilemma: a choice between the death of civilization and some kind of artificial adaptation, given that any natural, instinctive adaptation has failed.

Therefore, secondly, in order that civilization should not die, I proclaim,

The Need for Artificial Adaptation

What is artificial adaptation?

It is an act of sociological surgery. It is the violent transformation of sensibility as a way of enabling it to keep pace, at least for a time, with the progression of its stimuli.

Sensibility has reached this morbid state because it failed to adapt. Don't even think about curing it. There are no social cures. We must consider operating so that it can continue to live. That is, we have to replace the natural morbidity of misadaptation with the artificial health achieved by a surgical intervention, even if that involves some mutilation.

What do we need to eliminate from contemporary psychism?

It must, of course, be the mind's most recent *fixed acquisition*—that is, any general acquisition that occurred prior to the establishment of our present civilization, but only one recently acquired; there are three reasons for this (*a*) because, since it is the most recent of mental fixations, it is the least difficult to eliminate; (*b*) because, given that every civilization takes shape in reaction to the previous one, it is the principles of the previous civilization that are most antagonistic to the present one and are the greatest hindrance to the latter adapting to the newly appeared special conditions; (*c*) because, the elimination of the most recently acquired fixation will not wound the general sensibility as deeply as would the elimination or attempted elimination of some more deeply embedded mental deposit.

What is the most recent *fixed acquisition* of the general human mind?

It has to be Christian dogma, because the Middle Ages, when that religious system was at its height, immediately and enduringly precedes the eruption of our own civilization, and Christian principles are contradicted by the solid teachings of modern science.

Any artificial adaptation will occur spontaneously once we eliminate from the human mind the fixed acquisitions derived from its immersion in Christianity.

Thirdly, then, I proclaim

The anti-Christian surgical intervention

This involves the elimination of the three preconceptions, dogmas, or attitudes with which Christianity infiltrated the very matter of the human psyche.

A more concrete explanation:

1. ABOLITION OF THE DOGMA OF PERSONALITY—namely, that we have a Personality "separate" from that of other people. This is a theological fiction. The personality of each of us consists (as modern psychology knows, especially now that more attention has been given to sociology) of our intersections with other people's "personalities," our immersion in social currents and trends, and the embedding of certain hereditary "wrinkles," which derive in large part from phenomena of a collective nature. That is to say, in the present, the past, and the future, we are part of other people and they are part of us. For Christianity, the most perfect man is one who can most honestly say "I am I"; for science, the most perfect man is the one who can, with more justification, say: "I am all the others."

We should then operate on the soul, in order to open it up to an awareness of its interpenetration with other souls, thus obtaining a real approximation to the Complete Man, to Man as Synthesis of Humanity.

The results of this operation:

(a) *In politics*: The complete abolition of the idea of democracy, as per the French Revolution, according to which two men can run faster than one man, which is false, because *any man worth two men can run faster than one man*! *One* plus *one* doesn't come to more than *one*, whereas *one* plus *one* does not make that *One* called *Two*.—So, replace Democracy with a Dictatorship of the Complete Man, of the Man who contains the greatest number of Others; who is, therefore, the Majority. We will then have the Great Meaning of Democracy, completely contrary to what we have now, which never existed anyway.

(b) *In art*: The complete abolition of the idea that each individual has the right or the duty to express what he feels. Only the individual who feels through various others has the right or the duty to express what he feels in art. This is not to be confused with "the expression of the Age," something sought after only by individuals incapable of feeling for themselves. What we need is an artist who feels through a certain number of Others, all of them different, some from the past, some from the present, others from the future. An artist whose art is a Synthesis-Sum, not a Synthesis-Subtraction of his others, which is what present-day art amounts to.

(c) *In philosophy*: The abolition of the idea of absolute truth. The creation of a Super-Philosophy. The philosopher will become the interpreter of interwoven subjectivities, the greatest philosopher being the one who brings together the greatest number of other people's spontaneous philosophies. Since everything is subjective, every opinion is true for every man: the greatest truth will be the inner-sum-synthesis of the greatest number of true and contradictory opinions.

2. THE ABOLITION OF THE PRESUMPTION OF INDIVIDUALITY
—This is another theological fiction—that each soul is one and indivisible. Science shows us, on the contrary, that each of us is a group of subsidiary psychisms, a clumsy synthesis of cellular souls. For Christianity, the most perfect man is the one most coherent with himself; for the man of science, the most perfect man is the one least coherent with himself.

Results:

(a) *In politics*: The abolition of any belief that lasts longer than a particular state of mind, the complete disappearance of all fixed opinions and ways-of-seeing; the disappearance, therefore, of all institutions that depend on the fact that any "public opinion" can last longer than half an hour. The solution to a problem at one particular historical moment will be arrived at by the dictatorial coordination (*vide* the previous paragraph) of the momentary impulses of the human components of that problem, which is, of course, a purely subjective matter. The total abolition of the past and the future as elements to be relied on or even thought about when reaching a political solution. The complete breakdown of all continuities.

(b) *In art*: The abolition of the dogma of artistic individuality. The greatest artist will be the one who defines himself least, and who writes in the most dissimilar and contradictory of genres. No artist should have just one personality. He should have several, creating each one out of a genuine gathering-together of similar states of mind, thus destroying the vulgar fiction that he is one and indivisible.

(c) *In philosophy*: The complete abolition of the Truth as a philosophical concept, both relative and subjective. The reduction of philosophy to the art of having interesting theories about the "Universe." The greatest philosopher will be that artist of thinking, or rather of the "abstract art" (the future name of philosophy) that coordinates the largest number of entirely unrelated theories about "Existence."

3. THE ABOLITION OF THE DOGMA OF PERSONAL OBJECTIVISM
—Objectivity is a rough average between partial subjectivities. If a society were composed, say, of five men, *a, b, c, d,* and *e,* that society's "truth" or "objectivity" would be represented by

$$\frac{a+b+c+d+e}{5}$$

In the future, each individual should apply that average to himself. Each individual or at least each superior individual should seek to be a harmony between other people's subjectivities (of which his own forms a part) in order to get as close as possible to that Infinite-Truth to which the numeric series of partial truths should ideally aspire.

Results:

(a) *In politics*: The dominion of the individual or individuals who are the most skilled Makers of Averages, thus banishing completely the idea that any individual is allowed to have opinions on politics (or on anything else), because one can only have opinions about the Average.

(b) *In art*: The abolition of the idea of Expression, to be replaced by Between-Expression. Only a person fully aware that he is expressing the opinions of absolutely no one (the Average) can grasp this.

(c) *In philosophy*: The replacement of the idea of Philosophy by that of Science, given that Science is the concrete Average between philosophical opinions, the proof being its "objective nature," that is, its adaptation to the "external universe" which is the Average of all subjectivities. The subsequent disappearance of Philosophy in favor of Science.

Final, synthetic results:

(a) *In politics*: A Scientific Monarchy, antitraditionalist and anti-hereditary, absolutely spontaneous because of the always unforeseen appearance of King Average. The relegation of the People to their scientifically natural role as mere fixers of momentary impulses.

(b) *In art*: The replacement of the expression of an era by thirty or forty poets with (for example) two poets each of whom will have fifteen or twenty personalities, each of which will be an Average of the social trends of the moment.

(c) *In philosophy*: The integration of philosophy into art and science; the disappearance, therefore, of philosophy as a metaphysical science. The disappearance of all forms of religious feeling (from Christianity to revolutionary humanitarianism) because they do not represent an Average.

But what will those results mean for the men of the future, what Method, what form, will the necessary collective operation take? What would that initial Method or mode of operation be?

Only the generation for whom I am calling, for whom the oestrus of Europe is rubbing against the walls, only they can know what that Method will be!

If I knew, I myself would be all of that generation!

But I can only see the Path; I don't know where it is going.

I nevertheless proclaim the need for the coming of a Humanity of Engineers!

I go further: *I absolutely guarantee the coming of the Humanity of Engineers!*

I proclaim to an imminent future the scientific creation of Supermen!

I proclaim the coming of a perfect, mathematical Humanity!

I proclaim its coming at the top of my voice!

I proclaim its Work at the top of my voice!

I proclaim It, quite simply, at the top of my voice!

And I proclaim this too: Firstly:

The Superman will be not the strongest, but the most complete!

And I proclaim: Secondly:

The Superman will be not the toughest, but the most complex!

And I also proclaim: Thirdly:

The Superman will be, not the freest, but the most harmonious!

I proclaim this loudly and from above, from the mouth of the Tagus, my back turned to Europe, arms raised, gazing out at the Atlantic and abstractly greeting the Infinite!

A Warning on Morality

When the public learned that the students of Lisbon, in between making obscene remarks to any ladies passing by, were determined to make us all more moral, I could not suppress a cry of impatience. Yes—precisely the cry that you, the reader, have just made.

To be young means not to be old. To be old means to have opinions. To be young means to have no time for other people's opinions. Being young means blithely telling other people to go to the Devil with whatever opinions they may have, good or bad—good or bad, because we can never be sure which of these do go to the Devil.

Those students make comments about the writers who pass them in the street for the same reason they do about the women who pass them in the street. If they don't know the reason without my having to tell them, then they never will. If they did know, then they wouldn't pass comment on the ladies or the writers.

Why on earth should we have to put up with that! Children: study, have fun and shut up. Study science, if you study science; study the arts, if you study the arts; study literature, if you study literature. Have fun with women, if you like women; have fun in a different way, if you prefer. That's all fine, because it doesn't go beyond the body of the person having fun.

As for the rest, just shut up. Shut up as quietly as you can.

Because there are only two ways of being right. One is by shutting up, which is the method best suited to the young. The other is by contradicting yourself, but only someone older can do that.

Everything else is a real bore for anyone who happens to be present. And the society in which we were born is the place where we usually happen to be present.

3 [c. November 1924]

What is Metaphysics?

In the opinion of Fernando Pessoa, in his essay "Athena," philosophy— that is, metaphysics—is not a science, but an art. I don't agree. It seems to me that Fernando Pessoa is confusing what art is with what science is not. What is science is not necessarily art: it is simply not-science. Fernando Pessoa concludes, quite naturally, that since metaphysics does not, and apparently cannot, arrive at any verifiable conclusion, it is not a science. He forgets that what defines an activity is not its aim, and the aim of metaphysics is identical to that of science—identifying facts, and not that of art, which is to replace facts. The sciences achieve that goal—some more successfully than others—because the facts they are trying to identify are defined. Metaphysics is trying to identify facts that are un- or ill-defined. But until they are known, all facts are undefined; and in relation to those facts, all science is in the same state as metaphysics. That's why I would call metaphysics not an art, but a *virtual science*, because it seeks to know, but does not yet know. It will always remain virtual, even if it doesn't: if there is another "plane" or life in which it ceases to be virtual—those are things that neither I nor Fernando Pessoa can know, because the truth is we know nothing.

Fernando Pessoa comments that sociology is a science as virtual as metaphysics. What conclusions, if any, have been reached by sociology so far? None. A special conference on sociology, devoted to the task of defining sociology as a science, failed to do so. Modern politics is so complicated and confused because the modern mind obliges us (possibly for no reason) to find a science for everything, and since we don't have a science, merely the desire to have one, we take as absolute the very relative (not to say worthless) sociology that we invented or which, in garbled form, we assimilated from someone else equally ignorant. Fernando Pessoa compares the debates between the scholastics and, above all, the modern socialists, communists, and anarchists. It's the same madhouse speculativism, except that the scholastics are subtle, rationally disciplined, and inoffensive, and the modern "progressives" (as they call themselves, as if there can be "progress" where there is no science) are stupid, confused, and, given the pseudo-semi-culture of the age, inept. Discussing how many angels can comfortably stand on the head of a pin might be futile, but no more futile—and certainly more amusing—than discussing what would be the most humanitarian and equitable regime (why not antihumanitarian? why not even more unfair and unequal than the present one?) in which future humanity will live (what do we know, given that we are ignorant of all and any sociological laws, given that we therefore have no idea—even while under their influence—about the natural forces that currently rule us and are driving us who knows where, or what future humanity will be like, what it will want—because it might not want for itself what we want for it—or even if there will be a future humanity, or if a cataclysm will destroy our world and our still incomplete sociology, and all the humanitarianisms of a lot of pretentious, illiterate Byzantines?).

Fernando Pessoa notes the fact—which he comments on in another connection—that science tends to be mathematical as it grows more refined, to reduce everything to precise "abstract" formulae, in order to liberate itself as much as possible from "personal equations," that is, from the errors of observation and coordination produced by the fallibility of the senses and the understanding of the observer.* Now "abstract formulae" are precisely what metaphysics is after. And mathematics, at its "highest" level, does come very close to metaphysics

---

* For the benefit of laymen, I should say one thing about this, albeit slightly off the point. As sciences become closer to that "mathematical state," they become *more precise*: it is doubtful, however, that *because of that*, they become *more certain*. Both pure mathematicians and those with no knowledge of mathematics tend to attribute to that science a "certainty" which is not necessarily true. Mathematics is a perfect language, and that's as far as it goes. We need to consider the relativity of mathematical principles themselves—not a simple conditional relativity, long familiar to all those who know that for many a practical, that is, truly scientific application of mathematics it is necessary to introduce correction coefficients; but a truly unconditional relativity, more than proven, for example in geometry, by the existence of non-Euclidean geometries, which are as "certain," when applied, as the "classic" form. I should also mention, for the benefit of those same laymen, that the term "relativity" is used here in its traditional, logical sense, and not in the unfortunate, absurd sense of Einstein's theory of relativity, which is just that, a theory, first limited, then generalized, of relative *motion*. [Note by Álvaro de Campos.]

or, at least, to metaphysical ideas. None of this, of course, means that metaphysics will ever be anything more than a virtual science, or that it won't. It means only that it is not an art, but a virtual science.

Anyone who has read my "Ultimatum" in *Portugal Futurista* (1917) will be shocked by these remarks. The philosophy expressed there would seem to be exactly the same as that of Fernando Pessoa, although it does in fact predate it. This isn't quite true. The practical conclusion might be identical, but the theoretical conclusion, which, for a theory, is the practical conclusion, is different.

To summarize, my theory was (1) that philosophy should be replaced by philosophies, that is, change one's metaphysics as one might change one's shirt, replacing the metaphysical search for truth with the metaphysical search for emotion and interest; and (2) that metaphysics should be replaced by science.

It's easy to see that this theory, while, in practice, having almost the same results as Fernando Pessoa's, is in fact different. I don't reject metaphysics, *I reject all virtual sciences*, that is, all sciences that have not yet reached the "mathematical" state; however, in order not to waste those virtual sciences, which, because they exist, represent a human need, *I make art out of them*, or, rather, I propose that art should be made out of them—out of metaphysics, various metaphysics, trying to come up with coherent, diverting systems of the universe, but with no intention of creating something true, just as in art we describe and discuss some interesting emotion, without worrying about whether it does or does not correspond to any objective truth.

It is for that reason that I replace the virtual sciences by the arts in the subjective field, so as not to forsake the desire or human ambition that brings them into existence, and which, like all desires, demands satisfaction, however illusory, and replace virtual sciences with real sciences in the objective field.

Let me make still clearer the difference between me and Fernando Pessoa. For him, metaphysics is *essentially* art, and sociology, about which he doesn't speak, is, naturally, science. For me, they are both equally, *essentially* sciences, although they are not as yet sciences, and may never be, but for an extrinsic, not an intrinsic reason. I propose, then, that they be replaced by arts because they are not really sciences, which means that, between my theory and that of Fernando Pessoa, there may, in practice, be that coincidence of effects that is often found between theories that have not just diverged, but are resolutely opposed.

I will go further ... Metaphysics can be a scientific activity, but it can also be an artistic one. As a scientific activity, however virtual, it seeks *to know*; as an artistic activity, it seeks *to feel*. Metaphysics deals with the abstract and the absolute. Now, the abstract and the absolute can be felt and not just thought, for the simple reason that everything that exists can be felt. The abstract can be considered, or felt, as not-concrete or as directly abstract, that is, relatively or absolutely. The emotion of the abstract as non-concrete—i.e., undefined—is the basis, or even the essence, of *religious* feeling, and includes in that feeling both the religiosity of the Beyond, and the secular religiosity of a future humanity, because, once one forms a vision of a *definitive*, i.e., absolute humanity, or of a *definitive* i.e., absolute political ideal, you experience it non-concretely, because you experience it in relation to concrete reality, and in opposition to the "eternal flux and reflux" that forms the basis of that vision. The emotion of the abstract as abstract—i.e., defined—is the basis or even the essence of *metaphysical* feeling. Metaphysical and religious feeling are directly opposed, as one can clearly see in the metaphysical infecundity (for lack of any highly original metaphysical ideas) in ages such as ours, where speculations about utopian societies are the most noticeable phenomena, and there would be no metaphysics at all if there were not some deficiency in the other part of the religious spirit and in that freedom of thought that stimulates all speculation; or, as in the Middle Ages, it became lost in the adaptation of Greek metaphysics by theology, apart from the metaphysical star of an occasional heresy shining briefly in that caliginous night.

Religious feeling defies rationalization, and there can be no theology or utopian sociology without deceit or disease. Metaphysical feeling can be rationalized, as can any feeling for some definable thing, which only has to become *entirely* defined to be transformed into rational or scientific matter. All I propose is that metaphysical matter, as long as it is not entirely defined, and is therefore in the process of being thought and therefore on its way to becoming a science, should at least be *felt* and metaphysics should therefore be an art; given that everything, good or bad, true or false, does, because it exists, have a *vital* right to exist.

The aesthetic and social theory I expounded in "Ultimatum" can be summed up like this: in the irrationalization of activities that are not (at least not yet) rationalizable. Since metaphysics is a virtual science, and sociology another, I propose the irrationalization of both— that is, metaphysics becomes art, which irrationalizes it because it deprives it of any finality; and sociology becomes pure politics, which irrationalizes it because it makes practical what it is only theoretical. I do not propose the replacement of metaphysics with religion or sociology with social utopianism, because that would be not to irrationalize, but to subrationalize those activities, giving them not a diverse finality, but an inferior degree of finality.

This, in short, is what I was defending in "Ultimatum." And the entirely new and original political and aesthetic theories that I propose in that proclamation are, for an entirely logical reason, entirely irrational, just like life.

4   [c. December 1924–January 1925]
Notes for a Non-Aristotelian Aesthetic
I

Nowadays (once they've been told), everyone knows that there are so-called non-Euclidean geometries, that is, ones that are based on postulates different from those proposed by Euclid, and that reach different conclusions. Each of these geometries has its own logical development: they are independent interpretative systems, independently applied to reality. This process of multiplying "real" geometries and coming up, so to speak, with various types of abstraction based on the same objective reality has proved very fruitful for mathematics and beyond (Einstein owes a lot to it).

Now, just as we can create—if we choose to and if they prove useful—non-Euclidean geometries, I see no reason why we don't create—why we don't choose to and why they wouldn't prove useful—a non-Aristotelian aesthetics.

A long time ago, and without even realizing, I formulated a non-Aristotelian aesthetic. I wish to set down the notes I made in perhaps immodest parallel with Riemann's thesis on classical geometry.

I call Aristotelian aesthetics one that believes that the aim of art is beauty or, rather, the production in others of the same feeling as that provoked by the contemplation or sensation of beautiful things. For classical art—and its derivatives, Romantic, decadent art, etc.—beauty is the aim, although the paths to that end may diverge, just as in mathematics there can be different proofs of the same theorem. Classical art gave us great, sublime works, which is not to say that the theory behind the construction of those works is correct, or is the only correct theory. In both theoretical and practical life, it often happens that one can arrive at a correct result via incorrect or even faulty processes.

I believe I can formulate an aesthetic based not on the idea of beauty, but on *force*—using that word in its abstract, scientific sense; because were I using it in its vulgar sense, it would, in a way, merely be beauty in a disguised form. This new aesthetic, while accepting many classical works as excellent in their own right—but doing so for a different reason to the Aristotelians, which was, of course, also that of their creators—allows for the possibility of constructing new kinds of art unimaginable or unacceptable to any supporter of Aristotelian theory.

For me, art is, *like any activity*, a sign of force or energy, but, since art is produced by living beings, and is, therefore, a product of life, the force manifested in art is the same as that manifested in life. Now, vital force has two aspects, that of integration and disintegration—anabolism and catabolism as physiologists call it. Without the coexistence and equilibrium of those two forces, there would be no life, because pure integration is the absence of life and pure disintegration is death. Since these forces oppose each other and balance each other in order for there to be life while it lasts, life is an action accompanied automatically and intrinsically by a corresponding reaction. And the specific phenomenon of life resides in the automatic nature of that reaction.

The *value* of a life—i.e., the vitality of an organism—resides, then, in the intensity of its reactive force. Since, though, that reaction is automatic, and balances the action that provokes it, the force of the action, namely, de-integration, has to be equally strong. In order for there to be intensity or vital value (the only possible value in the concept of life) or vitality, these two forces must be equally intense, because if not, there can be no equilibrium, with one being less than the other. Thus, the vital equilibrium is not a direct fact—as the Aristotelians want (this is, after all, the point of these notes)—but the abstract results of the encounter between two facts.

Now art, which is made because it is felt and in order to be felt—if not, it would be science or propaganda—is based on sensibility. Sensibility, then, is the *life* of art. However, within sensibility there must be the necessary action and reaction that make art live, the disintegration and integration which, in balance, give it life. If the integrational force in art comes from outside sensibility, it would come from *outside life*; it would not be an automatic or natural reaction, but a mechanical or artificial one.

How can we apply to art the vital principle of integration and disintegration? This is easy enough; as with most problems it is enough to see precisely what the problem is. If we look at the fundamental aspect of integration and disintegration, that is, its manifestation in the so-called inorganic world, we see that integration manifests as *cohesion*, and disintegration as *frangibility*, that is having a tendency, for (at this level) almost entirely macroscopically external reasons—and which are, to a greater or lesser degree, perpetually active—for the body to split, to break up, to cease to be the body it is. In the so-called organic world, these two forces coexist, changing their names depending on how they manifest.

As for sensibility, the principle of cohesion comes from the individual characterized by that sensibility, or, rather, by that form of sensibility, because it is the *form*—taking that word in its abstract, complete sense—that defines the individualized whole. In sensibility, the principle of frangibility comes in many different forms, most of them external, and these are reflected in the individual psyche through the non-sensibility, that is, through the intelligence and the will—the former tending to de-integrate the sensibility by disturbing it, inserting into it elements (ideas) that are general and so necessarily contrary to the individual, making the sensibility human rather than personal; the latter tends to de-integrate the sensibility by limiting it, removing from it all elements that are redundant either because excessive to action itself or because superfluous to rapid, perfect action, thus making the sensibility centrifugal rather than centripetal.

Sensibility reacts against those disruptive tendencies in order to cohere and, like everything in *life*, it reacts with a particular form of cohesion, that of *assimilation*, that is, the conversion of the elements of extraneous forces into personal elements, into its own substance.

So, contrary to Aristotelian aesthetics, which demand that the individual generalizes or humanizes his necessarily private and personal sensibility, in this new theory the opposite is true: the general must be particularized, the human must be personalized, the "external" must become "internal."

I think this theory is more logical—if logic exists—than the Aristotelian theory; and I believe this for the simple reason that art thus remains the contrary of science, which is not the case with Aristotelianism. In Aristotelian aesthetics, as in science, one moves in art from the particular to the general; in this theory, one moves in art from the general to the particular, which is not what happens in science, in which one moves from the particular to the general. And since science and art are, intuitively and axiomatically, opposing activities, so, too, are the ways in which they manifest themselves, and the theory that shows these ways as being truly opposed is more likely to be correct than one that shows them as convergent or similar.

Above all, art is a social phenomenon. Now, in man there are two clearly social qualities, that is, qualities that impinge directly upon his social life: the gregarious spirit, which makes him feel equal or similar to other men, and to want to reach out to them; and the individual or separatist spirit, which makes him distance himself from them, place himself in opposition to them, to be their competitor, their enemy, their half enemy. Any individual is both individual and human: different from all the others and similar to all the others.

A healthy social life comes from a balance between those two feelings: the healthy, social man is defined by an aggressive fraternity. Now, if art is a social phenomenon, it already contains that gregarious element, but where is the separatist element? We cannot look for it outside of art, because then there would be no extraneous element in art, which would diminish it as art; we have to look for it inside art— that is, the separatist element has to manifest itself in art too, and *as art*.

This means that, in art, which is, before all else, a social phenomenon, the gregarious and the separatist spirit have to take on *a social form*.

Now, of course, the separatist, antigregarious spirit has two forms: the withdrawing from others, and the imposition of the individual on others, the superimposition of the individual on others—isolation and *dominion*. Of these two forms, the second is the *social* one, because to isolate oneself is to cease to be social. Art, therefore, is, above all, *an effort to dominate others*. There are, needless to say, various ways of dominating or trying to dominate others: art is one of them.

There are two processes involved in dominating or winning—seduction and subjugation. Seduction is the gregarious way of dominating and winning; subjugation is the antigregarious way of dominating and winning.

All superior social activities involve these two processes, because there can be no others; and, if I refer specifically to superior social activities, it is because these are the ones that involve the idea of dominion. There are three superior social activities—politics, religion, and art. Each of these branches of superior social activity involves seduction and subjugation.

In politics there is democracy, which is the politics of seduction, and dictatorship, which is the politics of subjugation. Any system that exists to please and to seduce is democratic—whether it be the oligarchic or plutocratic seduction of modern democracy, which seduces only certain minorities, which includes or excludes the real majority; or whether it be the mystical, representative seduction of medieval monarchy, the only truly democratic system, since only the monarchy, given its essentially mystical nature, can seduce both majorities and groups that are organically mystic in their innermost lives. And any political system that exists to subordinate and subjugate is dictatorial—whether that is the artificial despotism of the tyrant wielding physical, inorganic, and unrepresentative power, as in decadent empires and *political* dictatorships; whether it is the natural despotism of the tyrant wielding mental, organic, and representative power, the hidden envoy, when the time comes, of a people's subconscious destinies.

There is also a metaphysics of religion, which is the religion of seduction, because it tries to insinuate itself through reason, and explaining or proving are both evidence of a desire to seduce; and there is "proper" religion, which subjugates through unproven dogma and inexplicable ritual, thus taking direct, superior advantage of the confusion in men's souls.

As in politics and religion, so in art. There is an art that dominates by seduction, another that dominates by subjugation. The former is art according to Aristotle, the latter is art as I understand and defend it. The former is naturally based on the idea of *beauty*, because it is based on what *pleases*; it is based on *intelligence*, because it is based on what is general and comprehensible and, therefore, *pleasurable*; it is based on the artificial unity, *constructed* and inorganic, and therefore *visible*, of a machine, and is therefore *valuable* and pleasurable. The latter is based naturally on the idea of *force*, because it is based on *subjugation*; it is based on *sensibility*, because sensibility is private and personal, and it is with what is private and personal in us that we dominate, otherwise, to dominate would be to lose one's personality, or, in other words, to be dominated; and it is based on the spontaneous, organic, *natural* unity that can be felt or not felt, but never seen, never visible, because it is not there to be seen.

All art begins with sensibility and is based on that. Whereas the Aristotelian artist subordinates his sensibility to his intelligence, in order to make that sensibility human and universal, that is, to make it accessible and pleasurable, and thus *seduce* others, the non-Aristotelian artist subordinates everything to his sensibility, converts everything into the stuff of sensibility, thus making his sensibility as *abstract* as his intelligence (without it ceasing to be sensibility), as *transmittable* as the will (without it ceasing to be the will), thus becoming a *transmittable, abstract sensible focus* that forces others, whether they want to or not, to feel what he felt, dominating them by an unexplained force, the way the stronger athlete dominates the weaker, the way the spontaneous dictator subjugates a whole people (because it is a synthesis of him and therefore greater than the sum of him), the way the founder of religions dogmatically and absurdly converts other people's souls to the substance of a doctrine which is, basically, *him*.

The true artist is a dynamogenic focus: the false or Aristotelian artist is a mere transformer, destined merely to convert the direct current of his own sensibility into the alternating current of another's intelligence.

Among "classical," that is, Aristotelian artists, there are true and false artists; and among non-Aristotelian artists, there are true artists and mere simulators—because theory does not make the artist, you have to be born an artist. However, what I understand and defend is that every true artist falls within my theory, whether he thinks of himself as an Aristotelian or not; and every false artist falls within the Aristotelian theory, even if he is trying to be a non-Aristotelian. That is what I still need to explain and demonstrate.

Unlike Aristotelian aesthetics, whose very foundation is the idea of beauty, my theory is based on the idea of force. Now the idea of beauty can be a force. When the "idea" of beauty is an "idea" of sensibility, an *emotion* and not an idea, a temperamental inclination towards sensibility, that "idea" of beauty is a force. Only when it is merely an *intellectual* idea of beauty is it not a force.

Thus, the art of the Greeks is still great even according to my criterion, *especially according to my criterion*. For the Greeks, beauty, harmony, and proportion were not intellectual concepts, they were the fruit of their inner sensibility. That is why they were *an aesthetic people*, searching for and demanding beauty *from everyone, in all things, always*. That explains the violence with which they *broadcast* their sensibility to the future world, a sensibility to which we remain subject. Our sensibility, though, is so very different—having been worn away for so long by so many social forces—that we cannot receive that *broadcast* with our sensibility, but only with our intelligence. This aesthetic disaster stems from the fact that we mostly received that *broadcast* through the Romans and the French. The former, although close to the Greeks in time, were always so incapable of aesthetic feeling that they had to use their intelligence to *receive* that broadcast from Greek sensibility. The latter, with their narrow sensibility and pseudo-intellectualism, were capable of "taste," but not of aesthetic emotion, and so they distorted the already distorted Romanization of Hellenism, elegantly photographing the Roman painting of a Greek statue. A great gulf—which defies measurement—already exists between the *Iliad* and the *Aeneid*—so great that it is evident even in translation; the gulf between a Pindar and a Horace seems infinite. An equally large gulf separates a two-dimensional Homer like Virgil or a Mercator-projection Pindar like Horace from the deadly tedium of a Boileau, a Corneille or a Racine, from all the unbearable aesthetic trash of French "classicism," the same "classicism" whose posthumous rhetoric still suffocates and distorts the admirable transmissive sensibility of Victor Hugo.

However, just as for the "classicists" or pseudo-classicists—i.e., the "Aristotelians"—beauty can be the fruit not of their sensibility, but of the musings of their reason, so for the fake non-Aristotelians, force can be an idea born of the intellect and not of the sensibility. And so just as the mere intellectual idea of beauty does not help in creating beauty, since only the sensibility can truly create, because it really does *broadcast* itself, so the mere intellectual idea of force, or of non-beauty, does not help in creating the force or the non-beauty it is trying to create. This is why there are—and in great abundance too!—simulators of the art of force or non-beauty, who create neither beauty nor non-beauty, because they are incapable of creating anything; they make neither fake Aristotelian art, because they don't want to, nor fake non-Aristotelian art, because there is no such thing. Unwittingly, though, and very badly, they do end up making Aristotelian art, because they make art with their intelligence and not with their sensibility. The majority, if not all, of the so-called realists, naturalists, symbolists, and futurists are mere simulators, I won't say entirely devoid of talent, but certainly, albeit few in number, with a talent for simulation. What they write, paint, or sculpt might be interesting, but only in the way an acrostic is interesting, or a drawing done with a single line and other such things. As long as you don't call it art, that's fine.

Up until now—which marks the first appearance of an authentic doctrine of non-Aristotelian art—there have been only three true manifestations of non-Aristotelian art. The first is to be found in Walt Whitman's astonishing poetry; the second in the even more astonishing poems of my master Caeiro; and the third in the two odes—"Triumphal Ode" and "Maritime Ode"—that I published in *Orpheu*. I don't even consider this to be immodesty on my part. It is quite simply true.

5   [c. 4 June 1927]

Ambience

No age can pass its sensibility on to another age; it can only pass on the intelligence implicit in that sensibility. It is through emotion that we become ourselves, whereas through intelligence we become other. Intelligence disperses us; that is why it is through what disperses us that we survive. Each age gives to subsequent ages only what it was not.

A god, in the pagan, that is, the true, meaning of the word, is only the intelligent sense that a being has of himself, because that intelligent sense of himself is the impersonal and therefore the ideal form of what he is. By making of ourselves an intellectual concept, we make of ourselves a god. Few people, however, do form an intellectual concept of themselves, because the intelligence is essentially objective.

Even among the great geniuses, there are very few who existed for themselves with complete objectivity.

To live is to belong to others. To die is to belong to others. To live and to die are the same thing. But to live is to belong to someone outside ourselves, and to die is to belong to someone inside. The two things are similar, but life is the outside of death. That is why life is life and death is death, because the outside is always truer than the inside, since the outside is the visible part.

All true emotion is a lie to the intelligence, because emotion doesn't occur there. All true emotion wears a false expression. To express yourself is to say what you don't feel.

The cavalry horses are the cavalry. Without the horses, the riders would be pedestrians. The locus makes the locality. To be is to exist.

To pretend is to know oneself.

6   [c. 14 August 1929]

Novella

My friend Moreira owned an old country house with a garden, and he once commissioned an elegant kennel to be made for a dog. A carpenter agreed to do the work, and, attracted by the strangeness of the commission and by the supposed madness of the man asking him to take on the task, he constructed a kind of chalet that would, without exaggeration, have cost a fortune.

When the kennel was ready, Moreira came to inspect and approve his work. He praised the carpenter and then left to ponder the matter.

Days later, when the carpenter appeared with the bill, Moreira asked him to go with him into the garden. When they reached the kennel, he said sweetly.

"Look, carpenter, leave the bill in the kennel. The dog will pay."*

---

* In old-fashioned Portuguese, the word for "dog" (*cão*) could also mean "trap" or "trick." We've attempted at least to make a joke of it, but a different one. The original Portuguese text ends thus: "*Ela é que é o cão.*" (She [the kennel] is the dog.) —Trs.

7

All art is a form of literature, because all art is saying something. There are two ways of saying—speaking and remaining silent. The visual arts are not literature, they are the projections of an expressive silence. In every art that is not literature one must look for the silent sentence it contains, or the poem, or the novel, or the drama. When we say "a symphonic poem," we are speaking very exactly, and not in some trite or metaphysical way.

This seems to be less straightforward when it comes to the visual arts, but if we think of lines, planes, volumes, colors, juxtapositions, and contrapositions as verbal phenomena spoken without words, or rather through spiritual hieroglyphs, we will understand how to understand the visual arts, and even if we don't manage to understand them then, we will, at least, have within our grasp the book that contains the cipher and a soul that can contain the decipherment.

That will do until the rest arrives.

8   [c. November 1935]

Brief Note

The superior poet says what he actually feels. The average poet says what he decides to feel. The inferior poet says what he thinks he should feel.

None of this has anything to do with sincerity. Firstly, no one knows what he really feels: it's possible to feel relieved at the death of a loved one, and to think that we are feeling grief, because that is what you should feel on such occasions. Most people feel conventionally, albeit with great human sincerity, not, however, with any kind or degree of intellectual sincerity, that is what matters to the poet. So much so that in the whole long history of Poetry, I don't think there have been more than four or five poets who said what they truly, and not just effectively, were feeling. There are some very great poets who never did, who remained incapable of doing so. At most, certain poets have moments when they do say what they feel. Here and there,

Wordsworth does. Once or twice Coleridge does: for *The Rime of the Ancient Mariner* and *Kubla Khan* are more sincere than the whole of Milton, even, I would say, than the whole of Shakespeare. I have one reservation as regards Shakespeare, and that is that Shakespeare was essentially and structurally factitious, which is why his constant insincerity manages to be constant sincerity, whence his greatness.

When an inferior poet feels, he feels by the book. He might be sincere in his emotions, but what does that matter if he is insincere in his poetry? There are poets who pour their feelings into their verse, never checking to see if they ever did feel those feelings. Camões mourns the loss of a sweet soul, and it turns out that the person doing the weeping is Petrarch. If Camões had felt an emotion that was genuinely his, he would have found a new form, new words, anything but the sonnet form with its ten-syllable line. But no, he wrote a sonnet in decasyllables in the same way as he would don mourning in real life.

My master Caeiro was the only entirely sincere poet in the world.

9 [c. January–February 1931]
Notes in Memory of My Master Caeiro
(Some of them)
[1]

I met my master Caeiro in exceptional circumstances—but then all of life's circumstances are exceptional, especially those that are nothing in themselves, but in their results come to be everything.

I was almost three-quarters of the way through my Scottish course in naval engineering, when I left for a journey to the Orient; on the way back, I disembarked in Marseilles and, feeling a great reluctance to continue by ship, I traveled overland to Lisbon. One day, a cousin of mine took me to Ribatejo, and there I met a cousin of Caeiro's, who did business with him, and it was in that cousin's house that I finally met the man who would be my master. That's all there is to say really, because it was a small thing, like any act of fertilization.

I can still see him, with all the clarity of my soul, undimmed by

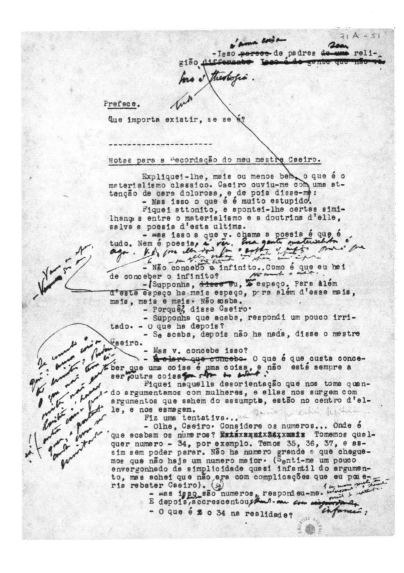

- Isso ~~parece~~ de padres ~~de uma~~ reli-
~~gião differente~~ ~~Isso é de gente que não ~~

Preface.

Que importa existir, se se é?

- -

Notes para a "ecordação do meu mestre Caeiro.

Expliquei-lhe, mais ou menos bem, o que é o
materialismo classico. Caeiro ouviu-me com uma at-
tenção de cera dolorosa, e de pois disse-me:
- Mas isso o que é é muito estupido.
Fiquei attonito, e apontei-lhe certas simi-
lhanças entre o materialismo e a doutrina d'elle,
salve a poesia d'esta ultima.
- mas isso a que v. chama a poesia é que é
tudo. Nem é poesia, a ver.
- Não concebo o infinito..Como é que eu hei
de conceber o infinito?
- Supponha, ~~disso eu~~, o espaço. Para além
d'este espaço ha mais espaço, p ra além d'esse mais,
mais, mais e mais. Não acaba.
- Porquê, disse Caeiro.
- Supponha que acaba, respondi um pouco irri-
tado. - O que ha depois?
- Se acaba, depois não ha nada, disse o mestre
Caeiro.
- Mas v. concebe isso?
- ~~Não sei que concebe.~~ O que é que custa conce-
ber que uma coisa é uma coisa, e não está sempre a
ser outra coisa.
Fiquei naquella desorientação que nos toma quan-
do argumentamos com mulheres, e ellas nos surgem com
argumentos que sahem do assumpto, estão no centro d'el-
le, e nos esmagam.
Fiz uma tentativa...
- Olhe, Caeiro. Considere os numeros... Onde é
que acabam os numeros? ~~Extxxxxxixxxxxxxix~~ Tomemos qual-
quer numero - 34, por exemplo. Temos 35, 36, 37, e as-
sim sem poder parar. Não ha numero grande a que chegue-
mos que não haja um numero maior. (Senti-me um pouco
envergonhado de simplicidade quasi infantil do argumen-
to, mas achei que não era com complicações que eu pode-
ria rebater Caeiro).
- mas isso são numeros, respondeu-me.
E depois, accrescentou
- O que é o 34 na realidade?

memory's tears, because that vision is not an external one … I see him before me, and I will perhaps see him eternally as I did that first time. First, those childlike blue eyes that know no fear; then the already rather prominent cheekbones, his slightly pale complexion, and his strangely tranquil Greek air, which came from within not from without, because it was neither an expression nor his actual features. His almost abundant hair was fair, but in dim light, it took on a chestnut tinge. He was of average height, tall rather than short, and slightly stooped. His face was quite pale, his smile was what it was, his voice the same, uttered in the tone of someone who wants only to say what he is saying—neither loud nor soft, but clear and free of intentions, hesitations, timidities. His blue eyes were always looking. If there was something lacking in a remark we made, he would find it out; his forehead, while not particularly broad, was strikingly pale. Yes, that pallor made it seemed larger than his pale face, which had a certain majesty. His hands were rather thin, but not excessively so; the palms wide. The expression of his face was the last thing you noticed—as if, for him, speaking was less than to exist—it was a smile like the one that, in poetry, one might attribute to beautiful inanimate objects, simply because they please us—flowers, large fields, sunlight on water—a smile that simply exists, not a smile that is telling us something.

My master, my master, lost so early. I can see him again in the shadow that I am inside myself, in the memory I preserve of what is dead inside me …

It was during our first conversation … I don't know how it came about, but he said: "I know a young man called Ricardo Reis, who I'm sure you'd like to meet: he's very different from you." And then he added: "Everything is different from us, which is why everything exists."

These words, spoken as if they were a proverbial saying, were like a sudden seductive jolt, like being possessed for the first time, and they entered the very foundations of my soul. However, unlike a real seduction, their effect was to receive in every one of my sensations a virginity that had not previously existed.

337

[2]

When discussing the clear and direct concept of things, which characterizes Caeiro's sensibility, I quoted to him, with friendly perversity, what Wordsworth believed to be a description of an insensitive nature:

> *A primrose by a river's brim*
> *A yellow primrose was to him,*
> *And it was nothing more.*

And I translated these lines (omitting the exact translation of "primrose," because I don't know the names of flowers or plants): "*Uma flor à margem do rio para êle era uma flor amarela, e não era mais nada.*"

My master Caeiro laughed. "That simpleton had a good eye: a yellow flower really is only that, a yellow flower."

Then, suddenly, he thought and said:

"There is one difference. It depends on whether you consider the yellow flower to be one of several yellow flowers or just that single yellow flower."

And then he added:

"What the English poet meant was that, for that particular man, seeing the yellow flower was an ordinary or everyday experience. And that's not good. We should see everything as if for the first time, because it really is the first time we're seeing it. And so every yellow flower is a new yellow flower, even if it is the 'same one' as yesterday. We are not the same, nor is the flower. Even the color yellow is no longer the same. It's a shame that we don't have the eyes to know this, because then we would all be happy."

[3]

My master Caeiro wasn't a pagan: he was paganism itself. Ricardo Reis is a pagan, Antonio Mora is a pagan, I am a pagan; Fernando Pessoa himself would be a pagan were he not such a tangled skein inside himself. But Reis is a pagan by nature, Mora by intellect; I am a pagan out of sheer rebelliousness, that is, by temperament. There was no explanation for Caeiro's paganism, only consubstantiation.

I will define this the way one defines indefinable things, by taking the coward's way out, and giving an example. One of the things that most clearly sets us apart from the Greeks is their absence of any concept of infinity, their distaste for infinity. Well, in that regard, my master Caeiro shared that same un-concept. I give below what I believe to be a very precise account of the astonishing conversation in which he revealed this to me.

He was telling me—in fact, developing what he says in one of his poems in *The Keeper of Sheep*, that someone or other had once called him a "materialist poet." I didn't particularly agree with this description, because my master Caeiro is not definable in that way, but I told him that the description wasn't entirely absurd. And I tried to explain to him, as best I could, what classical materialism is. Caeiro listened to me intently, but with a pained look on his face, then he said brusquely:

"But that is just very stupid. It's the sort of thing that priests with no religion come out with, and there's no excuse for it."

I was taken aback, and pointed out various similarities between materialism and his own doctrine, although not including his poetry. Caeiro protested.

"But what you call poetry is everything. It's not poetry, it's seeing. Materialists are blind. You say that they say: space is infinite. Where did they ever see that in space?"

And somewhat confused, I said: "But don't you conceive of space as being infinite? Can't you conceive of space as being infinite?"

"I don't conceive of anything as infinite. How can I possibly conceive of anything as infinite?"

"Listen," I replied, "imagine a space. Beyond that space, there's more space. Beyond that, still more and more and more … It doesn't end."

"Why?" asked my master Caeiro.

I suffered a kind of mental earthquake. "But what if it does end," I cried. "What lies beyond that?"

"If it ends, there's nothing beyond," he replied.

This sort of argument, childish and feminine and therefore unanswerable, tied my brain in knots for a few moments.

"But can you imagine that?" I said at last.

"Imagine what? That a thing has certain limits? Of course! Something without limits cannot exist. To exist presupposes that there is something else, which means that everything is limited. What's so hard about thinking that a thing is a thing and not always something else beyond it?"

At this point, I had the physical sensation that I was speaking not with another man, but with another universe. I made one last effort, a detour that I convinced myself was legitimate.

"Listen, Caeiro ... Think of numbers. Where do numbers end? Let's take any number—34, for instance. Beyond that, we have 35, 36, 37, 38, and so on, without end. There's no large number that doesn't have a still larger number following it ... "

"But that's only numbers," my master protested.

And then he added, looking at me like a formidable child:

"What is number 34 in Reality?"

[4]

There are certain sudden phrases, which are deep because they come from the deep, which define a man or, rather, a man defines himself indefinitely by them. I will never forget what Ricardo Reis said in this regard. He was talking about lying, and he said: "I hate a lie, because it is inexact." That contains all of Ricardo Reis—past, present, and future.

Since my master Caeiro only ever said what he was, he can be defined by anything he wrote or said, especially after the period that begins midway through *The Keeper of Sheep*. However, among all the many things he wrote that were published, among all the many things he said to me and which I have told or not told, the words that contain him most simply are those he said to me once in Lisbon. He was talking about something or other to do with how we each relate to ourselves. And I suddenly asked my master Caeiro: "Are you content with yourself?" And he replied: "No: I am content." It was like the voice of the earth, which is everything and no one.

[5]

I never saw my master Caeiro sad. I don't know if he was sad when he died or in the days preceding his death. I could find out, but the truth is I've never dared to ask those who were with him when he died about his death or about how he faced it.

Anyway, it is one of the great griefs of my life—one of the real griefs in among so many fictitious ones—that Caeiro should have died without me by his side. This is stupid, but human, and true.

I was in England. Ricardo Reis was no longer in Lisbon, having gone back to Brazil. Fernando Pessoa was there, but it was as if he wasn't. Fernando Pessoa does feel things, but he isn't moved, not even inside.

Nothing can console me for not having been in Lisbon on that day, apart from the spontaneous consolation that thinking about my master brings me. No one can be inconsolable when remembering Caeiro or his poetry; and in my dear master's work and the memory of him, even the idea of the void—the most terrifying of all if you think of it with your sensibility—has something luminous and lofty about it, like the sun shining down on the snow of unreachable peaks.

10   [c. 1930*]

One day, Caeiro said something truly astonishing. We were talking, or, rather, I was talking about the immortality of the soul, and I was saying that, even if it were false, I found this a necessary concept, in order to be able to bear existence intellectually and to see in it more than just a pile of more or less conscious stones.

"I don't know what being necessary means," Caeiro said.

I responded without responding: "Tell me something. What are you for yourself?"

"What am I for myself?" Caeiro repeated. "I am a sensation of me."

---

* From this prose text onwards, none were published during Pessoa's lifetime.

I will never forget the feeling of shock as those words collided with my soul. My soul is prepared for many things, including things that go counter to Caeiro's intentions. But this was, after all, so spontaneous, like a ray of sunlight falling without a thought as to why.

11 [c. 1930]

My master Caeiro was a master for anyone capable of having a master. Anyone who was close to Caeiro, who spoke with him, who had the physical opportunity of knowing his mind, was a changed person after encountering that unique Rome from which you did not return the same as when you went—unless that person did not make the journey, that is, unless that person was, like most people, incapable of being an individual except in the sense of being a body separate from other bodies and symbolically corrupted by the human form.

No inferior man can have a master, because the master has nothing to give to such a man. That is why strong, clearly defined temperaments are easily hypnotized, why normal men are relatively easy to hypnotize, but not idiots, imbeciles, the weak and incoherent. Being strong means being capable of feeling.

As you will have gathered, the three main people around my master Caeiro were Ricardo Reis, Antonio Mora and me. I am flattering no one, not even myself, when I say that we were, and are, three individuals completely distinct, at least brainwise, from the current animal humanity. And all three of us owe the best of the soul we now have to our contact with my master Caeiro. We are all different—that is, we are ourselves more intensely—after passing through the sieve of that carnal intervention of the Gods.

Ricardo Reis was a latent pagan, detached from modern life and detached from the ancient life too, into which he should have been born—detached from modern life because his intelligence was of a different type and quality; detached from ancient life because he could not feel it, for one cannot feel what is not here. Caeiro, the rebuilder of Paganism, or, rather, its founder insofar as it is eternal, brought him the sensibility he lacked. And Ricardo Reis found the pagan in himself that he already was. Before he met Caeiro, Ricardo Reis had not written a single line, and when he met Caeiro, he was already twenty-five. After meeting Caeiro and hearing him recite *The Keeper of Sheep*, Ricardo Reis came to realize that he was, organically, a poet. Some psychologists say that it is possible to change sex. I don't know if this is true, because I don't know if anything is "true." However, Ricardo Reis did cease being a woman to become a man, or ceased being a man to become a woman—as you prefer—when he came into contact with Caeiro.

Antonio Mora was a shadow with speculative tendencies. He spent his time chewing over Kant and trying to see with his mind if life had any meaning. Indecisive, like all strong men, he had not found the truth, or whatever for him was the truth, which comes I think to the same thing. He found Caeiro and found the truth. My master Caeiro gave him the soul he lacked; placed a central Mora inside the peripherical Mora that he had always been. And the result was the reduction of Caeiro's instinctive thoughts to a system and a logical truth. The triumphant results were those two treatises, marvels of originality and of thought: *The Return of the Gods* and *Prologomena to a Reformation of Paganism*.

As for me, before I met Caeiro, I was a nervous machine making nothing at all. I met my master Caeiro later than Reis or Mora, who met him, respectively, in 1912 and 1913. I met Caeiro in 1914. I had already written some poetry—three sonnets and two poems—"Carnival" and "Opiary." Those sonnets and those poems show what I was feeling when I lacked support. As soon as I met Caeiro, I found myself. I arrived in London and immediately wrote "Triumphal Ode." And since then, for good or ill, I have been me. Even more curious is the case of Fernando Pessoa, who does not, properly speaking, exist. He met Caeiro shortly before me—on March 8, 1914, according to him. That month, Caeiro had come to spend a week in Lisbon, and it was then that Fernando met him. He heard him read *The Keeper of Sheep*. He went home with a fever (his own), and wrote, in one fell swoop, "Oblique Rain," all six poems. "Oblique Rain" is nothing like any of my master Caeiro's poems, apart from a certain rectilinear quality in the rhythm. But Fernando Pessoa would have been incapable of plucking those extraordinary poems out of his inner world if he had not met Caeiro. And yet, moments after meeting Caeiro, he experienced the spiritual shock that produced those poems. Instantly. Because he has an excessively quick sensibility, accompanied by an excessively quick intelligence, Fernando reacted at once to the Great Vaccine— the vaccine against the stupidity of the intelligent. And that group of six poems, "Oblique Rain," is the most admirable thing in Fernando Pessoa's work. Yes, he might write greater things, but never anything more original, never anything newer, or, who knows, greater. More than that, there will never be anything more truly Fernando Pessoa, more intimately Fernando Pessoa. What could be a better expression of his always intellectualized sensibility, his intense inattentive attention, the warm subtlety of his cool self-analysis, than those poem-intersections, where the state of the soul is simultaneously two, where the subjective and the objective are both separate and one, where the real and the unreal fuse in order to be completely distinct. Fernando Pessoa made of these poems a true photograph of his own soul. In a moment, a unique moment, he managed to have his own individuality—which he never had before and never will again, for the simple reason that he doesn't have one.

Long live my master Caeiro!

12   [c. 1930]

I marvel at Antonio Mora's doctrine and, with a delicately dismissive gesture, I totally disagree with it. The trouble with all these men—Ricardo Reis, Antonio Mora and Fernando Pessoa, and, yes, because I consider myself to be beyond idolatry, my master Caeiro too—is that they see only reality. They all see it with diverse clarity; all are objectivists, even Fernando Pessoa, who is also a subjectivist. But I don't just see reality—*I touch it*. That is why they are, more or less overtly, polytheists, and I am a monotheist. The world when seen with the eyes is essentially diverse. When you use touch, though, there is no diversity.

They are all, diversely, more intelligent than me, but I am profoundly more practical than them. That is why I believe in God. I sometimes think that Milton could only ascend to a sublime sense of the Divinity when, deprived of sight, he returned to the great primitive world of touch, to the great unity of matter. And Satan himself, who is only the distorted shadow of God cast by the light of the apparent, can see best when his eyes have become black night.

The variety of the world is only variety when there is an implicit contrast with some kind of unity. And that intuited unity is God.

13 [c. 1930]
All ancient pagan civilization, which, for Caeiro, was the very blood of his soul, was, and is, for Reis, a beloved childhood memory—an education deeply embedded in his being.

14 [c. 1930]
I felt bewildered at first by this man singing gaily about things, whether true or imagined, which fill everyone with pain or horror—materiality, death, the unbeyond. I felt bewildered, too, that he not only did this joyfully, he communicated that joy to others. When I'm very sad, I read Caeiro and it's like feeling a gentle breeze. I immediately feel calm, filled with song and faith—yes, after reading the poems of that atheist of God and that man with no terrestrial beyond, I feel faith in God, in the soul, in the transcendent smallness of life.

Why? Because the personality behind the work vitalizes it with something other than the ideas that are there, and through which that personality apparently manifests itself. It's the poet Caeiro, not the philosopher Caeiro, who loves us. What we really receive from those verses is a child's sense of life, with all the direct materiality of a child's ideas, and all the vital spirituality of hope and growth, which belong, body and soul, to the unconscious life of childhood. That work is a dawn that wakes us and cheers us up; and that dawn is, nonetheless, material, rather than antispiritual, because it is an abstract effect, pure vacuum, nothing.

Apart from that, though, Caeiro's work has a critical effect. Those verses of direct sensation contrast his soul with our concepts that lack all naturalness, our artificial, mental, pigeonholing civilization, they tear up all the rags we thought of as clothes, wash our face clean of chemicals and our stomachs of pharmaceuticals—they burst into our house and show us that a table made of wood is wood, wood, wood, and that a table is a necessary hallucination of our industrial will.

Happy is the man who manages, even for a moment, to see the table as wood, to *feel* the table as wood—to see the wood of the table without seeing the table. He may "know" afterwards that it is a table, but he will never again forget that it is wood. And he will love the table, as a table, even more. That was the effect Caeiro had on me. I didn't stop seeing the appearance of things, their divine or human artificiality, but I also saw the material soul of the material they were made of. I was set free. Ever since then, I was like one of those Rosicrucians, of whom we have read the legend or the truth, and who, while superficially similar to all human beings and conforming to the customs and manners of the egalitarian world, knows the secret of the Universe and always knows where "the escape route" is, and the magic of essentiation.

15 [c. 1930]

Fernando Pessoa wrote at full tilt—at full human tilt—those very human and very complicated poems, yes, Fernando Pessoa, who, when he writes a quatrain puts industrial effort into seeing how he will place the number of syllables it must, by law, contain; who, when he feels something, immediately snips away at it with a pair of highly critical scissors pondering why the second line contains a disparate adjective and how, given that "but" is not the right word at that point, he is going to make "except" have only one syllable.

At that moment, this man, so pointlessly gifted, living constantly in the parabulia of his own complexity, finds his liberation. If one day he should go so far as to publish a book, and should that turn out to be a poetry book, with the brief poems all dated, you will see, then, if there is anything different about those dated after March 8, 1914.

Ricardo Reis listened, but he seemed not so much attentive to what Caeiro said as to some remote consequence or distant echo of those words. When I read what Reis wrote, I understood. The rising sun was illuminating the cornices of ancient temples, and blood was dripping from the desiccated entrails of that soul's divinations. In some previous incarnation—real or metaphorical—the ancient gods had been a reality for that being; and he could see them again, revealed now by that grown-up child, and he knew they were real.

In his way, Reis was waking up too.

Being, as I so profoundly am, a disciple of my master Caeiro, I am an intelligent disciple and, therefore, critical. He would not want to be followed in any other way, because he did not like mere animals.

Thus, I never accepted that criterion of Caeiro's—and which is, besides, not the most original of his ideas—that there is a distinction to be made between the natural and the artificial. There is no distinction, because both are real. I understand the distinction between dreams and life, although I agree that a good metaphysician could confuse the two. But the distinction between a tree and a machine has always seemed false to me. It seems that the tree and the machine are different because the former is the immediate product of nature, and the latter an intermediate product, with the human intelligence as intermediary. In reality, though, every product is intermediate: the tree appears out of the seed, the machine out of someone's intelligence. Both seed and intelligence are elements of reality. And if we say that the tree springs from the seed and the machine from the brain, we will have reduced everything to material terms and established their equal rights as matter.

No, I never accepted Caeiro's criterion of artificiality, nor his views on humanitarianism. Caeiro despises the artificial because it was not born of the earth, and he despises humanitarianism because it is not born of egotism. But the blossom on a tree is born not of the earth, but of the tree, and a love of humanity is born not of egotism but of a weariness with egotism. Everything is natural but with a wider circumference.

I can still hear, in my heart's memory, that voice, so placid and cool—and yet so full of all the inner warmth of reality!—saying, with all his inner simplicity: "Álvaro de Campos, I believe in what I have to accept." And I adopt those words letter for letter. I believe in the machine because I have to accept it just as I do the tree.

Yes, I know that Nature is the refuge, that the fields harbor all kinds of tuberculars from every part of the body, that the wind stirring the trees, etc., etc. But I have withdrawn to the hubbub of a large factory; I have fled from the world into a large international café; I have already been a hermit in the hermitage of no one knowing who I was in a provincial town whose name I didn't know and still don't know.

18   [27 February 1931]

It has become customary to say, ever since someone first started saying it, that, in order to understand a philosophical system, you need to understand the temperament of the philosopher. Like all things with a very confident air about them, and that are widely circulated, this is utter nonsense; if it weren't, it would not have circulated so widely. Philosophy gets confused with its formation. My temperament could lead me to say that two and two are five, but the statement that two and two are five is false quite independently of my temperament, whatever that might be. It might be interesting to know how I arrived at this falsehood, but this has nothing to do with the falsehood itself, it only has to do with the reason for its appearance.

My master Caeiro was a temperament devoid of philosophy, and that's why his philosophy—for, like everyone, he had one—isn't even susceptible to silly intellectual journalism. It's true that, since he was a temperament, that is, a poet, my master Caeiro expressed a philosophy, that is, a concept of the universe. That concept of the universe, though, is instinctive, not intellectual; it cannot be classified as a

concept because it isn't there, and cannot be classified as a tempera-
ment because a temperament defies classification.

An attempt to define, with more or less logical success, the ideas
organically concealed in my master Caeiro's poetic expression can be
found in certain of Ricardo Reis's theories, or in my own, or in the
philosophical system—this time perfectly defined—of Antonio Mora.
Caeiro is such fertile ground that, even though each of us owes all of
our soul's thoughts to our shared master, we each produced an inter-
pretation of life entirely different from each other. We really have no
right to compare my metaphysics and that of Ricardo Reis—which are
mere poetic vagaries struggling to explain themselves (unlike Caeiro,
whose soul was made up of poetic certainties that made no attempt
to explain themselves)—with Antonio Mora's system, which really is
a system and not an attitude or a mere fumbled attempt. However,
while Caeiro stated things which, being true as regards each other (as
we all understood), using a logic that exceeds our comprehension—as
does a stone or a tree—they were not coherent in their superficial
logic, both Reis and I (we won't speak of Mora, who was our superior
in this matter) were trying to find a logical coherence in what we were
thinking or imagined we were thinking about the World. And what
we were thinking or imagined we were thinking about the World we
owed to Caeiro, the discoverer of our souls, the souls later colonized
by us.

Properly speaking, Reis, Mora, and I are three organic interpreta-
tions of Caeiro. Reis and I, who are fundamentally, although diversely,
poets, make interpretations that are still tainted with temperament.
Mora, purely intellectual, interprets with his reason; if he has feelings
or a temperament, he disguises it.

Reis's concept of life can be seen very clearly in his odes, because,
whatever his defects, Reis is always clear. His concept of life is nonex-
istent, unlike Caeiro's, which is also nonexistent, but in a topsy-turvy
way. Ricardo Reis thinks that we can know nothing of reality, except
that it is here and that this universal matter was given to us as being

real. Without necessarily accepting this universe as real, we have to accept it as such, because no other universe was given to us. We have to live in this universe without metaphysics, without morality, without sociology or even politics. We must accept this external universe, the only one we have, just as we would accept the absolute power of a king, without discussing whether it's good or bad, but simply because it is what it is. Let us reduce our activity to the minimum, shutting ourselves up as much as possible in the instincts that were given to us and using them so as to cause as little discomfort to ourselves and to others, because they have just as much right as we do not to feel discomfort. A negative morality, but clear. Let us eat and drink and love (without becoming sentimentally bound to food or drink or love, because that would bring elements of discomfort later on); life is a single day, and night is certain; let us do neither good nor evil to anyone, because we do not know what is good or evil, and we don't even know if we are doing the one when we assumed we were doing the other; the truth, if it exists, lies with the Gods, that is with the forces that formed or created or that govern the world—forces which, given that by their actions they violate all our ideas about what is moral and all our ideas about what is immoral, are patently beyond or outside any concept of good and evil, and so we should expect nothing from them for either good or ill, neither belief in the truth nor belief in the lie; neither optimism nor pessimism. Nothing: a landscape, a glass of wine, a little loveless love, and the vague sadness of understanding nothing and having to lose the little that is given to us. That is the philosophy of Ricardo Reis. It is a harsher version of Caeiro's philosophy, falsified by stylization. In another way, though, it is very much Caeiro's philosophy: the concave aspect of that same arc of which Caeiro is the convex aspect, the turning in on itself of what, in Caeiro, is turned towards the Infinite—yes, towards the same infinite that he denies.

This—this basically negative concept of things—is what gives Ricardo Reis's poetry that hardness, that coldness, which no one could deny, however much they admire it; and those who do admire it—few in number—admire that same coldness. In this, though, Caeiro and

Reis are the same, with the difference that Caeiro is cold without being hard, and that Caeiro, who is the philosophical infancy of Reis's attitude, has the coldness of a statue or a snowy peak, and Reis has the coldness of a beautiful tomb or a marvelous rock so shady even moss does not grow there. That's why, given that Reis's poetry is rigorously classical in form, and totally devoid of vibration—even more so than Horace, despite the latter's great emotional and intellectual content. Reis's poetry is so intellectual, and therefore cold, that anyone who fails to understand one of his poems (which can easily happen, given how compressed their meaning is) will not feel the rhythm.

The same thing happened with me as happened with Ricardo Reis, apart from the fact that it was completely different. Reis is an intellectual, with the minimum of sensibility needed by an intellectual if his intelligence is not simply mathematical, with the minimum a human being needs for someone with a thermometer to confirm that he is not dead. I am exasperatingly sensitive and exasperatingly intelligent. In this respect (apart from having a smidgeon more sensibility and a smidgeon less intelligence) I resemble Fernando Pessoa; however, while in Fernando, sensibility and intelligence interpenetrate, merge and intersect, in me, they exist in parallel or, rather, they overlap. They are not spouses, they are estranged twins. Thus, I spontaneously formed my philosophy out of what is inferred by Caeiro, but which Reis ignored. I mean the part of Caeiro that is entirely contained in the line "And my thoughts are all sensations";[*] Ricardo Reis drew his soul from that other line that Caeiro neglected to write, "My sensations are all thoughts." When I described myself as a "sensationist" or a "sensationist poet," I didn't want to use an expression from the poetic school (a "school," God help us!); the word has a philosophical meaning.

I believe in nothing but the existence of my sensations; I have no other certainty, not even that of the external universe revealed to me by those sensations. I do not see the external universe, I do not hear the external universe, I do not touch the external universe. I

* Line 3 in poem 9 from Caeiro's *The Keeper of Sheep.* —Trs.

see my visual impressions; I hear my auditory impressions; I touch my tactile impressions. I do not see with my eyes, but with my soul; I do not hear with my ears, but with my soul; I do not touch with my fingers, but with my soul. And if anyone asks me what I mean by soul, I answer that I am my soul. That is where I fundamentally diverge from the fundamentally intellectual Caeiro and Reis, but not from the fundamentally instinctive and sensitive Caeiro. For me, the universe is merely a concept of mine, a dynamic, projected synthesis of all my sensations. I can see, or think I see, that many of the sensations experienced by other souls coincide with mine, and I call that coincidence the external universe, or reality. This doesn't prove the absolute reality of the universe, because there exists a kind of collective hypnosis. I once saw a great hypnotist convince a large number of people to see, really see, the same wrong time on clocks that were not there. From that I assume the existence of a supreme Hypnotist, whom I call God, because he succeeds in imposing his suggestion on the generality of souls, which, however, I do not know if he did or did not create, because I don't know what to create means, but it's possible that each of us can create something, just as the hypnotist can suggest that I am another person or that I feel a pain that I cannot say I don't feel because I do feel it. For me, being "real" consists in being susceptible to being experienced by all souls; and that forces me to believe in an Infinite Hypnotist, because he created a suggestion called the universe capable of being experienced by all souls, not just real ones, but even *possible* ones. Apart from this, I'm an engineer—that is, I have no morality, politics, or religion independent of the real reality of measurable things, and independent of the virtual reality of immeasurable things. I am also a poet, and I have an aesthetic that exists by itself, with nothing to do with the philosophy I have or with the morality, politics or religion I am occasionally obliged to have.

Now Antonio Mora did receive Caeiro's message in its totality and decided to translate it into philosophy, clarifying, restating, readjusting and altering it here and there. I don't know if Antonio Mora's philosophy is what Caeiro's would have been had he had a philosophy.

But I accept that it would be Caeiro's philosophy if he'd had one and had not been a poet and so could not have one. Just as the plant evolves from the seed, and the plant is not the seed magnified, but something entirely different in appearance, so the different, complex body that constitutes Mora's philosophy emerged naturally from the germ contained in the totality of Caeiro's poetry. I'm going to leave my exposition of Mora's philosophy for the next piece. I am weary of trying to understand.

19 [28 September 1932]

If children do not understand adults—who, besides, have nothing to understand because they are all the same, and anything that is the same as something else does not exist—it would be truer to say that adults don't understand children. Being an adult means forgetting that you were once a child. That is why parents punish their children for doing exactly what they did at the same age. When a father remembers how he was and does not punish his son, that is because he is behaving rationally: he believes that if he can remember what he was like, then he should not punish his son. In reality, he cannot remember. If he could, he would have remained a child.

This is apropos the, in one regard, dreadful result of Caeiro's influence on Ricardo Reis and how he received it. The absence of metaphysical concerns in Caeiro, natural in someone who thinks like a child, became in Reis's adult interpretation a monstrous thing. Like Caeiro, Ricardo Reis faces life and death naturally, but, unlike Caeiro, he thinks about them. That is the origin of those distressingly materialistic poems, distressing even for the person writing them. When Reis speaks of death, it's as if he were anticipating being buried alive. He considers himself to be nothing, apart from the entirely unnecessary effect of feeling the "damp earth" on top of him, and other equally suffocating ways of saying the same thing. The feeling that, in Caeiro, is a field with nothing in it, in Reis becomes a tomb with nothing in it. He adopted Caeiro's nothing, but was not wise enough not to allow it to rot.

To Ricardo Reis, growing old and dying seem to be the summation and meaning of life. For Caeiro, there is no growing old, and dying is over there, beyond the hills. This, I believe, is apropos the matter of influences.

Reis has no metaphysics. He adopted Caeiro's metaphysics, and that was the result. I'm not denying that he has an aesthetic side; but he cannot decently be read. Each of us should have our own metaphysics, because each of us is each of us. If we are influenced by others, then let us adapt them to our own rhythms, our own images, our own poems, but not our own soul!